W9-BRQ-635

Home on the Range

Also by Susan Fox

Body Heat

Caribou Crossing Romances

Caribou Crossing

Home on the Range

Gentle on My Mind

His, Unexpectedly

Love, Unexpectedly

Yours, Unexpectedly

Writing as Susan Lyons

Sex Drive

She's On Top

Touch Me

Hot in Here

Champagne Rules

Anthologies

The Naughty List

Some Like It Rough

Men on Fire

Unwrap Me

The Firefighter

Published by Kensington Publishing Corporation

A Caribou Crossing Romance

Susan Fox

PAPL
DISCARDED

ZEBRA BOOKS
KENSINGTON PUBLISHING CORP.
http://www.kensingtonbooks.com

ZEBRA BOOKS are published by

Kensington Publishing Corp.
119 West 40th Street
New York, NY 10018

Copyright © 2013 by Susan Lyons

All rights reserved. No part of this book may be reproduced in any form or by any means without the prior written consent of the Publisher, excepting brief quotes used in reviews.

If you purchased this book without a cover you should be aware that this book is stolen property. It was reported as "unsold and destroyed" to the Publisher and neither the Author nor the Publisher has received any payment for this "stripped book."

All Kensington titles, imprints, and distributed lines are available at special quantity discounts for bulk purchases for sales promotion, premiums, fund-raising, educational, or institutional use.

Special book excerpts or customized printings can also be created to fit specific needs. For details, write or phone the office of the Kensington Special Sales Manager: Attn. Special Sales Department. Kensington Publishing Corp., 119 West 40th Street, New York, NY 10018. Phone: 1-800-221-2647.

Zebra and the Z logo Reg. U.S. Pat. & TM Off.

ISBN-13: 978-1-4201-3190-1
ISBN-10: 1-4201-3190-7
First Printing: August 2013

eISBN-13: 978-1-4201-3191-8
eISBN-10: 1-4201-3191-5
First Electronic Edition: August 2013

10 9 8 7 6 5 4 3 2 1

Printed in the United States of America

Chapter One

"You're out of your frigging mind! You want me to go to a dude ranch?" Evan Kincaid glared across the table at the man who had, until two minutes earlier, been his favorite client.

"Calm down, you're making a scene." Gianni Vitale, a stocky, middle-aged man, flung out a hand in an extravagant gesture that encompassed the restaurant. Evan's gaze followed the hand. At one o'clock on a Thursday, Gramercy Tavern was filled with well-dressed people: businessmen like themselves, shoppers pausing for a break, and tourists gawking at the Robert Kushner murals and elegant décor.

The atmosphere was laden with garlic and gossip, and not a single person was staring at them. Why would they? Two typical Manhattan businessmen in suits and ties?

Evan turned back to Gianni and glared again. "I am not making a scene. And no way in hell am I going to a dude ranch."

"You're not listening. The Crazy Horse isn't a working ranch, it's a resort ranch. You won't have to play cowboy."

A ranch was a ranch. "I won't have to play anything because I'm not going."

Gianni blew out air. "You're worse than I was when Elena

told me where she'd booked our holiday. But trust me, it's great. You ride every day and you learn a lot about horses."

"Ride? No way." As a boy, growing up in Hicksville, he'd sworn no power in the world would get him up on a horse, and he'd stuck to that vow.

"There's also a wonderful spa. The facilities and staff are first rate." Gianni lowered his voice. "The food's even better than here. You'll have the time of your life. It's quite upscale. Upscale rustic." He took a sip of his dry martini.

"Upscale rustic?" Evan echoed disbelievingly. "Gianni, you don't have a hope in hell of persuading me." His client didn't know Evan had grown up in ranch country and hated it.

Gianni leaned forward, both elbows on the table, and did some glaring of his own. "Evan, you've been my investment counselor for five years. When Addison & Carruthers first assigned you to me, I protested—"

Evan's brows rose. "I didn't know that."

"It's true. But Winston Addison told me you were a rising star, and said your style would suit me. It did. Three years ago, when you left A&C to set up your own business, I was your first client."

It was true. When Evan's style had diverged too far from A&C's traditional one, he'd come to an amicable agreement with the partners. An agreement that allowed him to take a few clients with him in exchange for referring appropriate clients to A&C in the future. "I haven't lost my memory."

"You need reminding. I brought you millions of dollars of my own business and added more than a dozen clients to your list."

"And I've done very well for you and your colleagues, despite the recession. You've gotten your money's worth, and then some." Still, a sense of obligation niggled at Evan's conscience. There weren't many billionaires who would have left the security of an established firm like A&C to risk their fortune with an upstart, especially in a shaky economy.

Gianni leaned even closer. “I like to think we have become more than client and counselor. Are we not friends?”

Trust Gianni to play that card. “You’re breaking my heart.” Evan knew his words lacked conviction. Gianni wasn’t exactly a buddy, but their relationship was more than a strictly business one. And that was rare for Evan. Although he’d outgrown his childhood awkwardness, sociability still didn’t come easily. Besides, there was little time for developing friendships when you were on a fast track to the peak of the business world. But who needed friends? He’d had one once, and look how that had ended up.

“And you will break my heart, Evan, if you don’t give this opportunity a fair appraisal.”

“I didn’t say I wouldn’t appraise it. Just not on-site. Have this wrangler person e-mail me her financial analysis, her business plan, her projections, and I’ll give them full consideration. Though I have to say, I’m surprised. This is hardly your normal type of investment. What did you call it again? No-frills riding? What does that mean?”

“There are dude ranches where guests play cowboy, and resort ranches like the Crazy Horse, where Elena and I went. TJ Cousins wants to open a riding camp that focuses completely on horses and Western riding, with no distractions. Riding lessons every day, trail rides, horse care, communication with horses, and—”

“Yeah, yeah,” Evan broke in as an image sprang into his mind. A girl with chestnut hair pulled back in a ponytail sitting across from him in the high school cafeteria. Jess Bly. Animated, lunch forgotten, telling him her latest horse-crazy dream.

As always when he thought of Jess, he felt a flood of conflicting emotions. Predominant was a sense of loss. He felt that poignant emotion every time something major happened in his life and his first instinct—bizarrely—was to tell a girl he hadn't seen in ten years.

Annoyance with himself and his client put an edge in his voice. "God, Gianni, this reminds me of a girl I knew when I was growing up. She and your TJ Cousins sound like two peas from the same pod. And let me tell you, the pod might well have come from outer space."

It wasn't fair to tar the unknown TJ with a Jess Bly brush, but this no-frills horse stuff sounded like just the kind of kooky scheme his old pal would have dreamed up. Jess had been the sweetest, kindest girl—any happiness he'd experienced in his childhood was due to her—but she'd definitely not been the most practical person.

When she was eight, she'd wanted to breed racehorses, ride them herself, and win the Triple Crown. She'd just read *National Velvet*. When she was ten, it was a riding school that would make its students learn both English and Western style. When she was twelve—

Oh, what did it matter? Jess Bly was a part of his past. A part he tried not to think about. He had messed up badly, in so many ways. And paid the price, all these years. He'd lost his best friend. True, he hadn't deserved forgiveness after acting like such a shit, but all the same he'd have thought those years of childhood friendship would count for more than a cool e-mail dismissal from seventeen-year-old Jess. She'd said they should make a clean break, forget the past.

Forget? He wondered if Jess had managed to do that. For him, though he rarely thought of Caribou Crossing or his parents, it had proved impossible to forget Jess.

Gianni reached across the table and snapped his fingers, demanding Evan's attention. "I didn't write out a check; I came to you. The ideas are exciting, the woman is impressive, and I need you to tell me if it's a realistic investment. I don't need a huge return, but I want a reasonable prospect of success."

Putting aside his guilt trip down memory lane, Evan focused on his client. "How much money are you talking?"

"Investing between three and four million, I'd guess. She already has the property. We'd want to get things started with a few cabins, a lodge, a training ring, and of course great horses. It would expand from there. Also, TJ's idea is to have a sliding scale on the pricing, basically so guests pay what they can afford."

Evan snorted. Oh yeah, that was as businesslike as one of Jess's old schemes. Had Gianni left his brain back at the Crazy Horse? "As I said, have Ms. Cousins forward me the information."

Gianni shook his head emphatically. "You have to go there."

"That's absurd." Evan shoved away his unfinished black bass entrée. Delicious though it was, he'd lost his appetite.

Gianni pointed an accusing finger. "You don't get it. And you won't get it, not here in Manhattan. I wouldn't have gotten it myself if Elena hadn't dragged me to the Crazy Horse. You must talk to TJ in person and see her work with the horses. Her method draws strongly on Monty Roberts's techniques and—"

"Spare me the details." It was too much like talking to Jess, back when they were kids with big dreams. He remembered the hundreds of hours they'd spent together while she enthused over her horsy dreams and he expounded on how he was going to become king of the hill in the Big Apple. They had loved and supported each other. She'd been the only good thing about Hicksville. She'd been his first—*Damn!* Evan put the brakes on that train of thought.

"Let me get this straight," he said. "Ms. Cousins works for the Crazy Horse and she's soliciting guests to invest in a competing business?"

"No, no." Gianni shook his head vigorously. "Not competing. The two operations will be complementary, like your firm and A&C. Her concept would appeal to the more serious riders. And no, she's not soliciting guests, we just happened to get talking one day."

Yeah, sure. After this Cousins person had Googled Gianni and figured out how rich he was.

"I've never asked you for a personal favor," his client said.

Damn again. Gianni was pulling out all the stops.

"You're overworked, Evan. You need a holiday. I'll give you a paid one."

Now that was complete bull. "Cynthia and I were in Paris last month and Tokyo the month before."

"Those were work trips. Your estimable girlfriend doesn't take real holidays. Nor do you."

Evan shrugged. He hadn't thought of it that way, but what Gianni said was true. Every trip was business for at least one of them and often both. Her work as a corporate finance lawyer and his as an investment counselor often took them in the same direction. In fact, they'd met at a conference in Geneva.

Yes, they usually did plan their trips with an extra day or two to shop and visit museums and galleries, but they'd never taken a true holiday.

A holiday. For a moment, the idea was tempting. Oh, not to go to some idiotic dude ranch that reminded him of his crappy childhood, but perhaps to lie on a beach in the south of France. No, what was he thinking? He'd be bored out of his mind. He thrived on work. Sure, maybe he did get the occasional stress headache, but a good workout at the fitness club dealt with that. His personal trainer had even given him a set of stretches to do at the office, to ease out the kinks.

Hell, Gianni ought to be the first person to understand that holidays had no place on the fast track to success.

"When's the last time you had a vacation in the country?" his client asked.

"Never." When he'd lived in Caribou Crossing, it had been

anything but a vacation. "It sounds like sheer hell. Where is this Crazy Horse? Texas?"

"Canada. The interior of British Columbia. They call it the Cariboo. You fly into Williams Lake, then it's an hour or two drive."

Evan's heart jerked to a stop. Caribou Crossing—Hicksville, as he'd called it—was an hour or so from Williams Lake.

Dimly he was aware of Gianni waving at their waiter, and in a moment two martinis arrived. The waiter removed Gianni's empty glass. Evan didn't drink alcohol in the middle of the day, but his hand reached out automatically. Caribou Crossing, damn it. Miles and miles of open countryside, horses, Jess Bly. His mother.

His hand jerked back from the martini glass. His mother—and his abusive, runaway dad—were the reason he was so careful with alcohol.

Hell! He didn't need these memories.

And he sure as *hell* didn't need a holiday. He worked hard, yes, but he wasn't overworked or stressed out. He'd achieved his childhood dream and he relished it, building his business bigger and better—and not just making his clients more money but helping many support worthwhile charities. He and Cynthia led a jet-setting life. They had acquaintances to dine with in Paris and Rome, Hong Kong and Tokyo, London and Sydney. He lived in New York, the best city in the world, the boldest and bravest, the one place that had always drawn him, that still enthralled and impressed him on a daily basis. He was living his dream. No way was he going back to the hellhole where sheer misery had spawned that dream.

"Afraid you'll fall off a horse?" Gianni asked with pseudo-innocence.

"Don't be ridiculous."

"Elena's strongly in favor of the investment. She says I'm a new man since our holiday. Part of the deal with TJ is that we'd have a free cabin for a month a year, a place to unwind and to ride. To smell the roses, as they say at the Crazy Horse."

Evan recognized a threat when he heard one. "You're saying that if I don't go and meet this wrangler woman and analyze her proposal, you'll let Elena convince you to throw away several million dollars?"

Gianni grinned hugely and stretched his diamond-ringed hand across the table. "Good, you will go. Thank you, Evan, I knew you would protect my money."

"Wait a minute."

Gianni withdrew the hand and scowled.

"Where *exactly* is this place?" There'd been no Crazy Horse resort ranch anywhere near Caribou Crossing when he'd lived there.

A shrug. "I never looked at a map. What's the difference?"

Having transformed himself into the consummate New Yorker, Evan wasn't about to claim the Cariboo as his boyhood home. He shrugged. "Just curious." He drew in a breath and let it out. TJ Cousins . . . There'd been a bunch of Cousinses in the Caribou Crossing area—he'd gone to school with three of them, including Dave, the basketball star and class president—but there hadn't been a TJ. Chances were, this Crazy Horse was nowhere near Caribou Crossing. Even if it was, he'd never have to track down Jess. Or visit his mother.

Gianni really was his best client, and the closest thing he had—other than Cynthia—to a friend. He couldn't let the man throw away millions on some crazy scheme just because his wife, a normally sane woman, had developed a temporary passion for riding horses and smelling roses. "Okay," he said grudgingly, "you're on." This time he stretched his hand across the table. Gianni grasped it and pumped enthusiastically as Evan wondered what he'd gotten himself into.

"Free up your calendar for two weeks," Gianni ordered.

Evan snorted. "Two days."

"No, you'll need the full time to learn all you need to know. I don't want you going in as my investment counselor and grilling TJ. You'll go undercover, yes? As a regular guest. Take it slowly, get a feel for her and her methods. You can't understand the no-frills riding camp idea without understanding the context, the ambiance, the person behind it."

Evan frowned. Much as he hated to admit it, Gianni had a valid point. The success or failure of a new venture hinged not only on the business plan, but on the person behind it. His own company was a prime example. But a few days, a week max, should be sufficient.

"Have Angelica call me for the details," Gianni said. "Go as soon as possible, because Elena and I are anxious to get started on this, provided you approve it. The riding package starts on a Sunday, runs two weeks, and you return on a Saturday. The day after, you'll come to our apartment for Sunday brunch, thank me for the holiday, and tell us what you think of TJ and her plans."

Evan clenched his jaw. He wasn't used to surrendering control.

"Oh, by the way." His client's dark eyes sparkled.

He studied Gianni suspiciously.

"Take Cynthia if you want."

Chic Cynthia, at the Crazy Horse ranch. Evan's jaw unclenched and his laughter joined Gianni's rich chuckle.

The two of them left the restaurant together, then parted. After a short, brisk walk, Evan arrived at his sleek, modern office. He asked his assistant, Angelica, to phone Gianni and then call the Crazy Horse to see if it was possible to make reservations for a week. With any luck, the damned place would be booked up for the rest of the summer.

Toward the end of the afternoon, Angelica clicked across his marble-tiled floor. "You're in luck. There was a cancellation for next week at the . . . Crazy Horse."

Evan's lips twitched as the efficient Angelica's own lips—

colored a bizarre purple that he assumed must be the height of fashion—hesitated over the name. It was clear his assistant thought "crazy" was a fitting term to apply to him. He couldn't wait to see Cynthia's reaction when he told her at dinner tonight. Maybe he'd even pass along Gianni's suggestion that she join him, just to see her horrified expression.

"I booked you for two weeks."

"I said one."

Angelica held up a hand. "The Crazy Horse only books in two-week blocks. You can always find an excuse for leaving early. Like fall off a horse and break a leg?" She said it straight-faced, but he thought he saw a twinkle in her eye.

"You're a big help," he grumbled.

"Mr. Vitale told me to bill everything to your card and he'll reimburse you. He didn't want anything put in his name, since you're going undercover, as he termed it."

She handed over a file folder. "Here's your e-ticket and your confirmation number at the Crazy Horse. The price there is all-inclusive. At six thousand US dollars for a week, one would certainly hope so. I gather it's a world-famous, exclusive spot. I got you a few hundred dollars in Canadian money in case you want to do some shopping, though I can't imagine there's much to spend money on there." Her eyes were wide, and it wasn't with envy.

"Nor can I."

"The Crazy Horse e-mailed me their brochure and I printed it out for you. You should know . . ." She gave a little cough and he thought she might be stifling a giggle. It was a startling thought, because he'd never heard the all-business Angelica giggle. "Uh, with regard to clothing, you have to have . . ." She choked and this time he knew it was a giggle.

"Spit it out. This can't get any worse, can it?"

She let the giggle go and it soared buoyantly between them. "It can," she choked out. "Cowboy . . . boots. You . . . have to have Western . . . riding boots." She spluttered for a few moments, then managed to say, "I've put together a list of stores in Manhattan that sell them."

"Thanks, I think." He studied her, so sleek and chic. "Have you ever been on a horse?"

"I had a boyfriend who rode in Central Park and I went along once. I broke a fingernail and came back with my clothes smelling of horse. Disgusting. How about you?"

"Not once in my life." Yes, he'd lived ten years in horse country, and his best friend was the horse lover to end all horse lovers, but he'd refused to ever mount a horse. Partly, it was knowing that he, such an unathletic boy, would embarrass himself in front of Jess, but he'd also had a gut-level instinct that to ride would be to surrender. To accept that his life—his utterly miserable life in Hicksville—was all he'd ever know.

Riding. Damn it, this time he'd have to do it. But he was a big boy, and he could deal with it. He sure as hell wasn't going to turn into a country boy, and even if he didn't prove to be a skilled rider, there'd be no Jess to taunt him. Besides, he was no longer a klutz, and he would do his homework.

He was about to send Angelica to the bookstore when his brain flashed back to Jess teasing the shit out of him for trying to learn how to skate from a book.

"All right," he said. "I guess I'm really going." He glanced at his watch. Almost five o'clock. "First priority for tomorrow is to clear the calendar for next Monday and Tuesday. Maybe Wednesday. That should give me enough time to learn what I need to about Gianni's proposed investment." He rose and pulled on his suit jacket.

"You're leaving now?" She looked stunned.

No wonder. He rarely left the office before seven, after putting in at least a thirteen-hour day. "Going shopping. Have to find those cowboy boots," he said wryly.

She gave a hoot and departed in giggles.

Evan shook his head. Would wonders never cease? First,

Gianni had persuaded him to do something that, had he been asked this morning, he would have said was inconceivable. Then, the ultrapoised Angelica had been reduced to giggles. And finally, Evan Kincaid, the quintessential New Yorker, was heading out to buy cowboy boots and a how-to book on riding horses.

On the way past Angelica's desk, he asked, "Did anyone mention the nearest town?"

"Let me think. Something to do with deer. Or maybe moose. No, it was caribou. Caribou Crossing. Quaint, isn't it?"

"Caribou Crossing." The name had been on his mind ever since Gianni had started talking about horses, yet now it hit him like a sucker punch.

"Is something wrong?"

"No," he muttered, thinking things couldn't possibly go any more wrong. Then he squared his shoulders. So the Crazy Horse was near Caribou Crossing. As he'd resolved earlier, there was no reason in the world for him to lay eyes on his mother. Or Jess Bly.

Not unless he wanted to. Which he most certainly did not.

Chapter Two

It was his butt Jess Cousins noticed first.

Monday morning, and the latest group of resort virgins bustled and chattered in her barnyard like a flock of nervous magpies. Amid them this one guy stood still, his back toward her as he studied the row of horses tethered to one of the hitching rails. She took in pleasant impressions of height, ranginess, breadth of shoulder, length of leg, and a truly outstanding butt. Many of the Crazy Horse's guests were pudgy and a few were scrawny. It was rare to see an admirable physique and even rarer to see a world-class—

Jess snorted under her breath. What the heck was she doing, ogling a guest's backside? Was it just because she hadn't had sex in so long she'd almost forgotten what it was like, or was the backside in question really so outstanding? She was dragging her gaze away from the denim-clad object of her admiration just as the man turned around.

"Ev!" His name caught in her throat, emerging as a squeak. He'd changed a lot in ten years, but she recognized him instantly. Despite his pole-axed expression.

He strode toward her as his mouth formed her own name.

Her muscles locked her in place as he approached, and all her brain could do was repeat, *Evan, my God, it's Evan.*

She pulled herself together to demand, "What are you doing here?" just as he spoke the identical words.

He grasped her by one shoulder and herded her away from the group. Dimly she was aware of the milling guests, but it was hard to care about anything other than the fact that this man stood in front of her, his hand burning through the cotton of her embroidered Western shirt. Her heart thudded so fast she could barely breathe and her mind was a jumble of thoughts. For the life of her she couldn't pull a single one free and form a coherent sentence.

He gazed down at his hand as if only just realizing where it rested. Then he yanked it back as quickly as if he'd reached out to stroke a bull in a bucking chute.

Evan was at the Crazy Horse. Had he discovered her long-held secret? Was he here because he'd found out about Robin? The possibility stole what breath she had left. Finally, she managed to draw air and force out a few cautious words. "I work here."

"Oh." He seemed to be weighing the concept more carefully than it deserved. "They said the head wrangler would meet us here. TJ Cousins. That's . . . not you?"

Her breathing settled a little. He really did seem surprised to see her. No, he couldn't have known about Robin. And she mustn't say anything to give away her secret.

She nodded. "I don't use Jessica for my work. People kept making *Man from Snowy River* comments and it drove me nuts."

He shrugged, clearly baffled. "Huh?"

Hadn't she made him watch the movie, way back then? No, she must've had the sense to know Mr. City-bound wouldn't be interested in a film about horses and cowboys in the Australian Outback. He wouldn't know that the free-spirited, horse-loving heroine was called Jessica.

Now that she thought about it, they hadn't watched many movies. When he wasn't studying and she wasn't outside with the horses, the two of them spent most of their time talking. Sharing dreams. The dreams they'd always known would take them in opposite directions.

And now he was back on her turf. Looking like a man rather than a boy. A striking man rather than a cute but nerdy kid. A kid she'd believed to be the love of her life, yet known she had to give up.

Robin's father.

Jess had broken her heart over Evan Kincaid. How dare he come back?

He'd run away, and then—*finally*—e-mailed a couple of times from Cornell to apologize. *E-mailed*, didn't even have the decency to phone! She didn't remember the exact words she'd typed with such pain and deliberation, but she knew the essence of the message she'd sent: Get lost and stay lost.

"Cousins," he said on a note of revelation. "Dave? You married Dave?"

She lifted her chin. "Yup." No need to tell him they'd since divorced.

"You were friends in high school, hanging around with that *in crowd*"—he said it as disparagingly now as he had back then—"but I didn't think the two of you—" He broke off suddenly and she knew what he was thinking. She and Dave had been friends, but not romantically, or sexually, inclined.

Evan was remembering the night at Zephyr Lake—when she'd had sex with him, not Dave. Even after all these years, she could still read his mind.

No, of course she couldn't, nor did she want to. But the lake was so obvious. A pink elephant in her barnyard. Would they both tiptoe around it, pretending it didn't exist?

He cleared his throat. "I never connected TJ with Jessica."

Yup, Evan was going to tiptoe. Well, that was fine by her because her tongue was hog-tied, bound up good and tight by strands of conflicting emotions. Her bruised heart urged her to rail at him for rejecting her all those years ago, yet if she was going to be fair about it, she had rejected him, too. She'd refused his overture of continued, long-distance friendship. How could she write chatty letters to him while nursing a broken heart and holding back the huge secret of Robin's existence?

She'd done the right thing, and yet she'd missed him so badly. Even now, a part of her mushy heart yearned to envelope him in a gigantic hug.

But the strongest emotion, by far, was maternal instinct. She had to protect Robin, the product of that night at Zephyr Lake. *Jesus, this is Robin's biological father.* She'd thought she'd never see him again, but here he stood, strong and solid and very male.

Again, fear caught her breath. Why was he here? Evan, who had his own investment counseling firm in New York City—and yes, she'd Googled him. Evan, who'd sworn to never set foot in Hicksville again. Had he somehow found out? Come to claim his daughter?

But why on earth would he do that? He'd never wanted children.

She couldn't stand the uncertainty. "What in holy blue blazes are you doing here?" she demanded, her voice one notch south of a holler.

He shot a glance toward the dudes who chattered nervously as they eyed the horses tied to the hitching rails. She lowered her voice. "You're not a guest?"

He shrugged uncomfortably. "Actually, yes."

"Ac-tu-al-ly," Jess parroted the word, exaggerating the cultivated accent he'd acquired since she last saw him, "you're the last person I'd have expected. Back in school you couldn't wait to shake the country dust from—" She paused, snagged on another memory. This one triggered a surge of affection, a response as unexpected as it was undeniable. "From those beautifully polished leather loafers you hitchhiked into Williams Lake to buy, back in grade twelve."

Suddenly, the mess of unresolved issues flew out of her mind. All she could think of, in that moment, was that this was Ev, the guy who'd for years been her best buddy.

She smiled freely and, after his mouth fell open in surprise, he smiled back. "Good Lord, Jess, it's actually you. You look"—he eyed her up and down—"just great."

She read sincerity in his blue-green eyes. And something else, something that made her blood fizz.

Now came the scary memories. The memory of feelings she'd never experienced in the same way with any other man. Not even her ex-husband, Dave. She moistened lips that had gone dry. "You look good, too."

The package-creased tan denim shirt and well-worn designer jeans hugged a fine body. She'd always found him appealing—a scrawny kid with beautiful eyes and ears too big for his head—but now he was a total hottie. His face was craggy and his eyes were devastating. To her chagrin she remembered those eyes perfectly, the mingled blues and greens of brook water flowing over gray stones, flecked by sparkles of golden sun.

She closed her own eyes briefly, then looked again. He was beyond handsome; he was compelling. And sexy.

An image flashed into her mind. Evan's gangly young body rising above hers, the moon on his shoulder, as they made love on the lakeshore. She sucked in her breath and, afraid he could read her face, dropped her gaze.

Happily, the new image brought her down to earth. Literally. She saw exquisitely tooled chestnut leather Tony Lama boots. She cleared her throat. "They're not loafers, but I see you haven't lost your touch with the shoe polish. Hate to tell you, but the dust is going to stick. And we have far worse than dust to dish up at the Crazy Horse." She tilted her head and dared to look at his face again.

He glanced down to where his feet were planted in a

mixture of dirt and manure. His grimace of distaste was so typically Ev that she gave a snort of laughter.

"Okay, city slicker, enough of the chitchat. I have work to do." Jess strode toward the other guests, trusting that habit would carry her through.

Evan Kincaid. At the Crazy Horse. This couldn't really be happening, could it?

He hadn't mentioned Robin. If he'd come about her, surely he'd have said something by now.

Jess had made the decision not to tell him when she found out that those few rushed minutes at the lake, combined with her too old condom, had resulted in pregnancy. A baby would ruin all his long-held dreams. It wasn't fair to do that to him, and besides, it wasn't like things could have worked out for her and Ev. He'd have spent his life resenting her and their child for tying him to the place he'd scornfully called Hicksville.

Her own dreams were more flexible, and could easily, joyfully, bend to incorporate a child. Her and Evan's child.

No, not Evan's. Robin's father—the man who'd raised and loved her—was Dave Cousins.

Evan had never wanted kids. He wouldn't have wanted to know about Robin all those years ago, and he didn't deserve her. Not then, and not now. Nor could Jess have her daughter learn that her mom and dad had been lying to her ever since she was born.

To Evan it seemed like no time before Jess—he couldn't think of her as TJ—had inventoried the guests as to their riding experience, goals, and fears, and matched them up with horses. He admired her ability to relate to each person, deal with questions, soothe anxieties, and still elicit the information she needed.

He tried to shove aside the guilt that had swamped him

since he first laid eyes on her. He had, to use one of the country phrases he'd always shunned, "done her wrong." First, by making love to her at all, for giving in to his crazy lust and betraying their friendship, especially when he knew he'd be leaving for university. Second, by panicking and abandoning her at Zephyr Lake when he realized the damned condom had split. Third, by heading off to Cornell early, without talking to her about what happened. Not only was he a jerk, he was a triple jerk.

Evan hadn't known what to say to Jess, so he'd taken the easy road and not even tried. Except, that road hadn't ended up being so easy. Once he was at Cornell he'd missed her so much, and known he was no better than—he lifted a foot and glanced at his once pristine boot—horseshit.

And of course he couldn't get that split condom out of his mind. Surely one very hurried act of sex couldn't have resulted in pregnancy; still, he had to find out. So, a couple of months after he left Caribou Crossing, he e-mailed, apologized, and asked how she was, hoping with all his selfish heart that she wouldn't respond "pregnant." Hoping, too, that they could get their friendship—the only friendship he'd ever known—back on track.

That was when she'd told him she was doing great, and they should each go their own ways. All right, he'd thought, she wanted him to grovel some more—and she was entitled. So he'd e-mailed back and said he really hoped they could stay in touch and still share their lives and their dreams.

This time she responded, "Look, Ev, we always knew that this day would come. That you'd go to New York and I'd stay here. You're the one who wanted to leave, so just leave, damn it! Make a clean break. Forget the past."

He couldn't believe it. They'd seen each other almost every day for ten years. How could she dismiss that so easily?

In all the years he'd known her, he'd never seen this chilly side of her. They'd always promised that once he left for university they'd e-mail all the time. So he could only figure that she was totally pissed off at him for, quite literally, screwing up their relationship. When he'd taken their friendship to a place she hadn't wanted it to go, he'd lost that friendship entirely.

Now his gaze followed Jess as she moved nimbly among the horses and guests, whipped into the weathered barn and returned with hats and sunscreen, and exchanged quick words with her assistant, a pretty Native Canadian teen with striking features and long, straight black hair under a cowboy hat.

Jess herself was trim and businesslike yet indisputably female and attractive—attractive enough that he felt disconcerting stirrings of his teen lust. She wore faded jeans, a snap-fastened white shirt embroidered with red stitching, and brown cowboy boots that were plain and battered from use. She'd grown up exactly the way he'd have expected her to—and it seemed she was still spinning those crazy dreams.

He should have guessed that TJ Cousins was Jess. Now that he thought back, he did remember that Jessica was her middle name and that her first was something she hated so much she never shared it, not even with him.

Barely glancing at him, she gestured him over to a huge beast with an oddly colored hide—pinky brown with a few white splotches. If he'd had any vision of himself atop a noble steed, Jess had certainly put the kibosh on it. No doubt she was getting revenge for the way he'd treated her when they were seventeen, and he deserved it. But did she have to give him the ugliest horse?

As if reading his mind, the horse gazed sideways at him out of one liquid brown eye, then shifted position and plunked a gigantic hoof on the toe of Evan's boot.

"Ow!" He shoved the horse, to no avail. The animal opened its mouth, revealing frighteningly large teeth, and yawned. Evan drew back from those giant teeth and the gust of grassy breath. Or at least as far back as he could draw, given that he was anchored by one foot.

"Rusty!" It was Jess's assistant. She bustled over and gave the horse a gentle swat on the neck. It yawned once more and shifted position again, freeing Evan's foot.

"You all right?" the girl asked.

His boot was filthy and scarred, his toes were no doubt bruised, his nostrils twitched in protest at the smell of horse. "I'll live," he said curtly.

"You gotta be firm with him."

"I'll remember that." As if he had any idea how to be "firm" with a horse. He sent a silent curse winging in Gianni's direction. It wasn't the first to fly that route over the last couple of days, and he knew with certainty it wouldn't be the last.

Horses were bad enough. At least he'd been able to anticipate, and do some preparatory reading. But he hadn't anticipated Jess.

Back when they were seventeen he had, thanks to his adolescent hormones and stupidity, screwed up the finest thing he'd ever known.

The ugly horse stared at him sideways again.

"All right," he muttered. "Even if she did blow me off back then, I owe her a face-to-face apology. I'll do it as soon as I get the chance, and then I'm going home."

The horse shifted position, looked away, and snorted.

Evan was tempted to bail out on this ride, but that would raise questions. He didn't want to air his and Jess's personal business in public. He glanced over to where she was still engaged in pairing guests with horses. She was so *not* his type of woman, it made no sense that the sight of her quickened his breath and sent a heavy pulse of arousal through his blood.

She shoved the brown cowboy hat off her head so it hung on a cord down her back, and laughed at something a big-haired woman said.

God, but he'd missed that infectious laugh. It seemed to bubble from a wellspring in her very soul. Suddenly, his knees weakened and he leaned against the horse. He remembered how many times over the past years Jess Bly had popped into his thoughts.

She'd been his best friend, his staunch ally, since his first day at Caribou Crossing Elementary. He was seven; it was grade two; his family had moved to town three days earlier. His parents—Barbie-doll Brooke and dark-skinned Mohinder—were, as usual, hungover and fighting, so he'd walked to school by himself. An outsider, as always. Hating being in another new place; hating the dust and mosquitoes; hating having parents who smelled like stale booze, parents who hit each other and him.

And then magic happened. A little girl with a ponytail and sunny smile befriended him.

That same female, with the same hair and same smile, now clamped her hat back on her head and bellowed, "Okay, folks, listen up."

He shoved away from the horse and tried to focus, but his thoughts were more on Jess herself than on what she was saying. Superficially, she didn't look much different than she had as a teenager. Slim, fit, not too tall. Hair a glossy chestnut, hanging past her shoulders, bound with a leather thong so it fell in a gleaming tail. It was her face that had changed the most. It was unlined, yet wore a maturity that said she was a woman now. Was that why he felt so uncomfortable, so sexually aware of her? This was almost as unsettling as back when his childhood pal had first sprouted breasts.

"All right," Jess called. He focused yet again. She'd been giving instructions and he had missed the whole spiel. That wasn't like him. He had—as Cynthia teased him—a mind like a steel trap.

"Mount up. Just do what I said, and Madisun and I will

help you. When you're up, check your stirrups, then bring your horses over here by the gate."

"Mount," Evan muttered. He might not have heard her directions but he'd speed-read a book on riding during the lengthy trip from The Apple to Hicksville. He could do this. Left foot in the left stirrup. But the book hadn't mentioned that the stirrup would be hanging three feet off the ground.

"Up you go," the assistant—Madisun—said cheerily.

"Easy for you to say."

She chuckled and patted his horse's neck.

Evan grabbed hold of the stirrup and managed to force the toe of his once-shiny boot into it, then got a death grip on the saddle and hauled himself up, inch by painful inch. He settled into an unyielding leather contraption perched a mile off the ground atop a beast who obviously had a grudge against him.

"Great, you're all hunky-dory." The girl handed him the reins. "His name's Rusty and he's as gentle as a lamb."

"Tell that to my toes."

She laughed, her brown eyes sparkling in the sun. "You'll do great. Now, how are your stirrups? Feel okay?"

The boots pinched his feet, his toes were jammed through clunky metal rungs, his legs were twisted at an unnatural angle, and, to add insult to injury, he was sitting on top of a horse. "Just hunky-dory," he echoed through gritted teeth.

She turned the horse's head toward the closed gate in the wooden-railed fence that marked off the barnyard, and gave him another of her gentle slaps, this time on the rump. Rusty ambled over to where the other riders were congregating.

Evan tried to concentrate as Jess gave a few more instructions, but his mind still wouldn't settle. He'd give his Rolex watch—hell, he'd give a year of his life—to be back in Manhattan, wheeling and dealing in his glass-walled office.

"Any questions?" Jess called in a clear voice.

Oh yeah, he had questions. Questions about her business

plan, questions about why his hand tingled when it touched her shoulder, questions about what the hell he was doing here. As for questions about riding, he wasn't about to confess he hadn't been paying attention. Besides, he'd read his book and knew the basics: heels down, back straight, hold the reins in one hand. How tough could it be? With any luck, he wouldn't make a fool of himself in front of Jess, and this would be the first and only ride he'd ever take in his life.

"I'll be at the head of the line," Jess told the ten guests, "and Madisun will bring up the rear. Sing out if you have any worries. We'll walk for the first ten minutes to get the horses warmed up and everyone comfortable. Then we'll do a nice slow trot. Don't worry about grabbing on to the horn."

Jess sprang into the saddle of a tall black horse, her motions graceful and effortless. "After the first quarter hour we'll stop and Madisun and I will check and see how you're all doing." She reached down to unlatch the gate, swung it back, and rode through, motioning one of the guests to follow.

As Rusty strolled forward to take his place in the single-file line heading through the gate, Evan thought nervously about the waiver they'd all signed. It went against his nature to sign away his rights, but likely the thing wouldn't stand up if one of Cynthia's litigation colleagues got her teeth into it.

Not that Evan planned on having an accident. He curled one hand around the horn as the horses took a dirt trail winding through a forest of tall trees. Evergreens, he figured. He remembered something about needles indicating evergreens and leaves meaning deciduous, but that was grade three science. He'd never bothered to learn anything else about the vegetation that grew around Caribou Crossing.

After the first few minutes he realized nothing much was going to happen. His horse plodded along, the motion not exactly comfortable but nothing to be nervous about. The horse ahead plodded, the horse behind plodded. Now he could see why Rusty had been yawning. He released his death grip on the horn and patted the horse's neck. "Good boy."

He glanced at his hand, then lifted it to his face. Red dust was already working its way into the creases of his palm and there was a distinct odor of horse. He wrinkled his nose and wiped his hand on his jeans. Thank God the Crazy Horse had a laundry service.

His horse was three back from Jess's and occasionally he caught a glimpse of her hat or heard her laugh as she chatted to the person behind her. That laugh again, hearty and infectious.

So TJ Cousins was Jess Bly. Before he made a precipitous exit back to New York—before he let Gianni down—he needed to analyze the situation fully.

He'd come here predisposed to reject TJ's investment proposal. In Manhattan, it had seemed like pie in the sky. Now that he realized TJ was really Jess, he suspected the pie was half-baked. He and Jess had both been dreamers, but he'd had a solid grip on reality. With Brooke and Mohinder Kincaid for parents, reality was hard to ignore. So he'd done his homework, come up with a detailed plan, and developed the discipline and business savvy to turn his dream into a reality that was the polar opposite of the life he'd grown up with.

Jess, much as he'd cared for her, never had turned one of her dreams into a solid plan, not in the years he'd known her. He peered ahead, trying to catch another glimpse of her, but the trail twisted through trees and she was hidden from view. Was there any chance she'd changed?

People did change. Look at him. In the first couple of years of university, on scholarship at Cornell, he'd transformed himself from a hick into a reasonable facsimile of a cultured gentleman. Maybe Jess had transformed herself from a lovable nitwit into a woman with business acumen. He chuckled. And his heavy-footed horse could fly.

No, he figured she was just a girl who liked to play with

dreams. If her latest one didn't pan out, he doubted it'd be a big surprise—or a big loss—to her. Her wrangler job had the two things she'd always considered essential: It centered around horses and it was located in her "neck of the woods," as she used to phrase it. No, there'd never been any doubt about her priorities.

Nor had there been any doubt about his: He'd always wanted to take a gigantic bite out of the Big Apple. In the past ten years, he'd realized his dream. He had gone to university and graduate school, won a prestige job at a top investment firm, then struck out on his own and established a successful business.

He sucked in a deep breath. The air here smelled peculiar. Of dust and plants and horses. A far cry from Manhattan, where the odors of a dozen cuisines mingled with exhaust fumes and the burning-garbage smell of expensive cigars. Manhattan might stink, but it was the stink of life. Vital, cosmopolitan, hub-of-the-universe life. Never a dull moment. Rusty wouldn't have time to yawn.

Suddenly his horse lurched forward. Evan made a desperate grab for the horn. Was Rusty running away?

He regained enough composure to realize Rusty was still in line, and all the horses had picked up the pace. This must be a trot. It had to be the most uncomfortable motion in the world. He winced each time his backside whacked the unyielding leather. And it wasn't just his butt that was taking a pounding. Grimly, he wondered if he was doing irreversible damage to his male equipment. Could he feel any more miserable?

When he got back to Manhattan, he was going to kill Gianni. No, he was going to tell him to invest with TJ Cousins, and watch his client quickly go bankrupt. Except doing so would violate his professional pride and ethics. Evan flopped down, groaned, jounced up again. It would have to be murder.

Finally, as mysteriously as they had started, the horses stopped trotting and settled back to a saunter. So this was riding. Painful and utterly boring. Evan couldn't understand why some folks got so excited about it.

But Jess always had. When he first met her, she'd been riding for years. She boasted that she'd been comfortable in the saddle before she could walk, and he'd believed her. Especially after he met her parents, true horse lovers, too.

Looking back, he marveled at their friendship. They'd had nothing in common, but somehow they'd become the best of pals. The thought of her had sustained him through so many miserable nights in his sagging bed at the run-down shack his parents rented.

He realized Rusty had stopped. All the horses had, single file along a path through a grassy meadow. What a relief. His left knee was aching, so he took his foot out of the stirrup and stretched his leg. Christ, they'd been riding for only fifteen minutes. He was supposed to be in good shape, according to his personal trainer.

Jess rode back along the line having a quick word with each guest, her black horse prancing and fussing. Evan guessed the horse was as restless as he was.

When Jess reached Evan, she said, "How ya doin'?"

He hated to admit weakness but his knee really was killing him. And this was an hour-and-a-half ride. He pointed down. "Sore knee."

"Put your foot back in the stirrup."

"That's not going to help."

She gave an exasperated growl in the back of her throat. "Just do it, Ev."

After he obeyed, she shook her head. "Your stirrup's too short. Weren't you listening when I talked about stirrup length?"

"I, uh, guess I thought they were okay."

"Well, this one's not. Lift your leg."

"Huh?"

She rolled her eyes. "Kick your foot out of the stirrup again and hike your leg forward on the saddle like this." She demonstrated and he obeyed clumsily.

Then she leaned over and lifted the flap of leather that covered the stirrup. He glanced down and saw that the stirrup was held on to the saddle by a strip of leather that buckled like a belt. Jess pulled the end of the strap out of the buckle. The brim of her hat brushed his hip as nimble fingers worked the leather only a few inches from his thigh. Awareness of Jess as a woman surged through him and he sucked in a breath as his male equipment proved it was still entirely functional, hardening under his fly.

Jess did up the buckle, yanked the stirrup down, then replaced the leather flap and gave it a pat.

When she straightened, saying, "Now you're set," her cheeks were flushed. From bending over, or had she noticed his arousal?

For a moment they stared into each other's eyes.

Evan felt like he had as a teenager, when his body figured out that the tomboy he'd grown up with had overnight blossomed into a desirable young woman.

God help him, he'd wanted her, and he wanted her now. It had been irrational then, when their dreams were aimed in opposite directions, and now it was impossible. She was married, he was practically engaged, and he was almost certainly going to stomp on her latest dream as roughly as Rusty had stomped on his foot.

Jess clamped a hand on her hat, anchoring it more firmly, and turned her attention to the woman behind him. Evan found he'd been holding his breath, and now drew in air with a small gasp.

"What?" Jess called over her shoulder.

"Nothing. Uh . . . my knee feels better now. Thanks."

"Uh-huh. Next time pay attention."

He grinned. Jess could be patient, but she didn't suffer fools gladly. Must be tough, working with dudes. She was a naturally skilled rider; their ineptness must drive her nuts.

Like he had, as a kid. He'd never been the physical type, never fit in as a country boy and never wanted to. Jess had given up attempting to lure him into physical activity when she saw that the few times she managed to persuade him onto a bike or a frozen lake he only fell down.

Strangely enough, it was in New York he'd learned to value fitness. At first it was a necessity, when headaches and backaches impaired his ability to function. But once he'd strengthened a few muscles and felt better, he was hooked. He would never be a true athlete, but it was a kick to realize he wasn't as hopeless as he'd always believed. Just a late bloomer, he told himself, taking pride in watching his biceps flex as he pumped iron, or in giving agile Cynthia a run for her money on the squash court.

"If I can play squash, I can ride," he muttered to Rusty as the line of horses began to move. No way was he going to fall off in front of Jess.

She was good at her job. She'd found her niche and ought to stay here. Still, if he went home now and told Gianni not to invest, he'd be pulling the plug and sinking Jess's dream. And he would be doing it based not on who she was now, but who she'd been a long time ago—plus, to be honest, his own discomfort about being around her.

That wasn't fair. Not to her, nor to Gianni. And it would violate one of his own basic principles: to not judge a book by its front and back covers but to read the pages in between. He'd already treated Jess shabbily once. He owed her. But what he owed her was an objective assessment. He wouldn't be doing her a favor if he endorsed her funding and her business went belly-up.

Yet would Gianni even want him to stay at the Crazy Horse once he knew about Evan's prior . . . friendship with TJ

Cousins? It could be seen as a conflict of interest. He needed to phone his client as soon as the ride was over.

If the phone was available. The one damned pay phone. The Crazy Horse might be an internationally known resort, but it was still Hicksville in many ways. His picturesque cabin, charmingly decorated in something Gianni'd probably call "rustic chic," featured numerous amenities: healthy designer beverages in the fridge, a CD player with a stack of country and western music and relaxation CDs beside it, a goose-down duvet on the four-poster bed, thick towels and a terry robe, and an assortment of herbal bath products.

Evan cared more about what it didn't have. No cell reception, no telephone, no Internet, not even a television so he could keep up with world events. When he'd disbelievingly queried Will, one of the co-owners, who'd shown him to his room, Will said there was a pay phone and TV at the lodge, and a computer guests could use.

"That's it?" Evan had asked disbelievingly. "That's the full extent of the guests' ability to connect with the outside world?" Had he traveled back in time more than half a century? And a pay phone? Seriously? He was paying six thousand dollars a week, and he had to use a pay phone?

The older man, a chunky guy with tousled, gray-streaked dark hair, had responded cheerfully, "Yup. What we're offering is a getaway holiday."

Evan had squeezed his eyes shut, feeling a tension headache build. "A getaway?" It was the Cariboo that he wanted to *get away* from.

"Sure. After all, you're here to relax, and we make no bones about reminding you to stop and smell the roses."

How the hell could Evan relax without the Internet and his iPhone? What kind of place didn't have a sat tower? Oh, yeah: Hicksville.

Rusty stumbled over a root, calling Evan from his thoughts. "Pick up your feet," he muttered to the horse.

If he stayed here, he'd go stir-crazy.

He realized the horses ahead of him were filing back into the fenced yard by the barn. Jess had stopped her horse by the open gate and was sharing a word with each rider as they filed by.

"How ya doin', cowboy?" she drawled to Evan. "Rusty lookin' after you okay?"

Her cheeks glowed. Did she get prettier each time he looked at her? Before he could focus and come up with a snappy answer, his horse ambled into the yard and his opportunity was gone.

Why did Jess make him feel like a horny teenager? This was absurd. He was a healthy man with normal sexual appetites and a girlfriend who satisfied him completely. That was it—he'd think about Cynthia. Cynthia, stylish and clever, striking with her short blond hair and cool blue eyes.

Not Jess, married Jess, who in dress and manner epitomized all those country ways he'd been so eager to leave behind. Not Jess, with that infectious laugh and glossy fall of chestnut hair. Not Jess, with those heartwarming chocolate eyes . . .

If he stayed, it was going to be a very long week.

Chapter Three

Later that afternoon, as she gave a private lesson in the outdoor ring to a woman named Joan, Jess was amazed that she'd actually survived the day. Thank heavens for routine. She had followed the same pattern of activities so many times, she could do this stuff in her sleep—or today, when her brain was scrambled, her body and emotions in a turmoil.

She knew one thing, and it was the most important one: Evan wasn't here because of Robin. He hadn't said a word, hadn't dropped a single hint. He truly hadn't known Jess worked at the Crazy Horse. That was a huge relief, but now she had another major question: What was he doing here? Caribou Crossing was the last place in the world she figured he'd ever want to visit.

And, aside from the way he filled out a pair of jeans, it was pretty dang clear he hadn't changed. He hated every minute of being here.

Just like she hated every minute of having him here. Especially because she was still drawn to him.

Although she'd never forgotten him—how could she with Robin as a daily reminder?—she'd been sure she had resolved all her feelings, positive and negative. Now, dang it, seeing him in the flesh had reawakened every one of them. And, speaking of flesh, he'd awakened her body, too.

When she'd leaned close to adjust his stirrup—something she'd done hundreds of times over the years for riders—she had for the first time been aware of the intimacy of the act. She wanted to touch the firm thigh that strained against faded denim. To run her fingers up his leg toward the intriguing bulge under his fly. A bulge that was probably just an automatic physical reaction to her touch, not an indication that he was actually attracted to her. He was probably married to some elegant New Yorker. Or, since he didn't wear a ring, he had half a dozen of them as lovers.

"I'll think about him later," she muttered to herself. Under her, Knight shifted impatiently. She settled the restless horse and called encouragement and instructions to Joan, who circled the ring on a black-and-white horse named Mickey, after Mickey Mouse.

The first day with a new batch of guests was always demanding. She used the morning ride to make an initial assessment, then did any required juggling of horses and riders. Each rider would spend his or her entire two-week stay with one horse, learning about the bond that can exist between horse and human.

After the ride and continuing through the afternoon, each guest got a private lesson. Other than that, they were on their own for R&R, including getting a massage, taking a sauna, swimming in the indoor or outdoor pool, participating in classes in relaxation techniques and Pilates, or simply sitting in the sun with a cold drink.

She dreaded facing Evan again, which was why she'd scheduled his lesson last, after Joan's. Would he show? Maybe now that he realized Jess was the wrangler, he'd cancel his holiday.

Joan, a thirtysomething woman with an elaborate hairdo squashed under a straw cowboy hat from the Crazy Horse gift shop, called out, "Can we stop now? These new jeans are chafing."

"Okay, we'll cut the lesson short. If you have any old jeans with you, wear them tomorrow."

Brand-new designer jeans. What was the woman thinking? The brochure told guests to bring well-worn clothing. Jess had written the copy herself. Why didn't people take her advice?

As she and Knight led Joan and her horse, Mickey, toward the barn, she thought about Evan's wardrobe. The jeans that hugged his body so enticingly might have an expensive designer label, but they were faded and worn. The beige denim shirt was new, like his boots. She'd bet the city boy had never owned riding boots before, and probably he hadn't had any long-sleeved shirts that were appropriate for wear in the country. She'd specified long sleeves, to protect the guests from sunburn and scratches.

He'd read the brochure. No surprise there. Evan learned by reading, whereas she learned by doing. It was only one of the many differences between them. Once she'd thought the differences were cute, believed opposites attracted, but he'd proved her wrong.

Madisun met Jess and Joan at the barn, and helped the tired student dismount. They sent her hobbling on her way, and then the girl began to take off Mickey's tack. "Rusty's out back, tethered in the shade," she informed Jess.

"Thanks. When you finish with Mickey, go on home. I'll look after Rusty and Knight when the last lesson's over."

Jess stepped inside the barn and happily inhaled the familiar scent: a heady blend of hay and leather, apples and horses. In the miniature bathroom, she poured a glass of water and savored each chilly mouthful as it slid down her throat. She'd long ago stripped down to her T-shirt, and now she splashed cold water on her face and arms. Then she propped herself in the bathroom doorway, fanning herself with her hat as

Madisun hung up Mickey's tack and collected grooming brushes.

Maybe Evan was already on his way home to New York. If there was any guy who knew how to run away from Jess and Caribou Crossing, it was Evan Kincaid. She still remembered how much that had hurt, after their night at Zephyr Lake.

She had made love for the very first time, and with the boy she'd considered the love of her life. And he'd reacted like she'd tried to clamp a branding iron on his flank.

"Jess?" It was his voice, from the barnyard.

So he hadn't run this time. At least not yet. "Be right out."

She had to clear the air. No more, no less. Years ago he'd apologized—in a couple of stupid *e-mails*—and she'd told him to get on with his life. That obviously hadn't been enough for either of them, because the air between them had that heavy, tense feel, like just before a thunderstorm. If he was staying, she had to deal with this.

Jess strode out of the barn and came face-to-face with him.

He'd rolled up his sleeves and undone the top few buttons of his shirt. A strong neck, curls of tawny hair . . . She dropped her eyes and found herself gazing spellbound at his forearm. A muscled forearm. Again she marveled that Ev had acquired this new and utterly fascinating body.

"We have to talk." Fighting the impulse to run her fingers over his firm arm, she raised her gaze determinedly and stared into his eyes.

He nodded. "Jess, I owe you an apology."

A face-to-face apology. Her heart had been waiting a decade for this. So why was she irritated? Probably because she'd been all keyed up and ready to go, and he'd beaten her out of the starting gate. She glanced toward the hitching rail where Madisun was grooming Mickey. Satisfied that the girl was too far away to overhear, Jess opened her mouth to begin.

"I was a complete jerk," he said. "Please accept my apology. Can you forgive me?"

"I . . . Uh, what exactly are you apologizing for?" Running away, e-mailing rather than phoning, believing her when she said he should get lost?

"For violating our relationship, then running away like a coward."

Violating . . . What the heck was the man talking about? "Violating our relationship?"

"Jess, you were my best friend. From the moment I met you I felt a strong connection, and when we were kids it was great." Color tinged his strong cheekbones. "Then when I got older, hormones kicked in and . . . Look, I knew I was leaving town and you were staying. I never meant to be anything other than a friend. But then, at the lake, we had some beer and I . . . lost control. I betrayed you."

Was that why he'd run away right after they'd made love? He thought he'd betrayed their friendship? For her, she'd been honoring it.

"And I betrayed your parents," he went on.

"My parents?" she croaked disbelievingly. "How do my parents come into this?"

"They were so good to me. They trusted me and then I . . . took advantage of you."

Ooh! What an idiot he was! He didn't have a clue what had really gone on. She glared at him. "I seduced you."

"What?"

She took pleasure in how stupid he looked with his mouth hanging open. Hah! He might have beaten her out of the gate but she'd left him behind on the stretch.

"I had a silly crush on you," she said. "You acted like you weren't attracted to me but I didn't believe you." She had started out crisp and matter-of-fact, but slowed as she remembered the girl she had been. A crush? It had been full-blown love, but no way would she tell him that. "I wanted one night with you, Ev. I wanted you to—oh, it seems silly now that we're both grown up—to realize you cared for me. Not because I wanted you to stay in town. I absolutely did not want you to give up your dreams. I just needed to know the feelings were mutual."

He opened his mouth, but she rushed on. "I set it up. That picnic. I lied when I told you there was a party at the lake, and then lied when I said I'd made a mistake about the date. I brought the beer, figuring it would loosen your inhibitions. I even brought the c-condom." Her voice stuttered over the last word.

That damned condom. She'd bought it from a machine in the girl's restroom at school and carried it in her jeans pocket for so long, fingered it so many times, no wonder the stupid thing ripped just when it counted.

She'd always wondered if Evan had realized it had torn. He'd been as inexperienced as she had. When he'd first e-mailed, he'd asked how she was, not whether she was pregnant. And she'd responded in the same vein, saying she was great, terrific, never better.

Oh well, what did it matter whether he'd known? What mattered was that she hadn't told him about Robin then, and had no intention of telling him now.

Afraid he could read her thoughts, she said, "Yeah, Ev, I seduced you. It was dumb. And . . . well, I apologize." She let out a long breath, feeling like she'd crossed the finish line.

"But . . ." He shook his head, lagging a lap behind. "I don't get it."

She drew in a shuddery breath. "Like you said, there was this connection between us. It was kind of like brother and sister when we were kids, but when we were teenagers it turned into something different. For me, and I thought also for you. I needed to find out." Without thinking, she reached up to grip his shoulders.

He gazed down at her, and now the air between them was thick with tension.

Her hands became aware of the muscle and bone they gripped through the denim of his shirt.

The blue-green of his eyes deepened and a muscle twitched at the side of his mouth.

She found herself gasping for air. Dang it, how could the man have this effect on her?

Hurriedly, she dropped her hands and stepped away from him. "Okay, I admit I was upset when you skedaddled out of Caribou Crossing, and pissed when you e-mailed rather than phoned. But that's the past. Let's put it behind us."

Jess took another step backward. "Tell me, how *is* New York anyhow? All that you hoped for? And your career? You're doing well, achieving your goals?" She was babbling, but with each word she reminded herself that he didn't belong here. Didn't belong with her. No way was she going to let herself feel those old feelings again.

He'd been frowning a little as he watched her, but now he smiled as if he'd accepted her invitation to move forward. "Everything's perfect. New York's the best city in the world. I feel so alive there."

Yes, she could see that from the way his face became animated as he spoke.

"And my career—I'm an investment counselor—is all I'd dreamed of."

"That's great. I'm happy for you." And she meant that in all sincerity. Interesting, though, that he'd said nothing about his personal life. Maybe he didn't want to hurt her feelings. She forced a smile, determined to prove she was over him. "And are you married?" Google hadn't supplied her with that information.

"Not yet. I'm in a relationship, though. Her name is Cynthia Jefferson."

Of course he was in a relationship. How crazy to feel a sense of letdown. "I'm sure she's just lovely," she gushed. "And brilliant. That goes without saying." Unlike herself, who'd only scraped by in school because Evan helped her with her homework.

"All of that."

She tossed her head. "Well, enough chitchat. I guess we'd better get on with the riding lesson." Knowing she sounded like a total idiot, Jess clamped her lips shut and strode around the corner of the barn.

Silently, she tasted the name Cynthia—lovely, brilliant, *all of that* Cynthia—and it set her teeth on edge.

Evan watched Jess go. She'd caught him off guard and kept him off balance. He was still trying to get his brain around her announcement that she had seduced him, not to mention cope with the physical impact of her touch.

Damn Gianni for insisting he stay. When Evan had found time at noon to make a call without being overheard and had admitted to once being friends—yes, that was all he'd said, friends—with TJ Cousins, his client had brushed off the conflict-of-interest issue. Gianni said he was confident Evan would make an objective assessment as long as he didn't reveal to Jess why he was really at the Crazy Horse.

In order to make that assessment, Evan would have to spend a lot of time with Jess, which was proving to be unsettling. He was also uncomfortable with Gianni's insistence that he not let Jess know Gianni had sent him. Deception went against his nature, and he particularly hated to deceive Jess. It made him feel like a schmuck, yet he couldn't violate his client's confidence. What a mess this all was, and not least his attraction to Jess, which was strengthening by the moment.

"Evan?" she called from somewhere out of sight. "What's the holdup?"

He pulled himself together and went to find her. She was stroking Rusty, who was tied to a hitching rail under a leafy tree.

"I'm stuck with that horse?"

Rusty raised his head and Jess glanced over her shoulder. "He's one of our best. I trained him myself."

"He . . ."

"What?" She swung around to face him, her face showing pure exasperation.

"He tromped on my foot." As the words came out, he realized he sounded like a peevish little boy.

Jess's lips twitched and he had to grin in response. In a moment they were both howling with laughter. Now, at last, the air truly was clear.

"So," Jess said when she could talk again, "the first lesson is to always be aware of a horse's feet. I guess you've learned that one, so we can move on." She untied Rusty from the hitching rail.

Evan moved up beside her and, as she turned, his forearm brushed her arm. Heat surged through him and he jerked away at the same time she did.

"Where's your hat?" she demanded. "The brochure said to bring a hat. The afternoon sun is hot and you don't want to get sunstroke."

"I don't wear hats. You didn't used to, either." She'd said she liked to feel the wind in her hair. "But here you are in a Stetson."

"It's a Resistol and it's part of the job. Local color. I'll get you a spare hat. Or maybe you'd like a helmet?" she added in a teasing tone.

"Don't need a helmet. I'm not about to try anything dangerous."

"Riding a bike isn't dangerous," she taunted, "and yet you managed to fall off."

Annoyed by the reminder, he said grimly, "No helmet. No hat."

"Oh well, you've got a thick head. And you did sign the waiver. Mount up and we'll head into the ring."

He remembered something he'd read. "Uh, should I tighten the cinch?"

"Huh?" Jess gaped as if he'd started to spout Greek. Then she snapped her fingers. "You got that from a book."

Ruefully, he said, "You know me too well."

She hooted with laughter. "I still can't believe you actually thought you could learn to skate by reading a book."

He flinched, then summoned a wry grin. "I caught Brooke on a good day and she bought me secondhand skates." His mother had told him to call her Brooke because "Mom" made her feel middle-aged; she was a mere fifteen years older than him. "I practiced skating on the carpet, night after night."

"And then you went out on the frozen lake and fell splat on your butt. It was hilarious."

"I'm sure." He deliberated for a moment, then went on, for some reason wanting her to know the truth. "But to me it was horrible. I didn't want to confess I didn't know how to skate. I tried to learn, and I failed. The kids laughed, and I had to spend the rest of the winter pretending to my mother I was going skating. But the worst thing was, I believed I was a klutz."

The laughter had faded from her eyes as he spoke. But when he finished, she smiled again. Gently. "Ev, you have a brilliant brain, but you gotta admit you really are a klutz."

He shook his head. "You're wrong, Jess. You know what a self-fulfilling prophecy is? That's what you and I created. But it's not true. I'm as good at sports as the next guy. Not a natural like you, but not bad."

Her mouth formed a silent "oh."

"About riding . . . I wasn't trying to learn how from a book. I only wanted some background."

"Background is good." Her voice sounded choky and moisture sheened her eyes. "Gosh, Evan, I'm sorry. I misjudged you. I feel like . . ." She sniffed. "Like I ruined your childhood single-handedly."

He chuckled. This was vintage Jess. Her emotions ran close to the surface. "Don't overdramatize. But a person tends to live up to others' expectations, right? Well, have higher expectations of me."

She sniffed again, then smiled tentatively. "All right, I will." Then she touched his forearm. "I did notice you've, uh, developed some muscles."

His arm tingled. He looked down and saw three grubby fingers resting on his bare skin. There was dirt and he hated to think what else under her short fingernails. How could these fingers send such a zing through his blood? A zing that went straight to his groin.

"Squash," he blurted, moving his arm away and swinging an imaginary racquet.

Her cheeks were pinker than they'd been a moment ago. Had she felt that zing, too? "Running around a court chasing a ball? Boy, that sounds like fun."

He refused to apologize for preferring squash to riding. "It keeps me fit. And I run, lift weights. Ski." Away from her touch, his pulse slowed. A little. "Believe it or not, I skate at Rockefeller Center every winter."

"You used to say the only muscle a man needed to develop was his brain."

"My brain got so heavy, I had to build up some other muscles to support it."

She grinned. "I dunno about your brain, but your ears used to be pretty darn big."

They laughed together.

"Gosh, Ev, I've missed you. You know that?"

"Me, too." Now that he was standing next to her, he couldn't imagine how he'd survived ten years without her. Or how he would survive the next ten.

Her smile was so openhearted . . . and then, in a flash, it changed. As if she'd remembered something bad. Damn.

Guess it was too much to hope that they'd be able to put everything behind them.

He grabbed the reins from her hand. "Okay, teach me the trick for mounting this gigantic beast."

"Um, well, you should tighten the cinch first."

"You mean I was right?"

"Yup, actually. Madisun would have left it loose and—"

"Show me how."

But he regretted the request when her grimy fingers guided his own fumbling ones in hoisting the strap tighter around Rusty's belly. How could grubby hands possibly be so arousing?

He hiked himself on board, she sprung onto her black horse, and they rode over to the training ring. There, Jess told him to circle the perimeter, keeping Rusty close to the fence. Simple, repetitive, and it gave him time to reflect. He'd survived his apology, even though Jess had thrown in a twist he guessed would have him awake to all hours.

She'd seduced him? He didn't know whether to be flattered or insulted.

She'd cared for him. Not just as a friend, but romantically. Of course, she'd said it was only a silly crush, and she'd had no qualms about blowing him off in an e-mail a couple months later. Still, she'd cared. He had, too, though he'd never sorted out how much was friendship, how much was lust, and how much was . . . something else. A crush, like she'd said.

"Heels down and straighten your back!" Her voice broke into his musings, and he obeyed her instructions. Glancing over at her, looking so pretty and at home on horseback, he wondered if there was a chance the two of them might resurrect their friendship. Having found her again, he didn't want to lose her for the second time.

Jess was married, and surely Evan could get over his totally irrational feelings of attraction. Good God, he was dating Cynthia, who was exactly the kind of successful, classy woman he'd always wanted.

But even if he did handle the attraction issue, what about Jess's business scheme, and Gianni? He stretched his back, which ached from doing nothing more than sit atop a horse. He hoped Jess had developed a head for business and he could, in all good conscience, make a favorable recommendation. He hated the position Gianni had put him in.

He also hated how sexy Jess looked, sitting tall yet at ease in the saddle, a grubby white T-shirt hugging her curves.

"Take Rusty to a trot," she called.

"I hate trotting. It hurts."

"Of course it does if you flop around like a sack of potatoes. Come on, Ev, you have muscles now. Use them. Watch me."

Mesmerized, he watched her thighs and trim butt as she trotted her horse around the ring. Then, gritting his teeth, he gave it another try, and began to feel marginally more adept even though his muscles screamed in protest.

Finally, Jess said, "Okay, time to call it quits. You done good, Ev. There may be hope for you yet, cowboy."

They rode together into the deserted barnyard. Evan clambered awkwardly out of the saddle and winced as he landed on the ground.

"Sore?" Jess asked, swinging lightly from her own saddle.

"I'm finding new muscles."

She yanked the hat from her head, hooked it over a fence post, and pulled off the leather thong that held her hair in its tail. She tilted her head back and raised her hands to shake her hair loose, beaming with pleasure. The gesture was unaffected and purely sensual. It left him breathless.

"You should have a sauna before supper," she said, hands still at her head, torso stretching with abandon. "Remember, this is a resort and spa. The idea is to feel good and have fun, not to suffer."

He almost groaned. If she didn't want him to suffer, she shouldn't toss her hair that way. She shouldn't lift her arms high and wriggle around like that, so her T-shirt strained against her breasts.

Grimly he reminded himself of the reason he'd come to the Crazy Horse. "So tell me what you're up to these days, Jess. No more dreams of winning the Triple Crown?"

She shook her head, then flashed a quick, conspiratorial grin. "No, but I do have—" She broke off and her face sobered. "It's been a long day. I have chores to do before I go, and you don't have too long before supper. You really do need a sauna. And I'd bet, this close to mealtime, you can find a masseur or masseuse who's got an opening. Just think how good a massage would feel."

Oh, yeah. Every muscle in his body was begging. Resigned, he shrugged. "We'll talk tomorrow."

"Sure. See you in the morning."

"See you." He began to make his painful way toward the lodge.

"Evan?"

He turned back to find her staring at him.

"Why are you here in Hicksville?"

She'd asked before and he knew he'd eventually have to respond, so he had worked out an answer. It was even three-quarters true. "I belong to a young businesspeople's association. A number of us are around the ten-year mark in terms of when we left home to pursue our careers. One of the men came up with the idea of a ten-year plaque to celebrate our achievements. One of the women threw out a challenge. Before we could qualify for the plaque, we had to achieve something we were afraid of or backed down from or failed at as a kid."

Jess's forehead scrunched up. "What a weird idea."

He'd thought so, too, which was why he'd voted against Harriet Prince's proposal.

"You couldn't have settled for skating?" Jess asked. Then she shook her head. "No, that would be too easy. It had to be riding."

He nodded. "It sounds ridiculous."

"It'll make for some interesting stories when all you big successes get back together and report on your return to childhood."

That was pretty much what Harriet had said. And that was another reason he liked Cynthia; she'd agreed that the idea was absurd. Now it occurred to him that, if he really did learn how to ride, he could actually earn the stupid plaque. Not that he wanted it.

"So you need a trophy to prove to you how far you've come," Jess murmured.

"Of course I don't." Annoyed, he turned away again and began to hobble along the unpaved road, wishing he could just peel his boots off and toss them into the bushes. He glanced over his shoulder and saw that she stood still, staring after him. He raised a hand and, after a moment, she raised her own.

Evan took a deep breath, then continued along the road to the lodge. It was uphill, of course, which he figured was a fair analogy to this whole Crazy Horse experience.

Jess had cut herself off when she'd begun to reveal her latest dream. She didn't trust him enough to pour out her heart as she had when she was a girl. The truth was, he didn't deserve her trust. But if he couldn't get her to tell him about her no-frills riding camp, how the hell could he evaluate it? What's more, he felt like a pile of horseshit for deceiving her. And he felt as guilty as hell for being attracted to her.

He needed to hear Cynthia's voice. He hadn't talked to her

since he'd arrived. When he'd tried yesterday, his call had gone to voice mail. Now—he made the calculation quickly—it would be evening in New York. She'd probably be out for dinner. Oh well, at worst he could listen to her recorded voice. Maybe that would restore his sanity.

As he approached the picturesque log lodge framed by lush hanging baskets and a garden full of brilliant flowers, he tried to evaluate it through Cynthia's eyes. He remembered Gianni's term: upscale rustic. Yes, it was. If it was a ski lodge in Switzerland, Cynthia might like it, but when you combined it with heat, dust, and the smell of horses, he knew she'd be unimpressed. On the other hand, the spa facilities were world class. Maybe he should ask her to join him.

The lobby was quiet and he claimed the chair by the old-fashioned pay phone. He positioned the chair to face out the side window, though there wasn't much to see but a mass of tall trees, and called Cynthia.

A bird hung on to the side of one of the trees, banging its beak into the trunk. The word woodpecker flashed into his mind, surprising him because he was no more a bird person than a tree expert. Was the creature beating its head against a brick wall, just as he was? No, likely it was hunting for bugs. Doing something productive.

It was a pretty bird, with a red throat and black and white spotted markings.

"Cynthia Jefferson."

"It's really you. I was half expecting voice mail."

She laughed, a husky, sexy purr. "Darling. You called to talk to my voice mail? Shall I hang up?"

"Don't, please. I just wanted to hear your voice, in any form."

"Homesick?"

"Yeah." Oh yeah. He'd been feeling frustrated and restless, and now homesickness hit him like a punch in the gut. He stopped watching the stupid bird. If he were in Manhattan, he could be sitting with Cynthia in one of their favorite restaurants. He imagined waiters bustling around, other diners negotiating deals or flirting across the table. Cynthia, full of energy, just like the city, telling him about the latest merger she'd negotiated. Looking amazing, all sleek and sophisticated. Immaculate, from her short, elegantly styled blond hair to her perfectly manicured fingernails and pedicured toenails.

"Tell me you're finished and you're coming home," she said.

"Don't I wish."

"You can't just interview this wrangler person, get her business plan, make an assessment, and fly home?"

"Gianni's determined that I not reveal why I'm here, and immerse myself in ambiance. He calls it ambiance, I call it horseshit."

She chuckled. "Sounds utterly disgusting."

"Pretty much. And I ache in muscles I didn't even know I had." Calling her had nixed the possibility of a sauna, so he would shower and do the stretches his personal trainer had given him, though they'd been designed for a desk-bound CEO, not a beginner rider.

"Poor baby. Still, it's true there are factors to consider other than purely financial ones, and you can often assess better by observing."

"You're right," he admitted. He always valued Cynthia's intellect and her opinion.

"It's harder for a person to deceive you. If this woman is going to run the type of operation she pitched to Gianni, she needs quite the package of skills. Strong organizational ability, excellent business planning and budgeting, marketing, people skills, as well as the actual, um, horsy talents, whatever those entail. So, what do you think so far?"

How much should he tell her? "Something unexpected

happened. It turns out this TJ Cousins is actually a girl I knew when I lived here. Do you remember me mentioning Jess Bly?"

"Of course. Your best friend when you were children. Good Lord, Evan, is she the person you're investigating? That'll make it difficult."

Cynthia didn't know the half of it, thank God. He'd never told her about his adolescent lust, nor the night at Zephyr Lake. "It does. I feel like I'm doing something underhanded."

"Hmm. Of course you'd hate to mislead an old friend. But Evan, surely in this case your loyalty is to Gianni. He's the sole reason you're there."

"That's true. But he should trust me. I can tell Jess why I'm here, and still make an objective assessment."

"Darling, you're the best at what you do, but you've never had to analyze a friend's business proposal. She'll try to trade on your old friendship."

"She's not like that."

Another husky laugh. "Don't be naïve. Everyone's like that. The animal instinct for self-preservation. She may not even be conscious she's doing it, but you'll feel pressured."

It was true. He already did. But at least if Evan preserved his anonymity and Gianni decided not to invest, Jess would never know Evan was behind that decision. He grimaced. That didn't sit well with him either. How could he and Jess renew their friendship if the foundation was a huge lie? "I'm caught between a rock and a hard place," he muttered.

"You are. But you have excellent business sense. You'll make the right decision."

And she could help him stay objective, not to mention keep him from thinking dirty thoughts about Jess. "Why don't you come and join me?"

He listened to dead air for a moment, and then she said,

in a tone of disbelief, "You want me to come to the Crazy Horse?"

"There's a luxury spa. All sorts of seaweed wraps and manicures and massage. Pilates, too. You love that kind of thing."

"I love it because I'm a frantically busy lawyer who needs to destress on occasion."

"Destress now, here with me. I promise you'd never have to ride a horse."

"You can bet on that. But seriously, Evan, you know it's impossible. I have a full schedule. By the way, Bob Graham's coming in tomorrow. From Weston Ventures? He's thinking about buying that up-and-coming software company, Dynamite, and it could be quite exciting. Hush-hush, of course."

"Of course." They often discussed confidential matters, and trusted each other implicitly.

"Now, darling, I must run. I'm in a cab and it's just arrived at Nobu. I'm having dinner with Vanessa and Yul."

"I'm envious." The food at the Crazy Horse actually was gourmet, but he yearned for the sophistication of New York eateries.

After he hung up, he sprawled back in the chair and thought about Cynthia's analysis of his situation. She thought Jess would, intentionally or unintentionally, try to trade on their prior relationship. He had once accused Cynthia of being cynical and she'd given him a condescending smile. "No, darling, just realistic. It's another thing we have in common. It's part of the reason we're both so successful."

He knew her assessment of him was correct. Yet he did believe—as he knew she did—that decent people could promote their own interests without being unethical or dishonest. That's why it bothered him so much to keep quiet about his reason for being at the Crazy Horse.

And Cynthia was wrong about Jess. Jess would never manipulate him. She was honest and completely without guile.

Except that she had seduced him by means of a rather complex deception, and only confessed ten years later. . . .

Damn. He didn't want to think of Jess as a schemer, any more than he liked keeping secrets from her.

He rose creakily to his feet and glanced out the window, noticing that the colorful bird had disappeared.

Chapter Four

Jess sat at the kitchen table at Bly Ranch, eating her mother's roast chicken, taking a second helping of the parsley-sprinkled boiled new potatoes her father passed, but mostly watching Robin as she ate supper and chattered about her day at school.

Tonight, the similarities between her daughter and Evan seemed particularly pronounced, though no one else had ever noticed. The touches were subtle—the Bly genes had taken over the dominant features like bone structure and color of hair and eyes—but Evan's signature was there. When Robin screwed her face into a grimace as she told about some icky boy's gross joke, she mirrored Evan's expression when he'd seen the manure on his new Tony Lamas. When Rob's young brow furrowed with concentration as she described the science project she was planning, it was Evan's look as he listened to Jess describe the correct riding posture.

Evan's genes had definitely gone into creating this unique, fantastic human being.

Should she have told him back then? Given him a chance?

No, of course not. In the past ten years, he'd achieved the life he always dreamed of, and that wouldn't have happened if he'd known about Robin. Evan, whatever his flaws, was an honorable guy. He'd have insisted on marrying Jess, and they'd all have been miserable. This way, they were all happy. Yes, she'd done the right thing.

"Mom?"

She surfaced. "What, Rob?"

"Can I get a new pair of black jeans for our rodeo exhibition? Mine are too short."

"You're shooting up like a weed," Jess's father said to Robin. "You're going to be taller than your mother."

"You're right, Wade," her mom, Miriam, agreed. "The child has her mom's build but her dad's height."

Her dad. Yes, Evan was tall. But of course, her parents were talking about Dave, because they thought he was Robin's father. And he was, in every way that counted.

"Jeans," she said quickly. "Yes, sure. Pick them up the next time you're in town staying with your *dad*." She heard her voice emphasize the last word needlessly.

Robin spent half her time with her mom and grandparents at Bly Ranch, and the other half with Dave, who lived in a comfy two-bedroom suite at the Wild Rose Inn, the charming heritage hotel he owned. Although Jess and Dave were divorced, they were still the best of friends, and both adored Robin.

Should she tell Dave that Evan was in town? It would upset him, even if she assured him Ev had no clue Robin even existed.

Was there any chance the two men might bump into each other? Probably not. Dave was too busy to visit the Crazy Horse, and Evan wasn't likely to go into the town of Caribou Crossing. Unless . . . Would he go to see his mother, Brooke? It would be really nice if they reconciled. But what were the chances? Evan's bitterness ran bone deep, and for good reason. Still, he didn't know about Brooke's amazing turnaround. . . .

"Mo-ther!"

"Sorry, what did I miss this time?"

"I asked if Kimiko can come over after school tomorrow."

"Sure. Do you want to ask her for supper?" Jess didn't have to consult her mother, who did most of the cooking. Miriam Bly delighted in feeding any of Robin's or Jess's friends.

"I did."

Jess grinned. Her daughter operated under the same assumption of hospitality.

"But she can't," Robin went on. "Her brother's got some dorky game at seven, and her parents are dragging her along."

Jess smothered another grin. She could just imagine that, in two or three years' time, Kimiko's good-looking, athletic brother might be hero material for her little girl. She was grateful that day was still a ways off.

Or maybe Rob would take after her mother. Jess had never been impressed by the jocks. She couldn't see the point of games like football and basketball. When you'd galloped a horse across an open meadow and jumped a split-rail fence, squabbling over a ball seemed ridiculous.

It wasn't Dave's prowess at basketball that had attracted her. He was just such a darn nice guy. The nicest boy in school. He'd asked her out in grade eleven and she'd said no, telling him she wasn't ready to date. The truth was, her heart belonged to Evan, who showed not the slightest interest in dating her. But Dave was a good friend. When Jess wasn't hanging out with Evan, she spent a lot of time with Dave and his pals—a group Evan disparaging called "the in crowd."

The most she and Dave had ever done was exchange a peck on the cheek. He respected her wishes and she trusted him. That was why it was Dave she went to when she discovered she was pregnant. Evan had been gone almost two months and she hadn't heard a word from him.

He'd left her that night at Zephyr Lake, the unathletic Evan taking off at a flat-out gallop. He'd yanked off the condom, pulled on his pants, and disappeared into the darkness, leaving her his mom's old clunker of a car but not the keys, which must have been in his pocket. Leaving her in tears, wondering how such a beautiful night could have gone so wrong. Had sex with her been that awful? Or had he realized the condom had broken, and in an instant seen his entire future come crashing down?

She had finally pulled herself together enough to walk out to the highway and hitch a ride home. She didn't hear from him, and then, two days later, her mom came back from the grocery store with the latest gossip. Evan had caught an earlier bus than he'd planned and was already on his way across the continent to Cornell. Jess felt utterly betrayed. He had denied her the one thing she wanted: a beautiful memory of a mutual exchange of love. Instead she had the memory of her own stupidity, and his rejection.

Jess had thought distance might heal the wound. She and Ev had squabbled many times over the years, but always made up quickly. She'd waited for him to call or e-mail, but it was ages before she got his e-mail with that stilted apology and inquiry into how she was. Like he was a stranger writing a courtesy note.

Even at that, she might have given him another chance, but by the time he e-mailed again, Jess knew she was pregnant and planned to keep the baby. How could she write back and forth to Evan and pretend everything was normal between them? How could she share some details of her life but leave out the most important ones? Far better to make a break, no matter how painful.

"Jessica!"

She jerked upright, startled to find that her father and Robin had left. Her mother stood beside her, hands planted firmly on her hips. "I swear, you haven't been so moody since you were pregnant. There're bills to pay and horses to tend to. Are you going to daydream all night?"

She probably was. But first she had work to do. The ranch was a busy place and they all had their own set of chores. What with the job at the Crazy Horse and her work here, there was little time left over for pursuing her dream of setting up a no-frills boot camp for humans and horses. The dream she'd almost started to tell Evan about that afternoon.

Her mother squeezed her shoulder. "Feeling okay, honey?"

She jerked to her feet. "Fine. I'll be out in the barn."

As she followed the path through her mother's lush flower and vegetable garden, Jess thought about the way she'd started to open up to Evan about her riding camp ideas, just like in the old days. He'd been the recipient of all her dreams—except the ones about making love with him. But now . . . Now, the plain truth was that he intimidated her. When they were kids, they were equals because both had big dreams and—at least so she'd thought—an equal chance of achieving them. Now, ten years later, he had succeeded and she had . . . not failed, just not gotten there yet.

If she hadn't had a child, if she and Dave hadn't divorced, if her father hadn't had a stroke . . . Yes, she had excuses. But all the same, she feared her riding camp plan would sound like another childish dream to Evan. His mother, Brooke, had shown her the business card he'd enclosed with one of the checks he'd sent. He owned his own company. She envisioned a ritzy office, rich clients, sophisticated investments, international finance. Evan was miles out of her league.

And he'd done it all in ten years. Yes, the man did deserve a plaque.

Jess firmed her jaw. Okay, so she hadn't "made it" in ten years. But she would.

Dinner at the Crazy Horse last night, Sunday, had been quick and quiet, with most people travel-weary. That had been fine by Evan, who still, in social situations with strangers, felt some of the same awkwardness as when he was a misfit kid. He could talk investments, world affairs, and theatre, but personal small talk didn't come naturally.

Monday night, when the ten guests were seated around a polished maple table, the owners, Will and his wife, Kathy, pulled up chairs and joined them.

"Okay, folks," Will said, "it's time for introductions. Thérèse and George, how about you start us out, since this is your second time here."

A fit-looking middle-aged couple exchanged smiles, then the woman said, "We're from Switzerland and last summer we wanted to see Canada." Her English was flavored with a charming French accent. "Also we had a yen to try Western riding. We surfed the net for a place that was small, and focused on riding."

"But didn't make beginners round up cattle and camp out on the trail," George added, with a laugh.

"This was perfect," said Thérèse, "and so here we are again. Last year we traveled on to Banff and Jasper, and this year, after our stay at the Crazy Horse, we are going to Vancouver, then Victoria."

A plump, vibrant young woman, said, "You should come south of the border to Seattle. That's where I'm from. I can tell you all the things to see and do."

She glanced around the table. "I'll go next, seeing as I'm already talking. I'm Sandy, a software developer. I wanted a change from computers and the city, and I've always loved horses. I read about the Crazy Horse in a resort magazine. It sounded relaxed, friendly."

Next came Sylvia and Aaron from Chicago, both lawyers, who said friends had recommended the Crazy Horse.

"The Weissmans, right?" Kathy inquired.

"That's right. They were coming with us but had to cancel at the last minute because his mother had a heart attack."

"We were sorry to hear about that," Will said. "Hope his mother is okay."

"She's recovering," Sylvia said, "enough to kvetch about the diet and exercise program they're lining up for her."

Kathy laughed, then said, "Since they had to cancel, we acquired Evan."

Everyone turned toward him.

"I'm from New York," he began. He couldn't tell them someone had recommended the place, or they'd ask for a name. And he didn't want to tell the silly plaque story. He contented himself with saying, "I'm an investment counselor and, like Sandy, needed a break and thought I'd try something different."

The conversational ball passed to Joan, the thirtysomething woman with big hair who'd been limping up to the lodge when Evan walked down to the barn for his afternoon lesson. In passing, she'd said, "Hope you survive better than I did."

Now Joan said, "I've been a stay-at-home wife and mom, and the youngest kid just flew the nest. My husband, a real estate developer, never takes holidays so I'm giving myself a treat, riding horses plus getting some spa pampering." She wrinkled her nose ruefully. "At least I thought it would be a treat until I spent a couple of hours on a horse."

"It gets easier," Thérèse said. "Trust me."

That left Ann, an orthopedic surgeon from Toronto, and two middle-aged women whose names were Beth and Kim. They said they were partners who owned a bookstore in Vancouver, and from their affectionate manner Evan assumed the partnership to be personal as well as business. Ann, Beth, and Kim all confessed to being outdoors gals at heart.

These people weren't the country bumpkins he'd, for some reason, been expecting. He remembered now that Angelica had said the resort was exclusive and world famous, and the price tag was hefty. He should have known the other guests would be people who had either made or inherited a fair bit of money.

Before Evan knew it, he, Ann, and George, the CEO of a medical supply company, were deep in a discussion of the differences between health care systems in different countries, and how that impacted George's company's sales.

It seemed the social aspects of this trip might not be so bad after all. Who knew, he might even get some new business. Though he mustn't forget his real purpose: his mission for Gianni.

The mission that required deceiving Jess, while somehow persuading her to trust him again.

Evan groaned as hot shower water pounded muscles that had stiffened overnight. Today's program was light: a morning trail ride, then a free afternoon. Over dinner last night, guests had been making plans for massages and spa treatments, and Kathy was giving a cooking class, but Evan had no interest in such things. A few were going into Caribou Crossing, which was the last thing he wanted to do.

He missed his work.

This whole situation was absurd. He wanted to go to his New York fitness club and work out the aches and pains, then have a doppio—a double-shot espresso. He wanted to put in a thirteen-hour day at the office, then meet Cynthia for drinks and stimulating conversation. They'd part with a quick kiss—no sex, because they only made love on weekends, when they didn't have to get up at the crack of dawn. In New York, his life was organized. It made sense.

Quickly he dressed and headed for the lodge, where he dialed his own office number. After a ten-minute rapid-fire chat with Angelica, he felt even more frustrated. Damn it, things were happening in the world and he was stuck in Hicksville, missing out.

Because there was only one computer for guests, he couldn't monopolize it, and besides, Internet reception was slow and spotty. He asked Angelica to try to summarize everything in one e-mail each day, with attachments. He'd copy it to his USB drive and take it to his room, review everything on his laptop, type notes in response, then take his USB back to the guest computer and e-mail the file to her. Clumsy. Clunky. Frustrating. Inefficient. But it seemed to be the best he could do.

The lodge was coming to life, and he followed his nose into the dining room. At home, breakfast was usually a toasted bagel and a doppio to go, and yesterday the Crazy Horse buffet had been intimidating. His stomach hadn't been up to facing fruit salad, granola, bacon and eggs, sausages and pancakes, porridge with brown sugar and cream, and a basket of fresh breads and muffins.

Today, he was surprised to find he was really hungry, and the food looked tempting. He took small servings of several items before seating himself at the communal table, a slab of wood the size of the glass-topped table back in his own boardroom.

Socializing first thing in the morning was another rarity, and he wished for a private table, a *New York Times*, and his iPhone. By the time the table had filled up, he was finished eating and excused himself, his quiet voice barely audible amid the babble of excited chatter.

He headed back to his cabin to exchange comfortable sneakers for boots. Maybe if he went down to the barn early, he could get Jess talking about her no-frills riding camp.

His expensive boots looked almost as good as new. After yesterday's riding lesson, he had overcome his disgust and cleaned and polished them. But when he tried to wedge his sore feet inside, he decided that either the boots had shrunk overnight or his feet had expanded. Then, the moment he limped outside, reddish-brown dust rose as if magnified, to coat the gleaming surfaces. He stalked down to the barn, feeling distinctly out of sorts despite the gentle morning sun.

Jess and Madisun were bustling around the horses, and Jess barely spared him a smile. A smile that seemed more noncommittal than enthusiastic. Maybe the air between them wasn't as clear as he'd hoped.

Evan kept well away from the animals and leaned against a tree, drumming his fingers restlessly against the bark, then grimacing when he noticed his skin was sticky. Was there anything in this godforsaken place that wasn't dirty?

After a minute or two, he realized Jess wasn't going to come anywhere near him, and he could see she was far too busy to talk. He growled in annoyance, then hiked painfully back to his cabin, where he sat on the couch, glaring at his computer, which was virtually useless without the Internet.

When he returned to the barnyard half an hour later, most of the other guests were there, paired off with their horses. He went over to stand beside Rusty, keeping clear of the horse's feet. When Jess yelled, "Mount up!" he glanced at the cinch that ran under the horse's belly. When he had trouble squeezing his hand under it, he decided Jess or Madisun must have tightened it. He thrust his foot into the stirrup and hauled himself aboard.

The group left the barnyard by the same gate as yesterday, but then took what he thought was a different path. It was hard to tell; all the trees looked the same.

He concentrated on the things Jess had taught him in his private lesson—muttering "ear, shoulder, hip, heel" and "elbow, wrist, bit"—and thought he was actually improving. But after a few minutes, restlessness set in. He wasn't used to doing nothing. He was a multitasker. At home, if he was walking down the street or riding in a cab, he'd be transacting business on his iPhone. Even when he and Cynthia got together, as often as not one of them would be bouncing work ideas off the other.

Well, he could multitask here, too. In the unlikely event he did advise his client to invest in Jess's project, Gianni would have to sell some of his current interests. Evan made a mental review of Gianni's holdings, assessing the pros and cons of selling each.

He really had done a good job for Gianni. And Gianni seemed so keen on this no-frills riding thing. Gianni could afford a loss. What would it hurt to give Jess her chance?

He shook his head vigorously. It would hurt his sense of ethics. And if the program failed, it would hurt not only Gianni's pocketbook but Jess's reputation, not to mention his own.

Rusty trotted again, and Evan imagined the portly Gianni bouncing along in a rigid saddle. Gianni was the last guy he would have figured for harboring cowboy fantasies.

Evan's concentration was interrupted briefly when the horses loped. He had to admit he got a kick out of the powerful motion of Rusty underneath him. This gait was easier on his body than the trot.

When the string of horses returned to a walk, he turned his focus to investment strategies for the Alzheimer's care facility a client had started as a charitable project. Evan was on the board and—in a voluntary rather than paid capacity—in charge of managing the foundation's funds. Before he knew it, the ride was over.

Amid the milling horses and people, Evan made his way to Jess. "I was hoping you'd have time to talk."

"Evan, I have work to do."

Her answer didn't surprise him. But he had a Plan B. "The brochure said that guests can each have a couple of extra private lessons. Any chance of getting one this afternoon?"

She shoved her hat back and gaped at him. "You want *more* riding?" Then she snapped her fingers. "Ah. The plaque."

After a moment's deliberation, she said, "I have to head home for a while but I could come back later. Say around four?"

"Perfect. Thanks."

"No problem." But the way she looked at him said she thought maybe it would be.

As he made his way up to the lodge, he wondered about "home." Where did she and Dave live? It irked him to know so little about her, and to know he had only himself to blame.

Yesterday, he'd been almost tempted to ask Will and Kathy about her, but it had seemed like an invasion of her privacy. Bad enough he was deceiving Jess; he wouldn't go behind her back to gather information.

He cursed, and Joan, who'd been walking up the hill near him, shot him a startled glance. "Sorry," he murmured. "My backside's killing me."

She grinned. "Boy, do I know that feeling. So are my feet. I'm heading to my cabin to soak them."

It sounded like a great idea to him.

Evan spent the afternoon in his room on his laptop, working through the lengthy e-mail from Angelica. He felt alternately frustrated at being so cut off and pathetically grateful that the Crazy Horse did have one guest computer. He copied his completed file to the USB drive and went over to the lodge.

Kathy raised her eyebrow when she saw him at the computer again, so he said, "I'm trying to keep up with work."

"It's a pity you can't leave that behind and just enjoy the holiday," she said sympathetically.

He figured it wouldn't go over well if he replied that work was the only thing that made this "holiday" bearable.

Half an hour later, as Jess put him and Rusty through their paces in the outdoor ring, he thought grimly that when he was back in NYC, he'd be able to claim that damned plaque if he wanted to. It might be the only thing he had to show for the week. His teacher seemed no more inclined to chat with him about her horsy dreams than she had earlier in the day.

The sun that had been gentle in the morning had turned

vicious. Jess had stripped down to a figure-hugging tank top the same blue as the sky, and wasn't wearing her hat. When the lesson finally ended and she slid off her horse and came to assist him, his gaze caught on her bare shoulders and the nape of her neck peeping out from under her glossy ponytail.

Suddenly, he remembered the sight of her at Zephyr Lake, naked in the moonlight. She'd taken his breath away then, and she did now. She was slender but strong, her firm muscles a perfect compliment to her gentle curves. There was something ineffably female about her body, something earthy and so different from Cynthia's fashionable, gym-toned sleekness.

Arousal stirred his blood and guilt consumed him. He swung awkwardly off Rusty and tied the reins to the hitching rail as Jess instructed.

"You're done," she told him brusquely. "Good job, Evan. See you in the morning."

She had tied her own black horse to the right of his, and now turned her back on him and walked over to unsaddle it. He watched her over Rusty's back, admiring her natural grace and the slenderness and deftness of those grimy fingers. Why did he keep imagining those fingers touching him intimately?

Clumsily, he loosened Rusty's cinch. He hoped the activity would tame his growing erection, but his body had a mind of its own.

"Don't worry about it." At her words he jerked upright and saw she'd come to peer across Rusty's back.

"The saddle," she said. "Leave it. Aren't you ready for some R&R?"

His body was indeed sending him that message, unequivocally, but the R&R it craved wasn't the same thing she was talking about. He wasn't about to walk out from behind Rusty anytime soon and reveal his aroused state. "I want to learn," he muttered. For whatever reason, he needed to prove to both of them that he could become at least semicompetent at this horse stuff.

"Good for you. I'm impressed by your willingness."

She carried her horse's saddle toward the barn and Evan, watching the firm curves of her butt, groaned. If she had any idea how willing he was, she'd be shocked.

He fought with the unfamiliar bits of leather and metal on Rusty's saddle, and his pulse rate returned to normal.

Jess came back, carrying something he recognized from his reading as a halter, and went back to her horse. "Are you coming on the hayride tomorrow night?" she asked over her shoulder.

A hayride. Could there be a bigger waste of time?

As if he'd spoken aloud, she said, "Didn't think so. Too hokey, eh?"

"Does it have anything to recommend it?"

"A ride in a hay wagon, a sing-along, some dancing. With any luck, a clear sky and stars on the ride back. You have to experience it to believe it."

He figured it was an experience he could happily live without. He hauled the saddle off Rusty. "Shall I put this in the barn?"

"Thanks. I'll show you where." She hooked her horse's bridle over her shoulder and started across the yard.

Carrying the saddle awkwardly, he followed. "Are you going on this hokey hayride?"

She tossed a grin over her shoulder. "You betcha. I even have to wear a fringed buckskin skirt and vest."

"Sounds . . . cute."

She snorted. "Playing dress-up isn't my favorite part of the job, but it beats wearing a tie every day."

"In your humble opinion," he said mildly. Evan wore silk ties, expensive tailored suits and shirts, and Italian leather shoes proudly, as symbols of how different life was from the miserable childhood he'd left far behind.

As they walked into the cool, dark barn, he thought it smelled pleasant—of something grassy, with undertones of leather and apple. There was a faint stink of horse, but mingled with all the other scents it was quite bearable.

Jess turned, and her eyes twinkled in the dim light. "If you come on the hayride, you can laugh at me in my Annie Oakley getup."

He dumped the saddle where she indicated, on a wooden bar bearing Rusty's name. "Hard to say no to an offer like that, but it doesn't sound like my kind of thing."

She gave him a level stare. "What's the matter, Ev? Scared you might loosen up and actually have fun out here in Hicksville?"

He grimaced at the disparaging term he'd once flung about with such abandon. Why had she been so nice to him when they were kids, when he'd been such a little shit?

She moved away to hang up her horse's bridle. The peg was above her head and Evan watched her stretch up. The tail of her tank top pulled out of her jeans. She finished with the bridle, gave a haphazard shove to the shirttail, and Evan's mouth went dry.

"She's married," he whispered to himself. And then, belatedly, "And I'm with Cynthia."

He was making an utter mess of this. He was supposed to be doing his homework for Gianni, which meant pumping Jess about her business plans. Instead, he was lusting after a married woman when he was almost engaged to Cynthia.

Jess headed out into the sunshine, where she showed him how to swap Rusty's bridle for his halter. Then they went back to the barn, the bridle slung over Evan's shoulder. She pointed to a peg beside the one she'd used earlier. "Here, Rusty's is beside Knight's."

"Knight is the horse you ride? Is he yours?"

"Nope. He belongs to the Crazy Horse. I bought him for Kathy and Will a couple of months ago and I'm still training him. He's skittish. Not ready for guests yet."

"You do all the buying and training?"

"It's one of the best things about the job."

"Let me guess. Along with the Annie Oakley costume, the dudes are the worst."

She collected a couple of rubber brushes he guessed were used for grooming. "They have their good points, but sometimes they try my patience. It's great that they like horses, but they're not real horse people. It's a holiday experiment, not real life. That's why I want—" Abruptly, she cut herself off.

He knew she was about to tell him about her no-frills riding idea, the camp she wanted to create for real horse people. Why did she hold back? "This isn't where you dreamed of ending up," he commented, hoping that would prompt her to share her latest scheme.

Jess walked outside again, with him trailing behind. When they reached the horses, she said "currycomb" and handed him a brushlike rubber tool with short teeth on one side. "Go in circles to work out dirt and stimulate his skin. Avoid his face and legs; the skin's too thin there."

She walked over to Knight, then glanced back. "I haven't given up on the dreams yet." She disappeared behind the horse.

"Oh? Tell me the latest."

"Some other time."

He frowned, sensing that if he pushed, she'd retreat further. Puzzling over the problem, he slid his hand into the grip on the currycomb and began to brush Rusty. The repetitive motion proved to be surprisingly soothing. The sun pressed down on his head and shoulders. Rusty leaned into him slightly, Evan pushed back gently, and there seemed to be an equilibrium between them. If Cynthia could see him now.

Cynthia. He'd hardly thought of her all day. Only when he was feeling guilty about being turned on by Jess.

Jess had said she had a crush on him, back in high school. That blew his mind. Thank God he hadn't realized back then; the knowledge would've shot his hormones completely out of control.

Obviously she'd grown out of it. She'd ended their friendship two months later. At some point, she'd married Dave. She'd ended up loving Dave.

Most of the girls in their class had been crazy for Dave Cousins. He was good-looking, a good student, captain of the basketball team, class valedictorian. To top it off, he'd been nice. Even to Evan the geek. But Evan had spurned him, professing to consider him a dumb jock. The truth was, he'd envied Dave. Back then, Dave had it all. And later, he won Jess Bly.

"You two about finished?" Jess asked.

He looked up to see her holding out an apple. "Uh, thanks."

She swatted his shoulder. "Idiot. It's for Rusty. To help the two of you bond."

"Oh, sure. I knew that."

He handed her the currycomb and took the apple, hefting it gingerly. "What do I do?"

She demonstrated, feeding Knight his own apple, then wiping her hands on her blue-jeaned backside. Evan tore his gaze away from those seductive curves and cradled the apple in his palm, noticing how its curves mirrored the lines of her butt. He managed not to jerk away as Rusty's huge lips descended toward his hand. The horse took the apple politely and crunched it.

"That wasn't so bad," Evan said.

Rusty eyed him calmly, then snorted, blowing a froth of crushed apple and juice all over the front of Evan's shirt.

Jess gave a delighted hoot. "Applesauce."

He scowled down at himself. "Disgusting. Thank God this place has laundry service."

She touched his shoulder again, this time a quick, gentle squeeze. "You've done great today, Ev. I never would've believed it. Don't spoil it and get all hoity-toity, okay? Why don't you go and strip off those dirty clothes and have a nice relaxing sauna?"

He forced himself to breathe deeply and imagine a cold shower. Her touch, together with her suggestion that he strip, had set his blood to boiling again. "How about you? You're heading back home?"

"Soon as I turn these guys out to pasture."

He was achy and filthy, not to mention struggling with lust. A cold shower, then a massage—from a masseur, not a masseuse—and a sauna sounded like bliss, yet he found himself following Jess as she led the two horses across the yard to a fenced pasture. That curvy backside had the most seductive sway in those formfitting jeans. . . .

"How is Dave?" he asked abruptly. He didn't really want to know. He could pretty much guess. President of the chamber of commerce, no doubt. Evan just needed to make the fact of her marriage more concrete.

She glanced over her shoulder. "Dave? He's fine. Owns the Wild Rose, the best hotel, dining room, and bar in town."

"President of the chamber of commerce?"

She gave a puzzled frown. "No. He was, a couple of years ago, but now he's heading up the Heritage Committee. And coaching high school basketball on a volunteer basis."

"Yeah, he would be," Evan muttered.

"What?"

"I said, good for him. And the two of you are, uh, happy?"

He told himself he really wanted Jess to be happy. And he wanted—no, needed—to think of her as happily married.

She didn't reply. Instead she opened the gate and led the horses into the pasture, where she removed the halters and gave each horse a slap on the rump to send it away. With the fence between herself and Evan, she turned to face him. "We're good friends. But we're not married anymore."

His stomach lurched and his heart raced. "I didn't realize. Sorry."

"No problem."

Jess wasn't married. What was he going to tell his hormones now? Cynthia. He had to keep reminding himself of her.

Jess turned away and whistled loud and clear. In a moment a horse appeared, running toward her. Jess greeted it with a hug as it head-butted her. "Speaking of good friends, this is Conti. He's mine. Isn't he fantastic?"

Evan stared at the horse, which looked pretty much like any other horse. "Fantastic."

"He's part Arab and part quarter horse. I've had him five years."

He thought of the first horse she'd owned, the one she'd raised from a foal. "I guess Rascal is . . ."

"Yes." She gave a nostalgic smile. "He lived a long and happy life, died of old age, and is now in horse heaven."

"I remember the Christmas your parents gave him to you, before he'd even been born. You were so excited."

"It was the best gift ever." She turned as another horse came up to her and nudged her shoulder. This one was blond, and moved more slowly than Conti.

"Another of yours?" he asked.

"No, Petula belongs to the Crazy Horse. She's semiretired." She hugged the horse's neck and kissed her on the forehead.

"Aren't you, sweetie?" she said to the horse, who bobbed its head, either in reply or in a request for an apple.

Jess produced apples for both horses, then said to the blond one, "Go hang out with your friends, Pet. See you tomorrow."

Pet turned away and Jess came through the open gate with her own horse, Conti, following. She swung Rusty's and Knight's empty halters, but didn't put one on Conti. After closing the gate, she headed toward the barn with the horse trailing her like an overgrown dog. "I rode him over this afternoon, so I'll saddle up and we'll ride home."

"Where's home these days?"

"My folks' place. I moved back after Dave and I split up. Pa's health isn't what it used to be and I help out with the ranch. And Mom helps out with—" She moved away quickly.

"Pardon? With what?"

Jess stopped, and a long moment passed before she turned. For a rare moment, her face was expressionless. "With Robin. Dave's and my daughter."

A mother! That was an even greater shock than her divorce. "I had no idea. How silly of me. I always knew you wanted kids." Ten years had passed, and she'd been married. Of course she'd have a child.

"And now I've got one and she's terrific. And Dave's a *wonderful* father." She turned on her heel and stalked into the barn, leaving him standing beside Conti. He'd follow, but her body language was as effective as a slammed door.

After a few minutes, he called, "You coming out?"

"I have things to do. Go get cleaned up for supper."

Odd. But then so was everything between him and Jess now. Conti gazed at him and he shrugged. "See you later," he called into the barn.

"Yeah."

He hobbled toward his cabin, each step making him more

aware of pinched toes and muscles seizing up. Plus, he stunk of apple juice and was attracting the attention of a couple of huge wasps. What a day it had been. Gianni Vitale was going to owe him, but big.

A noise made him turn around. He saw Jess and Conti go flying down the road in the other direction.

So Jess had a daughter. Evan was pretty sure he didn't want children, though that was a topic he and Cynthia had yet to resolve. But still, when he thought about Jess and her daughter, he felt the oddest sense of yearning.

Chapter Five

Jess freed her hair from its ponytail and let the wind whip it back as she rode home.

It was so unfair that Evan Kincaid still got to her. When she'd seen him grooming Rusty, her heart had turned over. For a moment, she'd almost envisioned a different future, a future that didn't have him returning to New York.

She hadn't been that stupid back when she was a teenager. Evan had known where he belonged and she'd believed him completely, and wanted it for him. Her love for him had been that strong.

She hadn't planned to tell him she had a daughter—her tongue had raced ahead of her brain—but in retrospect she was glad. Someone, Madisun or Will or Kathy, would mention Robin, and Ev would wonder why she hadn't said anything. And, after all, what was the big deal? Why would he suspect that Jess and Dave's daughter had anything to do with him?

All the same, she'd best make sure Evan and Rob never met. She'd have to find an excuse for canceling the Saturday afternoon exhibition she and her daughter traditionally put on for the Crazy Horse guests: she and Robin with their horses, Conti and Concha, doing cowgal tricks.

A part of her was curious to see Evan and Robin together. Father and daughter. Just once. But she couldn't take the risk.

Thanks to a school project last year, Rob had an e-mail pal in New York City and was long-distance crazy about the city. She'd be all over Evan like fresh horse dung on a newly polished boot. They might bond, and then . . .

Then what? Ev wouldn't notice the clues any more than anyone in Caribou Crossing had. Rob was Dave's daughter. She'd picked up some of his facial expressions and turns of phrase, and they shared a number of personality characteristics.

The risk might be slim, but Jess couldn't take it. She owed it to all of them, not least to Evan. He'd always been clear that he never intended to have children. When she'd first seen him at the Crazy Horse, she'd panicked and wondered if he was here for Robin, but now that she'd spent time with him, heard him talk about his life in New York, she knew differently. She was as sure now as she'd been ten years ago that he wouldn't want to know he'd fathered a child.

At her parents' ranch, she found her daughter in the kitchen, Taylor Swift singing on the radio as Robin chopped celery. Robin gave her a big smile. "Hi, Mom, you just missed Kimiko and her mom."

"That's too bad." She washed her hands and face at the kitchen sink.

"Kimiko and I did our homework. So I can help you work Mystique tonight, okay?"

The gray filly—a quarter horse–Tennessee walking horse cross—had recently been sent to Jess by her friend, Ty Ronan, who lived down in the Fraser Valley. He was a healer who worked with rescue horses. If their personalities were right for the Crazy Horse, he sent them on to Jess after he'd worked his magic. The Crazy Horse paid a token sum and Jess trained them for trail work with dudes.

"Sounds good to me." She was so lucky her daughter

shared her love of horses. "What're you making?" She glanced into the bowl where Robin had tossed the celery, and saw chunks of apple. "Waldorf salad?"

"Uh-huh. Could you get me some nuts?" As Jess obeyed, Robin said, "You know, there's this really elegant big hotel in New York called the Waldorf Astoria? Caitlin's grandmother took her there for brunch for her birthday. I wonder if that's where the salad got its name?"

Did *everything* have to remind Jess of Evan? "Maybe. You could ask Mitch. You're at your dad's tomorrow, right?" Mitch was the chef at the Wild Rose Inn.

"Yup. Dad's going to help me with the assignment I have to do on the solar system."

Jess grinned, happy Dave had fielded that one. There was a lot to be said for sharing parenting responsibilities. "Where are your grandparents?"

"Gramps was out riding and he went to take a shower. He's going to barbecue hamburgers to go with my salad. And I think Gran's on the phone with Mrs. Baxter, planning the bake sale."

Jess smiled again, thinking how lucky she was. Although Evan had a successful career, she was the one who had truly "made it" in terms of having a happy, fulfilling life. Loved ones always came before work.

Not that she was ready to shelve her no-frills boot camp plan any day soon.

On Wednesday, Evan woke early, feeling anything but relaxed. He was addicted to the fast pace of life in Manhattan, and withdrawal was hell.

Before breakfast he placed a long call to Angelica, then tried Cynthia again. Last night, he'd gone to voice mail, and the same just happened again. He slammed the old-fashioned receiver into the cradle, then felt ashamed of himself. Cynthia had a busy career and a busy social life. She didn't center her life around him. He'd never wanted a woman who would do that. But her busyness only emphasized how dull—and futile—his own life had been this week. He had one and only one mission, and was no closer to accomplishing it than he'd been back in Manhattan.

He'd never have guessed that Jess, who as a girl would babble for hours about her dreams, could be so closemouthed. But then again, the days of being best friends were ten years in the past, and though that fact pained him, there was no way to change it.

After breakfast he returned to his cabin. He had time to spare, but not enough to concentrate on a work project. He did a few stretches, then paced restlessly. Boredom definitely didn't suit him. Even though he figured Jess would be too busy to talk, he decided to head down to the barn.

Despite the stretches, his muscles were stiff, he noted gloomily as he strode down the hill. It'd be a miracle if he could get his right leg over Rusty's back.

The scene that greeted him was similar to the previous day's, except he didn't see Madisun, and Jess's "Morning" was even more curt, and accompanied by a frazzled expression rather than even a noncommittal smile.

No, they weren't best friends anymore.

He stood to one side, feeling useless and frustrated, and in a few minutes was surprised to see other early-comers, Thérèse and George. Jess, hurrying past them, tossed off another quick greeting as the Swiss couple headed over to their horses and fed them carrot sticks. Then the pair went into the barn, emerged with saddles and bridles, and began getting their horses ready. They'd been here last year, Evan remembered, and clearly knew their way around. He felt even more out of his element.

After dashing past him a couple of times, Jess said, "You

can bring the tack out. I'm going to do Chipper next. You know how everything's marked."

"Sure," he growled. He was a paying guest. They were supposed to wait on him, not the other way around. Still, he'd rather be doing something other than standing and fuming. He went into the barn, located the saddle and bridle marked Chipper, and took them to her. He watched as her fingers flew through motions she'd obviously done thousands of times.

"Where's Madisun?" he asked.

"Must be running late." Her words were casual, but a flicker of concern crossed her face.

"If a person takes a job, they should be responsible about it. Maybe she's too young."

Jess paused a moment. "Madisun may only be eighteen, but she's mature." Was he imagining it or did she sound rather grim? She hauled the cinch up. "I'll do Mickey next."

He headed back to the barn. A gofer. The CEO of his own very successful business and he was gofering for a dude ranch wrangler. If he'd been in a better mood, he might have found it funny.

When he returned, she said, "You do this one and I'll watch. After this, you're on your own."

"But . . ."

"What?"

"Nothing." He wasn't used to being in a bad mood. It never happened in New York. Or, if it did, he was too busy to notice.

He dumped the saddle on top of the pad that already rested on Mickey's back. Joan's horse, he thought. He was actually beginning to tell the animals apart.

Jess popped around the other side of the horse, gave a tug, and said, "Make sure it's sitting straight before you do the cinch."

He felt like a total fumble-fingers under her scrutiny, and was aware of her barely concealed impatience. Finally, he had the bridle fastened to her satisfaction. "Okay, now you can do Rusty." She hurried away and he headed back to the barn, wondering if his bad mood had more to do with her seeming indifference to him than with being put to work.

The sound of an engine made him turn as a beat-up car rattled up, a clunker that reminded him of his mom's old car, the one he'd learned to drive in. Madisun got out and rushed over to Jess. The two exchanged a few words, and he wondered if the girl was getting a reprimand. If Jess wanted to manage a business, she had to know how to discipline her employees.

He went into the barn and was taking down Rusty's bridle when Madisun darted in and grabbed a saddle and bridle. "Morning," he said coolly.

"Good morning, Evan." Her voice sounded cheerful—determinedly so—and he noticed she was wearing dark glasses even in the gloom of the barn. A fight with her boyfriend, and she'd been crying all night? Or perhaps she was hungover? His childhood had given him a lot of experience with hungover people, so he knew to stay out of her way.

The morning ride was longer than the previous ones, and Evan's muscles loosened up more quickly. He took a certain pleasure in noting he'd become more attuned to Rusty's trot, or more skilled at "sitting it," to use Jess's term. But aside from those small differences, the ride was pretty much like any other. Rather than let it be a total waste of time, he focused on one of the items Angelica had e-mailed him. He was on the board of directors of Gimme a Break, a charitable foundation that funded scholarships for underprivileged kids. Angelica had sent him and LeVaughn Duvalle a batch of applications.

Thanks to LeVaughn's sizable startup endowment, their fund-raiser's competency, and Evan's own investment wizardry, Gimme a Break had lots of money to give away. The problem was, there were so many deserving kids, far more than the foundation could ever support. What Evan and LeVaughn looked for when they vetted the applications wasn't so much marks or even a clean record. It was the sense that the applicants had the drive to succeed, that they weren't looking for a free ride but would use the opportunity to truly make something of their future the way LeVaughn had. The guy had been an inner-city kid, his most likely destiny a gang and drugs, jail and an early death. But thanks to a strong mom, an amazing teacher-mentor, and his own talent and discipline, he was now a basketball star.

When the ride finished, most of the guests limped away, saying they were going to rest and relax before lunch. The Swiss couple remained behind, tending to their horses.

Evan longed for a lot of things—the Internet, cell reception, and a shower, among them—but something held him back. He told himself that if Gianni wanted him to immerse himself in the ambiance, he'd damned well do it. "Can I help?"

Jess eyed him skeptically, then shrugged. "Sure, if you want. Thanks. We need to loosen off cinches, swap bridles for halters, and make sure the horses have food and water."

"I think I can handle that."

She strode away and he noticed Madisun leaning against one of the horses as if it was propping her up. She'd taken her sunglasses off. Her eyes weren't puffy and red, but her brown-skinned face looked tired and strained. As if to confirm his impression, she gave a huge yawn. Then, realizing he'd seen, she hurriedly covered her mouth. "Sorry."

"Late night?"

She ran her hands through her long black hair and sighed. "My little sister was sick. I didn't get much sleep."

He felt rotten for having guessed a hangover. "That's too bad. I hope she's feeling better."

"Me, too." She frowned. "Had to leave her with a neighbor. I hated to, but I couldn't leave TJ in the lurch."

Where the hell were the parents? It seemed that, in addition to holding down a full-time job, Madisun was playing surrogate mom for her sister. Jess had said she was mature. Perhaps her mother had died, and she'd had to grow up early.

Madisun was gnawing on her lip.

"Don't worry," he said. "The neighbor will call the Crazy Horse if there's a problem, right?"

She smiled, suddenly looking less troubled. "Yeah, you're right. Thanks, Evan."

While they'd talked, he'd dealt successfully with Rusty's bridle and halter.

Madisun took the bridle from him. "Good work, cowboy."

Cowboy. That would be the day.

Jess went about her chores, but kept an eye on Evan. It was normal, over the course of the first week, for guests to get more involved with the horses. Still, she hadn't expected it of him. She couldn't figure him out. Sometimes he seemed to resent being there, even though he'd been the one to choose riding as the challenge that would win him his ten-year plaque. But then he'd drop the chip on his shoulder and get into the swing of life at the Crazy Horse. His riding was coming along and he moved among the horses with increasing confidence as he took off saddles and bridles and eased halters onto horses' heads.

When the work was done and Thérèse and George headed off to clean up, Madisun said, "I'm going to run home and check on my sister. See you this aft."

Evan had ended up back with Rusty, untangling his mane. He gave the horse's neck a pat. "See you this aft, too, pal." Another ride, shorter than the morning one, was scheduled.

Jess joined him as he moved away from the strawberry roan. "I know you, but I don't," she blurted out.

He gave her a warm smile. "You knew a boy. Now I'm a man. I've changed."

She considered that. "In some ways. But I bet the core is the same. You were a loyal, generous, protective kid, and—"

"I was? Seems to me I was an obnoxious little shit."

She chuckled, eyes dancing. "That, too. But you were passionate and driven about your studies and your career. I bet you're still all of those things—the good ones anyhow—just more fit and confident, more open to experience and vulnerability."

"Vulnerability?" He sounded offended.

"Trying something new and not being paranoid about doing it perfectly."

"Oh . . ." He took a few moments to mull that over, then said slowly, "I'm not sure Cynthia would agree with you on some of those attributes. Like protective and vulnerable."

Cynthia again. "Maybe she doesn't call out those qualities in you. You always said your ideal woman was strong and successful."

He nodded. "Yes, and Cynthia is. She's a top-notch lawyer with one of the top firms in Manhattan. With her and me, there's almost a sense of competition. Friendly competition. For example, whoever gets a new client buys dinner. It's one of the great things about our relationship."

"Mmm." It sounded pretty darn different from her own relationship with Dave. The two of them were a team, just as she and Evan had once been. Ev had seemed to like it that way, back when he was a kid. "But . . ."

"What? Say it."

She bit her lip. "Don't you ever want to be vulnerable? Don't you want to be with someone who can be vulnerable? I mean, if neither of you is ever vulnerable, why do you need each other? It's one thing to have fun together, to celebrate successes, but isn't the true friend the one you can turn to when you're down, when you're feeling beaten or just plain stupid? When you've done something dumb, and you need to confess to someone who will sympathize? After all, we all do dumb things, we all have fears, we all have bad days. Don't we?"

"I guess."

He didn't seem to be getting her point. She felt like a hick, a country girl with only a high school education. Cynthia was a high-flying Manhattan lawyer.

But Jess was stubborn. She didn't mind—well, she didn't mind horribly—if someone disagreed with her, but she hated it when the person didn't understand what she was driving at. Time to stop with the abstract stuff and give him something concrete, something that hopefully he could relate to. "You and me, when we were kids, we were a team. Right? Each of us was fine on our own, but when you put us together there was something bigger and stronger and brighter." She stopped, distracted by the thought of Robin: the product of the two of them, and the brightest light in her life.

She rushed on. "When two people care about each other, you form something new." Dang, why did everything she said lead back to Robin? She quickly added, "Remember when I had to give that speech in grade ten? I was petrified. I was sure I'd throw up onstage, or forget my lines, or . . . Well, I had a list of at least a hundred possible disasters."

"Oh yeah, you were a mess," he said in a fond tone.

"But you helped me. You rehearsed me and pep-talked me, you teased me and bullied me, and when the day finally came and I had to do it, it wasn't just me up there on stage. You were with me. It was like that line from the old song Mom loves: You were the wind beneath my wings, and that day I flew, Ev. Because of you." Her eyes grew misty.

He reached out a finger—a grimy, horsy one, her absolute favorite kind—and caught a tear as it spilled over. "Still cry at the drop of a hat." His hand lingered, cradling her cheek.

Such a tender, affectionate touch. It was all she could do to keep from pressing into his hand and asking for more.

"Remember when I broke Mrs. Gutterson's window?" he

asked. "I'd been fooling around with a softball, in the days before I swore off sports completely. I didn't mean to break anything, I was just clumsy. No one saw me. I could have gotten away with it. But I felt awful, and told you. You made me see I had to confess, whatever the consequences."

Jess nodded, scarcely able to breathe as he stroked the side of her face.

"You came with me," he went on. "You stood by my side while she cussed me out in German, and then you helped me mow her lawn every week, all summer."

She managed a choky little laugh. "Hey, that's what friends are for. Besides, I figured you'd probably chop off a finger in her horrible old machine."

His expression was affectionate. "Friends, Jess. I valued our friendship so much, and then I destroyed it. I've missed it—you—a great deal."

She could no longer resist leaning into his hand. "You mean, you thought about me after you'd gone?"

He drew a deep breath, then let it out. "Yes, I thought of you. When I had a problem—or a triumph—my first reaction so often was that I wanted to tell Jess."

Her heart did a somersault, and that recalled her to reality. She forced herself to step away from him. "Until you met Cynthia, I guess."

After a few seconds he said, softly but deliberately, "Even after I met Cynthia."

"Oh!" The heat and intensity in his gaze mirrored her own feelings. What was he saying? What were they doing? Was he trying to throw her off balance? Was *she* throwing *him* off balance?

No way could she deal with this. Quickly, she strode across the stable yard, tossing a quick order over her shoulder. "Go for lunch, Ev. I have work to do."

* * *

As lunch—delicious barbecued salmon and a wild rice salad, followed by strawberry shortcake—was winding up, Evan leaned close to Thérèse and whispered, "Where'd you scam those carrot sticks?"

"Scam?" she queried in her engaging French accent.

"Beg, borrow, or steal," he translated.

"Ah, yes." She winked. "Kathy keeps a supply in a dish just inside the kitchen door. Apples, too."

Evan wasn't ready to risk applesauce again, but helped himself to a pocketful of carrot sticks. He limped back to his cabin and sank down on the couch. How much more could his body take? And how much idleness would his mind survive?

He checked the schedule for the afternoon. A short ride, then several hours that he could devote to work, perhaps broken by a swim. Dinner and then the hayride. The hokey hayride. He wasn't actually going to go, was he?

As he did some stretches, he reflected on his last conversation with Jess. It was true that, even after he'd met Cynthia, Jess was often the first person he thought about when he wanted to talk to someone. Oh, not about the ins and outs of his job—that was an area where Cynthia was invaluable. But if it was a matter of feelings—like his anxiety before the first Gimme a Break board meeting, or his pride afterward—it was always Jess Bly.

This wasn't good. Nor was it good that he'd told her, nor that he'd caressed her cheek, the tanned skin so warm and supple under his fingers. She might think . . . What? That he was interested in her? Well, damn it, he was, but he certainly wasn't going to do anything about it. Not only was he committed to Cynthia, but, as a couple, he and Jess were as mismatched as they'd always been. The wrangler and the city slicker. Nope, not going to happen.

He relaxed from a stretch and lay flat on the yoga mat that had come with his room, linking his hands behind his head. Why hadn't Cynthia supplanted Jess in his mind when he wanted a friend to talk to? He'd put it down to a lingering childhood habit. But Jess's comments about vulnerability made him wonder. He'd always told himself he valued independence and wanted a relationship that was a partnership of two self-sufficient people. People who were the complete opposite of his dysfunctional parents.

In his relationship with Cynthia, he hadn't allowed room for vulnerability, nor had she. They both thought of it as a weakness. And yet, as Jess said, surely everyone, even the strongest person, had moments of vulnerability. Like his anxiety before that Gimme a Break board meeting, an anxiety he'd never confessed to Cynthia.

He remembered how he'd felt when Jess made that tenth-grade speech. As he sat in the audience, he'd fought back tears of pride and felt a warm glow, knowing he'd helped her overcome her fear. She was right. As kids, they'd been a team.

And, with a start of surprise, he remembered meeting with LeVaughn Duvalle when they were putting together the Gimme a Break Foundation. The basketball star was worth several million dollars, but the inner-city kid was still inside him, worried that his lack of finesse would jeopardize the foundation's success.

The thing was, LeVaughn was a dynamic, outgoing guy, much more than reserved Evan, and he was the perfect spokesperson. Evan had told him that, then said, "I'll make you a deal. I'll give the boring facts and numbers, but first you talk about our goals and your own experience. You motivate; I'll inform."

They'd each had their weaknesses and fears, and when they'd admitted to them the solution was obvious. And their foundation, not to mention their relationship, was the stronger for confessing their vulnerabilities.

He scowled. Damn. It had always been like this. Just when he thought he knew what he was doing, Jess made him rethink.

Cynthia did that, too, only on different issues.

The two women had something in common. And why wouldn't they? They were the only two women he'd ever cared about. Except for his mother, but caring for Brooke had been a loser's game.

Evan growled. This was why he hated "downtime." His thoughts made lousy company. He'd scrap the stretches and head down to the barn to feed Rusty carrots and help Jess and Madisun with the tack.

Chapter Six

Later that day, after an early dinner, Evan again headed for the barn, this time in company with the other guests. Hard to believe, but he actually felt mellow. Even his mangled toes were comfortable in an old pair of gym shoes.

He'd gone through a pile of work after the afternoon ride, so he was feeling productive. Then he'd indulged in an arnica massage and a eucalyptus sauna, ending up in near nirvana. Dinner had been excellent, especially the rack of lamb and the Blue Mountain pinot noir—though, as usual, he'd restricted himself to one glass. Unlike his parents, he would control his drinking, and not vice versa.

Beth and Kim, arm in arm, strolled beside him. Both wore souvenir T-shirts with Caribou Crossing's unofficial logo of a road sign like the ones in school zones but with "Caribou Crossing" and a black silhouette of the mammal on them. As a kid, he'd scoffed at the logo because the real live caribou moved to more remote territory more than a century earlier. Jess, he remembered, had loved the logo, as well as the wire caribou in the town square.

"We're really looking forward to this evening," Beth said to him.

"TJ told me it's special," he replied. And hokey, though he

didn't mention that part. The odd thing was, he felt a surge of pleasant anticipation himself. What was that all about? One glass of wine never gave him this kind of buzz. Was there some magic in the country air? Or was it Jess?

The week had brought surprise after surprise and, as he'd relaxed in the sauna, Evan had decided not to even attempt to resolve the issues. A confused mind couldn't make a sound decision. He had to step back and gather more information before he decided how to proceed. He was a highly intelligent analyst. There was no problem that could get the better of him, not even Jessica Bly Cousins.

"We went into town this afternoon," Kim said. "Did you know Caribou Crossing started out as a gold rush town?"

"Oh?" Of course he knew that. It was the town's main claim to fame, and the townspeople played it up to the kitschy hilt, along with the whole country and western thing. Tourism was big in Caribou Crossing. Businesses had names like Lucky Strike, Gold Pan, and Round Up, The sleazy bar his parents, then his mom, used to frequent was called The Gold Nugget Saloon. Was it still there? If so, that's probably where Brooke was at this very moment, he thought sourly.

"Wow!" Beth's exclamation drew him out of his thoughts.

They were nearing the barnyard, and there stood a huge, hay-filled wagon. It was harnessed to two sizable horses, their reddish-brown coats set off dramatically by blond manes and tails. Jess stood with a wiry bald man, barely her height, the two of them cooing to the giant horses. Garbed in a fringed buckskin skirt and vest, a beige cowboy hat, and a pair of fancy tooled Western boots, she made a fine picture. A picture that several of the guests were currently snapping.

"Hi, folks," she called. "This is Jimmy B and he's your wagon driver."

The guests approached the horses gingerly. "Jimmy B barely comes up to their knees," Sylvia murmured, just as the driver sang out, "Howdy, folks. Don't you be afeard of these critters. They're gentle as kittens, they don't bite, and they just love to be patted. Step right on up and meet Harry and Sally."

"When Harry met Sally!" Sandy cried, and the ice was broken. Soon everyone was clustered around the horses, stroking necks and making friends as they bombarded the elderly driver with questions.

Evan wandered over to the barn, where Jess was making notes on a clipboard. "Annie Oakley, I presume?" he teased.

"Told you it'd be worth a laugh."

Her smile gave him a twinge of yearning. A complicated yearning made up of affection and lust.

"It's not exactly Fifth Avenue," he said, "but here it's just right." He admired the detail work in the cinnamon skirt and vest and the embroidered Western shirt.

She pirouetted, the fringes on her skirt flirting with the bare skin above her knees, and he admired those knees, too. "My dress buckskins. Worn only on special occasions."

Their gazes held for a moment, and he knew that, at least for him, just being together made it a special occasion.

She drew in a breath, let it out, then turned on her heel and strode over to the group. "Okay, gang, let's get this show on the road."

After she and Jimmy B helped everyone scramble into the hay wagon, Jess hopped aboard on the opposite side from Evan. The driver made clucking sounds to get the horses going, then guided them down a dirt road through the trees. The scent of fresh hay filled the air, the horses' harnesses jingled, and a bird serenaded them.

"Jimmy B," Jess said, "why don't you tell the folks a bit about how Caribou Crossing got its start?"

"Like the old expression goes," the driver said, "there was gold in them thar hills. The Cariboo Gold Rush, back in the 1860s, brought a flood of people from all over the world. They walked and rode up the Cariboo Wagon Road, across some pretty tough terrain, and a passel of 'em ended up here."

“So the town started as a mining camp?” Sandy asked.

“Sure did,” Jimmy B said. “It was a town of tents and thrown-together shacks; of miners, mules, and mercantile stores; and of saloons, gambling dens, and brothels. But then Reverend Petty and the missus came along, and they knew just the thing to tame those miners. Anyone know what that might be?”

Evan, who’d studied the history of Hicksville in elementary school, kept quiet but Thérèse, seated beside him, called out, “Wives!”

“You know it, sister,” the driver said. “A wagonload of brides.” As Jimmy B went on with the story, Evan murmured to Thérèse, “You heard this story last year?”

She nodded. “And we’ll probably hear it next year, too. I think the Crazy Horse will be an annual thing for us.”

“You like it that much?”

“It’s so different from Zurich, and we go home feeling renewed.”

George, seated on his wife’s other side, leaned over to say, for about the tenth time, “It certainly does get into your blood.”

As Jimmy B carried on with his story-telling, Evan mused that, while the Crazy Horse was a very long way from being in his blood, it wasn’t as awful as he’d feared. As for renewal . . . well, he didn’t need anything to renew his enthusiasm for his life in New York City. But there was another possibility of renewal that excited him: the chance of reestablishing a true friendship with Jess. When they were teens, he’d let hormones ruin their friendship. Now, though his hormones still responded to her, he was damned if he’d give in to them. No, the more serious problem was his evaluation of her business proposal, the one he couldn’t get her to talk about.

The wagon arrived at its destination and people clambered down with oohs and ahs. In front of a forest backdrop nestled a small, deep blue lake, with a fair-sized tepee beside it.

Smoke drifted lazily out of a hole at the top, and the air had cooled off enough that the fire would be welcome. Over to one side, a wooden fence marked off a grassy meadow, and across the field the sun was setting in soft shades of peach and purple. Most of the guests made for the tepee, but a few headed over to lean on the fence.

Evan had never been one to admire—much less notice—scenery, but this gentle sunset drew him, and he found himself a spot at the fence, slightly removed from the others. A tangle of wild roses twined around a fence post, and their sweet scent complemented the view.

Jess saw Evan stroll over to the fence. Jimmy B would get the fire going in the firepit, and Marty, one of the kitchen staff at the Crazy Horse, would serve drinks, but Jess knew she should head into the tepee and play hostess. Besides, it was dangerous to spend too much time with Evan. Yet her boots had a mind of their own and carried her in his direction.

Avoiding a beautiful but prickly branch of wild roses, she rested her elbows on the top rail, then gazed at the setting sun. Her peripheral vision caught the movement when Evan turned toward her. She glanced at him.

He smiled and she smiled back. Her heart skipped. It had been doing that too dang much lately.

She turned back to the view and cleared her throat. "Tell me about Cynthia. It's a serious relationship?"

He nodded slowly. "We've been seeing each other for two years and we're talking about the future. We're perfect for each other."

There, she told herself, *he's committed. Don't go dreaming any schoolgirl dreams*. "What's she like?"

"She's from Boston, a wealthy background, but she's become a success all on her own."

"You said she's a lawyer?"

"Yes, a corporate finance attorney."

"Oh." Jess didn't have a clue what that was. It sounded way out of her league, and not very interesting. "And she's beautiful, I suppose?"

"Stunning. Scandinavian heritage. Blond hair, blue eyes, great bone structure. Very chic, excellent taste."

Jess tried not to wince. So far, she was pretty much hating Cynthia. "What about her personality, her interests? What does she do for fun?"

"She loves her work, but aside from that she enjoys theatre, gallery openings, travel. We both make lots of business trips and often go together, taking extra days to sightsee. Paris, London, Hong Kong. You know."

Jess snorted. "Of course I don't. And, as I'm sure you know, I have no burning desire to go to any of those places." To be perfectly honest, much as she loved horses, wild roses, and country sunsets, she wouldn't have minded some foreign travel. But she would never be rich, and family and horses would always be her priority. "I'm a homebody." Realizing she sounded defensive, she was annoyed at herself for comparing herself to his perfect woman.

"I remember." His tone was gentle and it calmed her.

She gave him a rueful grin. In some ways, no one would ever know her as well as Ev once had.

And she'd always known what kind of woman he wanted as his life partner, and it sure wasn't a country girl. Now he'd found his woman, and Jess told herself she was happy for him. Trying to sound enthusiastic, she said, "So you and Cynthia are perfectly compatible. That's great." When she'd felt the zing of sexual chemistry with him, it had obviously been one-sided.

"It is."

Despite the years of separation Jess knew this man, and heard the shadow of doubt. "Ev? Is there a problem?"

He gave a small, dismissive shake of his head. "It's not

really a problem. Just one area where we haven't reached complete accord."

Good heavens, he made their relationship sound like a business merger rather than a romance. "You've got me intrigued."

"It's personal."

She turned away. Absurd to feel hurt. They weren't kids anymore, no longer confidants. Why should he tell her his personal secrets?

Because he once had.

The sunset was in its final stages. A peachy glow lit the horizon line. She blinked hard to clear the moisture that fuzzed her vision.

His voice brought her gaze to his face once more. "When we were teenagers, you said you wanted marriage and kids one day. I said I wanted to share my life with a strong, intelligent career woman, but I didn't want kids."

Yes, it was just as she'd thought. Evan hadn't changed. She was relieved, Jess told herself. But then she worked through the implications—those for Ev—of what he'd said. Her mouth made a soundless "oh." "And Cynthia does?"

"Right now her career is her priority, but she's our age and she says she could see wanting one or two kids when she reaches her midthirties."

"Are you still sure you don't want to have children?"

"Pretty sure. And Cynthia's not even positive herself about wanting them. But if she did, well, her idea of parenthood isn't the same as mine."

Idea of parenthood? Either you were a parent, or you weren't. Well, unless you didn't know you were a parent . . . She shook her head, brushing that thought away. "How do you mean?"

"She says it wouldn't need to affect our lives much. We'd still have our careers, our travel, our social activities. We'd hire a live-in nanny."

"And have someone else raise your kids?" Jess's voice squeaked in protest.

"Lots of couples do," he said mildly, but she heard an undertone of doubt in his voice.

"Why bother having children if you don't want to spend time with them? If you don't want to be a *real* parent? That's unfair on the kids."

He swallowed, and she wished she hadn't spoken without thinking. Both his parents had made him feel unwanted and unloved. He'd always been reticent about talking about his folks, but Jess had been his best friend for ten years. She'd picked up on things. Things he'd made her vow to keep secret.

"Cynthia's parents weren't around much," he said, "but she and her brother were raised with all the privileges. The family gets along very well; they see each other several times a year. But . . ."

He turned to her, biting his lip. "I keep thinking of your family, Jess. Your parents were more affectionate with me than Cynthia's parents are with her. Oh, I don't doubt they all love each other in their fashion, but it's such a . . . cool, neat-and-tidy kind of love. You'd think that would appeal to me, but . . ."

Yeah, she would have. But it looked like Evan had more of a heart than he gave himself credit for. Jess kinked up one corner of her mouth. "Families are supposed to be messy."

"I don't know. Look at mine. That was way too much mess. There was no love at all and—"

"No!" Jess leaped in. Brooke had loved Evan; Jess knew that. But was it her place to tell him about his mother, and the amazing person she'd turned into?

"Jess, it's okay. I'm just saying, that's not the right model for a family. As for Cynthia's . . . well, there's affection, but their approach seems so dispassionate. Even though she says it worked beautifully for her."

And look how she'd turned out. It seemed Cynthia preferred

affection to passion. No fuss, no muss. "Isn't it odd," Jess mused, "that coming from opposite backgrounds, you and Cynthia ended up so similar?"

His forehead kinked into a frown as he reflected. Then he said, "Maybe it's not so surprising. Cynthia was always expected to succeed. She has, and she's determined to prove that it's on her own merits, not because of family connections. My parents didn't even want me, and had no expectations, so I created my own. I was driven to be the opposite of my parents. As for you—" He broke off.

She read his mind and finished his thought. "I, with the perfect loving family, never achieved much of anything."

He frowned again, then slowly said, "There's nothing wrong with what you're doing. Besides, you started to say you had some other plans?"

He remembered that? They'd been talking about the dudes and she'd said they weren't real horse people. She'd started to tell him about the boot camp, but had cut herself off. Ev had probed a little, and she'd said she hadn't given up on her dreams. She sure wasn't going to share her dreams with him now, after he'd branded her an underachiever.

The sun had set, the air was cool, and the mosquitoes were coming out. The other guests had headed into the tepee and they should, too, but the conversation about children didn't seem finished. She might not want him to be Robin's father, but that didn't mean he couldn't be a good father to other children, if he ever decided that was what he wanted. Tonight, for the first time, she'd heard ambivalence in his voice when he talked about kids.

"If you and Cynthia did decide to have children," she said, "there's nothing to say you couldn't be a real father. In five or ten years, you might be ready to cut back on your work hours, read to your kid, teach him or her how to skate."

He shook his head slowly. "That's part of why I don't want kids. I'd have no idea how to go about being a good parent.

I've no experience with children, and my parental role models were disastrous."

Oh God, this conversation was just too tough. And yet, he'd been her best friend. She truly cared what happened to him. And so she said, "That's a cop-out, Evan."

It was getting dark quickly now and she couldn't make out the details of his face, but she could feel his anger.

Fine, let him be mad, but she was going to have her say. "Be honest with yourself. If you really don't want children, that's fine. But if you're looking for role models, just think of my parents. Besides, all you'd really have to do is look inside yourself. You're a fine man, and . . ." She sucked in a breath, then told him the truth, a truth she'd just as soon not recognize herself. "I think you'd make a good father."

He didn't respond, but her instincts told her his anger was dissolving. Then, quietly, he said, "Thanks."

"Sounds like it's an issue you and Cynthia need to resolve. But I do see how hard it must be, both of you trying to guess how you're going to feel about things years down the road."

He moved closer, and his shirtsleeve brushed hers. "How about you, Jess? Do you think you'll get married again?"

"No." The answer came quickly. The only men she'd ever loved were Evan and Dave. Now, seeing Evan again, it was impossible for her to imagine loving anyone else.

Unmusical squeaks and squawks suddenly filled the night air. Recalled to her duties, she said, relieved, "Oh gosh, everyone's inside and the musicians are tuning up. I'm shirking my job. And you'd better go and get a songbook."

"A songbook?"

"We don't expect folks to know all the words, so we have them printed out. You'll see." She forced a smile and started toward the tepee.

Behind her, Evan groaned. "You did promise me hokey."

Inside, Jess made sure everyone was comfortable on the rustic wooden benches circling the crackling fire in the firepit. Marty was serving mulled wine and hot chocolate with her usual efficiency and cheer.

Jess participated in the standard introductory repartee with Hank and Gavin, the two local men who between them played guitar, banjo, fiddle, and harmonica, and sang as well. She helped Marty hand out songbooks and jolly the shyer guests into joining in on the first song, a catchy, rather ridiculous, old classic, "She'll Be Coming 'Round the Mountain." As usual, the Crazy Horse worked its insidious spell, and by the time they'd reached the line about killing the old red rooster when she comes, even Evan was singing.

Then the musicians began a sprightly fiddle tune and Jess and Jimmy B did a lively two-step. After a couple of minutes, each of them hauled a guest to his or her feet. She was tempted to pick Evan for her partner, but there were so many reasons that was a dumb idea. Instead she chose Aaron, a young married man who seemed game for anything.

After quickly teaching him the steps, she turned him over to his wife and selected another guest. Again, not Evan. He sat out the first number, then succumbed to Joan's pleas and joined in with good grace. There weren't enough men to go around and soon the women were dancing with other women, and then everyone began to change partners in a mad whirl. The tunes were lively and Jess swung from arm to arm, occasionally noticing that the arm, the smiling face, was Evan's.

When they were teenagers, she'd gone to the school dances with a group of friends and danced with the boys—all the boys except the one she really wanted to be with. Evan had boycotted the dances. How strange, now, to be whirling about in the same room.

When the music stopped, the guests were panting and laughing. Hank untied the red bandanna from his throat and wiped his sweaty face. "We're going to have a sing-along, folks; then it'll be time for me and Gavin to take a break."

Jess found herself on a bench between Evan and Sandy as Marty refilled everyone's mugs.

"Okay, listen up," Hank said. "We're gonna have a little battle of the sexes here. Anyone see *Annie Get Your Gun*?"

Several hands went up.

"Then you know that anything you can do, I can do better."

The people who knew the musical chuckled. Evan turned to Jess with a questioning look.

"It's a song from the show," she said, with a grin.

Hank said, "You gals, you're gonna sing Annie Oakley's part, and us men are gonna be Buffalo Bill. And we're gonna outholler you!"

"No, you're not," Jess called on cue. "'Cause anything you guys can do, we gals can do ten times better."

Amid catcalls and hoots of laughter, the musicians began to play and, after a tentative beginning, everyone was belting out the humorous song. Evan, too.

Jess thought of how many times she'd done this. She could go through the motions in her sleep. But tonight it felt different.

She always enjoyed these evenings, but now the fire smelled more pungent, the mulled wine was spicier, and the singing was more boisterous. The scent of Sandy's perfume was like lilacs on a summer afternoon. Evan smelled faintly of lime, which surprised her; she'd have expected something more sophisticated. As he turned a page in the songbook, his sleeve brushed hers and she shivered.

His voice was deep and rich. She'd never heard him sing before. Never seen him dance, much less danced with him. Never seen him on a horse.

If the old Evan had been attractive to her, this one—with the firm, pure-male body and the willingness to experience her world—was far more so. She shivered again.

He stopped singing and leaned close. "Cold?"

She shook her head. "I'm fine. How about you?"

"I'm good." His eyes held hers. "Very good."

Her heart turned a somersault. She forced herself to break the gaze, and stared at her songbook, at words she'd memorized years ago. No, no, no, she couldn't let herself fall into this stupid trap again. Couldn't toss her heart into the hands of a man who'd never be hers, who was in love with another woman.

When the song ended, Hank and Gavin said they were taking a short break, and Jess jumped to her feet. She had to socialize; it was her job. But mostly, she needed to get away from Evan's disturbing presence.

Evan sat still, watching the other guests mingle and chat or wander outside in search of outhouses. Jess had abandoned him and was chatting with Sandy, the software developer from Seattle.

The inside of the tepee was dim, lit only by the dancing flames of the impressive bonfire Jimmy B tended. The tent smelled of wood smoke with an undertone of something fruity. Didn't people burn apple or cherry branches sometimes, or was the aroma coming from the mulled wine Marty was serving?

Across the circle, Jess had moved along and was now talking to Aaron. Sylvia, Aaron's wife, sat on Evan's left, engaged in an animated conversation on orchid growing with Kim. To his right, Ann and Joan shared thoughts on raising children. Evan had nothing to contribute to the conversations on either side and felt as socially unskilled as when he was a teenager.

In Manhattan, conversations focused on business, world events, or critiquing a play or musical performance. People, at least in his crowd, didn't just chat aimlessly. They didn't waste time. The guests at the Crazy Horse often did talk business, but the relaxed evening atmosphere had turned people's thoughts to family and hobbies. He had neither.

This night really wasn't working out. Alone, he was uncomfortable with the other guests. With Jess, he was uncomfortable for a different reason. No, for several really bad reasons.

He wished he could leave and head back to his cabin, but he'd never find his way in the dark. He was stranded.

Stranded in this tepee, and stranded at the Crazy Horse. Out of his natural element, out of the city where he'd built a self-image as a confident, competent professional. Here he was just Evan Kincaid. No one knew him. Probably no one wanted to. Why would they? What was there to know, besides the fact that he was a successful investment counselor?

He was relieved when the musicians returned and started to play a song with a humorous name—"I've Got Friends in Low Places"—and a catchy chorus.

Evan did know how to dance—lessons had been part of his program to turn himself into a cultured man—but definitely not to this kind of music. Still, he didn't protest when Ann grabbed his hand and pulled him up. It was better than sitting alone.

When the next piece began, Beth and Kim each latched on to one of his arms and cried, "Line dancing!" He didn't know what line dancing was, but it proved to be an awful lot like an aerobics workout.

Next, a flushed Sandy claimed him.

Jess stood beside Jimmy B, both of them clapping time and cheering the dancers. After a few minutes, Sandy tugged Evan over in their direction. "No slackers now," the young woman panted. "If we're going to make fools of ourselves, so are you." She latched on to Jimmy B's arm and pulled him into the fray.

"Bet I can show you a thing or two, missy!" the elderly man shouted as he spun her away.

"He will, too," Jess said. "He's a great dancer."

"And I'm hopeless," Evan said. He stared at her for a moment, then decided it was silly to avoid dancing together. Or maybe he just couldn't resist a legitimate reason for putting his arms around her. So he grabbed her hand and tugged. "Teach me how to do a proper two-step."

And there she was, in his arms, all warmth and curves, but the two of them were moving too fast for him to really savor the experience. Just as well, or he'd have had a hard-on.

Laughing, almost shouting to be heard over the music and the other dancers, she called instructions. Once he knew the basic rules, he picked it up quickly.

By the end of a couple of sprightly tunes, everyone was panting. Hank said, "All righty, folks, catch your breath. We'll do 'Red River Valley.' "

When Gavin began to sing, his voice was so pure and true, such a perfect match to the plaintive words and music, that everyone held still, captured in the spell.

From this valley they say you are going
We will miss your bright eyes and sweet smile

Some of the dancers moved into each other's arms and began to drift slowly to the music. No way could he turn down the opportunity to gather Jess closer, and she went without protest.

She tilted her head up to him. "Thought you said you couldn't dance."

Talking. That was a good thing. Better than thinking about how good her body felt, only inches from his. "Not the two-step."

Gavin continued singing:

Just remember the Red River Valley
And the cowboy who loved you so true

Jess cleared her throat and moved back a couple of inches in the circle of his arms. "Dance a lot in New York?"

Right, he was supposed to be talking. "There's an occasional dinner dance or charity ball, but my social life tends more toward drinks, dinners, theatre."

He couldn't concentrate—at least not on anything but the sensation of Jess in his arms and the battle against the arousal surging through him.

"This is a pretty far stretch from what you're used to," she murmured.

"Yeah, it's different. But it's actually . . . fun." It was a revelation, and he missed a step. He caught the rhythm again. "I think folks are having more fun tonight than at clubs in Manhattan."

"That's nice of you to say."

Do you think of the valley you're leaving
. . . And the pain you are causing to me?

Had he caused her pain when he left Caribou Crossing? He must have, if she'd had a crush on him, then made love with him. If only he'd realized . . .

What would he have done differently? Not made love to her. Kept their relationship as "just friends."

Jess fit so easily in his arms as they moved to the poignant rhythm of the music. For him, this was a peak experience, one he'd remember the rest of his life. For her . . . He wondered how many men she'd danced with over the years. "Do you go dancing other than on these Wednesday night hayrides?"

"Occasionally at the Wild Rose Inn, Dave's hotel. The bar gets hopping on a Saturday night, and there's line dancing on Sunday evenings. Jimmy B and his wife give lessons."

"And whom do you dance with?"

"Whoever's around. Mostly Dave."

Dave again. "Sounds like you two are pretty tight." Ridiculous to feel jealous, but maybe a guy always felt a little possessive of the first girl he'd made love with.

"Yup. Neither of is into dating, so we hang out together."

He frowned. "You broke up, but you hang out together rather than date anyone else?" If they got along so damned well, why the hell had they broken up?

She shrugged. "That's how it is."

And if she'd broken up with Dave, why wasn't she dating other men? "So," he said tentatively, "why don't you date?"

"It's a small town. I know the guys and no one interests me that way."

He could relate to that. Manhattan was huge, but he'd had trouble finding a woman he found physically attractive and intellectually stimulating. Until Cynthia. He cleared his throat and moved slightly away from Jess. "What about the guests here? Or is that taboo?"

"There'd be no future in it."

"I suppose that's true."

Just like there had never been a future for the two of them.

He sensed she was thinking that, too. No future, and yet the present felt very good.

They stopped talking, but their bodies had a communication of their own going on, one that was subtle and too damned sexy. It was all he could do to resist pulling her that last inch or two closer, so their bodies would press together as they danced. He reminded himself of Cynthia. It was okay to dance casually with an old friend, but a clutch-and-grab was definitely not.

He was both sorry and relieved when Hank's voice broke in. "Grab a seat, everyone. We're gonna sing this next song together. It's the last one for tonight, and it's got a special place in our hearts."

The song turned out to be "Home on the Range."

As he sat beside Jess, Evan listened, rather than sang. Jess's voice was pure, and she sang the words with feeling.

I would not exchange my home on the range
For all the cities so bright.

It reminded him of the huge difference, the insurmountable difference, between the two of them.

She didn't look at him once, and as soon as the song ended, she sprang to her feet and went over to Jimmy B. "Time to round 'em up and head 'em out, pardner."

Evan trailed the group as they strolled to the wagon. He hung back as people hopped up and settled in. Knowing he was being stupid, he waited until Jess found her spot, then climbed up beside her.

She shot him a startled glance but said nothing.

"Oh my gosh, look at the stars!" one of the guests exclaimed, and everyone leaned back to do so.

Evan's "Wow" melded with the others' exclamations. Never had he seen a sky so clear and velvety black, studded with so many sparkling stars. Had the skies been like this when he was a boy, and he'd never noticed? Had he never looked up, all those times he walked home from the library when it closed at nine? Had his mother ever, just once, gazed up at the sky rather than getting plastered in the bar or sitting in front of the mind-numbing babble of TV, drinking beer and whining that there was nothing to do in this godforsaken place? Maybe if Brooke had seen the stars, she'd have taught him to look, too.

Jimmy B chirruped to Harry and Sally, and the wagon was on its way. Evan shifted to find a comfortable position and breathed in the earthy scent of fresh hay. During the ride to the tepee, Jimmy B had told stories and kept the guests chatting. Now he was silent and people spoke softly, in hushed tones of reverence for the miracle they were experiencing.

Evan listened to them marvel about the incredible canopy of stars, the purity of the air, and the virtuous ache of well-used muscles, their comments underlain by the jingle of the horses' harnesses.

Jess was beside him, lying back on the bed of hay, her hands behind her head. Her elbow brushed his hair.

And he thought, *This is Jess's life. Every day, every night, is like this for her. Does she take it for granted?*

The answer, he knew, was that she both did and didn't. She didn't often stop to marvel, but somewhere deep in her bones was a certainty that this was good and right, that this was part of who she was. Appreciation was an elixir that flowed in her veins. It always had. But she'd never been able to explain it in a way he could relate to. To him, like to his mother, Caribou Crossing had been Hicksville, and he hadn't seen—maybe hadn't let himself see—anything good in it. Except Jess herself, and her parents. Now, for the first time, he felt he really understood her. Without her speaking a word of explanation.

"Home on the Range" could have been written for her.

He gazed resolutely at the stars and resisted moving closer to her. This was intimate enough, lying side by side as if they were spent from lovemaking. Arousal pulsed through him, and he shifted position.

"Hey, city boy, bet you don't see stars like this in the Big Apple." Her voice, a whisper caressing his ear, stirred his already heated blood.

Stars. Who could think of stars when her warm breath was so seductive? Did she have any idea the effect she had on him?

"No." He gave a soft laugh. Keeping his voice low so no one could overhear, he said, "Well, different kinds of stars. Movie stars, stage stars, all sorts of celebrities."

"Whoopee," she murmured dryly.

"Don't sound so enthusiastic," he teased, rolling onto his side to face her.

She turned toward him and he saw the flash of her teeth and gleam of her eyes. Starlight illuminating Jess's smile. It didn't get any better than this.

"The beautiful people," she murmured. "I'd never *make it there*, would I?" Softly, she sang the words *make it there* to the tune of the Frank Sinatra song that played in every tourist spot in NYC.

"You, Jess, would make it anywhere." The words, which he had indeed meant sincerely, came out sounding too heartfelt. He added quickly, "That is, if you remembered to wash your face and comb your hair."

She punched his shoulder. "You big-city guys sure know how to flatter a gal."

He caught her fist in his hand. "Be careful who you beat up on, lady. I'm a lot tougher than I used to be."

She curved her hand so her fingers interlaced with his. "I thought about what you said. About the self-fulfilling prophecy? You're right, and I'm really sorry."

"It was a long time ago. Don't worry about it."

"But why did I do it? I'm not mean."

"No, you're not. Jess, you were kind to me."

"And yet . . . You know, I think it scared me, how bright you were. I felt dumb, and I don't like feeling second best. So I had to be better at something."

It was a lightbulb moment. "Damn." He gave a wry chuckle. "You and me both. I acted like a superior jerk because I was better in school. I had to play it up, because that's all I had going for me. When I compared the two of us, you were the one who had everything else. The great parents, the terrific personality, a ton of friends, your natural talent for physical activity."

"And I took all that for granted and just saw that I was a dummy compared to you. Amazing that we were friends."

"Like you said earlier, we supported each other. Maybe not as well as we could have if we'd each been more self-confident, but I think we did a fine job. Remember, we were kids, we didn't have the benefit of all these years of experience."

"True." She smiled. "You're right, experience counts for a lot. I'm doing a better job with Robin. I tell her she can do anything, but she needs to measure herself by her own standards, not anyone else's. She has to feel good about how hard she tried, not worry if she did better than others. I want her to be confident, to try things. I don't want to hold her back."

"Sounds like a healthy approach." And it did. But yet—and he felt a twinge of guilt for thinking this—might her philosophy result in another low achiever, just like herself? Well, so what if it did? Jess was happy and well adjusted. Not everyone had to be a blazing success in terms of a career.

Realizing this was the first time she'd opened up about her daughter, he asked, "How old is Robin?"

Her hand, which had remained twined in his, freed itself as she sat up abruptly.

"She's nine."

"Nine!" He jerked up, too. "I didn't realize she was so old. You and Dave—"

"Yeah, yeah," she muttered softly. "She wasn't planned; I messed up with birth control. But Dave and I loved each other and wanted to get married and have our baby. So we did."

She and Dave must have gotten together right after he left town. Or even before. No wonder she'd written that she'd never felt better, and that she and Evan should go their separate ways.

Trying to suppress bitter jealousy, he said, "Guess that makes sense. Except . . . you ended up getting divorced."

The unspoken question hovered between them. After a long moment, she answered it. "Dave met someone. They had the kind of love that comes around only once in a lifetime."

His bitterness dissipated. “That must’ve been hell.” Yet she’d remained friends with Dave. Jess was one strange woman.

“I understood. It wasn’t that he loved Rob or me any less. I know that sounds strange, but it’s true. Anyhow, we divorced; he was going to marry Anita. Can you believe I even liked her? And then . . .” She shuddered. “She was diagnosed with brain cancer. It was sudden, severe; she lasted less than a year. When she died, it nearly shattered Dave.”

“My God, that’s awful.” He shook his head. “Even so, I’m surprised the two of you are so close. I’d have trouble being so friendly with someone who had . . .”

“Dumped me for someone else? Yeah, I was upset. But the love between us wasn’t that special once-in-a-lifetime kind. It was . . . comfortable. So we ended up being friends, which is maybe how we should’ve kept it in the beginning.”

“But then there wouldn’t have been Robin.”

Her breath hitched, and then she said softly, wholeheartedly, “Robin is the best thing Dave and I have done together.”

Almost, she made him want to have a child of his own. He cleared his throat. “Your relationship is unconventional, but it sounds healthy for all three of you.”

She nodded emphatically. “It’s great. Dave’s the best.” Her voice held such warmth, he experienced another irrational surge of jealousy.

“He’s changed since Anita died,” she went on, sounding concerned. “He’s got this deep melancholy. He keeps busy, but he’s not happy. He’s overprotective of Rob. I worry about him.” She shook her head slightly. “But anyway, Rob has a great family. Mom and Pa are terrific, as you know, and Dave’s family is huge and wonderful. Rob’s surrounded by people who love her.”

Evan felt a rush of loneliness. And envy. Lucky Robin.

There had always been times when Jess could read his mind. Now she said, her voice a little scratchy, “Sorry. You know I'd have done anything to change the way you grew up." Moonlight showed the sincerity in her eyes.

"You're the only thing that made it bearable, Jess. You and your parents. You gave me the only affection I ever knew."

They gazed at each other for a long moment. He'd been fighting arousal all evening, but couldn't resist any longer.

Her eyes gleamed and her lips were mere inches from his. He wanted to lean forward and—

"All righty, folks," Jimmy B's cheery voice broke in. "Here we are, safe and sound. Everyone hop down, and you men give the womenfolk a hand."

The barnyard was dim, lit by the moon and stars. The magic spell still bound the guests as people clambered off the wagon.

Knowing he was insane, Evan pushed himself to the edge, vaulted out on legs that hadn't entirely stiffened up, and turned to Jess. He reached out his arms.

"I can g—" she started.

"Of course you can." He didn't step back.

After a long moment, she slid forward into his arms. Carefully he took her by the waist and lifted her from the wagon. He held her above the ground, reveling in the experience of, for the first time, feeling strong and masculine with her.

Slowly, he eased her down so the front of her body caressed his. She gasped and he knew she'd felt his erection. When he was a teen, he'd done everything he could to hide the fact she turned him on. Now, for whatever reason, he didn't want to.

Yesterday afternoon she'd said that when they were seventeen she'd wanted to know that he, too, was attracted. Maybe this was his way of finally telling her.

Their gazes locked; then she swallowed hard and moved away to speak to Jimmy B.

In hushed voices the guests bid the driver and Jess good night, then started toward the cabins. Evan hung back, behind the wagon. She hadn't said good night to him. Had she been offended by what he'd done? Had she thought he was making a pass?

Had he been making a pass?

With a final farewell and a jingle of harness, Jimmy B set the wagon in motion and Jess and Evan were left alone.

She walked toward him and he thought she was going to go straight past, but she stopped abruptly, about three feet away. She put her hands on her hips. "I was right all along. You *were* attracted to me."

He took a step toward her. "I was. I didn't want to be, but I was. You caused me many a sleepless night."

"Good! Damn it, Ev, if only you'd admitted it then."

He took another step and rested his hands on her shoulders. "Then what? I knew we had no future." He gave a little tug and she stepped close so she was touching him. To be more precise, she was resting her flat belly against his erection.

He groaned. "Jesus, Jess."

She looked up at him, her eyes mysterious pools.

He lowered his lips to hers.

She met him eagerly, without restraint. Her lips were soft and hot, and when she opened them he invaded her mouth.

Her arms went around him, one hand high on his shoulder, the other taking possession of his backside, urging him even closer.

He was way past wanting her. He needed her, right now. His hand slid under the loose fringed top, worked her shirt free of the waist of her skirt, and stroked the smooth flesh of her lower back. The night air was cool but her skin was on fire and so was he. His hand fanned out across her back, possessing as much of her as he could encompass.

He needed to take her quickly, but afterward he wanted her slowly, he wanted to touch and savor every inch of her body. At Zephyr Lake he'd barely had the courage to look at her, but now he would, with a man's appreciation, a lover's desire.

He thrust against her and her hips twisted, increasing the pressure. The ache inside him was building to epic proportions. He was going to have to do something soon, yet he wanted to prolong this moment forever.

Jess tore her mouth from his. "This is what it's supposed to be like between us, Evan." She sounded fierce, proud, passionate.

"You've persuaded me." His voice was ragged and his finger shook as he traced her cheek, the line of her jaw. "Better late than never."

Her body went still in his arms. Slowly, she removed one hand from his butt, then the other from his shoulder. She stepped back, leaving him lonely and aching for her.

"Not if it's a dead end," she said. "We still have no future, Ev. And we'd hurt someone else. What about Cynthia?"

Cynthia. He had completely forgotten. "Jesus." He let his breath out in a soft whistle. "I . . . don't know what to say. We're not . . . engaged."

"You and Cynthia are talking about the future."

"Only talking." He was rationalizing, behaving like an ass, and he knew it, but his craving for Jess was so strong. After years of suppressing it, its power was now irresistible.

"I'm not the kind of woman who does this." She put her hands flat on his chest and, with rigid arms, held him at a distance. "Yes, there's chemistry between us. But we're not going to do anything about it."

If she felt anything close to what he felt, how could she possibly stop now?

He put his hands over hers. She resisted for a moment, then submitted to his touch. "You cared about me when we were teenagers, Jess."

She jerked away. "I had an adolescent crush. *Had*. I'm not the same person."

"Don't tell me you don't still care."

She glared at him for a moment, and then her eyes closed. “All right, I care.”

Warmth, the heartwarming kind as well as the arousing kind, poured through him.

Then her eyes opened again and her chin tilted up. “But as a friend. Chemistry and friendship don’t mix. We proved that in grade twelve.”

“That was different.” But the moment he said the words, he knew they were a lie. He and Jess had no more of a future now than they’d had then. To begin a relationship would be unfair to her, as well as to Cynthia.

Damn. What the hell was he thinking? He groaned. The truth was, he wasn’t thinking. Just feeling. And he wasn’t used to feeling, so it wasn’t surprising he couldn’t handle it. How could he betray Cynthia? How could he treat Jess this way? What the fuck was he doing?

He nodded firmly. “You’re right. I lost my head. It won’t happen again.”

She nodded, too. “Good night, Evan. Let’s just . . . try to be friends.”

Chapter Seven

As Jess drove home, she congratulated herself. She should feel guilty for having indulged in that one searing kiss, but she didn't. Evan had owed her for a very long time. The kiss had confirmed what she'd always believed. Thank God she'd managed to pull back, though. She absolutely refused to fall in love again with Evan Kincaid.

But she had to wonder about the nature of Evan's relationship with his girlfriend. Jess got the impression that, when he'd kissed her, Ev had completely forgotten about the woman he was supposedly committed to. And how could he and Cynthia consider marriage if they didn't agree about something as important as children? Though perhaps, if they truly loved each other, they believed they'd find their way, together.

Love. It wasn't a word Evan used when talking about Cynthia. She'd heard respect in his voice, but not tenderness or passion. Of course he'd always been restrained about expressing emotions. In fact, he'd tried not to feel them because his parents had taught him that feeling led to pain.

With a shiver that rippled through her whole body, she remembered him gasping "Jesus, Jess" in a husky voice that was the essence of passion.

She pulled the truck to a stop by her parents' ranch house.

The house she'd grown up in, where she and Ev had done homework on the kitchen table, and where she'd cried into her pillow over him.

She made a fist and bopped herself on the side of the head. "What in holy blue blazes are you thinking, woman? Didn't you shed enough tears over the guy when you were seventeen? Don't go there again. Don't, don't, don't."

She was still muttering "don't" as she walked through the mudroom and into the kitchen. To her surprise, her mother—usually an early-to-bed person—was sitting at the table in her dressing gown, her hands cradling a mug of tea. She poured another mug and shoved it across the table as Jess sat down.

"You're up late. Is everything all right?" Jess asked.

Level gray eyes appraised her. "I was going to ask you the same thing. You've been acting oddly. What's going on, Trixie Jessica Bly Cousins?"

Yikes, her mother had brought out the full arsenal of names, including the dreaded Trixie. Who else had a mom who, as a girl, had been such a fan of Trixie Belden, girl detective, that she'd named her daughter after her?

Jess sighed and took a sip of tea. Apple cinnamon. Comfort tea. "Guess who's back, staying at the Crazy Horse?"

"Back?" Her mother shrugged, and then her face lit. "Oh, Jessica, not that Italian man who seemed keen on your riding camp?"

"Don't I wish. No, I haven't heard from Gianni Vitale. I suppose it was just the usual holiday-induced daydream."

"I'm sorry, dear." She patted Jess's hand, then said, "So, who's back?"

"Evan Kincaid."

Her mother's face brightened again. "Evan! Really? How is he?"

Jess had never told her parents about the way her relationship with Evan had ended. They had no idea that Jess and Evan had been onetime lovers, that Evan had deserted her so coldheartedly, that Robin was really his child. They'd thought it strange she and Evan hadn't kept in touch, but Jess had persuaded them she was too busy with her new husband and daughter and Evan was too busy at Cornell.

Jess bit her lip. "He's good. Can you believe he actually wants to learn how to ride?"

Her mother chuckled. "That doesn't sound like our Evan. What on earth brought him to the Crazy Horse? Did he know you were there?"

"He didn't have a clue."

"So . . . Oh. His mother?"

"I don't think so, but maybe that's part of it." They both knew Evan sent Brooke money.

"He knows her address," her mom said, "and she knows his, yet neither of them have ever written to the other." She "tsk-tsked." "That poor boy. And that poor woman."

"He says he's here because of some club he belongs to. They've got this challenge where you have to do something you were scared to do, or failed at, ten years ago. He says it's riding."

A realization hit Jess, making her feel stupid. "But there are riding places all over the States. If he came back to Caribou Crossing"—Hicksville, in his mind—"there can really only be one reason. Even if it's just a subconscious one. I bet he needs to come to terms with Brooke."

"If those two could only put the past behind them."

"You can't ever really put the past behind you."

Her mother gave her a sharp look. "Sounds like the voice of experience. You're right; I phrased it badly. I mean, it'd be nice if they could move beyond the past. Evan should see how much Brooke has changed. Do you think he knows she has bipolar disorder?"

"How would he, if they never communicate?"

"You could tell him."

"I know. But I'm not sure I should start the conversation."

Evan had faced up to Caribou Crossing and horses. Did he have the guts to deal with his mom?

"He was always touchy on the subject of his parents. For good reason."

The two women drank tea in silence for a few moments. Then Jess's mother said, "So what's got you upset? Does it have to do with Evan? Are you regretting not keeping in touch?"

Jess stirred restlessly. "I guess, a little. And it's nice seeing him, but . . . it's hard figuring out how to act together, after all these years."

"I guess it would be." Her mother nodded, then said, "Jessica, you invite him over for supper. Your pa and I would love to see him, and I'm sure Robin would like to meet your old friend."

"Robin." Jess leaped to her feet. No way was she letting her daughter and Evan sit down and talk around the Bly kitchen table.

When Evan had been in New York, Jess and Dave's deception had seemed so logical and been so easy to maintain. Now, she truly felt like she was in the middle of a tangled web, and she wasn't a very skilled spider. "She'd be bored," she said quickly. "All that talk about old times. Besides, I don't know if Evan can come. Maybe he's got other plans. Gosh, maybe it's supposed to be a secret he's here. I never asked."

Her mother's eyes narrowed. "He wouldn't keep it a secret from us. And we won't be telling Brooke. It would only hurt her if he doesn't get in touch. Lord knows, that woman's had enough pain in her life. Jessica, you invite Evan for supper. Maybe Friday?"

"I—"

"If you don't ask him, I'll call the Crazy Horse and do it myself. Just because you're feeling guilty for having cut off ties with an old friend, you shouldn't deny your pa and me an opportunity to catch up with him."

Oh great, now she was getting guilt from her mom. "Okay, I'll ask. Night, Mom."

Jess went to kiss her sleeping daughter. Then, as she brushed her teeth and washed her face, she stared at her reflection in the bathroom mirror.

Same old Jess. Country girl, plain and simple. Freckles, no make-up. Long dark lashes and well-shaped brows. A straight nose, full lips, a strong jaw. Not bad, but nothing that would compare to Cynthia. Yet Evan seemed to find country girl attractive. She'd been right that he always had, and she felt vindicated.

She tilted her head. Was she attractive, or had it always been about that inexplicable bond between her and Evan? When she'd loved him in high school, she'd known the girls considered him a nerdy know-it-all, a misfit who shunned their town and was shunned in return. Jess had focused on the beautiful eyes and his sweet, loyal personality, and she'd found him the most attractive guy in the world.

Now he really was gorgeous on the outside. Was that what drew her, or was it her conviction that the old Ev still lived inside the handsome new shell?

Aagh. "Don't," she muttered, and bopped herself on the head again. It didn't matter why she was drawn. There were so many reasons to resist the urge.

Tomorrow, she'd pass on her mother's supper invitation. If Evan accepted, she'd make sure Robin was at Dave's.

Did she want him to accept?

Evan couldn't sleep, and it wasn't just because of the mosquito bites. Tonight, knowing Cynthia waited for him in

Manhattan, he'd started to make love to Jess. His body still ached with unsatisfied lust.

Lust? Much as he'd like to think that was all it was, he couldn't fool himself that things would ever be that simple with Jess. What was it about the woman?

Partly, it was their history. She'd had an unwavering loyalty. She'd pushed and challenged and questioned, she'd teased him about his clumsiness, but the constant underlying theme was her faith in him.

No one else had ever thought so highly of him. His father—before he'd run out on Evan and Brooke—had called him a sissy and a failure. His mother had almost been worse. Every now and then, she'd be fun, exciting, affectionate, and he'd get sucked in. Sucked in to caring, to believing she might actually care for him. But those spells never lasted long, and she'd be back to the drinking, the long days in bed or in front of the TV. Back to whining about this stupid hick town and about Evan, saying he'd ruined her life.

Jess's parents . . . Well, they'd been great, but to them he'd always been their daughter's eggheaded little friend. The other kids at school had included him in activities only if Jess insisted.

It all came back to Jess. She'd been the firm center that held his faltering world in orbit.

Cynthia was her own self-contained world, just as he, in Manhattan, was his. Now he wondered if maybe they'd each been holding their emotions in careful check, afraid to surrender control. Control, versus love.

Did he love Cynthia?

He liked and admired her, and he certainly loved the *idea* of her. She was exactly what he'd always believed he wanted.

But as for real love . . . He wasn't sure what the word meant. When he looked back on his life, he realized the only time he'd ever come close to loving was when he and Jess were kids. His feelings for her had seemed so straightforward.

The only uncomplicated aspect of his life. But then they had hit their teens, and hormones had messed up even that one good thing.

Now here she was, in his life again. And he still had feelings for her. The childhood affection, plus the teenage lust in raging proportion, and maybe something more: a liking and respect for, and a curiosity about, the woman she had become.

As for the lust, he definitely had to sublimate that feeling. His commitment to Cynthia wasn't a formal one, but it was real. Besides, the fact was, he and Jess had always belonged in different worlds. They had no future as anything other than friends.

As she had pointed out. Damn, she was right. And she didn't even know his real reason for being here. If he revealed it, they might have no future at all.

Why did he care so much whether they did? And why didn't he feel the same things for Cynthia as he did for Jess? Was it simply a matter of time? His emotions for Jess were both more tender and more violent. In fact, with Jess, he was irrational. With Cynthia, he was utterly rational. There was a powerful lesson in that. He valued rationality.

Evan traded his sweaty pillow for a fresh one, and listened to the absence of sound. How the hell could anyone sleep in this place? He missed the constant background hum of traffic, the shrill of sirens, the bustle of a city always awake, always alive. Here there were no sounds to lull him to sleep, to distract him from the turmoil of his thoughts.

He swung out of bed, wishing for one of the forms of relief that would have been available in New York. But there was no Internet to surf, no e-mail to check, not even a TV with a twenty-four-hour news channel.

He clicked on a light and studied the photo of Cynthia that sat on the dresser. He'd come close to betraying her, and the knowledge shocked him. First thing in the morning he'd call her. A defense against Jess.

* * *

By the time he'd showered in the morning, Evan was able to view the previous night with crystal clarity. There was one, and only one, reasonable explanation. Temporary insanity.

He hurried to the lodge, dialed the phone, and it rang and rang. He was going to be stuck with voice mail again.

But no, she answered, sounding distracted.

"Cynthia, did I catch you at a bad time?"

"Evan, hello. I'm busy, but, no, of course I have a moment to talk, darling."

He could imagine her expression as she turned her focus from work to him, and he appreciated that she was making the effort.

"So," she teased, "are you walking bowlegged and singing country and western songs?"

He scratched a mosquito bite. The damned things itched like crazy. "Good guess. I'm definitely sore. Riding is hard on the body. And last night there was a sing-along. We ran through quite the repertoire of old favorites. Are you familiar with that song that goes 'She'll be coming 'round the mountain when she comes' "? He heard the sarcasm in his voice and winced. The lyrics were no more ridiculous than most opera librettos.

"I take it that's not some kinky sex analogy?"

He gave a snort of laughter. "Somehow I don't think so. Though in one verse she was wearing pink pajamas when she came."

She chuckled. "Poor darling. Culture deprivation. Take heart, it's only a couple more days."

And he'd learned absolutely nothing about Jess's proposal. What the hell was wrong with him? His work ethic was atrophying out here in the boonies.

"Jess doesn't seem inclined to discuss her proposal," he said. "Any suggestions?"

"Hmm. That seems odd, considering you used to be such friends. Maybe she's shy about it in light of your success."

He reflected. "That's perceptive of you."

This was what they did best. Brainstorm together. With a few words, she'd given him an insight from which he could work out a new approach.

"How about you?" he asked. "What are you working on?"

"Weston has decided to go after Dynamite, so I have a lot on my plate."

"Oh, right." How could he have forgotten a deal like that? "Tell me about it."

She didn't say anything for several seconds. Then, "Are you sure you're interested?"

"Of course. Why wouldn't I be?" He truly was. That was his world as well as hers, and he listened intently as she described the maneuvers she was planning. He asked a couple of questions, made a suggestion, and felt his hunger for home grow into a gnawing ache.

"I must get back to it," she said, "but before I go, I've heard good things about a one-man play that's in town next week. They're saying the performer's the new Woody Allen."

He grimaced. "I'm not a big Woody Allen fan." Understatement. He found the guy unbearably tedious.

"Right. I forgot. Oh well, I'll go with Tonia; she'll be keen."

"Great."

"Uh-huh. Got to go. Bye, darling."

"Bye, Cynthia."

They really were good together, he thought as he hung up. Even when their interests differed, there was no pressure. She'd be quite happy going to the play with her friend, and she'd share any interesting bits afterward. Their lives were a perfect balance of togetherness and separateness.

At breakfast the others rehashed the highlights of the hayride and sing-along, and Evan, in a New York state of mind, thought how naive they all sounded. He didn't have much appetite and left the table early.

As he tramped down the hill to the barnyard, he kicked a pebble and wished he was back home. He hadn't belonged in the Cariboo when he was a kid, and he didn't belong here now. The difference was, now he was a grown-up, a free agent, and he didn't have to stay.

Today he'd find an opportunity to get Jess alone. She had softened toward him last night, and, insane idiot that he'd been, he'd never even thought of exploiting that opportunity to ask about her business plans. Was Cynthia right, that Jess was overawed by his success? Maybe she'd feel less intimidated now, after he'd made a fool of himself last night. He'd apologize, play up his frailties and her strengths, and look for an opportunity to talk about her current dream.

Madisun gave him a subdued "Good morning" and he asked, "How's your sister?"

"She'll be okay. Thanks for asking." But her smile looked as forced as his had been.

Should he inquire further? No, he didn't want to be pushy. Besides, he had his own agenda. "Where's TJ?"

"In the barn, getting tack."

Squaring his shoulders, he strode inside. Jess had just hauled a saddle down, and the moment their gazes locked over the top of it, he felt a zing of sexual heat.

Quickly, he looked away. The next thing he knew, she was dumping the saddle into his arms. "This is Mickey's," she said brusquely. "You can saddle him up."

He got a grip on the saddle. "About last night . . ."

"Yes?"

"I behaved stupidly. I'm really sorry."

She shrugged, her expression noncommittal. "No problem. We both did."

She turned away, slung a bridle over her shoulder, and

picked up another saddle from a peg marked "Rambler." When she walked out of the barn, he walked beside her.

"My parents asked me to invite you over for supper," she said without looking at him.

He stopped dead. "Your parents . . ." When he'd had sex with Jess, he'd not only betrayed their friendship, but the trust her parents had placed in him. What had she told them—ten years ago, and now?

She stopped, too, and shot him a narrow-eyed glance. "Don't worry, they don't know anything about what happened when we were seventeen. I just told them we were both too busy to stay in touch."

"Thanks. That's more than I deserve."

"Yes."

What could he say to that? Instead, he responded to the invitation. "I'd love to see them, but I won't go if you don't want me to."

She gnawed on her lip, and then her face relaxed and she gave him a genuine smile. "I'd like you to come, too. I'm just feeling a little weird about . . . you know. Last night and everything."

"Me, too." He felt weird, as well, about the fact that despite his best intentions, his body was superaware of hers. "But you're right, we should concentrate on being friends. We made great friends once upon a time, and I'd like to get that back."

She sighed, then said softly, "Me, too."

Finally, here was an opportunity. "Then I want to get to know you again. You hold back with me, Jess. I know the basics, like your divorce, your daughter, living at your parents' ranch. But you don't tell me your hopes and dreams the way you always used to. I miss that."

She ducked her head a little, so the brim of her cowboy hat hid her eyes. "It takes time to rebuild trust."

Trust. Shit. "I guess it does." He *did* want to be her friend, to hear her hopes and dreams. He wanted to be a man she could trust. He couldn't manipulate Jess to serve Gianni's agenda, and he couldn't sit at her parents' dinner table and deceive the whole family. Cynthia would probably disagree with him, but he had to call Gianni, be more forthcoming about his friendship with Jess, and say that this undercover role didn't work for him. He needed to convince his client that he could be honest with Jess and still objectively assess her plans.

Jess glanced up, wrinkling her nose. "About supper, uh, there's something else. Pa asked me to tell you in case it makes a difference."

"Huh? Tell me what?"

She walked over to the dark brown horse Aaron rode, and Evan followed, still lugging Mickey's saddle. "Hey, Rambler," Jess crooned, then she eased her saddle onto the horse's back. To Evan, she said, "Do you know why your father left town, back when you were ten?"

His father? He never thought about Mo Kincaid. How had the man come into this conversation? "Didn't know why he stayed, didn't know why he went. All I knew was, I was glad. Brooke might have neglected me, but she didn't hit me."

Jess was tightening the cinch, and sent him a quick glance over her shoulder. "I didn't know this at the time, but it was my parents, Ev. They reported him to the cops."

"What? Did you—"

"No," she said quickly. "I didn't tell them. I didn't know that much anyhow, just that your parents fought more than mine did and you sometimes got hit. You didn't say much—"

"Damn right." His dad had drummed into him, with his fists, that family secrets weren't to be shared. Still, he'd been a little kid, Jess was his best friend, and he'd let a thing or two slip, then sworn her to secrecy.

"Everyone knew you were a klutz, but my folks got suspicious of all your bruises and cuts. Then when you had that broken arm and said you'd fallen out of a tree . . ." She shook her head. "You were no tree climber."

It had been a stupid story. Had he secretly wanted her parents to guess the truth that he was scared to tell?

Fingers busy with the saddle, she said, "The police questioned your father. He was drunk. He denied everything, and, uh, Brooke backed him up. But the cops didn't buy it. They told my parents they were going to charge him. Guess he saw it coming, because he took off."

Well. He might've been Jess's little eggheaded friend, but the Blys had cared enough about him to protect him. That was pretty amazing. As for his dad and Brooke . . . well, he'd always known they didn't give a damn what happened to him.

"Yeah," he said, "that makes sense. There wasn't much to keep him. A kid he didn't want, except as a punching bag. A wife . . . well, the same went for her. That's why Brooke would have kept quiet—she'd have been afraid he'd beat her up. God knows why the two of them ever got married in the first place. Well, of course that was because he knocked her up when she was barely more than a kid. Jeez, it's enough to put you off marriage for life."

She slanted him a gentle smile. "But then you look at my folks and realize that's how it's supposed to be. They had that bad patch back when I was seven or eight, but they loved each other, worked things out, and were stronger for it."

He nodded thoughtfully. "Yet you and Dave didn't make it. Guess there are no guarantees, are there?"

"No, but you can stack the deck," she said, taking the horse's halter off.

"For example?"

"Don't get married too young, to someone you barely know. Don't . . . well, I'm sure you can fill in dozens of others."

"Don't knock a girl up like my father did," he said bitterly.

She'd been buckling Rambler's bridle. Her fingers stopped dead. "Right."

Damn. What an ass. "Sorry, Jess. I forgot about you and Dave. Honestly."

"Yeah. Okay." She cleared her throat and picked up the task again. "Anyhow, Pa wanted you to know. In case you held it against them."

"God, no. They might have saved my life." The broken arm hadn't been the worst of his injuries, only the most visible.

"So, supper tomorrow?"

"I'd be pleased to come. It'll be great to see them again." It would, and so would meeting her daughter. At least, in that environment, he ought to be able to curb any feelings of lust for his old friend.

"You going to put that saddle on Mickey, or stand around lollygagging all day?"

"Oh, right."

As he got Mickey ready, and then Rusty, Evan reflected on parents: Jess's and his own. She was right that he had good role models in the Blys. He'd always been so positive he didn't want kids, but Jess's comments had started him thinking. Was it fear of being a bad parent that held him back? Should he tell Cynthia he was willing to reconsider the issue—if she was willing to reconsider her ideas about parenting? And yet, could he imagine himself and Cynthia with a family of their own sharing dinner at home in the same way he used to have dinner with the Blys when he was a boy?

"Mount up!" Jess's call interrupted his thoughts, and he swung into Rusty's saddle, feeling almost proficient.

When the group was out on the trail, Evan reflected on what he needed to do. It was Thursday morning. He should definitely go home on Saturday. Already he'd been away longer than he'd anticipated.

As soon as he got back to the Crazy Horse, he'd call Gianni.

Then, assuming his client gave him the okay, he'd reveal the truth to Jess, try to persuade her to forgive him for his deception, and find out all the details of her no-frills riding idea. Preferably before having dinner with the Blys.

His clients sometimes called him a miracle worker. But that was the Manhattan Evan Kincaid. The Crazy Horse Evan felt like an incompetent bumbler.

And even more so when, at the end of the morning ride, he asked Jess if they could get together sometime in the afternoon. By then he'd have talked to Gianni and be free to tell her the truth. But, with a head shake, she'd responded, "Sorry, it's an insanely busy day."

"It's important. Jess, I need to talk to you about something."

She'd looked mildly curious, but said, "Every minute's scheduled. But we'll have lots of time at supper tomorrow."

One evening. He had one evening to accomplish everything he needed to, before returning to New York. If that's how it had to be, he could handle it. Though he preferred to be organized and methodical, he also performed well in a crunch.

Once the horses had been dealt with after the morning ride, Jess whistled for Conti and rode into town.

After hitching her horse to the rail behind the Wild Rose Inn, she went in the back door. Poking her head through the kitchen door to greet Mitch, the cook, she filled her nostrils with a mouthwatering blend of cooking smells.

"What can I fix you?" Mitch asked. "Special today's Santa Fe chicken salad."

She groaned. "Sounds fantastic. But I don't have time to stop. It's one of my afternoons off from the Crazy Horse, and I've got a ton of work waiting for me at the ranch."

Dave wasn't in the manager's office, but then he rarely was. His style of management was hands-on and friendly, and today he was behind the front desk providing a family with directions to Gold Rush Days Park.

Dave waved a hand at Jess, who waved back, then settled into a chair in the lobby, which was cleverly decorated to look rustic yet have modern-day comfort. She watched her ex affectionately. At six foot two—a couple of inches taller than Evan—he was as handsome, rangy, and fit as he'd been in high school. His sandy hair still flopped over his hazel eyes. He was still one of the most decent guys you could ever hope to know, though since Anita's death he'd lost his vibrancy. He kept busy, but it was a busyness born of sorrow and emptiness rather than vitality. She wished she could help him.

He'd been there for her when she needed him most. When she found out she was pregnant, her first instinct was to get in touch with Evan. It wouldn't be hard. She knew he was at Cornell in student housing.

But then she thought it through. Ev had always been adamant about not wanting kids. He might return, marry her, ruin his life, and totally resent her and the child, as his parents had resented him. Or he might try to force her to have an abortion. Neither alternative was one she would consider.

The reality of being pregnant made her focused and practical. This wasn't a "someday in the future dream," like her various horse-oriented ones; this was real, and imminent. She knew that her parents, after they overcame their shock, would support her. She and the baby would live with them, she'd help out with the ranch, and her mom would teach her how to raise a child.

But before she told her folks, she wanted a guy's perspective—Dave's perspective—on whether she was being fair to Evan.

Watching Dave now, she noted how patiently he listened

to a little redheaded girl who was telling him some story that involved a lot of giggling.

He was such a sweet, even-tempered guy. And yet, when she'd told him about the night at Zephyr Lake and her pregnancy, he'd called Ev a lot of foul names she'd never heard him use before. He'd ranted about Evan not deserving anything except a sock in the jaw, which Dave would have been more than happy to deliver right to Evan's door in Ithaca, New York. She told him Ev wasn't to blame—which had him cussing and ranting all over again—and then she asked him to cool down and think it over for a couple of days.

When he came back, he stunned her by proposing marriage. He said he loved her and would love her baby, and he hoped and believed she'd come to love him.

It was Jess's turn to go away and think. She was fond of Dave and truly respected him. Next to her pa, he was her favorite guy in the world, now that Evan had so thoroughly disillusioned her. Of course she could love Dave. He was perfect.

She and Dave agreed to tell the world he was the child's father. While they hated to lie to their families and friends, the baby's welfare came first.

They were married and Dave was so wonderful that Jess indeed grew to love him. Two months after Robin was born, Jess came into Dave's bed for the first time, and over the next few months they experimented and played and learned to give each other pleasure. She told herself that was mature love—something quite different from the teenage lust she had felt for Evan.

Their marriage might have lasted forever if Dave hadn't met Anita. Not that Jess begrudged him. A love like Dave and Anita's came along only once in a lifetime.

A chorus of good-byes roused her from her reverie, and she realized the tourists were leaving.

"Hey, Jessie," Dave called.

"Hey, good-looking." She came over to the desk and leaned across to peck his cheek.

He tweaked her ponytail. "What brings you my way?"

"Can you take Rob tomorrow night?"

"Sure. She's spending the weekend with me anyhow. We'll just start early." A sandy eyebrow kinked. "Couldn't have asked me over the phone?"

"Uh, there's a bit more to it."

Now both eyebrows skyrocketed. "You don't have a date?"

"No." She bit her lip. "Mom and Pa invited someone for supper. He's staying at the Crazy Horse and . . ." She glanced around, making sure they were alone. "It's Evan."

Dave's mouth fell open. He started to say something, but his lips couldn't form words.

"It was a big surprise for me, too."

"What's he doing here?" he demanded.

"It's a long story. He didn't know I worked there. You ought to have seen his face. He didn't know I—you and I—had a child. Anyhow, when I told Mom he was around, she insisted I invite him over and—"

"And you don't want him to meet Robin."

"No."

He gave one firm nod, his eyes blazing with a fire she hadn't seen in a long time. "Good. I don't want him to meet her either. She's *my* daughter."

She nodded back. "Yes, she is. She always has been, from even before she was born. Remember how you used to rest your hand on my tummy and let her kick you, and you sang Willie Nelson songs to her?"

He grinned. Then his face went somber and he said, softly but vehemently, "I won't be losing her to him."

Jess shook her head vigorously and whispered back, "No, you won't. He doesn't know. He won't know. Not a soul knows but you and me, and no one else ever will. Not my folks, not Robin herself. We've always agreed on that."

He let out a long breath. "Thanks. I knew that, I really did. I trust you, Jessie-girl, more than anyone in the world. Guess I panicked for a moment." He stepped out from behind the desk and held out his arms to Jess.

She walked into them and they hugged long and hard.

When they separated, he touched her cheek. "How about you? How do you feel having him back in town?"

"Confused. God, but for Robin, I wish he and I had never hooked up. We were such good friends and we should have stuck with that. Teenage hormones can really mess you up. Now, well, maybe we're trying to find our way back to being friends."

His gaze flicked up and down her body. "No 'hormones' this time around?" She heard the quotation marks he put around the word *hormones*. He knew she'd cared deeply for Evan.

Her cheeks warmed and she dropped her head.

Dave lifted her chin with his index finger. "Don't let him hurt you again, Jessie."

"Of course not." She sounded too vehement. She knew it, and could tell from his concerned expression that he did, too.

"He's only here for two weeks?"

She nodded. "Then he'll go back to New York. He loves his life there. He's got a girlfriend and they're talking marriage."

"He's got a girlfriend, and yet you're blushing over him?"

"Don't worry, I won't make the same mistake twice. But it's funny . . ."

"What's that?"

"There are only two guys I've ever been seriously attracted to. You and him. Other men don't interest me. Is something wrong with me?"

He shook his head. "Not unless it's wrong with me, too. For me, it was just you and Anita." A shadow crossed his face, as it always did, when he mentioned that name. "I know there won't be anyone else."

She guessed he was right about that. When Anita died, he closed his heart to the possibility of loving again.

She gave him another, fiercer hug. "Got to go."

"You ride over?"

"Yup, Conti's hitched out back."

He walked out with her. Mitch popped out of the kitchen to give her one of her favorite sandwiches: rare roast beef and mustard on dark rye. In payment, he got a kiss on the cheek.

Dave held the sandwich as Jess swung into the saddle. He rubbed her horse's nose with gentle knuckles. "How you doin', Conti?"

When Jess was settled in the saddle, he handed her the sandwich. "Where and when should I pick up our girl tomorrow? From school?"

"Uh, let's see. No, it's a professional development day and Kimiko's coming out to the ranch. Maybe you could come by around five? Drop Kimiko off at home?" She unwrapped the sandwich and took a big bite.

"No problem. By the way, Rob and I are having supper with my folks on Saturday. A barbecue. My sibs will be there, and a couple of cousins, complete with families. You're welcome, too."

"Thanks, I just might. I'll let you know." The distraction of a big loving family might be exactly what she needed as an antidote for a week of Evan.

He gave her thigh a gentle swat. "You're the best. Just remember to think with your brain, right? Not your . . ."

She snorted, then turned Conti so quickly the horse's tail flicked Dave's face.

Chapter Eight

On Friday morning Evan woke feeling almost content. Perhaps it was because this was his last day at the Crazy Horse, or maybe it was because yesterday he'd convinced Gianni to let him tell Jess the truth.

He enjoyed the hearty breakfast and participated in the conversation. The guests sure were friendly and relaxed, compared to the people he and Cynthia worked and socialized with. It took some getting used to, but he was beginning to fit in.

He snagged a handful of carrots—still not trusting Rusty with an apple—then went back to his cabin to exchange his sneakers for the pointy-toed boots, which had loosened up enough to be almost comfortable. Outside his cabin, he met up with Ann and Sandy, and the three of them chatted companionably as they made their way to the barn. "I'm looking forward to the session on horse care and communication," Sandy said enthusiastically.

"It should be interesting," he said noncommittally.

Ann caught his eye and gave a snort. "Tell us what you really think, Evan."

The two women chuckled, and he joined in. "I'll try to keep an open mind." Besides, this was one of the things

Gianni had mentioned in Jess's plans for her riding camp. He'd have another opportunity to observe and evaluate.

Although Jess had yet to tell him about her latest dream, the week had given him ample chance to assess a number of relevant factors. She was great with the guests as well as with her assistant. Everyone who'd taken riding lessons was full of compliments for her skill and patience. She trained most of the horses herself, and they were all good tempered and well mannered, even if a few, like Rusty, had a sense of humor—but hey, that wasn't a bad thing.

Jess kept the tack and horses in great shape, and trail rides left and returned on schedule, or at least as much as possible given the unpredictability of both the horses and the guests.

He was convinced Jess made the perfect employee for a place like the Crazy Horse, or the camp she had in mind. What he needed to know now was whether the girl who used to hate homework could plan, administer, and market a business.

In the barnyard, he and the two women split up and went to their horses. Evan greeted Rusty with carrots and a pat on the neck, then saddled up and exchanged halter for bridle.

Madisun tossed him a grin. "You're a pro."

With an exaggerated groan he hoisted himself into the saddle. "And one day even this will get easier, right?"

"You'll be springing up effortlessly before we're done with you."

"I almost believe you. Now do you want to sell me a bottle of snake oil?"

Her delighted burble of laughter made him grin. He wasn't used to making women laugh. It could get addictive.

As the line of riders wound along the trail, he found himself savoring the sun on his face and shoulders, the scent of trees—pine, he'd heard Jess say—and roses. The wild rosebushes really were pretty, with their simple blossoms ranging from pastel to vivid pink. For the most part, the riders didn't talk and the only sounds were the clomp of hooves, creak of leather, and occasional chitter of squirrels and birds. It was boring, but somehow not quite as boring as it had been on previous days. In fact, it was rather peaceful. He worked a few investment plans in his head but had trouble concentrating, and eventually found himself content to just drift along.

He remembered thinking that he couldn't relax without the Internet. It seemed he'd been wrong. Just as well he was heading back to Manhattan tomorrow, before his work ethic eroded entirely.

Back in the barnyard, Jess and Madisun instructed several guests on how to remove tack. Each day, more people wanted to take care of the horses themselves. Evan felt smug at managing perfectly well on his own. He stroked Rusty's neck as he waited for the others to finish up.

Jess came out of the barn lugging a box, which she dumped on the ground. "We'll talk about communication, then we'll get to grooming." She lifted a wicked-looking spiked metal implement from the box, then let it drop back.

They were going to use that for grooming? He couldn't imagine Rusty being too happy about that.

"I know Thérèse and George know about Monty Roberts," Jess said. "Have any of the rest of you heard of him?"

Evan recalled Gianni mentioning the name. A couple of hands went up and Ann said, "The original horse whisperer."

Jess nodded. "He's been a groundbreaker in the way we think about—and treat—horses. You've seen old movies where cowboys 'break' horses with whips and spurs?"

Heads nodded.

"How would you feel about someone who treated your dog or cat like that?"

"I'd want to string him up," Kim called out, and others muttered agreement.

"Me, too. Now, how do you think an intelligent creature

would end up if they were treated that way? Obedient maybe, but . . . ?"

"Scared," Evan said softly, remembering Mo Kincaid's fists. Others added "mad" and "resentful." He was nodding and, across the barnyard, noticed Madisun doing the same. There was something about the look on her face . . .

But then Jess spoke again, and he focused on her.

"All of that," Jess said. "And when you're dealing with more than a thousand pounds of living animal, do you want that animal feeling scared and hostile? Or do you want him to be your willing partner?" She moved to a line of tethered horses, stroking noses and rubbing cheeks. "These are noble, courageous animals. If you treat them with respect, with love, you can enter into a partnership that's unique."

Like people, Evan thought. Like what he and Jess once had. Watching her, casually attractive and graceful in her Western garb, he noted that she'd developed presence, a natural confidence and ability to hold the group's attention. Now, if only she'd also developed a head for business, he could actually recommend that Gianni invest in her riding camp.

She faced the guests. "Those of you who have pets know what it's like to have that magical sense of bonding with an animal. But think of the difference. The horse is far bigger and more powerful than a dog. He can kill you. Don't ever forget that."

A few people glanced uneasily at the horses, but Evan shook his head. Not these animals. Not the way Jess had trained them. But he understood what she was doing. "Guess I'd better show you some respect," he muttered to Rusty.

Jess went on. "If you face a mugger on the street and he's got a knife, he has the power. What do you do? Make him mad? Try to scare him? No, you acknowledge his power. You respect it.

"Well, a horse has power. But—unless he's been mistreated

and his soul damaged—he wants to give that power to you, to share and use. He wants to please you. And he will go to amazing ends to do so. You've probably all heard stories of horses who have died for their masters. Their hearts are that big."

She paused and Evan knew she was fighting tears. Dear, emotional Jess. She must give this speech every two weeks, yet it still touched her heart. He wanted to hug her. Instead, he reached out to stroke Rusty's neck. The horse turned a liquid eye on him.

"Monty Roberts's most famous book is called *The Man Who Listens to Horses*. He learned by observing wild horses. He saw the way the adults, particularly the dominant mare—and yes, men, I did say the lady was dominant—taught the young ones. He learned the body language, he figured out what the horses were telling each other. And he applied those techniques to training horses. With amazing success."

She stood in front of the group and lifted her hands toward them, palms up. "And what are those techniques based on? The principles of acceptance versus rejection. Horses, just like us, hate to be ostracized. They want to be liked, accepted by their group, their leader."

Evan had wanted that, too, as a child. But it hadn't happened. Blame his flawed parents or his own proud, bull-headed personality. But the only place he'd ever felt accepted was with this girl, and her generous parents.

Jess went on. "If you're the trainer, it's your acceptance they seek. They want to be your friend. If you ask them to do something and they obey, you reward them with acceptance and friendship. If they disobey, you don't hit them, you simply shun them. You send them away until they tell you, with their body language, that they want to be forgiven, to try again."

When Evan had run out on her at Zephyr Lake, then

e-mailed far too late she'd shunned him. He had tried again, once, but she hadn't taken him back.

Jess glanced from face to face. "I'll be telling you more about Monty Roberts's techniques over the next week. You can watch his videos at the lodge if you're interested, and the gift shop sells his books."

Evan, still wondering about the parallels between their relationship and a horse and its trainer, was coming to understand why Jess was keen on her horsy boot camp. She'd like to give sessions on horse communication every day, not confine them to a few minutes here and there. She wanted to deal with what she called "real horse people," not horse lovers who wanted to do a little riding but also enjoy being pampered at a spa.

Jess rubbed her hands together. "Enough talk. Now you're going to work." She picked up the metal spike again and grinned mischievously. "Starting with the hoof pick."

Ten minutes later, head swimming with information about grooming tools, armed with his very own hoof pick, Evan gazed dubiously at Rusty's huge hooves.

"You'll feel better for this," he muttered to the horse. Feeling safer starting at the front, he attempted to lift one of the horse's legs, trying to remember how Jess had done it. She and Knight had made it look easy: she nudged, and the horse's leg rose.

Evan nudged. "Up now," he said encouragingly.

Rusty shifted position, momentarily raising the opposite hoof, then plunking it down solidly. Yeah, the horse did have a sense of humor.

"You're enjoying this, aren't you?" Evan said. "Don't you know you're a noble beast who's supposed to try to win my approval?"

He heard trills of female laughter, both from Ann, the

woman whose horse was next to Rusty, and from Madisun, who'd come to see how they were doing.

"Let me show you again," the girl said, demonstrating on Ann's horse.

Finally, Evan met with success. Then, balancing the horse's knee on his own, he did his best to scrape assorted disgusting, foul-smelling substances from inside Rusty's hoof. The horse's weight grew heavier and Evan's knees sunk lower toward the mucky ground. "If you think I'm going to kneel for you, you have another think coming, my friend."

Ann chuckled and he glanced over, noting tousled red hair, flushed cheeks, a plucky grin. "Wait until I tell the other docs how I spent my summer vacation," she said.

"Mastering new skills," he said.

"Developing manual dexterity. Can you believe I'm a surgeon?" She twirled her hoof pick clumsily.

"Honoring the amazing bond that is only possible between horse and human." His pick sent a chunk of manure flying, barely missing his face, and they both burst out laughing.

"You two are having way too much fun," Jess teased from behind them. "Come on, you've only got three hooves to go."

Ann squared her shoulders and turned back to her horse, Distant Drummer, whose coat had a pretty pattern of brown and white splotches.

Evan followed suit with Rusty, and Jess watched until they'd both managed to get their horses to lift the next hoof, then moved on to coach Sandy.

After a few minutes, Ann said, "You know TJ, don't you?"

"From a long time ago, though I didn't know she worked here when I registered."

"She's wonderful at her job. So patient with us, so knowledgeable. It's obvious she has a tremendous love and respect for horses."

"That's very true." He felt a rush of pride. "She's really something, that Jess."

"Jess?"

"TJ is her professional name, but her real name is Jessica."

"Jessica? Like the woman in *The Man From Snowy River*?"

He remembered Jess mentioning that movie, citing it as the reason she used TJ in her work. "You saw the movie?"

"I've seen every movie with horses in it. Haven't you seen it?"

"No."

"Oh, you have to, you'll love it. And *Return to Snowy River,* too. I know they're old, but they're a must if you love horses. I can't believe you haven't seen them."

"I, uh, only discovered horses fairly recently."

"I can't believe it. You're doing so well."

"Thanks." The astonishing thing was that he was enjoying it. Somewhere along the line, it had stopped being an intellectual and physical challenge and started to become a pleasure. Jess was entitled to a few "I told you so's."

He let down Rusty's last hoof and gave him a teasing slap on his flank. "That's four. And I bet you've got the first one filthy again, haven't you?"

To Ann, he said, "Don't let on about TJ's real name, okay? I gather she doesn't want any *Snowy River* jokes."

"The secret's safe with me."

Together they went to exchange hoof picks for grooming brushes and combs. They chatted for a while as they worked, then fell silent. There was something profoundly relaxing about the firm, even motions, the feel of Rusty's warm body, the undemanding companionship.

When everyone was finished, Jess lavished words of praise, then said, "That's it for the day, folks. Enjoy the time off."

"I'm looking forward to the demonstration tomorrow afternoon," Thérèse said.

"What demonstration?" Joan asked.

"Fancy cowgirl riding," Madisun said. "TJ is incredible and her daughter's a star."

"TJ, you have a daughter?" Sandy exclaimed. "I can't wait to meet her."

Nor could Evan. He was looking forward to his chance at dinner tonight. He hoped that Robin would be like the young Jess, and that he wouldn't recognize Dave in the girl. For some crazy reason, it hurt to think that Dave and Jess had created a child not long after he'd left town.

Jess yanked off her hat and fiddled with the brim. "I'm not sure Robin can make it."

The guests protested loudly, and for some reason Jess shot a quick glance in Evan's direction before she said, "I'll see what I can work out."

When the guests headed for the lodge, Evan hung back, hoping for an opportunity to talk alone with Jess. He needed to make his confession, and didn't want to do it in front of her parents and daughter. "Can I help you turn the horses out for the night?"

Madisun cocked her head toward Jess. "He's got good horse sense. I vote yes."

"Good horse sense." Jess shook her head bemusedly.

The three of them worked companionably together, and then Madisun headed into the barn to clean tack. Alone with Jess, Evan felt a physical pull to move closer to her. To touch her, even if it was just to brush her hand or to flick off the smudge of dirt on her cheek. He resisted, knowing he shouldn't be feeling this way. What he really needed to do was talk to her about Gianni Vitale.

He was trying to find a way to open that conversation, when Jess said, "About supper? I have some chores to do at the ranch. I'll ride home now, then drive back and pick you up at your cabin around six."

"I can catch a cab," he said automatically. "But do you have to leave right now? I'd hoped for a chance to talk."

"Can't now, I have too much to do. The ranch doesn't run itself, and there's a horse I'm training, too. We'll have lots of time to talk tonight. And as for a cab, you're not in Manhattan, city boy. Taxis are few and far between. 'Sides, Mom would tan my hide."

"Okay," he muttered unhappily. "See you later." How in hell was he going to handle this? Confess on the drive to the ranch, then pump her about her business plan while her parents and daughter listened?

He had walked a few steps when she said, "Evan?"

He turned back. "Yes?"

There was a soft, almost wistful expression on her face, and again he wanted to touch her. "You're really fitting in," she said. "I wish you'd been like this when you were a boy."

For a moment, he wished it, too. He and Jess could have ridden together, taken picnics into the backcountry. And that thought had him feeling like a horny teenager again. But no, he'd hated this place, hated his life. If he'd stayed, he'd never have become the man he was today.

Firmly, he shook his head. "I needed to be focused. Driven. I had to get out of here to find myself." And to escape his home life, but Jess knew that without him saying it.

"And maybe now you had to come back to find yourself?"

His immediate reaction was to reject the idea.

She must have read his face, or his mind. She grinned. "Think about it. And while you're thinking, have a sauna and massage. Tomorrow you'll be in the saddle for more hours than your body is used to."

"I hear you, boss." Turning to walk up the hill, he hated to think how she'd react when she learned the truth. Tomorrow, he wouldn't be in the saddle; he'd be on a plane to NYC. Would this tentative new/old friendship with Jess still be alive, or would she flat out reject him again once she knew he'd been lying to her all week?

Damn Gianni, anyway!

Jess said a quick good-bye to Madisun, gave the usual good-night treat to her old friend Petula, then leaped up on her own horse, Conti, for the fifteen-minute ride home. If she didn't keep up with the ranch chores, her father would overdo. There was an ongoing conspiracy between Jess and her mother to keep Wade Bly from overextending himself. They'd do everything they could to prevent another stroke.

She loved the powerful feeling of Conti surging forward between her thighs. Communication between them was a continual two-way street. It happened by instinct, by sensation, rather than by effort.

Why couldn't the chemistry between a man and a woman be as easy and natural?

She remembered how it had been with her and Evan, the one time they'd made love. Or, as she was sure he would term it, had sex. She'd expected magic under a canopy of sparkly stars, and though the physical act had been hasty and clumsy, just being intimate with him for the first time was its own magic. Until it ended so badly.

The other night, lying beside him on a mattress of hay with ten other people clustered around them, she'd felt magic again. And later, when everyone had gone and passion overcame them for a few precious, frightening moments . . .

Her feelings terrified her. Loving Evan had always been crazy and doomed. Now he'd found his success, his life, in Manhattan. There was no hope for them as a couple. Besides, there was the perfect Cynthia.

And Robin. Not to mention Dave. Why was she even thinking this way?

Why in holy blue blazes was it so impossible to look at

Evan and simply think "friend"? She managed it just fine with Dave, even after years of marriage and great sex.

Nearing Bly Ranch, she slowed Conti to cool him down. She only wished she could cool her fevered brain.

When she'd turned him out to pasture, she dashed into the house to say hello. In the kitchen, her mother gave her a quick, wet-handed hug, then went back to mixing the ingredients for meatloaf, her hips sashaying like a teen's to a Patsy Cline song on the radio.

In Robin's room, she and her friend Kimiko were on the Internet and didn't notice Jess as she stood in the doorway. Jess watched as her daughter busily clicked away amid a clutter of stuffed animals and posters ranging from Justin Bieber, dressed in black clothing way too cool for his age, to Elizabeth Taylor in *National Velvet*, a classic Dave had found for Rob's last birthday.

Now *this* was the definition of perfect. This beautiful, bright girl. Her and Dave's. Keeping Robin safe and happy was the most important thing in the world.

Choosing not to interrupt, Jess hurried out to the barn. No sign of her father, but his mare, Cadenza, who was Conti's sister, was gone. She would have loved to saddle up Mystique, the filly she was training, and ride out to join her pa, but instead she went into the office in the barn. Settling behind the desk, she saw that her mom, who handled the bookkeeping, had paid a bunch of invoices and put aside a stack of mail that needed to be dealt with. Jess started going through the mail and had almost finished when she heard the sound of a vehicle. Her watch told her it was five o'clock.

She hurried outside and greeted Dave with a quick hug. "I lost track of time. I hope the girls are ready."

"I'm in no hurry. Just as long as I don't run into—"

"You won't. I'm picking him up at six."

Together they walked to the house, where Miriam Bly gave

Dave a big hug and kiss. Then she handed him a knife and ordered him to slice apples for the pie she was making.

Jess went to Robin's room to roust the girls. As she had suspected, they were still tethered to the computer.

"Your dad's here," she told Robin. "Time to go."

She hustled the girls downstairs, but proceedings stalled as her mother packed oatmeal cookies for Dave to take home, and for Kimiko, whose parents kept a busy schedule as owners of the only Japanese restaurant in town.

"Drop Kimiko at home, then you two come back for supper," Jess's mother urged Dave. "You and Evan were classmates, after all."

A hiss escaped Jess, and Dave sent her a warning glance. "Thanks, Miriam, but I have plans for Rob tonight."

Finally, Jess gave Robin a last, especially tight hug and a big kiss, and waved until Dave's truck was out of sight. She ran a hand through her hair, dusty from a day of riding, wondering if there was time for a shower.

"Oh, Jessica," her mother said, "when you go for Evan, would you pick up some vanilla ice cream? For the apple pie."

Jess sighed. "Sure. And I need to gas up the truck, too, so I'd better get a move on." She'd hoped to look cool and collected; now she wasn't even going to achieve clean.

She did make it to Evan's cabin on time, which she considered an accomplishment. Then he opened the door and she felt at a distinct disadvantage. He'd had the sense not to overdress, yet he looked wonderful in pressed khakis and a crisp white cotton shirt with open neck and rolled sleeves. Five days of sunshine had tanned skin that was by nature a bit dark, an inheritance from an Indo-American grandmother on his dad's side. His tawny brown hair was acquiring golden highlights.

He looked absolutely delicious and she wanted nothing more than to go into his arms for a long, slow hug and kiss.

Not that he'd want to go anywhere near her grubby self. One touch, and dust would spoil his immaculate shirt.

She glanced at his feet. Tan leather loafers, polished to a glossy sheen. A total contrast to her grungy cowboy boots. She suppressed a sigh of regret. "Let's get going. I'm running late."

"Sorry to add to your list of chores."

She glanced up again, saw his sincere smile, and suddenly felt better. "Oh, Ev, you're not a chore. Come on, Mom's been cooking up a storm."

Evan's stomach growled, distracting him from thinking how cute, tousled, and sexy Jess looked. He remembered all the times he'd stuffed himself at the Bly kitchen table—then been sent home with a bag of leftovers, an unspoken acknowledgment that the cupboards at his own house were usually pretty bare.

"I can't wait," he said, grabbing the cabin key and the paper bag containing a bottle of wine that he'd bought from the Crazy Horse bar.

They climbed into her dusty truck and she drove down the gravel road toward the highway. Country and western music played on the radio and he remembered how he and Jess used to squabble over which station to listen to. Now, rather than joke about her taste in music, he needed to tell her about his relationship with Gianni. He reached for the knob and turned down the volume.

He'd just opened his mouth when Jess said, "Ev, you know the subject of your mother might come up?"

"I won't be the one raising it." Still, being so close to Caribou Crossing for the last few days, he'd thought of Brooke more than once. He couldn't resist asking about her. Striving for a casual tone, he queried, "So what's she up to? Still using the welfare checks to buy her beer?"

Jess shook her head. "No beer, and she hasn't been on welfare for years. Evan, you wouldn't believe how Brooke's pulled herself together. She works for Auntie Kate at her shop. The old Cut 'n' Curl is now Beauty Is You, and it's quite trendy. For Caribou Crossing, anyhow. Brooke's great."

"Wow." He tried to get his head around the idea of his mom not drinking, of her holding a real job. If he didn't know better, he'd think Jess was joking. But she would never joke about Brooke.

He tried to reconcile the picture she'd painted with the memories of his mother. "She did have a flair for that girly stuff when she wanted to," he said slowly. "When she wasn't . . . out of it. Sometimes she'd look so young and pretty." He shook his head, remembering. "Then before long she'd hit The Gold Nugget Saloon, drink until she ran out of money. She'd come back home messed up. Wouldn't comb her hair for days on end. Didn't get out of her dressing gown, and sometimes not even out of bed."

He didn't add the rest. During the frequent bad spells, she didn't cook meals, buy groceries, do laundry, clean the house. Evan had become self-sufficient. He tried to make himself unobtrusive, too, knowing that his mother hadn't wanted him, didn't love him. That she blamed him—along with his dad—for ruining her life.

When the welfare ran out, he didn't want to spend the money from his part-time jobs on food. That was his "escape Hicksville" fund, accumulating for the day he graduated from high school. No, he was always able to rely on Mrs. Bly's standing invitation for supper.

And now here he was, heading out to the ranch for one of those meals. How far he'd come . . .

"Memories?" Jess's voice was gentle.

"I don't know which were worse, the bad times or the good ones. When Brooke was happy she was amazing. She bubbled like champagne. She'd dress in bright clothes, do her hair up fancy. She'd get a job as a waitress or sales clerk, she'd bring home money and food, she'd hardly drink at all, and she'd—"

"What?"

"Say she loved me," he said ruefully. "It was like living in a beautiful dream. Pure illusion, yet time after time I'd get sucked in because I desperately wanted to believe."

He stared ahead, watching the two-lane highway unwind and noting that the scenery was the same as always: split-rail fences along the road, rolling ranch land with cattle grazing, an occasional house and barn, and low hills in the background. His peripheral vision told him Jess kept glancing his way.

"You should believe," she said. "The loving woman was the genuine one."

"Mothers who love their kids come to parent-teacher meetings and open houses. When you're little they tuck you in and read stories, and when you're older they wait up and ream you out for being late." He thought he'd gotten over the bitterness long ago, but its sourness tinged his voice.

Almost under his breath, he added, "Mothers who love their kids don't mind being called 'Mom.' "

Her hand darted out, touched his thigh, then retreated.

He appreciated her compassion, but he was grown up. Time to get off the subject of his mother. He needed to tell Jess about his reason for being here. How should he start?

"Evan? You realize Brooke was ill?"

Her question distracted him. "Ill? You mean alcoholic, right? Yeah, she and my dad were both alcoholics. I know that's a disease, but that's not a lot of consolation when you're the kid who suffers for it."

"I know. But it was more than that, Ev. All those days when she couldn't get out of bed?"

"Clinical depression? Probably so. But she didn't do anything about it. Never went to a doctor. Never took me either. Not even the time I broke my arm." He cleared his throat. "The time *he* broke my arm." The days of denial were long gone.

He glanced over at Jess's solemn profile, then said, "Brooke had to know she could get help for her problems. But she didn't want to get better. She enjoyed being miserable."

Jess swung the truck off the country highway onto gravel and he turned away from her to see the "Bly Ranch" sign. It was the same wooden one he remembered, just ten years more weathered. Oh shit, they were there already. He'd lost his opportunity to confess, and yet he couldn't regret hearing the news about his mother. "Jesus, I can't believe Brooke finally got it together."

Jess nodded. "She was in a car accident. She'd been drinking. Smacked into a tree, and no, she didn't hurt anyone but herself. Ended up in the hospital. She was manic, and the doctor diagnosed her as having bipolar disorder and put her on medication."

"Bipolar disorder." He whistled softly. "Jesus." He replayed the memories again. The dark, dismal spells, but yes, they alternated with the times when she was almost frenetically active and cheerful. "Damn. I should have realized."

"You were a kid."

"Afterward. I should have figured it out when I grew up." But he'd always avoided thinking about his parents.

Jess didn't comment.

Evan felt shell-shocked. "So, she was diagnosed," he said slowly, "and she's on medication?"

"Yes. It's been four years. She joined A.A. then, too, and has stayed sober. She goes to church every Sunday." Jess darted him a sideways glance. "She must like the person she's become—or the one she found inside herself."

He realized he was shaking his head slowly, not in disbelief but in wonder. "And who is that person?"

They weren't at the house yet, but Jess pulled the truck to

a stop on the side of the road and turned to him. "Why don't you see for yourself?"

"No!" It was one thing for Jess to tell him about his mother, and maybe he could even believe her. In the abstract. Good for Brooke if she'd built a new life for herself. He'd done the same. But there was no reason those two lives needed to intersect.

He shook his head firmly. "I have no need to, and why would she want to see me? I'm the kid who ruined her life. I'd remind her of a past she'd rather forget."

"Ev, she boasts about you."

"What? She doesn't know anything about me."

"She knew you were hell-bent on succeeding, and she knew you'd do it. She Googles you and knows a lot about your career."

"You talk to her?" Why did it feel like a betrayal?

"She cuts my hair." Jess gave a soft laugh and flipped her ponytail. "She despairs over me. All I let her do is whack an inch off the ends. And she keeps telling me I should get a manicure." She waved her right hand in his face. "These hands. Can you imagine?"

Her nails were short as could be, and would benefit from a nailbrush.

He tried to imagine her with a fancy manicure like Cynthia's, and laughed. "Some things don't change."

Jess shrugged. "Yeah, and I hate wearing make-up, and I often forget to put on sunscreen." She slanted him a mischievous glance. "I'm guessing Brooke would thoroughly approve of Cynthia." Her tone turned snarky. "But Cynthia probably pays ten times as much for a haircut as your mother charges, and would never condescend to let a hick-town stylist touch her precious locks."

He chucked her under the chin. "Catty." And why should his fingers burn from that slight touch?

"But true?"

"Yeah, true. Cynthia's appearance is an important part of who she is."

"Unlike some of us, who have better things to do with our time."

So did Cynthia. She put in just as long hours as Jess, and her hairstyle and manicure were as much a part of her work costume as Jess's Western shirts, boots, and Annie Oakley outfit. But he figured saying so would only hurt Jess's feelings.

"You look great," he said. "Just as great as she does." He meant it. He could have added that her natural, rather earthy style was even sexier, but no way was he saying that. He couldn't understand why he even felt that way, when Cynthia was exactly the kind of woman with whom he'd always envisioned sharing his life. "You're just different types. You're natural and she's—" He broke off, not sure how to phrase it.

"Yes?" That catty gleam still lurked in her eye. "Were you going to say 'artificial'?"

"I wasn't. And she isn't." Cynthia was as genuine in her own way as Jess was. "Sophisticated."

She flipped her ponytail again. "Okay, I'm not insulted. The last thing I want to be is sophisticated."

He grabbed that flirty tail and tugged it. "Lucky for you, because it's the last thing you'll ever be."

She stuck out her tongue, and then they were both laughing. He did love Jess's laugh. Like the woman herself, it was bighearted and engaging.

As they held their gaze, their laughter turned to smiles. Smiles that softened at the edges into uncertainty. On his part, into longing.

He had no idea what Jess felt, but she suddenly busied herself getting the truck back on the road.

Also as suddenly, he realized he'd let himself get distracted again. "Jess, could you stop again for a couple of minutes? There's something I need to talk to you about."

"Hah! And risk Mom's wrath? There's ice cream melting in the back." She pressed more firmly on the gas pedal.

Resignedly, Evan took in the view: green fields marked off by neat split-rail fences; a herd of cattle grazing in the distance; three horses in a paddock. The line of trees over by the creek was taller than he remembered, but that was about all that had changed. He'd never paid much attention to the Bly cattle ranch, but he'd been there so often he must have absorbed images by osmosis. "Cottonwoods," he murmured.

"I can't believe you remember that."

"I didn't. Not consciously. I heard your voice in my head. We were playing down by the creek, and there was fluffy white stuff all over the ground. It smelled odd. I asked what it was and you said it came from the cottonwoods."

She didn't say anything, but her lips curved in a smile.

When Jess shut off the engine, a dog rushed up. It was medium sized, mostly black but with some white in its coat, and it had pointed ears and a long, rather bushy tail.

"This is Pepper," Jess said, squatting down to stroke the wriggling body. "He's our cattle dog, an Australian Blue Heeler."

"He's just a young one."

She peered up at him. "How did you know that? You were never an animal person."

"I remember you telling me if a dog's feet are too big for him, he isn't full grown. It stuck with me." He grinned. "Besides, look at him. He's got absolutely no dignity. Everything about him screams puppy." He bent down and got in a few strokes, finding the dog's warm hide pleasant to the touch. He was less pleased with the sloppy licks that landed on his hand.

He stood up and wiped his hand gingerly on his pant legs. "What happened to Dandy-girl?" The Bly's Border Collie had always tried to sleep on Jess's bed at night, and often succeeded.

"She died last year. Old age. It was hard for all of us.

Especially Rob." With Pepper at her heels and Evan trailing, she headed for the back door.

The moment they went from the mudroom into the kitchen, Mrs. Bly dropped her paring knife. "Evan!" She hurried forward and wrapped him in a warm embrace, and he hugged her back, memory and affection bringing a swell of moisture to his eyes.

Fortunately, she stepped back before he embarrassed himself. "Let me look at you," she said. "Little Evan Kincaid, all grown up. I can't believe how you've filled out. Hasn't he, Jessica?"

"He has," Jess said dryly from behind him.

Jess's mother hadn't changed much herself, still trim in a loose shirt and jeans, only now there were gray threads in her wavy hair blending in with the sandy ones. "Mrs. Bly, it's so kind of you to invite me."

"Nonsense, dear. The moment Jessica said you were here, I insisted she bring you around. Why, the thought that you'd visit Caribou Crossing and not come see us! I'm dying to hear everything that's happened since you left town. And by the way, call me Miriam, okay?"

"I need a shower," Jess said. "You two can catch up."

"Not without your father. He'd never forgive me. Jessica, you go wash up. Evan, Wade's out in the barn, in the office. Would you bring him in? I just have to finish the salad, and then we'll be ready to eat. Ice cream, Jessica?"

"Oh, shoot, it's in the truck. I'll get it."

She'd forgotten the ice cream? He realized he'd forgotten the wine. A fine pair they made. "I'll do it," Evan said.

But a few more minutes wouldn't hurt. Anxious to see Jess's dad, Evan walked the familiar pebbled path through the Bly vegetable and flower garden, down to the barn, where one end had been converted into an office.

He found Wade Bly hunched over a pile of papers, tugging thoughtfully at his short silver-streaked beard. Jess's father didn't hear him, and Evan paused in the doorway, watching the older man. Where Mrs. Bly—with her sandy hair, freckles, and abundant energy—seemed hardly to have aged, her husband looked like a different man. Or, perhaps, the father of the vigorous man Evan had once known.

But, when he glanced up and saw Evan, Wade's smile banished the years. "Son, it's good to see you." He strode toward Evan, hand outstretched. His walk was a little lopsided now, but his handshake was firm.

"You, too, sir."

The older man laughed and his eyes—Jess's expressive chocolate ones—twinkled. "Sir? I may look older than the hills but I don't need to be reminded of it. Call me Wade, now that you're a grown man."

"Mrs., uh, Miriam said supper's almost ready. She wants you to come up to the house."

"This morning Miriam had all her cookbooks out. She was worried she couldn't compete with those fancy New York eateries. I told her you'd probably appreciate some good old-fashioned home cooking. Figured you wouldn't have changed all that much?" He kinked an eyebrow.

"That wasn't her world-famous meatloaf I smelled?"

"And mashed potatoes and gravy, biscuits, glazed carrots."

His stomach gave an approving growl. "My favorites."

"I guess. Though it seemed to me you were happy to eat pretty much anything she put in front of you." The older man's expression turned serious, saying something without exactly putting it into words.

Evan nodded. "That's the truth. And I'm very grateful." For more than just the food, he meant, and he knew Wade Bly understood.

Wade nodded. "We were happy to help. You were our Jessie's friend and a fine boy in your own right. You were, and always will be, welcome in our home."

The two men glanced at each other and then away. Evan

had to clear the lump in his throat before he could say, "That means a lot."

"Well, let's not keep Miriam waiting."

As they started up the path, Evan again noticed the other man's slight limp. "How have you been, sir?"

At the older man's exaggerated scowl, he amended, "Sorry, I mean Wade."

"I'm doing all right, but I put a scare into the womenfolk. Had a stroke a few years ago and it took me some time to come back from it. Jessie's a saint. Might've lost the ranch, but for her. She still takes on more than her fair share. Those dang women are always at me to slow down."

Evan had thought Jess impractical and unambitious for not having achieved more in the last ten years, when in fact she'd been helping her parents keep their ranch. "I was surprised to see Jess at the Crazy Horse. Never figured she'd end up babysitting a herd of dudes."

"It's a good job. She still has dreams, though." He gave a fond smile. "You know our Jessie."

"Wouldn't she make a good partner in this ranch? She could gradually take it over, and then it'd be hers when you retired." That might be a more reasonable, achievable dream than her no-frills camp.

"You'd think, wouldn't you? But she turned me down. The girl's got no love of ranching. A person should do what they love. If they can." He paused to pick a couple of dead blossoms off a trellised rose. "But I don't need to tell you that. You were the most single-minded boy."

Pepper bounded out to greet them. Wade bent slowly to pat his head and Evan squatted to stroke him.

"Didn't think you were too fond of animals," Wade commented.

"They made me uncomfortable. I didn't know how to act around them." He gave the dog a final pat on its rump.

"Don't have to act any particular way. Especially with

dogs. Just be friendly and they'll be thrilled to bits." He put a casual arm around Evan's shoulders. "Glad to see you've loosened up some."

As they neared the back door, Evan snapped his fingers. "You go ahead. I have to get something from the truck."

He welcomed the opportunity to be alone, to cope with the unaccustomed emotions that threatened to swamp him. After years of absence and silence, he couldn't believe how unquestioningly the Blys had welcomed him. He didn't deserve their generosity.

Especially given the reason he was here in Caribou Crossing.

Chapter Nine

As he reached into Jess's truck for the tub of ice cream and the bottle of wine, Evan thought about dinners at people's houses back home in Manhattan. Bright but superficial greetings; meals that were often more trendy than tasty, catered rather than cooked, and often calorie-wise.

They didn't compare so well to Miriam Bly's warm hug and her husband's firm handshake. Or, he thought as he hurried back to the house, to the savory smell of meatloaf.

He put the ice cream in the freezer and handed Wade the brown paper bag. Miriam came to look. "Wine. What a treat."

He had, in consultation with Will at the Crazy Horse—not saying that he was going to Bly Ranch, just that he wouldn't be eating with the guests and needed a special bottle of wine—chosen a Syrah from a BC winery called Red Rooster. He should have known that whatever choice he'd made it would have been welcomed with equal delight.

Evan was washing his hands at the kitchen sink when Jess joined them, her hair damp on the shoulders of a sleeveless blue shirt she wore with beige cotton capris. As she passed, he smelled something citrusy, the kind of fresh, natural scent that came from shampoo or body lotion, not perfume.

Cynthia was always first to try Calvin Klein's latest offering. He'd never had the heart to tell her he found the perfume cloying. Sometimes after he'd been with her, he wished he could scrub the inside of his nose to get rid of the lingering smell.

With Jess, he wanted to lift her hair, bury his nose in the nape of her neck, and breathe her in. Then kiss the soft skin and—damn, even with her parents there, he was getting aroused.

Leaving Wade to work the corkscrew, Evan glanced around the kitchen. It looked the way he remembered it, with pale yellow walls and brown tiles on the floor. The kitchen table was the same old one where he and Jess used to do homework, but the appliances were new. So was the artwork. He went over to the fridge to inspect an unframed watercolor of horses in a pasture, which was clipped to the door. It was childish, yet the artist had done a great job of capturing a sense of spirit and motion. "Your daughter?" he asked Jess.

"What?" Wineglasses clinked together as she hurriedly turned from the cupboard where she'd been lifting them down.

"The artist's your daughter?" he clarified.

She saw where he was looking. "Oh. Yes, that's Rob's."

"Your school notebooks were filled with horse sketches."

"So are Robin's," Miriam said. "She's a lot like her mom. Except Robin somehow also manages to do her homework and get good marks."

"Our Jessie did keep getting distracted," her father said, laughing.

Miriam turned to Evan. "Remember how we always had you over for supper before a test? To make sure she studied?"

"That's certainly one thing Robin got from her father," Wade said. "She's exceptionally well organized."

Glasses clattered together again, and they all turned to look at Jess. "Sorry," she muttered. "I'm clumsy tonight."

"Where is Robin anyhow?" Evan asked.

"She's at her dad's tonight," Jess said.

He'd been curious to meet the girl, and now it looked like he never would. Unless he decided to stay a few days longer. And he might have to, to carry out his mission for Gianni. "That's too bad," he said. "I wanted to meet her."

"Jessica figured we'd be talking grown-up talk, so she sent Robin away to Dave," Miriam said. "Though I must say the child is almost as mature in her conversation as you were at that age, Evan."

"It came out of books."

"With Rob, it's her dad's influence," Jess said quickly. "Dave talks business with her just like she was an adult."

"Supper's ready, everyone," Miriam said. "Evan, you sit down and take first dibs."

"My mouth is watering." By habit, he took the chair he'd always sat in, and the others did the same, which put Jess across from him.

"You're so polite," Miriam said. "This food isn't what you're used to."

"Thank heavens for that." He cut a healthy serving of meatloaf. "I've eaten in places where half a quail is considered a sizable entrée." Soon he had them laughing as he described, in outrageous terms, various Manhattan meals. The funny thing was, he exaggerated only a trifle. Much as he loved New York, the restaurants Cynthia chose did better at feeding a svelte woman like her than a big guy like him.

He reached for the gravy, but Jess had gotten there first. "Nice to see a woman with a healthy appetite," he commented as she slopped gravy over a pile of mashed potatoes.

"I wear off every calorie. If a gal actually *works* for a living, she can afford to enjoy her food." She shoved the gravy over. "I gather Cynthia is fashionably skinny?" Before he could answer, she said to her parents, "Ev's lady friend is a lawyer."

"Oh?" Miriam said. "A friend of mine and her husband

have a general practice law firm in Caribou Crossing. What kind of law does Cynthia practice?"

"Corporate finance," Evan said.

"My dad handled commercial lending for his bank," Miriam said. "But I admit, Bly Ranch books are as complicated as I've ever managed when it comes to finance. I'm not quite sure what corporate finance law is."

"Well, it's . . . Oh, never mind, it's not very exciting." He felt disloyal, because Cynthia's job was indeed exciting, at least to both of them, but here with the Blys it would make for dull dinner conversation. So would his own job.

When Wade said, "And you're a successful investment counselor," Evan shrugged. "I match up people's short- and long-term goals with a portfolio that best meets them."

"Sounds challenging. And worthwhile."

Worthwhile. He'd never thought of his career in terms of worth—not the kind of worth Wade meant—only achievement.

He glanced to his left, then his right, noting the slight tremor in Wade's hand and the lines beside Miriam's mouth. Simple folks, trying to hang on to their ranch, provide for their retirement, put something by for their daughter and granddaughter. Simple folks with simple goals. Unlike many of his wealthy clients whose goals were avoiding tax, buying bigger and better businesses, and justifying the cost of owning private jets.

It startled him to realize it could be satisfying to help people like the Blys.

"I'm sure you're wonderful at your work," Miriam said.

"I've done well," he said quietly. "I have my own company."

"An impressive achievement, son," Wade said.

"But we always knew you'd be a success," Miriam chimed in.

Across the table, Jess tipped an imaginary hat to him, and the gesture seemed sincere, not mocking. Evan felt a glow of warmth, reveling in these people's regard for him. They were hardly a demanding audience, but their opinions mattered.

He actually felt as if he'd come home.

It was another startling thought. One that brought another of those disconcerting rushes of moisture to his eyes. He concentrated for a few minutes on eating the delicious dinner and regaining his composure.

Damn it, he didn't want to mislead these people. He didn't want to disclose his relationship with Gianni here and now; that was something to be discussed privately with Jess. But he could be frank about his career, and the light he'd just seen it in, thanks to this conversation. "In all honesty, I spend most of my time making rich people richer."

Jess and her parents exchanged glances, obviously hunting for polite words.

"I know it's a tough job, but someone has to do it," he said dryly.

That earned him a few uncertain chuckles.

He found himself wanting to tell them about his pet projects, not so much to prove he had a decent side, but because he figured they'd understand. "My clients aren't all spoiled rich folks, though. One of them's a basketball star. LeVaughn Duvalle? Don't know if you've heard of him?"

"Sure have," Wade said promptly. "That man has real talent. He's a good team player, too."

"Yes, he is. Well, we were talking over lunch about how poor his mom, who raised him after his dad was killed in a gang fight, had been. He said he felt almost guilty for making so much money. I had the idea he might want to help other kids who were born with the deck stacked against them, and he was very keen. We set up a scholarship fund for underprivileged kids, the Gimme a Break Foundation."

He was talking too fast but couldn't stop. "Another client, who was shattered when her husband was diagnosed with Alzheimer's, set up a foundation to fund a facility for patients who can't afford proper care."

Jess beamed at him as her father said, "Very commendable."

"And rewarding," Miriam added. "How good you must feel to be a part of those projects. To make a real difference."

Yes, that was one of the best parts of his job. He smiled at the others around the table. "Your turn. Catch me up on what you've been doing."

After they had discussed the ranch, the garden, and the growth of the town—with the subject of his mother never being raised—Wade said, "And of course Jessie has a grand plan for a business she'd like to start up."

Jess's father had given Evan the perfect lead-in. He hated to pump Jess before revealing his mission, but it would seem unnatural not to ask about this grand plan. "I remember that story." He took a sip of wine as he inwardly cursed Gianni, and the lack of an opportunity over the past couple of days to tell Jess the truth. "What's the current plan, Jess?" he asked.

"A riding camp." She shot him a wary glance.

"Camp? You mean, a place where you'd give riding lessons?"

"Well, yeah, but more than that."

Her mother raised her eyebrows. "Jessica?" She turned to Evan. "Normally she'll go on and on about it."

"I'd like to hear," he said. Remembering Cynthia's suggestion that he intimidated Jess, he added, "Though I bet the Crazy Horse would really miss you. I'm very impressed by what you do there. The riding program and the horses are excellent, and you're great with the guests." It was the truth, and he hoped it would bolster her confidence and her willingness to share her ideas.

Her smile was warm. "Thanks. I count it one of my biggest triumphs that you're turning into an accomplished rider."

She took a deep breath. "Okay, here's my plan. Ev, one day you asked if the guests at the Crazy Horse drive me nuts. Well, no, they're great, but I'd rather work with true horse lovers. I want to set up a camp where people can come for two weeks or more and focus totally on horses and riding." She leaned forward, elbows on the table, eyes sparkling. Here, in the relaxed atmosphere of her own kitchen, she was finally opening up.

"It'd be no-frills," she went on. "The guests wouldn't be playing cowboy on cattle drives, and there'd be no fancy spa. I'd have the basics to stay fit, like massage and a whirlpool, but nothing fancy. Natural, rustic, no luxuries. And the guests would work hard. They'd be on horses most of the day, taking lessons and going on rides. It'd be a boot camp for Western riders, and it'd include looking after your own horse and tack, and learning about communication with horses."

Her enthusiasm was contagious. As a boy, he'd listened to her dreams and supported her, but not really understood. Now, after a few days' exposure to her horsy world, he had a better grasp of what she was talking about. "Sounds intriguing." Reflecting, he said, "Is there a market for it? I mean, seems to me a lot of people who are serious about horses are already riding, and the others are more casual about it, like the group at the Crazy Horse."

She glanced away from him. "I think there's a market." The spark had left her voice.

She *thought?* Seemed as if this was what he'd feared: dreams, with no substance. "You could do an Internet search. See what's out there now, in other parts of the world. What audience they're targeting, what programs they offer." *Come on, Jess*, he pleaded silently, *get your act together*.

"In my spare time?" she muttered.

Wade glanced at her, then back at Evan. "Actually, Robin has some ideas. The school term's almost over and she says she's going to do some comparative market research this summer."

"Smart kid," Evan said with respect.

"Her dad's been teaching her about how he runs the Wild

Rose," Wade said, "and she's really cottoned on to business principles."

More than her mom, obviously.

"I don't want it to be a place that's just for the rich," Jess said. "I want to make the opportunity to ride available to people who make less in two or three months than what the Crazy Horse charges for a week. I think being out in nature, bonding with an animal, learning to be competent at riding, getting fit—all those things—can make a real difference in people's lives."

"I think you're right." And that was what Gianni had meant about ambiance. If Evan hadn't been here these past few days, he'd never have understood that. "Are you talking about kids or adults?"

"Adults and families, to start. It'd be less complicated, but once it's established I'd like to expand to include a kids' summer camp program. The place would be based on the philosophy that those who can afford to pay more will do it willingly so their fees can subsidize the less fortunate."

"It's an interesting idea." Could it work? If there was really a market for it, and if she got start-up funding, and . . . There were a lot of ifs. "So, what's your plan?" he asked her. "Where would you locate it?"

"Here. Mom and Pa have put me on the title for the ranch, and I'll use a corner of it, just up the road, for the cabins and other facilities. We'll share paddocks and the large-scale equipment."

And she'd no doubt keep trying to run the ranch while she ran her own operation. Unless she could persuade her father to hire an assistant. "That'll cut down a lot on your start-up costs."

She nodded. "And I'd start small. A small lodge with a kitchen, dining room, and office. A bunkhouse for singles and a handful of cottages for couples and families. All designed to allow for expansion over the years in a way that'll be practical and attractive. A barn, of course. Horses that I can pick up cheap and train. Evan, I told you about Ty Ronan, down in the Frasher Valley, who's working with rescue horses, healing them physically and emotionally. We've talked about me taking some of his horses. I'd get them super cheap, and train them."

"That all sounds good," Evan admitted. "It'll be a lot of work, though, even to get going on a small scale, and it'll be a hefty investment."

"I'm looking for investors. If they're horse people, they get a month's free stay each year plus, hopefully, a return on their investment when the camp is established."

"Uh, maybe not so much return," he said, "if you're subsidizing some of your guests."

Her eyes narrowed in challenge. "You're saying no one would invest?"

Not if their goal was the best possible financial return. He didn't want to come right out and say that, so he hedged with, "Have you had any luck finding investors?"

"I've had a few people interested, but so far no one has come through. Sometimes I get talking to one of the Crazy Horse guests about it." She added quickly, "Not trying to poach clients from Kathy and Will, but we figure if I get my place going, our two operations will be complementary, and we'll do mutual referrals. Anyhow, there've been a few guests who were really excited. But there's a *but*."

"What's that?"

"Folks come to the resort and get bitten by the magic, then they go home, it all seems so far away, and they're back into their busy lives. They lose interest. I never hear from them again."

"Do you follow up? Send them a business plan? Keep them enthused?"

She shook her head. "I don't want to push. If they're not really keen, it wouldn't work."

He figured it was her job to make them really keen. If she truly believed in her camp, why wouldn't she sell it to the best of her ability? But maybe she didn't really believe; maybe it was just another dream. "Do you have a name for this camp? A really catchy, marketable one?"

"We've tossed a few around. 'Boot It' is the current favorite."

"Hmm. Not bad," he said. "It's cute, but it doesn't convey much information. That works for a name that's already well established, but not so well for a start-up business. You know about branding, right?" he said.

Wade and Miriam, who'd both been listening quietly, chuckled. Wade said, "You forgotten you're on a cattle ranch, son?"

Evan laughed, too. "Not that kind. Well, yeah, kind of. Each cattle brand is unique, right? And the purpose is to identify the animals. Every business needs the same kind of thing. So do charities, like Gimme a Break. Something distinctive, memorable, that conveys the message."

Jess was nodding, but why on earth didn't she already have a name for her business?

As he sat at her family's kitchen table, enjoying their hospitality, his heart sank. Her dream wasn't necessarily hopeless, but she hadn't done the tough work needed to make a go of it. He couldn't recommend it to Gianni. Not as a solid business investment that would in any way rival the ones in his client's current portfolio. Troubled, he raised his glass. "Here's to you. I hope it works out."

Her parents said, "Hear, hear," and drank the toast.

Then Wade said, "Maybe we go back to 'Riders Boot Camp.' Robin had that idea for the cowboy boot logo."

"It's informative," Evan mused. "Jess, you said the camp would be no-frills? Well, that's a no-frills name. It could fit, especially with a boot logo. Good play on words: boot camp and cowboy boots."

She nodded. "It could work."

"Great," Miriam said with a smile. "It's decided. Now

here, Evan, you haven't had one of my biscuits." She passed the basket.

He took one, added a generous swipe of butter, then bit into a puffy, golden-topped piece of heaven. "Miriam, you could make your fortune selling these in Manhattan. We have bagels and croissants, but nothing like this."

"Oh, get on with you, Evan. They're just plain-old baking powder biscuits."

"They don't taste plain to me," he said.

Now that the spotlight was off her, Jess could relax. She watched and listened as Evan ate with obvious pleasure and chatted with her parents. He fit in so well. Better than he had as a boy. Then he'd been skittish, sometimes timid and insecure and sometimes verging on arrogant as he spoke of getting out of this hick town and making a name for himself.

Now he'd achieved his goal and both the arrogance and the insecurity had disappeared.

She wondered, looking back, why she'd been so crazy about him. Maybe because he'd been the underdog, the stray puppy. When he moved to town, she befriended him and he became hers, in rather the same way as Rascal, the first foal her father had helped her train. What kind of love was that?

But that wasn't all there'd been to it. It was the things like her tenth-grade speech and Mrs. Gutterson's window. At heart, Evan had been a nice boy, and he'd been there for her as much as she'd been there for him. They might have been as different as night and day, but it took both night and day to make up a proper twenty-four hours.

Now, when she looked at the adult Evan—did he always have to look so good, whether it was in worn designer jeans or a crisp white shirt with rolled sleeves?—or when their bodies touched, her feelings came alive in a way she hadn't experienced in ten years. Was it just the old emotions, an echo of past longing? Somehow Jess didn't think so. Sure, her old affection for Evan was mixed in, but now she was looking at a grown man she barely knew. It was this man she was attracted to, this man she wanted to get to know. This man she wanted to touch. She remembered the press of his aroused body against hers. A shiver wrenched through her.

"Jess?" His eyes, a startling blue-green against his tanned skin, looked concerned. "You all right? You've gone quiet on us."

"I'm fine."

"You've stopped shoveling food down your throat at the speed of light."

"Just tired." She jumped to her feet. "Is everyone finished? I'll clear the table; then we can have some of Mom's fabulous apple pie, à la mode."

Without waiting for answers, she began to gather dishes. Oh God, surely she wasn't falling in love with him again. She couldn't let that happen. There was too much at stake, too much she was hiding. But how could she prevent it?

For the rest of the meal, she avoided meeting Evan's eyes, which was difficult when he sat directly across from her. She ate pie and drank coffee and wished he hadn't come. Almost as much as she wished he would stay forever. But when her mother said, "Now tell us, is New York everything you dreamed of?" his enthusiastic and long-winded response told her exactly how likely that was.

Feeling depressed, she said, "It's getting late. Evan, I'll drive you back."

He turned to her mother. "Miriam, let me help with the dishes. If you'll remember, I wield a wicked dish towel."

"I wouldn't think of it. But Evan, do come back again if you have the time. Our door is always open to you."

Her father seconded the invitation.

Jess stood in the doorway, watching them. If only, if only, if only . . .

Her father shook Evan's hand warmly and her mother gave him a big hug.

"Come on," Jess said abruptly. "Let's hit the road."

As Jess started up the truck, her motions were jerky. Evan felt a buzz of tension in the air and couldn't figure out whether it was positive or negative. He had to talk to her about Gianni, but first they both needed to relax. He looked for a neutral topic of conversation. "I'm sorry I didn't meet Robin."

The truck lurched as Jess's foot slipped on the gas pedal.

"She sounds like quite a girl," he added.

She was concentrating on the road, her hands gripping the wheel tightly. "She's wonderful. Dave and I are lucky."

Lucky. He'd bet they hadn't felt that way when they were teenagers and found out Jess was pregnant. He thought about his own sheer terror when he'd realized the condom had split that night he and Jess made love, and the incredible relief when Jess had written that she was okay.

"This isn't any of my business. . . ." he started.

"But that's not going to stop you, is it?"

"It must have been a shock, finding out you were pregnant."

"You can say that again."

"Did you consider abortion?"

"No!" Her eyes flashed his way, and then she turned her head back to the road. "I wanted that baby."

"And Dave did, too? Or was he just doing the right thing?"

Her lips curved up. "He was wonderful. He said he wanted to marry me and be the baby's father."

"Not to split hairs, but he was already the father. Whether he married you or not. Paternity isn't something you can just . . . undo."

"I suppose that's true." Her voice had an edge. It lost it

when she went on. "But don't you see, he was there for me. He was the best friend I could have wished for."

It struck Evan as a pretty odd way to describe the man she loved, the man who had fathered her baby and married her. Yet when he saw her profile in the dim light, the glow on her face told the story.

"You and Dave still love each other." Why did the idea make him unhappy? Stupid to be jealous when he and Jess would never be more than friends.

"Yup, we do. Jeez, Ev, he was my husband. He was there when Rob was born, holding my hand and coaching me all the way. It was the greatest night of my life, and I shared it with him. We both cried when we saw her. He's always been there for me. He's the dearest man in the world. Well, him and Pa."

Once, he'd been on that list. But he sacrificed his place when he bolted in fear ten years ago. "I can't believe you weren't shattered when he dumped you for Anita." His words were crude, but he was feeling pretty damned crude.

She ignored his rudeness and said calmly, "I already told you about that."

"Yeah, yeah. A once-in-a-lifetime kind of love. Generous of you. But he had a daughter."

"Robin knows how much we both love her. Dave and I share custody. It's completely amicable."

"You're too darn civilized. It doesn't seem natural."

She laughed. "To me it's perfectly natural that two people who loved each other would keep some part of that love even if they split up. It always seems weird to me that people can go from love to hate in an instant when they divorce. They couldn't have really loved each other in the first place."

He shook his head. "You have a unique way of looking at things." He gazed out the window at the country night, marveling at the absence of streetlights and traffic.

"It was incredibly hard on Dave when Anita died," she said.

Reflecting on that, he said, "Yeah, it must be horrible to watch someone die when you love them that much."

"Yes, but . . . it seems to me you count your blessings for having known them, and you store up all the memories to treasure forever. But I guess that's another of my odd little theories. It didn't work that way for Dave. It's like something inside him—his spirit—died along with her."

He had to ask, "Would you consider getting back with him if he could get over the damage?"

She took a moment before she answered. "No. We make good friends, but that's it."

"You're friends with him and you want to be friends with me. Jess, don't you ever want something more?"

Again, she was quiet for a bit. "Sometimes. But I don't want to be in a relationship again unless it's the kind Dave had with Anita. And that kind hasn't come my way." She paused, glanced in his direction. "Ev, is that what you have with Cynthia?"

He didn't have to think before he answered. "It's not what I want, Jess. I'm not the same kind of person as you. You're ruled by your heart and I'm ruled by my head. So is Cynthia. That's how we like it."

"Mmm. I guessed you'd say that. But I wonder if you're selling yourself short, and her as well. You do have a heart, Ev. I don't think it's that you can't feel things deeply, it's that you won't let yourself."

"Not everyone wants to live on an emotional roller coaster," he said curtly. She should consider herself damned lucky she'd always been surrounded by loving people, and never had her heart snapped around like a yo-yo, the way he had with Brooke. Christ, even the ex who'd dumped Jess still loved her in his fashion.

She glanced his way, then determinedly back at the road. "When you were a kid, the only way to survive was to avoid caring too much. If your father was mean to you or your mom ignored you, you told yourself you didn't care. Emotion meant hurt so you learned to turn it off."

Whatever. "It seems to me that was a pretty good lesson to learn."

"But, Ev, emotion can also mean joy, love, the greatest feelings in the world. You don't let yourself experience those things."

Let himself? She was making it sound like he had a choice, like people were throwing joy and love at him every day, and he was choosing to dodge. She had no idea what his life was like. "This is who I am," he snapped. "There's no reason to change. I'm happy."

"Are you?"

"Yes! I've got everything I ever wanted. Great career, great girlfriend, great life in Manhattan."

"Do you have seconds when you have supper with Cynthia? Do you laugh with your friends in Manhattan the way you laughed at my folks' house?"

No, he fucking didn't, damn it. He glared at her. "What are you saying? That I should stay here because I'll feel more . . . alive in Hicksville?" The moment he said the words, he knew that in some ways they were true. But only in some ways.

"No. Just that . . . maybe you're not hanging out with the right people or doing the right things in Manhattan. I know you love the place, but it seems to me you're shortchanging yourself. Emotionally."

"You're a fine one to speak. Your most meaningful relationship is a platonic friendship with your ex. And you tell me *I'm* playing it safe."

"I—"

Ten minutes ago, his goal had been to help both of them relax, and now the cab of the truck was filled with even more tension. He had to tell her about Gianni, but how could he raise the subject now? Jess didn't speak either as she drove toward the Crazy Horse.

Although they were on the highway, traffic was sporadic. It wasn't dark in the cab of the old truck; the dashboard instruments provided a dim light and the headlights of oncoming vehicles strobed them occasionally. Even so, he could see the stars.

In Manhattan it never got dark at night. The city lit up the sky. New York City was that dynamic. Here, the stars and moon provided the night light and the country faded away under that brilliant canopy. It was a different kind of vitality than in the Big Apple, but it had its own energy. Serene rather than frenetic.

Why hadn't he noticed the stars when he was a kid? Probably because he hadn't wanted to see anything good about Hicksville. But now, despite the heated exchange with Jess, he was admiring the stars.

He wondered if Brooke, too, had learned to appreciate the stars.

He turned to Jess. "If she finally got it together, why did she stay here?"

She glanced toward him. "Huh? Oh, your mother."

"Brooke hated the country. She and my father were from L.A. She said she was a city girl through and through. She was furious with him for making such a mess of their lives. You knew he joined the US Army, right, then deserted? And that's why they came to Canada. We lived in all these little towns, he kept getting bottom-end jobs and losing them, and then we hit Caribou Crossing, and for some reason we stayed. But Brooke hated it." If he'd had a dime for each time she'd complained about Caribou Crossing, he'd have had enough money to pay his way through university.

"So," he went on, "if she got her act together, why didn't she move? She could be a hairdresser in L.A."

"Beauty consultant."

He raised his eyebrows. Jess couldn't have seen him because she was focused on the road, but she responded anyhow.

"Have a little respect, Ev. She does her job well, and it's more than being a hairdresser. Lots of women—and men—feel better about themselves because of her. She may not be a high flyer like you, but she's doing something people value."

Jess sent him a challenging look and he knew she was thinking about the dinner conversation, when he'd said he mostly made rich folks richer. Yeah, where did he get off looking down on his mother's work, or on Jess's impractical dreams? He'd thought he had it made, but tonight he'd realized for the first time that his successful career wasn't all it was cracked up to be.

If he told Cynthia that, she wouldn't get it.

Jess's voice pulled him out of his thoughts. "I didn't know your mom had been so fond of big cities. Didn't know she'd hated the country. I never realized that's where you got it from."

"I . . ." He'd never thought of it that way. In his mind, he'd rejected everything about his mother. Tonight was sure as hell an evening for uncomfortable revelations.

She shrugged. "Anyhow, when Brooke cleaned up her life, I never heard her talk about moving to a city and looking for work. When I spoke to Auntie Kate—"

"*You* spoke to your aunt?" he interrupted.

"Well, yeah. I knew your mom was turning her life around. I figured someone ought to give her a chance. Auntie Kate has a big heart and—"

"And so do you, Jess Bly," he said with a shake of his head. He couldn't decide whether to be grateful or annoyed she'd helped his mother.

She ignored the comment. "Brooke seemed happy to take a job here. Maybe Caribou Crossing finally grew on her. Maybe there was nothing left—no one left—for her in L.A. Maybe she didn't want to tackle a strange city like Vancouver or Seattle. Or New York." She paused, then said deliberately, "You'd have to ask her."

When he didn't respond, she said, "Why do you send her money?"

"What? She told you that?"

"Yes. Checks every six months."

He shrugged. "She fed and clothed me, provided a roof over my head. I wanted to repay the debt."

"It's not debt between a child and his parent."

"She didn't want me. She was stuck with me and"—he shrugged—"maybe she did her best. Who knows?" It was another new idea. "God knows why she even kept me rather than let the government take me away. But she did keep me, and she spent money on me. I wanted to repay the money, plus interest. It was my way of finishing it."

"You must have paid the debt years ago, yet you never called it finished. You kept sending money. And you came back. There are guest ranches all over the country. You chose the Crazy Horse." Jess gestured and he saw they'd reached the resort sign. She turned down the gravel road.

He'd run out of time. He had to tell her now. If they discussed Gianni and her riding camp proposal now, he could still leave tomorrow with a relatively clear conscience. "Stop the truck for a moment, Jess."

"Why?" But she obeyed, pulling down the lane to the barn and stopping in the yard.

Evan took a deep breath, knowing everything was going to change. "It wasn't Brooke who brought me back. And it wasn't that idiotic ten-year plaque, though what I told you about it was true. It was Gianni Vitale."

"Gianni Vitale? You know Gianni? Oh, did he recommend you come . . ." Her voice trailed off and her eyes widened in shock. Yeah, she was getting the picture.

She groaned and grabbed her head with both hands. "He's a client of yours." She glared at him. "I'm an idiot! I should have known. Of course it would be work that brought you back here. Jesus, Evan, you've been spying on me!" Her voice screeched upward in anger.

"Yes. Yes to all of it."

She punched him in the shoulder, not at all gently.

He rubbed the sore spot, guessing he'd have a bruise. "I didn't know it was you when Gianni asked me to check out TJ Cousins's proposal. You know that, Jess; you saw how surprised I was on Monday."

She nodded grimly. "Right. And then you spent the next five days deceiving me."

"Yes. On Monday I phoned Gianni and told him you and I used to be friends. He wanted me to stay, and to keep you in the dark, and—"

"I hate the both of you!" she spat out.

"Jess, he's not one of the guests who forgot you as soon as he got home. He and Elena have been talking about your riding camp. But he's a businessman. He has to check things out. And I'm his investment counselor, so I'm the one to do it for him. I had to honor client confidentiality, but I hated lying to you—"

"Oh, that makes me feel *so* much better!"

"After a few days I decided I couldn't do it. I called him and told him so. For the last two days, I've been trying to tell you but whenever I said I wanted to talk to you, you were too busy. Remember?"

She gave a grudging nod. "But you didn't say it was important. I thought you just wanted to chat, and there'd be lots of time for that."

He had told her it was important. She just hadn't paid attention. "I'm going home tomorrow."

"What? But . . . Oh, of course." Her jaw tightened. "Tonight over supper, you decided the camp was just another of dumb old Jess's stupid ideas."

"I never planned on staying this long. I figured a couple of days, tops."

"Another of your little secrets."

"For the record, I don't think you're dumb. You're just not always the most businesslike person. And I don't think your idea's stupid. But you need to do more homework." He found himself adding, "Maybe I can help you with that."

"You?" Her voice rasped. "After what you've done to me, you think I even want to speak to you again?"

He couldn't help noticing the way her breasts heaved up and down as she sucked in quick, shallow breaths. "I just thought—" Actually, he hadn't thought before speaking.

"Get out of this truck, Evan Kincaid. And get out of my life. Go back to Manhattan and tell Gianni to take his millions and invest in some boring stock that'll make him a bundle more money. Because I know he and Elena will never get as much enjoyment out of that stupid money as they would out of participating in my project!"

She glared at him and he stared back at her. "You may well be right, Jess, but—"

"Get out!"

Her whole body vibrated with anger. Reluctantly, he reached for the door handle. "Are you sure?"

"Ooh!"

It seemed she was.

Chapter Ten

The guests had been told to rise at dawn and assemble in the lodge for a quick muffin and cup of coffee. After that, the plan was to ride for a couple of hours to a viewpoint where they'd be served a trail breakfast. They would eat and relax, then ride home again.

Evan's own plan had been to check out, get a cab to Williams Lake, and fly home. He'd told Cynthia he wouldn't be back in time for Saturday dinner, so they planned to get together for brunch on Sunday. He would spend the rest of Sunday in the office.

Instead, after a sleepless night, Evan decided he couldn't leave now, with matters as they currently stood between him and Jess. He felt terrible about their fight, and knew how hurt and angry she was. Maybe she'd be calmer today, and if he apologized again, surely they could work things out. Evan had lost her friendship once, because he'd given up too easily. He wasn't about to let it happen again.

He hurried to the lodge at the crack of dawn, wanting to make a call before the others began to assemble.

"Evan," Cynthia answered. "Are you at the airport, darling? Good God, it must be the middle of the night there."

"There's been a small setback. I'm going to have to stay another day."

"What's wrong? Is your old friend still holding out on you?" Did he detect an edge to her voice when she said "old friend"? Was Cynthia's patience wearing thin?

"Well . . . Actually, we have talked a bit about her plans. I had dinner at her place last night and—"

"Sounds cozy." Now the edge was sharp enough to cut glass.

"It's not what you're thinking. She lives with her parents. They're old friends, too."

"She's still with her parents? A grown woman? How quaint."

He frowned. "Her father had a stroke and she helps run the family ranch. And her parents help with her daughter, which is a far better arrangement than some anonymous after-school care facility."

Cynthia didn't reply for a moment, and Evan realized his comment could be taken as a criticism of her preferred method of child rearing. It was a discussion they needed to have, but in person. He stifled a groan. Now he had two women mad at him.

"Daughter?" Cynthia sounded more pleased, probably figuring he wouldn't be interested in a woman with a child. "You didn't mention she had a child. Where's the father?"

"They split up, though they're still friends."

"Hmm. So you had dinner with the family at the ranch. . . ."

"Yes, though Robin, the daughter, wasn't there. I'll meet her today." That was another benefit to staying—assuming by then he'd made up enough with Jess that she'd introduce him to the girl.

"Another meal with the family?" she asked grimly.

"No, it's one of the Crazy Horse activities. Jess and her daughter are putting on a cowgirl display. Roping and barrel racing. It should be fun. And this morning, since I'm staying, I'll go on the breakfast ride."

"Breakfast ride? And will that be fun, too?" Her voice had lost some of its grimness and she sounded genuinely curious.

"Yeah, actually I'm kind of glad I'm staying for it," he confessed. "The guests are interesting people, and the scenery is terrific. Jess assigned me this funny-looking strawberry roan called Rusty, and he's turned out to be great. I've even learned to saddle and bridle and groom him. Lord, Cynthia, you ought to see me wield a hoof pick."

"Hoof pick," she echoed disbelievingly.

"Yeah, it's a curved metal tool for cleaning the gunk out of a horse's hooves. To prevent infection." Suddenly self-conscious, he gave a strained laugh. "I'm boring you."

"Actually, it's very educational. But Evan, you still haven't said why you're staying another day. I gather it's not just so you can participate in this breakfast ride, and see the cowgirls barrel race."

"Oh, I omitted the important part. I told Jess that Gianni had sent me, and she told me to get lost."

There was a lengthy silence, then, "You broke your promise to Gianni. And, because Jess told you to get lost, you decided you have to stay."

He realized that their last couple of calls had been so rushed he hadn't filled her in on the latest development. "No, I cleared it with Gianni first. I told him that I was uncomfortable deceiving an old friend, and that I could make a better assessment if I was honest with Jess so she and I could discuss her plans openly."

"Discuss her plans openly? After she told you to get lost?"

That was an excellent point. "Guess I'll find out. In the old days, she didn't hold a grudge. She reacted quickly, emotionally, then she'd get over it."

"Hmm. So the bottom line is, you're planning to fly home tomorrow?"

"Yes, definitely." Or at least hopefully.

"I see."

"The flight won't arrive in time for dinner, though. Sorry."

"Take however long you need." Her voice held no inflection.

"I said I'll be back tomorrow."

"Call me when you get in." And she hung up. No goodbye. And he realized that, since she'd first greeted him, she hadn't called him "darling" again.

Things would be fine once he got home, he told himself. He'd make her understand. But his first task was to get through to Jess.

Outside the window, the sky was beginning to lighten, and he heard voices as other guests approached the lodge. They all collected blueberry muffins and cardboard cups of coffee, then, eating and drinking as they went, trooped down to the barn. The guests, so clean and pressed on Monday morning, so antsy and on their best behavior, were now disheveled and casual. His own clothes were clean, but he hadn't bothered to use the iron in his cabin. Others had stained jeans, sunburned noses, and hair combed any which way, often topped by a cowboy hat. Ponytails had become popular among those—including Aaron—with hair long enough to tie back.

As he approached the barnyard, he looked around for the only ponytail that interested him. When Jess emerged from the barn, his heart thumped with pleasure and anxiety. He hurried over and urged her back inside.

"You're here!" Her face, tired-looking around the eyes, showed amazement and . . . was that pleasure? Whatever the expression, it was quickly replaced by a scowl. "I thought you'd be on your way home."

"I couldn't go. Not until we cleared the air."

"I've been up half the night—" she began.

"Me, too," he broke in. "Jess, I'm really sorry. I never wanted to deceive you, and I feel rotten. We're friends. We shouldn't keep secrets."

Her face went still, almost guarded. "It hurt. I felt betrayed." She spoke slowly, as if she was choosing her words carefully. "But I know that people keep secrets sometimes, thinking there's a good reason."

Relieved that she could understand this, he pled his case. "Gianni put me in an untenable position. He's my client and he's paying for this trip. He didn't want me to tell you because—"

He broke off as Aaron and Sylvia came into the barn and said good morning. When they had gathered their tack and gone out, he began again. "This isn't a typical investment." For the first time, he truly understood what Gianni meant. "What you said last night is true. Gianni and Elena would likely make more money from some other investment. He's savvy enough to know that. But those investments are impersonal. This one would be personal, fun; they'd have a place to visit where they could see the horses. They'd feel a part of the whole thing."

He was speaking quickly, putting it all together. "That's why Gianni told me I had to come in person, soak up the ambiance. He wanted me to understand everything this investment represents to him, not just a bunch of figures on paper."

"That doesn't explain why you couldn't be up front with me," she said implacably.

"The boot camp would depend so much on you. How you are with people, with horses. Your vision and your personality are key to success. Gianni wanted me to see you being natural, not trying to impress me."

She gave a wry laugh. "Guess you got what you came for then. I sure didn't do much to impress you."

More people were coming into the barn, picking up saddles and bridles. He lowered his voice. "That's not true. I'm very impressed. By you." Impressed, attracted, and confused. "As for your camp, we need to talk some more about that, to see if it's really feasible." At the moment, he didn't think it was, but with some hard work she might develop a realistic business plan. If she wanted this badly enough, and didn't merely enjoy playing with a new dream, he could help her get organized.

"You're impressed by me?"

"Yes, Jess. And I want to be your friend." Though his feelings for her made him uncomfortable, he couldn't bear the thought of losing her a second time. "Can you forgive me? I never wanted to hurt you."

"I want to believe that."

He could see that in her expressive chocolate eyes. "Come on, Jess." Trading on old knowledge, he said, "You know you're rotten at holding a grudge."

She gave a small, rather sad, grin. "We know each other too well. Even after all these years."

"Some things don't change."

She ducked her head, then lifted it again, and he saw she was no longer smiling. "And some do. We're different people now. You've made your success, and I've yet to make mine. I don't think Gianni Vitale is the right route for me."

"He still might be if you put some more work into your proposal. Last night, I said I was willing to help you. I mean that."

She tilted her head higher. "Evan, I do have some pride. I don't want your help." She turned and walked across the barn toward the open door.

"Jess?"

She froze in the doorway, then after a moment looked over her shoulder at him.

"Can we still be friends?" He held her gaze, letting his eyes tell her how much that meant to him.

Her lips quivered, then she said quietly, "I guess time will tell," and headed out into the barnyard.

Evan sighed, but tried to be optimistic. Horses and open

country would sweeten her mood. She'd think through what he said and find it in her heart to forgive him.

He went through the now-familiar steps of getting Rusty ready, then swung into line behind Sandy. Early morning light stretched pale fingers through the treetops as they started out.

After half an hour, the horses emerged from the woods and clustered around Jess, who'd stopped Knight. She sat tall and straight in the saddle, her body flexing as Knight shifted restlessly from foot to foot. Behind her, green hills rolled into the distance, kissed by the morning sun. He froze the picture in his mind, to hold on to when he was back in the city.

She swept her arm toward the hills. "This is perfect for galloping, but I'll guess not all of you are comfortable with belting off into the wide open spaces."

"What if Mickey runs away?" Joan asked anxiously.

Damn, Evan thought. He wanted to gallop Rusty down the middle of those gentle hills and feel the wind rush past them.

"We're going to split into two groups," Jess said. "Madisun's will skirt the meadows and take a lovely trail through an aspen grove. You'll do some trotting and a couple of nice long canters, but in line along a trail just like we've been doing all week. If you're good, Madisun will let you dismount and pick berries. There's absolutely no flavor in the world like sun-warmed wild strawberries."

"That's for me," Joan said, and a few others agreed.

"And your group, Jess?" Aaron asked eagerly.

"We'll gallop across the meadows. You won't have to ride single file, but stay away from the area over there." She waved an arm to the left. "There are gopher holes."

She studied the guests from under the brim of her Resistol hat, her gaze pinning one, then the next. "No racing. No passing me. Hold on to the horn if you want, but always keep a firm grip on the reins. If your horse is going faster than you're comfortable with, pull back on the reins, shift your weight back in the saddle, and say 'whoa.' The horse will obey.

"If you feel at all scared of galloping, don't do it. This isn't a competition. It's about having fun and being safe. Not about getting the shazam scared out of you."

The guests chuckled, but Jess didn't. "Understand?" she asked, and waited until she'd gotten nods from everyone.

"Okay." Her smile flashed white against her tanned skin. "Madisun, gather your group. We'll wait until you head out."

Evan didn't feel scared. Excited, yes, and a touch nervous, but definitely not scared. He was going with Jess's group. So, he found out, were Thérèse, George, Sandy, and Aaron.

Jess studied Evan for a moment, then grinned. "Why am I not surprised, city boy?"

In that moment he sensed she was on the road to forgiving him. With a huge sense of relief, he grinned back.

She gave a few final words of instruction, then aimed Knight up the meadow and took off like an arrow out of a bow. The five who'd been left behind gaped at each other, then Evan touched his heels to Rusty's sides and soon they were flying in her wake.

By now he knew Rusty's gait. They were going faster than ever before, but he realized there was nothing to fear. He heard someone whoop and glanced to his right, where Aaron was belting along, ponytail flying just like Rambler's tail, smile wide enough to split his face. Evan laughed with sheer joy, and soon all five of Jess's charges were whooping and hollering.

She grinned over her shoulder. Her hat had come off and bounced on her shoulders, and tendrils of chestnut hair whipped free from her ponytail. Evan urged Rusty on, coming up beside Knight. "This is great!" he shouted into the wind. And the very best part was sharing this with her and seeing the pleasure on her pretty face.

"Told you so!" she yelled back. Then she glanced down at his hands and whooped. "Look, Ma, no hands!"

He hadn't even thought to grab the horn. Instead his

posture mirrored hers, one hand holding both reins, the other resting on a thigh. His body had learned to synchronize with Rusty's rhythm and he didn't need the horn for balance.

When Jess slowed Knight, the others pulled up abreast. Evan, still beside her, said quietly, "I should have tried this years ago. I missed so much."

"You might've done it if I hadn't made you believe you were a klutz."

"I didn't have to believe you. Let's let bygones be bygones." All of them.

She gave him a crooked smile, indicating she knew exactly what he meant. "Sure. Why not?" In a quick motion, she pulled off the Resistol that hung on her shoulders and handed it over. "Time you got yourself one of these, cowboy, but for now you can borrow mine."

Evan might never have been a hat guy, but he slid this one on his head with pride, like he'd earned a gold star from his favorite teacher. He was beaming as Jess motioned everyone back into single file, then led them into the woods. A few minutes later, the trees thinned, giving way to a cluster of sweet-scented wild rosebushes, and the riders emerged beside a small lake. It wasn't Zephyr Lake, but it looked similar enough that it gave him a twinge.

Jess turned in her saddle and waved an arm toward the lake. "See the beaver lodge?"

He gazed at the mess of branches, noting that the small trees in the surrounding area had been cut into stumps with roughly pointed ends, like crudely sharpened pencils. He found himself wondering where the beavers were. What was their lodge like underwater? Were there young ones? He'd never seen a beaver lodge before. Why had he been such a closed-minded kid?

"The tepee!" Thérèse cried, and Evan turned to see where she was pointing. Across the lake, near the shore of a tiny bay, was their sing-along tepee.

If Brooke hadn't prejudiced him against the country, might he have grown up singing goofy songs, riding a horse, maybe picking wild roses to give to Jess?

"Everyone ready for another gallop?" Jess called, and his negative thoughts whisked away on the breeze Rusty created as they took off. The five horses pelted in single file along a trail by the lake. When they slowed to a trot, then to a walk again, Evan leaned down to stroke Rusty's neck and murmur words of appreciation. What a fine way to spend a morning.

Jess stopped Knight at the end of the lake and slipped from his back. "Madisun's group isn't the only one that's got wild strawberries."

Evan slid down and peered at the ground, seeing scraggly tufts of grass, reddish tendrils that snaked out from patches of green leaves, and here and there tiny red berries. He knelt with the others and picked a couple of the red beads, trying not to care how grubby his hands were. When he crushed the berries between his teeth, flavor exploded in his mouth, sweet and intense. With the flavor came a memory.

Jess had fed him wild strawberries at Zephyr Lake.

He glanced over to where she was hunkered down, popping berries into her mouth.

And he realized something. He'd always avoided thinking of that night. Whenever his mind had ventured near, he'd been overcome with guilt. But in truth there had been positive aspects. Jess had been his loving friend and she'd shared herself with him on a level no one else had ever done, before or since.

Yes, Evan had felt he was betraying their friendship. Yes, he'd behaved in an utterly despicable fashion. But there had been good things. He should remember them, too, and let Jess know he appreciated the gift she'd given him.

She glanced up and caught him staring at her. "What?"

He realized he was smiling. "It'll keep."

She looked puzzled, but shrugged, and said, "Okay," and went back to the berries.

It didn't take the six of them long to demolish all the ripe berries in the small patch. They mounted again, and soon were urging the horses along a steep trail that zigzagged up a sizable hill. Jess reminded them to lean forward, taking their weight off the horses' hindquarters. Evan patted Rusty's neck as the horse doggedly plodded uphill, head down. "Thanks, pal. I'd never make it up here on my own."

When they arrived at the top, they found that Madisun's group had beaten them. Horses grazed contentedly while the guests clustered around a campfire tended by Will. The enticing aromas of bacon and coffee drifted through the fresh morning air.

"Loosen off the cinches," Jess instructed. "Untie the reins and drop them. The horses won't go anywhere."

Evan gave Rusty a farewell pat on the rump before heading over to a rocky outcropping to check out the view. He whistled as he saw the panorama spread beneath him. The wooded land, serene under morning sunshine, was dotted with gleaming lakes, ribbons of road, and the occasional building.

He remembered how, when he'd first arrived in New York City, he'd gone up the Empire State Building and been blown away by the view. This one was so different, but equally spectacular.

Jess and a couple of other guests came to stand beside him. After making enthusiastic comments, people wandered over to collect breakfast, leaving Evan alone with Jess.

She pulled the elastic from her messy ponytail, tossed her head so glossy chestnut waves gleamed in the light, and gave a joyous laugh. "Can you believe they pay me to do this?"

"Sounds like the job's not so bad."

"It's great. But . . ." She stared out at the view, no longer laughing.

"But?" he prompted, studying her familiar profile and thinking she was even lovelier than the view.

She chewed her lip. "I want to achieve my dream." She turned her gaze on him. "At least I think I do. But then I look at you. You've made your childhood dream come true, and yet, last night, I sensed maybe reality can't measure up to the dream?" She ended on a questioning note that made him reflect.

A couple of days ago his answer would have been easy. He'd had two dreams: his career and the perfect woman. He'd realized both, and they were great.

But yet, neither made him whoop or laugh with joy. At the Crazy Horse he'd learned he had the capacity to experience—and express—pure, uncomplicated joy.

Needing to be honest with Jess, he mused, "I wonder if dreams are moving targets. You think you know what your dream is, but when you get there you find you want something more, or different. Maybe that's how it has to be, if you're not going to stagnate."

She nodded, her brown eyes serious. "That makes sense. When you were talking about your investment work last night, you did sound a little, uh, cynical. But then you talked about that Alzheimer's facility, and the scholarships for low-income kids, and you came alive."

She'd seen that? He felt a warm glow at her perceptiveness, and at the realization that yes, there were things in his work that were worth whooping over, now that he'd learned how. He nodded. "I'd like to do more of that kind of work. And I'm thinking of shifting my client base—" He stopped abruptly. He'd barely considered the idea, and if he said it aloud then . . . Well then, he'd darn well have to make it happen.

He smiled at his onetime best friend. "Shifting my client base away from the rich folks. Oh, some of them—like Gianni and Elena—are wonderful and I'll happily help them make more money, and encourage them to spend some of it on worthwhile, and of course tax-deductible, causes. But I'd like to work with some . . . hmm, let's see . . ."

"Poor folks?" She tilted her head, curiosity lighting her eyes. "But they don't have the money to invest."

"Everyone has money to invest. It's a matter of priorities. Is your priority a day-to-day lifestyle, or is it something future oriented, like a meaningful—and maybe early—retirement? A good education for your kids?" He grinned at her. "Or starting up a business you've always dreamed of?"

She grinned back, her eyes warm with affection and approval. "Evan Kincaid, I think you've found a new dream and it's even better than the old one."

And this, too, was a moment worth whooping over. Though at the moment, he felt less like whooping and more like tugging her closer and kissing those smiling lips.

Gradually, the smile softened, her lips trembled, and she caught her breath. She'd read his mind. Did she want that kiss as badly as he did?

Suddenly, her head jerked and he became aware the others were calling them. "Time for breakfast," she said breathlessly.

She turned to walk away, but he stopped her with a hand on her shoulder. "There's something I need to say."

She turned back, expression uncertain. "Yes?"

"About that night at Zephyr Lake."

"Oh!" Her face went pink.

"Thank you."

"What?" Apparently it was the last thing she'd expected.

He squeezed her shoulder gently, feeling the warmth of her body through her red checked shirt. "For making love with me. Sharing yourself. It was special, and I was a fool not to appreciate that. I do now. I wanted you to know."

Feeling awkward, yet relieved to have gotten the words out, he dropped his hand and hurried over to the campfire.

It was a few minutes before Jess joined the group. She'd twisted her hair back into a neat tail, and was unusually quiet.

But she did shoot him one shy smile, which told him that for once he hadn't totally screwed things up.

Breakfast was fantastic. Kathy, Will, and Marty turned out piles of buckwheat pancakes, fluffy scrambled eggs, crisp bacon, and sizzling sausages and kept pots of coffee simmering on the fire. There was real maple syrup for the pancakes, rich cream and raw sugar crystals for the coffee, and pitchers of fresh-squeezed orange juice and pineapple juice. Fresh air and exercise had fueled everyone's appetite. The food disappeared in amazing quantities and the mood was as mellow as Evan had ever experienced.

Satiated and relaxed, he topped up his coffee mug, then wandered over to a rocky outcropping where he could sit and marvel at the landscape spread out beneath him.

After a few minutes he heard footsteps. "Mind if I join you?" Madisun asked.

He glanced up. "Please do."

She hitched herself up on a stump. "I love this view."

"I can see why." Curious, he asked, "Do you ever get tired of this?"

"Not tired, but . . . restless. I haven't been anywhere, haven't done anything. And I want to."

Jess, who had been checking the horses and filling her head with the tang of pine, stepped out from a cluster of trees to see Evan and Madisun. Their backs were to her and they didn't notice her arrival. She paused, enjoying the picture. Madisun perched on a stump, her knees up and her arms encircling them, long black hair cascading halfway down her back. Evan sprawled on a rock near her feet. He'd taken off the Resistol and the sun-bleached highlights in his hair glistened like the gold that had first attracted miners to this country.

Madisun said, "It must be wonderful to live in Manhattan."

"It's a terrific place. It's vibrant and it truly does never sleep. But Caribou Crossing's got a lot to recommend it, too." He waved an arm at the panorama below them.

"Yeah, but it's the only place I've ever lived. And it's so small town. Like, can you believe my parents actually christened me Mary-Anne? Mary-Anne Joe. I mean, what kind of small-town dorky name is that?"

"Madisun is far more sophisticated," he agreed.

Jess smothered a laugh, feeling only a little guilty about eavesdropping.

"I picked it because of Madison Avenue. But I spell it with a *u*, like the sun."

"Imaginative, and distinct."

"I'm going down to Vancouver to university next year," the girl said. "I'm saving up and if I'm really careful I'll have enough by then."

"What are you going to study?"

"Haven't made up my mind yet. I'll meet with a career counselor once I'm accepted."

"Hmm. From what I've seen, there are a few things about you that stand out. First, you love horses."

"And I'll miss them like crazy in the city, but I want more. More of a life than I've got now. More than my parents, that's for sure." There was bitterness in the girl's voice and Jess, who knew a little about the family, understood.

"Good for you," Evan said. "And you can make it happen. From what I've seen, you're organized and efficient, but you're also warm and personable. People do what you want and don't realize they're being handled. You picked that up from TJ?"

The girl nodded emphatically. "She's taught me so much."

"Do you have any kind of head for business?"

"Well, I try to handle the money in my house. My parents are . . . hopeless."

What she wasn't telling Evan, Jess knew, was that when

her father had a job, if Madisun didn't get her hands on his pay checks, he'd drink up every penny he earned. That left her mom, a high school dropout, with nothing to feed and clothe the nine kids. Nothing except the money Madisun brought in, which she was trying so hard to save for her education.

"What about business administration?" Evan suggested. "Develop those business skills to go with your people skills, and combine all that with your love of horses." He grinned up at Madisun. "Get a job managing a place like the Crazy Horse, and maybe own one yourself one day."

She gasped. "Holy sh—I mean, holy cow. I never even dreamed of it."

"Dream, Madisun. That's what I did when I was a teenager. I dreamed my dreams, made them very specific, then went out and made them happen."

"Wow." Jess couldn't see Madisun's eyes, but guessed there was hero worship in them. The girl said, "You've made your dreams come true. That must feel . . . like, wow!"

"Sure." He paused, and Jess guessed he was revisiting their earlier conversation. "But don't think it's just about dreaming. You have to put those dreams together with some concrete planning and hard work. Dreams on their own never make anything happen."

Jess winced. She'd come across like a nitwit last night when he asked about her no-frills boot camp. She actually did have some concrete ideas, but it was hard for her to verbalize that stuff when Ev was so damned brilliant. And he was right that she hadn't done as much research as she needed to, but research and finance had never been her strong points.

He'd offered to help. . . . But nope, that wouldn't work. She felt too stupid around him.

She straightened her shoulders. She was darn well going to get more businesslike about pursuing her objectives. Evan had given her some ideas and she'd bet Dave would help her follow through. He'd know how to prepare a business plan.

She'd find other potential investors and have something solid to offer them.

She backed into the trees, leaving Evan and Madisun alone. It was time to help Kathy, Will, and Marty clear up and load the SUV they'd driven up the gravel road. Then she'd round up the horses and guests and ride back, down the zigzag trail.

Her thoughts turned to the afternoon demonstration with Robin. She hadn't been able to come up with a good excuse, one that would satisfy Rob, in particular. She'd just have to keep Evan away from her—*their*—daughter. Thank heavens Rob was staying with Dave this weekend, and would be in a hurry to get back so they could head over to his folks' place for the barbecue.

After the long ride, a number of the guests went for massages, saunas, or other spa pampering. Evan showered, then sat on the deck of his cabin for an hour. He tilted his chair back, rested his bare feet on the wooden railing, and did not much of anything. The printout of the last e-mail from Angelica sat on the table inside, but he didn't bother to look at it. He'd deal with it tomorrow on the long flight home.

His bird—he'd verified with Will it was a woodpecker—joined him for a time, busily drilling holes and harvesting insects, and he didn't envy it its industriousness.

Then he pulled on his boots—which he hadn't bothered to clean after the morning ride—and ambled toward the barn for another session on horse communication. The concept was catching his interest. At breakfast, Thérèse had shared some things she'd read in Monty Roberts's book. As a result, several of the guests planned to watch one of the Monty Roberts videos in the lounge after dinner. Evan had thought of buying the book and boning up, but for once was less inclined to read than simply to experience.

When the guests were assembled in the barnyard, Jess led an unfamiliar bay horse from the barn. The horse danced about, hooves never still, eyes rolling.

"This is Nevada," she said, "and he's had a sad time of it. He's wary of people because they've taught him he can't trust them. He'll learn differently at the Crazy Horse, but it's a slow process to build trust after someone's shattered it."

And yet it seemed Jess had forgiven Evan for his own misdeeds. Yes, she had a generous soul.

She led the horse into a small fenced ring and turned him loose as the guests clustered along the fence.

"Don't stare a horse in the eye," Jess said. "It's not like with humans in Western society, where it's a sign of self-confidence and respect. With horses, it's a threat. Predator and prey. Likewise, don't approach a horse directly. To them, it's an act of aggression."

She demonstrated how Nevada shied away when she walked straight toward him, then she went back and approached again, slowly, on a zigzag path.

For the next half hour, Evan watched and listened, intrigued by the idea that each species had its own way of communicating. The concept was obvious, but he'd never spent time thinking about species other than humans. Of course, each human communicated uniquely, too.

Watching Jess with the horse was not only an education but a pleasure. She was in her element, so natural and beautiful that his heart filled with admiration and pride. Unfortunately, his body also pulsed with arousal. Why did that always happen when he was around her? Normally, he could compartmentalize. Sex had its place in his life, and it didn't intrude at inappropriate times and places.

It never had, not with Cynthia nor any of the other women

he'd dated. But with Jess, it was like being back in high school. He was constantly horny.

He was both sorry and relieved when she glanced at her watch and said, "Okay, that's enough for now. I have to change. Robin'll be here any moment." She took Nevada back into the barn.

The guests discussed Jess's lesson while they waited. Soon a horse appeared, trotting down the road. It was a bay, similar to Jess's but a little smaller. At first Evan couldn't make out the figure on its back, except for a cowboy hat. As horse and girl got closer, he saw a fancy embroidered cowgirl shirt above black jeans, but the brim of the hat hid her face.

The girl dismounted in front of them, dropped the reins, and patted her horse's neck, then came forward. "Hi. I'm Robin, and this is my mare, Concha."

No lack of confidence, Evan thought. Good for her.

Then she eased the hat off and let it dangle down her back.

His mouth dropped open. It was Jess. Jess at the age of nine. He stared in fascination. No, he could see subtle differences. Robin was taller, and her nose turned up like Miriam Bly's. But the slender build and athletic way of moving were her mother's, also the chestnut hair and sparkling brown eyes.

He was moving forward to introduce himself when Jess, dressed in a costume identical to Robin's, rushed to join the group. "Hi, Rob. Come talk to me a sec." She put her arm around her daughter's shoulders and steered her away. "I have a couple of ideas for this afternoon's exhibition."

As the full-size and miniature models crossed the barnyard, Evan's eyes followed them, seeing his old friend in a new light. Slender, fit Jess, who at times looked no older than the girl he remembered, really was a mom, with a pretty, confident daughter.

The two took their horses into the ring, which had been set

up with three big barrels in a triangle as well as a dummy of a calf, and the guests leaned against the fence to watch.

Robin was a skilled rider, looking like she'd been born in the saddle as she and her mom raced their horses around the barrels. The dummy calf was automated, moving around and kicking up its heels, and mother and daughter roped its head and its legs, as well as the fence posts around the ring.

As Jess and her daughter interacted, the love between them was obvious, in a way that was as natural as breathing.

He tried to imagine Cynthia with a daughter. Himself with a daughter. Could they be good parents? Jess and Dave had been kids themselves, fresh out of high school. You'd think age and life experience would count for something, but Evan couldn't bring a picture to mind of him and Cynthia with a baby, a toddler, or a child like Robin.

As soon as the exhibition was over, Robin called, "Bye, folks," and trotted Concha down the road. Again he'd missed the opportunity to meet Jess's daughter, and for some reason—especially after having actually seen Robin—he really regretted not being able to talk to her. There was something compelling about the girl that made him want to get to know her.

Because he was leaving tomorrow, Evan hung back while the rest of the guests headed up the hill and Madisun drove off. Jess turned Nevada out to pasture, did her apple-and-a-hug routine with the old palomino called Pet, and brought Conti in.

She was bridling her horse when he came up beside her. "Your daughter's a keeper."

Her eyes widened in surprise, then, for some reason, narrowed. "Dave and I think so."

"I wish she'd stayed. I'd like to have met her."

Jess's eyes narrowed a bit more. He had the sudden impression that she didn't really want him to meet her daughter.

Or maybe she was just skeptical of his sincerity. After all, he was the guy who'd said he didn't want kids.

"Rob has a busy day," she said. "She's staying with Dave this weekend, and they're going to his folks' for dinner." She finished buckling the bridle and hooked the knotted reins over a post. "I'll probably go, too. His family's great."

Earlier today, he'd felt close to Jess, sensed she'd forgiven him. Now she was being abrupt and distant. He sighed. "Jess, you and Dave manage to be friends. It can't always have been easy. I know I'm not perfect, I've acted like a jerk, but I really hope we can stay in touch and be friends, too. I really missed you, all these years."

Jess closed her eyes for a moment, and when she opened them her face softened. "Yeah. Me, too."

Oh, damn. He hated it when the two of them were at odds, but when they weren't, the feelings of attraction and arousal snuck up on him. The ones he wasn't supposed to experience.

She took a deep breath, then let it out. "And, Ev, thanks for saying what you did about that night at the lake. Thanks for understanding what I was doing. I didn't mean to be dishonest, to manipulate. I just wanted, like you said, to share my feelings with you."

"I wish I hadn't been so dense at the time."

"It's okay. Like you said, you're not perfect."

He smiled. "I deserve that."

They gazed at each other.

His blood thickened with the need to kiss her.

She glanced away and mumbled, "I'm not perfect either." Then she squared her shoulders and met his gaze again. "So, I guess this is good-bye."

Evan wasn't ready to say good-bye yet, but what other choice did he have? "I guess it is." He held out her Resistol. "I won't be needing this."

She waved it away. “Keep it. A souvenir. A reminder to stop and smell the roses.”

He slung it over his neck so it hung down, resting on his shoulders. “Thanks.” He’d miss those roses. And the wild strawberries, even the woodpecker. Rusty. Most of all, Jess. “We’ll stay in touch this time, right?”

“I hope so,” she said softly.

Maybe he couldn’t kiss her the way he wanted to, but friends could hug, couldn’t they? He reached out and pulled her into his arms. “Jess, this week has been—”

“Yeah, yeah,” she muttered, returning the hug fiercely, then pulling away. Turning away from him.

“You’re sure I can’t help you with the boot camp thing?”

She looped the reins over Conti’s neck. “Nope. But thanks.” With an agile spring she was in the saddle, and in the next instant the horse was flying down the road.

He watched until she was out of sight, feeling an immense sense of letdown. Something inside him, something he hadn’t even been aware of until recently, had gone hollow and achy.

Slowly, he began to walk up to the lodge. Jess didn’t seem all that distraught about him going. But what had he expected? A marshmallow-hearted girl blubbering in his arms? God, he never did know what to do when she cried.

Besides, what was the point of sentimental farewells? They’d reestablished a tenuous friendship and that was what counted. Still, a touch of emotion from her would’ve been nice.

He plucked a wild rose from a bush beside the road and held it to his nose. The scent was perfect. Sweet and somehow innocent, as enticing as a fresh, sunny morning. So much more appealing than hothouse flowers or artificial perfume. Would he ever smell a wild rose again? Ever see Jess’s lovely smile?

To distract himself, he planned out the rest of the day. He’d have dinner with the guests, then watch the Monty Roberts video. Get Will to check into flights, then give Cynthia a call, see if he could get back into her good graces. Tomorrow, he'd be back in Manhattan. Life would get back to normal. So why did he feel so depressed?

Chapter Eleven

Jess couldn't see for the blur of tears, but Conti knew his way home and by the time they arrived, the tears had dried. She told herself she was happy with the way things had turned out.

She and Evan had rediscovered their friendship and cleared the air on so many issues. Except for Robin, of course. Jess had spent a lot of time last night thinking about Robin. What right did she have to be mad at Evan for being secretive about his relationship with Gianni when she'd been keeping a far bigger secret for the last ten years?

She was still convinced Ev wouldn't want to know he had a child. It was in no one's interests to tell him. Her position was 100 percent justifiable.

And she was rationalizing far too much.

Evan said he still didn't want to have children, but she wasn't sure she believed him. He was like a damaged horse, letting fear rule him: the fear that he'd screw up as badly as his parents had, the fear that love might again slap him in the face. When it came to emotion, he chose the safe course and denied himself the most fulfilling one.

She wanted more for him.

Evan had learned some things this week, whether or not he

realized it yet. If he carried through with his plan to shift the focus of his business, he'd be happier in his career.

And what about Cynthia? Did Jess really want him finding a deeper, more emotional relationship with his girlfriend? Having kids with her?

A surge of jealousy made her grit her teeth. Absurd to be jealous, when she knew Evan wasn't the man for her. Or, to be more accurate, she wasn't the woman for him.

He was her friend, and she wished him happiness. If he could find it with Cynthia, then good for him. But he'd better not expect Jess to attend their wedding.

She strode toward the house, but stopped when her mother, weeding carrots, called, "Hi. How was the demonstration?"

"Good."

"I bet Evan was surprised to see how much Robin looks like you did at that age."

"He said she was a keeper." She didn't mention that she'd told Rob not to stay and chat with the guests as she usually did.

"Mom, you know I mentioned the barbecue at Dave's folks' place? I was thinking I'd go." Tonight, she needed to be close to her daughter. Besides, socializing with Dave's big family would keep her from wallowing in self-pity. "You and Pa could come, too."

"Thanks, but I'm hoping to get him to take me to a movie."

Jess showered, dressed in shorts and a cotton shirt, and headed off in the truck. Dave's parents had a sprawling, ranch-style house on about four acres of land north of town. When she pulled into the driveway, the presence of Dave's Jeep told her he and Robin had already arrived.

She hurried around to the back, where people clustered around the large patio. On the lawn, Robin was playing with a couple of cousins and a golden retriever pup.

"Hi, Jessie," Dave, who was talking to his sister, called. He came over and they exchanged a quick hug and kiss. “How are you?” he murmured. “Is Evan gone?”

“He’s leaving tomorrow. And I’m fine.”

“Honest?”

She nodded. “And I’ve got lots to tell you, when there’s a chance.”

He raised an eyebrow. “Anything serious?”

“Nothing bad. Nothing about Rob. Just . . . I want to tap into your business expertise.”

“Tap away,” he said, with a relieved smile, as his parents came over to greet her with hugs.

“You look tired, dear,” Sheila Cousins said.

“It’s been a long week.” She smiled, very glad that she’d come. “So I gave myself a treat and came over here.”

“We’ll look after you, honey,” Ken said. “Find yourself a chair. The barbecue’s warming up and Sheila’s got steak marinating.”

Since she and Dave had announced their engagement, his parents had treated her like one of their own children. The divorce hadn’t changed that.

“Son, get the girl a beer,” Dave’s father ordered.

“Yes, sir.” He saluted. “Coming right up.”

As Dave walked away, his parents exchanged troubled looks.

“He goes through the motions, doesn’t he?” Jess murmured. “But his heart’s not in it.”

They nodded. “It’s got to get better with time,” Sheila said, leaning into her husband. His arm came around her as she said, “It just has to. I can’t stand seeing him this way.”

Jess touched her shoulder. “I know it hurts, but it doesn’t do him any good if we get depressed, too.”

Sheila nodded. “You’re good for us, Jessica. You have such a positive outlook. You never let yourself wallow.”

Wallow? Jess suppressed a smile at just how close she’d

come to doing that very thing tonight. But instead, here she was, and feeling better already.

As Jess made her way across the lawn toward Robin, she reflected that she and Dave really did have different personalities. Even if her heart was breaking—and that's how she'd felt when she was seventeen and Evan left—she did get on with life and make her own happiness.

"Mom!" Robin rose from the grass.

Jess hugged her. "Hi, hon. Cute puppy. Whose is he?"

"Mary and Jason's. His name is Happy, because he always is." She glanced behind Jess. "Hi, Dad."

Jess turned and saw Dave approaching. He handed her a bottle of beer and said to Robin, "Oh, so now you're speaking to me. I figured you'd deserted me for good when you saw that dog."

"Dad, you know how at Mom's place we've got Pepper? Well, maybe at your place we should have a puppy, too."

"Uh-oh." Jess nudged Dave in the ribs.

"But Rob," he responded, "it wouldn't be fair on a dog to live at the Wild Rose."

"He could hang out with you in your office, and you could take him for walks. He'd keep you company when I'm not around." Robin turned to Jess. "Mom, don't you think it's a good idea?"

"I'm staying out of this." But the truth was, she agreed with her daughter. A puppy's silly, rambunctious nature, its unconditional love, might do Dave good.

"We're not making any decisions right now," he said firmly. "This pup's an unfair influence. Now come on, Pop's got the steaks on, and Mom's dishing out baked potatoes."

He put an arm around each of them as they walked up the lawn to the patio. "What have you two got planned for tomorrow?" Jess asked.

"We're going to ride out to Trout Lake and have a picnic," Robin announced.

"Good. Malibu doesn't get enough exercise." Malibu, a palomino gelding, was Dave's horse, whom he kept stabled on the outskirts of town.

"Then we're going to Arigata to have dinner with Kimiko and her family," Robin said.

"Checking out the competition?" Jess asked Dave. Arigata, Kimiko's parents' restaurant, was one of the best in town, as was the dining room at the Wild Rose Inn.

"You could come, too, Mom," Robin said, hopping up the steps ahead of them.

"I've already horned in on one of your nights with your dad."

"But I like it when we're all three together."

Jess and Dave exchanged glances. It was about the only disadvantage to how well they got along. Robin kept hinting they should get married again.

Jess leaned close and whispered into her ex's ear, "Or we could change the subject back to the puppy."

He gave a snort of laughter and she grinned. Dave's laughter was a rare thing these days. She squeezed his waist. "This is just what I needed tonight."

"Steak and baked potatoes?" Robin asked.

"Absolutely."

The three of them assembled their dinners. During the meal, Jess moved from group to group, catching up with Dave's family. But when Sheila served glazed strawberry pie and Ken poured mugs of coffee, Jess and Dave gravitated to the front porch, away from the crowd. They sat side by side on the top step.

She savored a bite of Sheila's pie. "Remember me mentioning a guest a few weeks ago who seemed interested in investing in my boot camp idea? Well, Evan's his investment counselor. That's why he came."

"What? You didn't tell me that before. Jess, you mean there's an investor who's seriously interested?"

"You sound surprised."

"Uh, well . . ." He stuffed a big forkful of pie into his mouth.

She wondered for the first time if anyone had ever taken her seriously when she babbled on about her horsy dreams. No, she hadn't done the hard work to put together a serious proposal, so maybe no one believed she would work to achieve those dreams. "Well, apparently Gianni was interested enough to send Evan here undercover to check me out."

Dave stared at her. "Undercover? You mean, you didn't know?" Sounding increasingly outraged, he said, "Evan was checking you out behind your back?"

"Yeah. Though when he came, he didn't know I was TJ Cousins."

"Man, that's . . ." He shook his head. "I don't know what to say. But he did end up telling you?"

"Yeah, and it hurt. But I could see his side, too. Besides, it's not like I've been exactly honest with him."

"Yeah, but—"

"I know. A kid's a different thing than a business deal. Anyhow, the bottom line is, I know he won't recommend me to Gianni."

"That's too bad." He was cutting another piece of pie, not meeting her eyes.

"You're not surprised, are you? You know I don't have the stuff an investor's looking for. The research and analysis, a business plan."

Dave nodded slowly. "Jess, you do need those things if you're going to attract serious investors. I've mentioned that a time or two, but I don't know if you even heard me. You're always more interested in talking about horses than business."

She cut a forkful of her pie but didn't lift it to her mouth. "I guess I've never really grown up. I always spun dreams, but now I realize they aren't going to come true unless I put in the hard work to make that happen. I want to do that, Dave, but I don't know how. I've never been to business school."

"Ah. That's what you meant about tapping my expertise."

"Would you help me?"

"Heck, Jess, you put up with my night school and correspondence courses when I was getting my degree. You ought to reap some of the rewards. But I'm surprised—"

When he broke off, she prompted, "What?"

He put down his empty pie plate and picked up his coffee mug. "Evan could have offered to help."

She bit her lip. "He did."

"Oh. Then you don't need me." Dave sounded hurt and jealous.

Jess reached out to grip his arm. "I turned him down."

"Why? Oh. Too complicated? What with you still, uh . . ."

"Being attracted to him? That's not the problem. After all, the assistance would be long distance, and he has this girlfriend in New York—Cynthia—who's his perfect mate." She took a sip of her own coffee, finding it unusually bitter.

"Then . . ."

"My pride won't let me. It's like I need to prove something to him. I'll never be the huge success he is, but I do want to achieve my dream and I want to do it on my own—or at least without his help."

"But you'll take mine."

"Gladly. I don't have anything to prove to you."

He studied her face. "Are you sure you have something to prove to Evan? I mean, I'm the last one to take his side, but the two of you did used to be best friends."

"And we're finding our way back to a friendship. But I feel like we're not equals. When we were kids, we were equal, and now he's a success and I'm not."

"That last point's debatable, but so's the previous one. When you were kids, you were a success and he wasn't."

"Oh, come on, he was the brightest kid in school."

"And the other kids accepted him only because of you. You were the popular one, the well-rounded one. He just tagged along." He drained his coffee mug and picked up hers. "You drinking this?"

"Go ahead. Look, Ev helped me as much as I helped him. I'd probably have flunked high school if he hadn't helped me with my homework."

"Maybe. But not because you were dumb, just because you couldn't be bothered to sit down and study."

"Whatever. He did get me through school."

"And you got him through, in a different way."

"Which made us equal. But now it would all be one way. There's nothing I can offer him."

"Isn't your friendship enough?"

"It doesn't feel like it to me." It was dusk now and she had trouble reading Dave's face. "What are you saying? You don't want to help me? You want me to ask Evan?"

"No. I do want to help. I just don't want you running yourself down, or thinking he's better than you. You're a fine woman, in all ways, Jessica Bly Cousins."

Before she could thank him, people started to drift around from the back of the house, heading for their cars.

When Robin came to say good night, Jess gave her an extra-long hug. "Have a good day tomorrow, sweetheart."

"See you Monday, Mom."

Monday seemed an awfully long way away.

Sunday, Jess's one full day off from the Crazy Horse, was so packed with ranch work and horse training that she barely had time to think. Or to miss Evan. It was only on Monday morning, when she rattled up to the resort in her truck—she'd driven rather than ridden because she had truck-type errands to run later—that she felt a serious pang. A week ago, she'd gazed around the barnyard, taking a quick preliminary inventory of the new gang of dudes, and she'd seen Evan's butt.

She shook her head, bemusedly. Today that butt—the one that looked so fine in faded denim—would be clad in the pants of a designer business suit. He'd be sitting behind his desk in some New York skyscraper—

Or he'd be strolling down the hill from the lodge, Jess's Resistol on his head, laughing as he listened to Beth.

Jess stuck her head out the truck window and blinked to clear her vision. As a group, the guests raised their hands to wave, Evan among them. She squinted and saw that his smile was as wide as when he and Rusty had pelted across the green meadow.

A wave of joy surged through her and a grin split her own face as she waved back. She pumped her foot down on the gas and sped into the yard, needing a couple of minutes to pull herself together before everyone—Evan—arrived.

Evan watched as Jess's expression of disbelief turned into a big, genuine smile, and relief washed through him. He had hoped she'd be glad he was staying but hadn't been sure until now.

Saturday night, he'd watched a Monty Roberts video with the other guests, munched Kathy's popcorn, and had a second glass of an excellent red wine, breaking his one-drink rule because he didn't feel driven to prove his self-control. When the guests said their good nights and headed back to their cabins, he realized he hadn't gotten around to asking Will to book him a flight for Sunday.

He'd thought about what a hokey Saturday night it was, about what he and Cynthia might be doing in New York. And it dawned on him that he was in no great hurry to rush back. Yes, Manhattan was home and he did miss it. But he sensed there were still lessons to be learned here. Gianni Vitale had been wiser than he'd given him credit for.

Besides, there was Jess. They'd struggled their way to a

tenuous friendship, and he wanted to cement the bond. Maybe he'd win her trust enough that she'd let him help with her boot camp plan. Hell, it was still possible that, when he met with Gianni and Elena in a week's time, he might be able to make a positive recommendation.

Somehow he knew that whatever happened over the next week it would turn him into a better man.

Now he let the others head off to greet their horses and he sauntered over to Jess, who looked fresh and pretty in a blue checked Western shirt. "Mornin'," he said, unable to keep the corners of his mouth from twitching.

"What the heck are you doing here?" she demanded, a slight frown tugging at her brow. Then she gave her head a quick shake. "Seems to me I said pretty much the same thing a week ago."

"Pretty much." He couldn't hold back the grin. He felt so damned good, being with her—everything out in the open between them, able to be honest with each other. Or at least to be honest about everything but the attraction they both felt, the one they had both sensibly been trying to ignore.

She smiled, too, her eyes gleaming with happiness. "Let me guess, you've decided riding isn't enough to earn that ten-year plaque. Now you want to learn roping."

He laughed. "Something like that."

"Why didn't you call me and let me know?"

"Wanted to surprise you."

"You did." Together they walked into the barn to get their tack. "Yesterday, I imagined you flying home."

He hoped she'd felt a twinge or two of regret. "Yesterday, I slept in, then Kathy and her crew served us an amazing brunch. I did some work my assistant had e-mailed me, then went for a run to work off the brunch. A few of us hiked a couple of miles to a lake, with a picnic lunch supplied by Kathy. In the afternoon . . . I don't really remember what I did. Dinner was a barbecue and we spent hours at it."

Her eyes had widened as he spoke. "You relaxed," she said disbelievingly.

"Yeah."

She looked almost as surprised by his easy agreement as she had by his recitation of Sunday's activities.

"We'd better get going," he said. "Everyone's keen to get riding, after a day without."

"Right." She still looked a little stunned.

"Say, Jess, can I book a private lesson?"

"Sure. But you're doing so well, you don't really need it."

"Thanks, but you're going to teach me how to rope, right?"

Her brows flew up; then she caught on to the joke and gave a ringing laugh.

His heart expanded at the sound of her laughter, and he knew that staying had been the right decision.

Cynthia certainly hadn't been pleased, he reflected as he went to get Rusty ready. In fact, she'd been downright snippy, which was unlike her. Normally, she handled even the most serious crisis with equanimity. He'd have to call her again, later in the day.

As for Angelica, she'd been mildly annoyed at having to rearrange more appointments, but had ended up saying, "Have a good holiday, Evan, you deserve it. But you owe me, and you can pay up by bringing me a photo of you on a horse."

He swung into the saddle, thinking how easily the motion came now. He'd have to remember to get Joan or Sandy, who always carried cameras, to snap his photo.

The morning passed quickly and enjoyably. Even the cloudy weather was a pleasant change from the past week's heat, bringing a fresh coolness to the air. Evan found he was more attuned to his environment now that he wasn't doing mental multitasking.

That afternoon, when he took his riding lesson and worked diligently on improving, he said, "I'm actually going to miss this when I go back home. I'll have to check into riding in Central Park."

Jess, sitting atop Knight, snorted. "I suppose it's better than nothing. But that'll be English tack, Ev. It's quite different." A smile twitched her lips. "You'd better read a book."

"Or maybe I'll just take a lesson."

She tilted her hat and peered at him with a guileless expression. "Figure you'll get Cynthia to go along?"

He laughed. "Nope, but I bet Gianni and Elena will."

A shadow crossed her face, and then she forced a smile. "Say hi to them from me."

"Jess, I'm still willing to help you."

She shook her head. "Thanks anyhow. Well, time's up."

They rode back to the barnyard, where they took off their horses' tack. Evan felt a sense of letdown. What had he expected? That Jess would leap up and down, carry him off for dinner with her family, introduce him to her daughter, eagerly accept his offer of assistance?

Oh well, he was really enjoying the company of the other guests, and tonight the plan was to watch *The Man from Snowy River* and eat more popcorn.

It struck him that he'd been at the Crazy Horse for more than a week and he hadn't set foot in the town of Caribou Crossing. Nor did he plan to. Aside from Jess and her family, there was no one else he wanted to see. Not really.

Not Brooke. She'd hurt him too many times.

After he and Jess turned their horses out to pasture, he said, "You got my mother a job?"

"She got it herself." She gave him an appraising look.

He answered the unspoken question. "No, I don't plan to get in touch."

"Too bad."

"You've been generous to her. Putting her in touch with your aunt at the beauty salon."

"It's easier for me than for you. She didn't hurt me, not directly. I knew she hurt you, but I could also see how much she'd been hurting herself. I respect her for having the guts to make such huge changes. For staying sober."

She rested her elbows on the top rail of the fence and he did the same, wanting to bump his elbow against hers but instead making sure there were a couple of inches between them.

"You know what you said about Brooke being so keen on the city?" she said. "I wonder if it was L.A. she missed, or the life she had there? She was a pretty, popular girl. Not well off, but a bit spoiled. Then she fell for your father, who was one of those sexy bad boys. Once she got pregnant, everything changed."

"I guess it always does." He added, "She never talked to me much about those times. She just complained."

"We've been alone in the salon a few times when she's cut my hair, and she's shared some things. I think she likes me because you and I used to be such good friends. Being with me kind of makes her feel close to you."

Softhearted Jess might think so, but Evan had trouble believing it.

"Do you want to hear the story?" she asked.

Mostly he wanted to walk away from even thinking about his mother, but a part of him needed to know. He gazed at the horses, which were grazing peacefully. "I guess."

"You know her and Mohinder's parents forced them to get married? Everyone pressured him to get a job and he joined the army. Then he couldn't take the discipline and deserted. He paid for forged ID papers and took you and your mom to Canada."

This was all old news. "He never lasted long at any job. We spent my early years drifting around."

"Think what that was like for Brooke. In L.A. she'd

been a spoiled princess, and now she was alienated from her family, having to cope with a baby and a husband who couldn't hold a job. A husband who beat up on her when he was in a bad mood. She wasn't even eighteen when they left the States."

He nodded slowly. "Yeah, I guess it was tough. I don't remember much. Except being on my best behavior so no one would get mad at me."

"I bet. You were a clever kid. I'm sure you learned that lesson early." She moved closer and rested her hand on his forearm, below where he'd rolled up his sleeve.

Grubby fingers on a bare arm: such a simple thing. She probably intended her touch to be comforting, and it was, but it was also arousing.

He didn't move away.

"Anyhow," she went on, "your parents drifted their way to Caribou Crossing, and here they stayed."

"I never knew why they settled here."

"Brooke put her foot down. They'd moved so often. She said each place was as bad as the last, so they had to pick one and stay, so you'd have some stability."

"I never knew that." His mother had actually looked out for his interests? "But she was so unhappy here."

"Guess she'd have been unhappy anywhere, what with her bipolar."

He felt guilty for never having guessed his mother might be ill. Yes, she should have gotten treatment, but maybe she'd never had the courage to ask for help. It was a tough thing to do. Even when he was a kid, he'd never admitted he needed help. Thank heavens Jess and her parents had been so intuitive.

"She has so many regrets, Ev." Her hand tightened on his arm, drawing his gaze to her face.

He saw melting brown eyes, a pleading expression. "You think I should see her."

"She really does love you. It's like . . . all that nasty stuff has been stripped away, and underneath is a kind, gentle woman who wishes she'd lived her life differently. Do you realize she's hardly more than forty?"

"What?" Damn it, Jess was right. Good Lord, his mother was barely middle-aged. "She could start again. Get married, even have a kid."

Jess shook her head. "She lives a narrow life. Work, her A.A. meetings, church on Sunday. Her home." She paused a moment, then went on. "Her garden, her cat. She lives like she's in her seventies. I guess she's scared of making the same mistakes. Or maybe she's doing penance." She shot him a meaningful look.

"You're suggesting I could relieve some of her guilt."

She shook her head. "That's your decision. I know how badly she hurt you. You don't owe her anything, much less absolution."

"Thanks for understanding."

"She does, too. She'd be the first to say you can't undo the past. But, Ev, it might be good for you to see who she's become. To feel how much she loves you. Maybe there's a future for the two of you."

A future. With his mother. Experience made him cynical. "I doubt that very much."

Jess bit her lip. "I'm not sure you want to hear this, but she's living in the rental house on the ranch property."

His jaw dropped. He remembered back when he and Jess were kids, how some neighbors had helped her parents build that house. The rent would be a regular source of income to help buffer the ups and downs of ranching. How bizarre that his mother now lived there. "Figures that your family would take her in." They had soft hearts, the Blys. A hell of a lot softer than his.

She shook her head. "It's business. She's an excellent tenant."

Hard to believe. But so was everything else she'd said about Brooke.

When he didn't respond, Jess sighed and took her hand from his arm. "I have to head home."

Such a simple thing: a bare arm with no grubby fingers on it. And for whatever reason, he felt bereft.

Jess had been busy all day, but Evan's decision to stay another week was always on her mind, giving her daily tasks a special buzz of pleasure. He'd chosen to stay, and she believed it wasn't just about riding; it was about solidifying their friendship.

Friendship. When she'd first seen him this morning, she'd had to remind herself that was all it would ever be. There were dreams you could maybe make come true if you worked hard enough, but she and Evan as anything more than friends wasn't one of them.

After dinner, when Rob was in her room doing homework, Jess told her mother about Evan.

Miriam promptly said, "Oh, invite him for supper again. How about tomorrow?"

Robin would be home. "I have a ton of work," Jess said. "And Wednesday's the hayride. Maybe Thursday?" When Rob would be at Dave's.

"That's our bridge tournament."

Friday, Rob would be back at the ranch. "Friday's no good either," Jess said. "It's the guests' last night at the Crazy Horse, and Kathy and Will always do a special dinner. Evan shouldn't miss that."

Miriam Bly sighed. "I suppose it won't work then. Too bad. He's grown into such a fine young man."

Jess felt guilty. She was pretty sure Evan would have relished another visit, just as her parents would. But she couldn't let him spend an evening with Robin.

When she fell into bed that night, she remembered that tomorrow was a lunch ride. Now that the guests were more comfortable on horseback, the rides were getting longer. The group would start midmorning and ride out to a lake—not Zephyr—where Kathy, Will, and Marty would meet them with a picnic lunch.

When she'd first worked out the schedule with Kathy and Will, she had avoided mentioning Zephyr Lake. Just as she'd avoided going there since her visit with Evan ten years ago. Fortunately, the countryside was dotted with scenic little lakes. Although only one—the one with the tepee and beaver dam—was actually on Crazy Horse land, others were accessible by a combination of public access routes and trails owned by generous neighbors.

Jess thought about what she and Madisun would need to do in the morning. The late start gave them a perfect opportunity to check all the horses for cuts, limps, and infections. Even the older ones like Pet, who were semiretired.

She frowned, remembering she hadn't noticed Petula that afternoon. The sweet-tempered palomino always hurried over to greet her when the horses were turned out to pasture, but Jess had been distracted by Evan.

Jess had a bad feeling about not seeing Pet, and she trusted her instincts when it came to horses. She threw back the covers. No way could she sleep, not without knowing Petula was okay. Hurriedly she dressed, then tiptoed downstairs.

The roads were almost deserted and she made good time. Once she slipped through the gate in the pasture fence, she called softly, "Petula? Wake up, sleepyhead."

Clouds flitted across the sky, dimming the illumination from the moon and stars. Jess made her way cautiously across the rough ground toward a grove of trees where the horses spent the night. Shapes materialized and moved toward her. "Hi, Mickey, Distant Drummer, how ya doin'? Hey, Rusty, Knight, Rambler. Where's Pet? Anybody seen Pet?"

The horses were making sounds, little whickers of greeting, requests for food, but one voice made her heart race. The sound of a horse in pain.

The palomino was a pale shape, curled at the base of a tree. She turned her head toward Jess and scrabbled pitifully with her forelegs but didn't rise. Jess sank down, stroking the soft skin of the horse's cheek. "Hey, baby, what's wrong?"

The horse twisted her head, bit at her side. Jess ran a hand over Petula's belly, finding it swollen and hard. "Damn!" She leaped to her feet, realizing she'd left her cell phone at home.

Despite the poor light and rough footing, she took off at a run, pelting through the pasture, scrambling over the fence rather than stopping to unlatch the gate, and tearing into the barnyard. She grabbed the phone in the barn and dialed the vet.

"Yes?" The female voice that answered was calm, giving no sign its owner had been asleep.

"Sally, it's Jess. I'm at the Crazy Horse. Petula's down. I don't know for how long but I'm afraid it's been hours. I think it's colic." She ran through the symptoms quickly.

"Sounds like you're right. You know what to do. I'll throw on a pair of jeans and be there in a flash."

Jess grabbed Petula's halter and ran back to the pasture. The blond head turned her way and Jess quickly buckled on the halter. "Up, girl, you have to get up."

It took some effort but she managed to get the horse to her feet. "We have to walk. I know you feel rotten but you have to keep walking." She tugged on the rope and Pet, normally the most obedient of creatures, balked.

"Please, Pet," Jess begged, raising a hand to swipe at tears. Slowly, the horse moved toward her, and Jess could imagine the pain of every movement. Damn it, damn it, damn it, she should have checked Petula earlier.

"Please be all right," Jess whispered, resting her cheek against the horse's shoulder as they walked together. "Don't die on me, Pet."

Evan had slept soundly. He was getting used to the sound of silence—or, rather, the myriad sounds of branches whispering in the wind, frogs peeping, birds welcoming the dawn.

Whistling, he made his way to the lodge and claimed the phone, grateful he was the only early riser among the guests. "Morning, Gianni."

"Evan, how's it going? Was I right or was I right?"

Evan laughed. "About some things." His woodpecker was on the tree outside. He tapped gently on the window, and the bird cocked its head in his direction. "Thanks, Gianni. I needed this."

"Uh, you're welcome." For once the self-assured billionaire seemed at a loss for words. Then his tone sharpened. "You're recommending the investment then?"

"You're still keen, I take it?"

"Of course. Let's move ahead."

Evan said firmly, "No, not now. TJ's plans are too vague."

"Damn. It sounded so exciting. Something Elena and I could actually be involved in."

"That's true. And it may still work out. I just said not now. There are a couple of things I want to see happen first. One is that you take more time to think about it. When the glow of holiday excitement wears off, you may not be so keen."

"Why do you think I waited a month after coming back before I contacted you?"

"I didn't realize that. In any case, my other objection still holds. TJ's concept is too vague and she doesn't have a solid business model and a business plan."

"Hmm. That's troubling. I admit, we talked about the

general idea, not the business side. I wanted to leave that to you, but I assumed she had the facts and figures in place."

"She needs to do some work on that." Evan paused. "Gianni, did she tell you about her idea of, basically, having the rich guests pay for the poor ones?"

"Elena and I really like that idea. Not everyone's as privileged as us."

"I like it, too, but it's not a moneymaker. So tell me what you think of this idea." Over the past couple of days, he'd been playing with a different concept. "What if her camp, or at least part of it, was a charitable foundation? Donors would get tax receipts so that, perhaps more than making money, you'd be saving money with a big tax deduction."

"I like that. TJ didn't mention that to me."

"I don't think she's thought of it. But I could suggest it to her if that's all right with you." He laid his cards on the table. "You're my client and she's my friend. I know that's a potential conflict of interest. But you're interested in the boot camp, and I think you know by now that I'd never advise you to invest in something that wasn't solid. If I worked with Jess—TJ—in some fashion, and she put together a strong proposal for a company, a foundation, or both, then—"

"It's the best-case scenario for all of us," Gianni broke in.

"I think it could be."

"Still," his client said slowly, "if she's going to make this fly, she has to know how to do financial analysis and business projections herself, or at least hire the talent."

"Agreed."

"Morning, Evan." It was Ann, coming through the main door.

"Have to go," he told Gianni. "I'll talk to her again and get back to you." Or at least he hoped Jess would talk to him. Even if she didn't want his assistance, she should consider the idea of a charity, and she needed to find a professional who could help her organize a businesslike proposal.

He shelved his concerns for the time being and went into the dining room for breakfast. Each day he found himself more receptive to the group-style meals. Although first-thing-in-the-morning sociability might not be his natural style, he was holding his own and he enjoyed participating. This morning, the talk centered around last night's video and the morning ride.

Gianni had been absolutely right about that ambiance thing. Each event at the Crazy Horse seemed special, and the guests were getting horse-crazier by the moment. Already a couple were talking about buying a horse when they got home. Over breakfast, Evan heard everyone swear they'd be coming back to the Crazy Horse next year.

He noticed Kathy grinning as she refilled coffee cups. He pushed back his chair and followed her to the kitchen door. "How many actually come back?"

She put down the coffee urn. "Three or four in ten. Some don't make it every year, but come now and then. We have a couple of groups who come back together for the same week every year."

The idea made him smile.

Kathy grinned. "It's appealing, isn't it?"

"I admit it. But right now everyone is so hyped. That can't last."

"No, but we hope that in their time here—and that's why we only book in two-week blocks—people learn some lasting lessons about themselves. More confidence, especially physical confidence. Increased love and respect for animals. More of a focus on the outdoors and physical health. And most of all, the ability to stop and smell the roses."

First Gianni, then Jess, and now Kathy had used that phrase. "You have some fine roses here," he said, meaning far more than the pretty, sweet-smelling pink ones that grew wild.

"Don't I know it."

"You've done a great job in designing this concept and

marketing the place. I understand it has a terrific reputation, internationally."

She nodded with satisfaction. "Will and I set out to create something exclusive. Of course we wanted to make money, but also, we figure rich folks need this kind of holiday as much as poor ones. Look at you, Evan. A New York investment counselor. That's your real life, right? But I'm betting that when you go back to it you'll make some changes. You wouldn't have come here if there wasn't something inside you that was drawn to a slower pace, different priorities."

She gestured toward the tousled guests, chatting animatedly around the big wooden table. "And look at the business benefits. You could meet people like them at management seminars in Manhattan. You'd be wearing your power suits, talking business, pressing business cards into each other's hands, making notes on your smartphones. You'd never relax enough to get to know each other. Here, you're making friends and business contacts who are meaningful. Right?"

He nodded. Yes, Evan was going to check into George's company, with an eye to recommending it to his investors. George planned to hire Sandy to design a program for them. Joan's husband wasn't happy with his current investment counselor, so she would recommend Evan. The group of guests was forming lots of business connections.

He smiled at Kathy. "You really know what you're doing."

"Living in a beautiful place, making a fine living, meeting fascinating folks, and actually making a difference in some people's lives. What more could we ask?"

"Don't people forget to smell the roses once they get home?"

"Some do." She gave an impish grin. "We remind them, though. Once you're on our mailing list, Evan, it's hard to forget about the Crazy Horse. We e-mail a quarterly newsletter. It has news about us and the horses, a couple of recipes, some health tips and exercises, information about alumni."

"Really?"

"Be sure to keep us posted on what you're doing. It's good networking. We also send postcards periodically, with photos of Jess, Madisun, and Robin on their horses, Will and me in the kitchen, guests gathered around the fireplace in winter, wild roses blooming, and so on. And we e-mail you about special package deals."

Kathy and Will knew what they were doing when it came to developing their brand and marketing it. Why didn't Jess follow their example? Was it because, unlike her bosses, she lacked confidence in her product? Or because she just enjoyed dreaming?

Chapter Twelve

Today's ride had a later start time than usual, yet when Evan reached the barnyard, only half the horses had been brought in from pasture and hitched to the rails. There was no sign of Jess, although her truck was there, the driver's door hanging open.

Madisun looked frazzled as she turned to face the guests, four halters dangling from her hands.

"Running late?" George asked her.

"A little. Glad you folks turned up to lend a hand." Her grin seemed forced.

"What can we do, Madisun?" Evan asked. "Without getting in your way?"

"Uh, let's see. Why don't you tack up the horses I've brought in, and I'll get the rest of them."

She'd barely finished speaking when the guests stampeded toward the barn. She sprinted toward the pasture and was fumbling with the gate when Evan caught up with her. "What's going on? Where's TJ?"

When she turned to him, she was brushing tears from her cheeks. "I shouldn't tell you." She gave a hiccupy sob.

"What's wrong, Madisun? Tell me, I'm a friend."

A louder sob burst out, and then she swallowed hard. "We had to have a horse put down. P-Petula, one of our old favorites."

The palomino Jess called Pet. Oh God, Jess would be shattered.

"It was colic," Madisun said. "A t-twisted intestine. TJ was with her most of the night, but she and the vet gave up early this morning and had to p-put her down." She took a shuddery breath. "We had to get Pet's b-body taken away before the guests showed up. We don't want anyone to know, don't want to spoil the holiday mood. Oh Jesus, I shouldn't have told you!" She dragged a ragged tissue out of her pocket and blew her nose.

Evan touched her shoulder. "It's okay, I won't tell anyone. Where's TJ?"

"Up at the lodge. She's showering. But she's a mess, Evan. She couldn't stop crying."

Softest heart in the world. He remembered.

Madisun turned anxious eyes on him. "I don't know if she's going to be able to cope."

"She will," he said with certainty. "She has guts. And so do you. I'll do what I can to help. Let's keep the guests busy, and try to keep attention away from TJ until she pulls herself together."

Madisun leaned forward and rested her forehead against his shoulder. Then she drew back. "Thanks." She sucked in a breath, then exhaled. "I'll bring the rest of the horses in."

He studied her. "You're pretty strong for your age, aren't you?"

Eyes that were far older than eighteen met his. "Sometimes you have to be." She flicked her head, long black hair lifting, then settling. "I'll bring the horses to the fence. You can get them to the hitching rails?"

"No problem."

Soon everyone was working industriously, and Evan was glad for every moment he'd spent learning how to deal with the horses.

He was helping Joan put on Mickey's bridle when George's voice rang out again with "Running late?" Evan turned to see Jess entering the yard. Her clothes were fresh, her hair was damp, and her hat was pulled low, shadowing her face.

"Sorry about that," she said, voice ragged at the edges. "But I see Madisun has everything under control."

Evan broke in. "We've been practicing our skills." He put on a corny Cockney accent. "By George, mate, I think we've actually got it."

Jess's mouth opened in surprise.

He almost laughed. Yeah, he was acting out of character, but if playing the fool would help her and Madisun, he was glad to do it.

"TJ?" Madisun called out. "Can you help me over here?"

The guests went ahead with their tasks, and in a few minutes everyone was mounted, forming their usual line. "It's my lucky day," Madisun said as she swung into her appaloosa's saddle. "TJ's letting me be trail boss so Raindance and I will take the lead."

She went through the gate and the others followed, but Evan held Rusty back. When Jess drew up beside him on Knight, he said, "How're you doing?"

She tilted her head to look at him, and he got a good view of her face. He ached to see the shadows under her eyes, the puffy redness.

"Madisun shouldn't have told you." Her voice was husky from crying.

"Yes, she should. She's a trooper, but she was barely hanging on."

Jess swallowed so hard he could see it. "She told me how you helped out. Thanks."

"You're welcome." He wished there was some way to comfort her. But, knowing that what she needed most was privacy, he urged Rusty forward, leaving her to follow at her own pace.

Jess closed her aching eyes and held Knight back. The horse, used to being in the lead, danced in place and fussed with the bit. "Okay, boy," she murmured soothingly, leaning forward to stroke his neck. "You'll have a chance to run, but for now could you take it easy? I'm feeling fragile."

Normally she welcomed the challenge of working with the new horses like Knight, but right now she longed for the steadiness of a Rusty. Or a Petula.

Jess drew a quavery breath. Death was a natural event, but the elderly horse had still had a few good years in her. Quality years, hanging out in the pasture with the other horses or taking little girls for rides.

Jess eased up on the reins and Knight bounded forward. She held him to a walk, but he strode along so quickly he soon caught up with the guests. He argued over her command that he stay behind Rusty, tossing his head, prancing, and fidgeting. She kept her hands steady and her signals firm and he grudgingly conceded.

Evan glanced over his shoulder, gave her a quick smile, then faced front again.

She returned the smile, giving it to his denim-clad shoulders. It was a relief to have nothing more to do than control Knight and watch the gentle rhythm of Evan's strong back as he moved with Rusty. She drew in a deep breath of forest, deliberately expanding her lungs. The morning was gray and she smelled rain. Hopefully, it would hold off. She and Madisun had been too distracted to remember to hand out ponchos for the guests to tie to the backs of their saddles.

The horses trotted briefly, settled back to a walk, then,

coming into an open stretch, cantered. Knight kept wanting to pass, to take what he considered to be his rightful place in the lead. "Discipline is good for you," she murmured. Normally, after she'd trained a new horse, she passed the animal along to Madisun to ride at the back of the line for a couple of months. The Crazy Horse animals had to learn to keep their place, not compete for leadership.

Schooling Knight helped Jess focus. And, as always, just being on horseback out in the countryside was a healing experience. Her grief settled into a dull sense of melancholy.

When the riders reached the open meadows and split into two groups, as usual she took the advanced group. She gave Knight his head. His desire to run coincided with her own, and by now she knew her little band of guests could keep up without danger or fear.

The wind's fingers caressed her cheeks and stroked her drying hair. She rode silently, barely hearing the whoops of her companions, but when she pulled up and they joined her, she gave them a smile that felt real. "Everyone okay?"

The enthusiastic response made her smile again.

Her gaze lingered on Evan, clad in denim and cowboy boots, the Resistol hat looking perfectly at home atop his sun-streaked hair. Just as Evan looked perfectly natural and at ease in the saddle. City boy turned cowboy. Thank God he was here today. His simple presence made her heart feel a tiny bit lighter.

Jess's group joined up with the others and Madisun called out, "Follow me, now. We'll ride for another five or ten minutes, then make a pit stop. Then another hour to our picnic spot."

Jess sent a grateful smile in her direction. The teen had loved Petula, too, and felt her loss deeply. But Madisun was handling it better. She had a core of steel, that girl. Had to, with the stresses her parents laid on her.

Madisun led the group onto an overgrown dirt road. There

was room to ride two abreast, and most people did so, taking the opportunity to chat.

Jess forced Knight to remain at the end of the line.

Evan held Rusty back, too, then guided his horse in step beside Knight. "Feel like company, Jess?"

What would she have done this morning without Madisun and this man? This old friend, this handsome man who looked like he belonged here.

If he'd been more open to her world as a boy, would both their lives have been different?

No, she couldn't think that way. Today was already too stressful. She'd just enjoy the sight of him, her friend Ev riding beside her. "Yours, yes," she told him. "But I don't feel like talking." She was still too fragile. If she talked, she'd cry again.

"No problem."

They rode in companionable silence, broken only by the creak of leather, the jingle of harness, the horses' occasional snorts.

A few drops of rain splattered their shoulders. Jess glanced up. "Dang, we should've brought ponchos."

"We'll survive."

The drops soon stopped, thank heavens, and by the time they reached the lake, the sun was playing hide-and-seek among puffy white clouds.

Will, Kathy, and Marty awaited them with a barbecue set up beside coolers and wicker picnic baskets. The guests loosened off cinches, unknotted the reins and let them hang loose, spoke a few private words to their horses, then strode eagerly toward the picnic site.

"You've got them well trained," Evan said.

"It's more than that. You can see they love it. They're becoming part of this world, even if it's only temporary."

"I know the feeling."

She smiled, feeling sad. "I can see that." Today, in her

melancholy mood, it seemed particularly poignant that Evan could discover the wonders of the country yet be so committed to live in his huge city.

"Go get some lunch," she urged, and he obeyed.

Madisun came over and the two women hugged. "You're wonderful," Jess said. "I owe you big-time."

"I like being trail boss." But the girl's eyes were shadowed.

Jess put her arm around Madisun's shoulders. "Let's have some food."

The spread was, as always, luscious. Will barbecued hamburgers, basted with Kathy's secret sauce. The rest of the spread included crisp fried chicken, rich potato salad, tangy coleslaw, fresh-baked rolls, and an assortment of fruits and cookies.

People perched on rocks and logs by the lake and wandered back and forth as they replenished their plates.

Madisun was unusually quiet, and Jess noticed when she wandered into the woods. Jess always kept an eye on folks who headed for the shelter of the trees to answer calls of nature. Bears, wolves, and coyotes were rare, but not unknown. And so Jess noticed when Evan, too, headed off toward the woods close to where Madisun had entered.

She heard him call something. He stood in place a moment, then disappeared into the trees.

Curious, a little worried, Jess rose and brushed off her backside, then ambled in his wake. Treading softly, she moved between tall Douglas firs. A flash of red caught her eye. Madisun's shirt. About to call out, she moved a couple of steps closer, then drew to an abrupt halt.

The girl was in a clinch. With Evan. Jess's mouth dropped open and adrenaline coursed through her veins. She'd kill them. Both of them.

But then her senses sharpened. She heard choky sobs, saw how Madisun's sleek dark head was burrowed into Evan's shoulder, and how his hand was doing "there, there" pats on her back.

Jess sank down on her haunches, not wanting to intrude, yet wondering if she could help.

Finally, Madisun pulled away. "I'm so embarrassed." She fumbled a tissue out of her pocket and blew her nose loudly.

"Nothing to be ashamed of. You've held up so well all morning. Guess you'll really miss Petula."

"Yeah, but . . ."

"But?"

"I loved her, and I'm totally torn up about her dying. But it's not just Pet, it's . . . Oh damn, I'm never going to get out of here!"

What? Madisun was planning to go to university down in Vancouver.

"Why do you say that?" Evan asked.

The girl gave a despairing sigh. Then, "Sorry, I shouldn't be talking this way. You're here for a holiday, not to listen to my problems."

"Madisun, I'm TJ's friend and I'd like to be yours. Friends talk to each other, and not just about the cheery stuff."

The girl hung her head.

"What's the problem?" he prompted.

Speaking to the ground, she muttered, "Dad lost another job yesterday, and I can just see I'll have to fork over my savings to feed the kids."

Jess winced. Damn the man.

"Won't he get another job?" Evan asked.

Madisun glanced up quickly, then down again. "He'll go on a bender. A long one. He's that whole drunken Indian cliché. It'll be weeks, maybe months, before he'll work again."

Another long pause. "And your mother is, uh, dead?"

"No! Why would you think . . . oh, because I was looking

after my sister. No, Mom was just out of town for a few days because her own mother was ill."

"She doesn't have a job herself?"

"With my eight younger brothers and sisters at home? And *him* to look after? Not hardly. 'Sides, he knocked her up when she was in grade eleven and she never finished school. The only work she'd ever get hired for wouldn't pay much."

Evan let out his breath in a low whistle. Jess wasn't close enough to see the expression on his face, but she could imagine what he was thinking. Imagine the parallels he'd be drawing between Madisun's home life and his own childhood.

"Sorry," the girl said again. "I keep thinking I'm making progress, but then something like this happens." She sighed. "I'm never gonna get out of here, and it's stupid to think I will. I have a damned good job and I should be grateful."

He touched her shoulder. "It is a good job, and I'm sure you are grateful. But don't give up on the dreams, Madisun. I'm betting you will get out of here." He drew a long, audible breath. "I did."

Jess sucked in her own breath. She'd have bet Evan never, but never, talked about his origins.

Madisun's head came up. "What?"

He nodded. "This is just between us, okay? I grew up in Caribou Crossing—that's how I know TJ—and my parents weren't much different from yours. He knocked her up when she was in high school. He drank, had trouble holding a job. Best thing he did was abandon us. Then there was just Broo—my mother and me. She was like your mom, didn't have many job skills. Or, uh, the personality to hold a job. We had some hard times. But I knew one day I'd get out." He gave a small, wry laugh. "Recently, an old friend said I was the most single-minded boy. I was, and I did it. Got out, and made my dream into reality."

Madisun slanted a cynical gaze his way. "White boy. That makes it easier."

"Don't cop out. You're bright and talented, you have what it takes to succeed. Maybe you'll have to work a bit harder, but for each person who judges because you're female, or aboriginal, you'll run into someone else who'll bend over backward to give you a chance. You just need to find the good people, work hard, and never lose confidence in yourself."

She shrugged. "Yeah, okay, you're right. I already know that from how the teachers at school treat me. The thing that's really going to stop me is money, and my home situation. Last night really brought it home."

"What happened?" Evan asked softly.

"He came home after the bars closed, drunk as a skunk. . . ." She trailed off.

Evan's body tensed. "Did he hit you?"

Madisun gazed at the ground and slowly shook her head. "Not this time." She lifted her head and stared at him. "It was just that I saw . . . he's never gonna let me go."

Jess's muscles had clenched. She honestly hadn't known Madisun's father beat her, but she should have. Damn it, she wanted to punch him out, and she knew Evan felt the same. Somehow, she had to get the girl away from her father and help her find her way.

Madisun was still staring at Evan. "Your dad hit you?"

"Sometimes."

She nodded, as if she'd already known.

Jess's eyes filled with tears as she rose and tiptoed away. The two of them shared something that, thank God, she could never fully understand.

As the group rode home after lunch, Evan felt the tension in the air. Jess's grief, Madisun's despair, his own anger over the girl's sad plight. And of course, some lingering memories of his father's fists.

The other guests didn't seem to pick up on the undercurrents.

They were mellow, even sleepy, after hours of riding and fresh air, not to mention an excellent repast.

Trying to put his negative feelings aside, he pulled Rusty up beside Jess and Knight. To his surprise, she gave him a big smile, so warm it almost knocked him out of the saddle. She didn't say anything, though.

After a few minutes he said, "Want to tell me about Petula?"

Her mouth formed an O, then shaped itself into a crooked grin. "Yeah, I do. Thanks, Ev." She began to talk softly, almost as if to herself. She told him how she'd first met the horse, how sweet-tempered Pet had always been. She told funny stories and moving ones.

He was listening to a eulogy, given by someone who had known the deceased well and loved her deeply. A horse, yes, but what difference did that make?

With a start, he realized that finally he'd entered Jess's world, where horses could be almost as important as people.

Here she was, babbling on to Evan about a horse. Just like the old days. He'd always listened then, too, but she'd known it was because he was interested in *her*, cared about her, not because he gave a damn about horses.

"Anyhow," she wound up, shooting him a guilty look, "that was Petula, and I'll miss her."

"Of course you will." He gave a sympathetic smile. "Thanks for telling me. She was a great horse."

Simple words, and yet they sounded sincere. Yes, Evan had changed. He was actually relating to the whole horse thing. "Thanks for letting me talk about her. It was just what I needed." He'd known that; he'd given her that gift. Damn it, if she'd been crazy about the old Evan, how much more dangerous was this new one?

Sudden raindrops, fat, hard ones, pelted the top of her cowboy hat. "Yikes!" The sleeves of her shirt, the denim at her thighs, darkened in big splotches. Up ahead, guests exclaimed in dismay, and the line moved into a trot. Jess decided to let Madisun keep the lead rather than take over from her. The girl knew what she was doing, and it would boost her confidence.

She assessed the clouds, which were a threatening slate gray. "We're really in for it," she told Evan. "Stupid not to have brought ponchos. I wasn't thinking."

"It's just water," he replied.

Sure enough, as the rain splattered down harder, and people got wetter and wetter, she heard more laughter than complaints.

In fact, the cool rain was refreshing, and she enjoyed the rich, dusty scent as it splashed onto the dry ground. Fortunately, they weren't far from home. The ground wasn't slippery and Madisun let them lope slowly for a fairly long stretch. The group returned to a walk as they neared the barn. Both the riders and the horses were soaked, and the horses' legs were coated in mud.

When they reached the barnyard and dismounted, Jess said, "Go get warm and dry, folks. Madisun and I will look after the horses."

It pleased her when the guests ignored her command. Joking with each other, flicking wet hair out off their faces, they fumbled with damp leather straps and slippery buckles. They made short work of getting the tack off, wiped down, and stored in the barn, as Jess and Madisun turned the horses out to pasture.

"Hot chocolate!" Kim exclaimed. "Let's change into dry clothes, and then we'll invade Kathy's kitchen. I bet she'll let us make hot chocolate."

"TJ, Madisun," Ann said, "you should come with us."

"Sounds good to me," Madisun said. "TJ?"

Hot chocolate sounded like a fine idea. But at home in the bath, alone. Followed by bed and, hopefully, a sound sleep. "Thanks, but I'm going to pass."

As the others left, Evan lingered behind. "You're beat. Let me drive you home."

She gave him a tired smile, thinking that the only thing better than hot chocolate and going to bed alone would be sharing them with this man. "Thanks, but I'm okay. I need some time on my own."

"You're sure there's nothing I can do?"

He could be a different man, a man who wanted to stay here rather than return to New York. He could be a man who loved her.

At the moment she wanted nothing more than to fling herself into his arms and stay there forever. Instead she shook her head. "You've done it. I don't think I'd have survived today without you. You're still a darn good friend."

"Get some rest, Jess. Call if you need anything. Promise?" He leaned down and pressed damp lips to her wet forehead. She put her arms around him and clung, allowing herself one brief moment of contact. It was all she could handle, feeling the way she did about Evan right now, and knowing how emotionally fragile she was.

As Jess drove away, Evan stood in the rain wishing he could somehow ease her pain. He respected Jess as a strong, independent woman, and yet he wanted to protect her. He never felt protective around Cynthia.

He took a long shower, then dressed and sprinted through the drizzle to the lodge. Voices told him the others were hanging out in the kitchen, but he headed straight for the phone.

Fortunately, she answered.

"Hello, Cynthia. Are you busy?"

"Evan. I'm at the office and of course I'm busy. The Dynamite deal? Remember?"

"Sure. Sorry for bothering you."

"You're not bothering me!" Her exasperated tone told him that if he hadn't been before he certainly was now.

Biting his lip, he glanced out the window. Despite the rain, that bird was there, its head cocked toward him. It seemed to be asking a question. And now, finally, he knew the answer.

"Cynthia, I've been doing a lot of thinking since I got here, and—"

"Wait." He imagined her holding her hand up, the way she did when she needed to think. He obeyed. For a couple of long seconds. Then she said, "You're a square peg."

"Pardon?"

"We both thought you were a round one, but you're not. We aren't ever going to fit together, are we?"

His reaction stunned him. He felt a heady surge of relief and found himself smiling. Then he sobered and said quietly, "I suppose not. I'm sorry. I should have realized sooner, but I honestly thought our relationship was exactly what I wanted."

"I know. Maybe you had to go back home to figure it out." Her tone was flat. He couldn't read what she was feeling. "This woman, Jess," she continued. "You love her."

"No! Well, yes, in a way. I mean, I always have. As a close friend." And an object of his lust, but he wasn't going to mention that.

"That's not how it sounds from here."

"Cynthia, nothing's happened." He winced, feeling guilty about the half-truth, but if he mentioned the kiss, it would only hurt her.

"I know you wouldn't cheat on me. But that's not the point. The point is, our relationship is going nowhere." She sounded exceptionally calm.

"So . . . I guess we're breaking up?" It was what he'd intended, but she seemed to have taken control.

She gave a humorless laugh. "That's what 'I've been thinking' means, isn't it? Besides, you're right. It's for the best. For both of us."

He'd known the two of them weren't emotional people, but he couldn't believe she could be so calm about this. "You aren't . . . angry, or hurt?"

She gave another laugh, and this one actually held a note of humor. "What would be the point? You know me, Evan. I'm eminently practical. I hate to waste time, or emotion. You and I did all right, but it's time to move on. Separately."

It felt anticlimactic. Not that he wanted a scene, but two years ought to at least end with a whimper, if not a bang.

Damn. This was just how he and Jess had finished ten years ago. Except they'd done it by e-mail—even more impersonally.

He couldn't let it end like this. "Cynthia, are you really all right?"

"Of course. Disappointed, but to be honest I'd suspected it wasn't going to work."

He wondered if she was rewriting history in her head, but it didn't matter.

She went on. "And when you told me you were going home—"

"It's not *home*! New York is home. I only came here to check out this investment."

"Oh, Evan, you don't fool me. Don't fool yourself. You had things you needed to find out. It sounds to me like you're getting in touch with a part of yourself that's been buried deep for far too long."

It wasn't like her to play amateur shrink, and that fact, as much as her words, gave him pause. Besides, she was sounding very much like Jess had, when she'd said that maybe he had to come back to Caribou Crossing to find himself.

"Maybe you're right," he admitted slowly. "But I'm confused."

Had he just, for the first time with Cynthia, admitted to vulnerability?

If so, she brushed it off, saying briskly, "You'll sort things out." She paused a moment. "Have you seen your mother?"

"No!" Good God, what was up with this woman? She'd turned from fiancée to shrink in less than five minutes. Was this her way of shoving aside her emotions and pretending he hadn't hurt her?

"Hmm," she said thoughtfully. "Well, I think you need to. You left home when you were still a boy, Evan. You need an adult resolution of the whole thing, even if it's a decision to sever all ties."

She and Jess really did have some things in common. He felt ganged up on. "I'll think about it."

"Mmm-hmm. Well, do what you need to do. Now I must run. Let's see . . . I have some things of yours. I'll drop them off at your apartment, pick up the items I've left there, leave your keys. You can courier my keys to me when you get back to town—or perhaps we'll meet for a drink one day."

Good old efficient Cynthia. "Sure, that sounds fine."

"Bye for now."

"Cynthia?"

But she had already gone.

He hung up the phone. Who was the woman he'd just spoken to, just broken up with? Was she really so pragmatic, so adaptable, or was she saving face? It irked him that after two years together, he couldn't tell what she was feeling. Before, he'd admired her emotional restraint. Now, oddly, he wanted to know her better. He cared about Cynthia and believed that, behind her reserve, she cared about him. When he got home, he'd ask her for that drink. Perhaps he could be a better friend than he'd been a lover. Somehow, things were coming into focus this week.

He glanced out the window. The bird was pecking busily, and the sound of laughter drifted in from the kitchen. So did the scent of chocolate. Suddenly, he felt lighthearted. A mug of hot chocolate was exactly what he wanted.

* * *

Evan slept like he'd never slept before. Usually, he was awake before his alarm went off, but on Wednesday morning he actually managed to sleep through its buzz. Too late for breakfast, he dashed into the lodge and picked up a muffin and a cardboard cup of Kathy's delicious coffee. He also snagged a couple of apples, one for himself and one for Rusty.

When he reached the barnyard, he was pleased to see that both Jess and Madisun had clear eyes and genuine smiles. He could barely suppress an urge to hug each of them, for very different reasons. Although he'd known Madisun just over a week, she almost seemed like the sister he'd never had. As for Jess . . . his feelings were far from brotherly. And now, finally, he could admit that to himself without feeling guilt. He was a single man; she was a single woman. There was nothing wrong with being attracted.

He let his gaze linger on her, appreciating everything about her. She might not be a fashion plate, but damn, she looked terrific. Ancient jeans hugged slim, feminine curves, a light blue shirt bared strong, tanned forearms and a lovely throat. A wide leather belt showed off her slim waist and emphasized the curves above and below. Ponytailed hair gleamed in the pale sunlight.

But the best thing—the captivating thing—was her face. Its lines were clean and strong, yet ineffably feminine. Her mouth was generous and expressive, almost as expressive as those chocolate eyes that could sparkle with laughter, melt with tears, or sizzle with passion.

Passion. He'd seen it in her eyes, the same passion he'd felt and tried to repress. What were they going to do about it?

"Evan," she called, a quizzical smile on her face. "Somebody hog-tie you so you can't move?"

She had. "Just enjoying the morning," he said, then headed to the barn to get Rusty's tack.

As soon as the group was on the trail, his thoughts returned to Jess. Now that he was single, could the two of them be more than friends? Well, why not do an analysis?

Fact 1: He was attracted to her. That was undeniable. Even thinking about her made him harden, an undesirable condition for a man seated on an unyielding leather saddle.

Fact 2: Though Jess said she just wanted to be friends, he knew she felt the same attraction he did. The passion in that kiss last week, the affection in her glance, told him that. But he'd been with Cynthia, so they'd both held back. Which led him to the next point.

Fact 3: They were now both single. So far, so good.

Rusty made a grab at the leaves of a wild rose, thorns and all. Evan yanked sharply on the reins. "Forget it."

The words echoed in his head, and he sighed. He'd been avoiding consideration of the single most important fact. The one that had always been there.

Fact 4: Jess lived in Caribou Crossing. More than that, she belonged here. Just like Rusty, those pink roses with their heady perfume, and the squirrel that scolded from a fence rail. Her heart was here—with her daughter, her parents, that damned Dave Cousins, and her beloved horses. In New York, she would slowly wither, the way one of those pretty pink blossoms eventually would if he snapped it off its stem.

He couldn't do it twice: make love to her, then abandon her.

She knew it, too, he realized, and was protecting herself. When she'd said she wanted them to be "just friends," it wasn't only because of Cynthia. Jess knew that anything more would lead to pain—and perhaps another ten long years of loneliness. If they were friends, at least they could stay in touch.

Were they naive to think they could make a friendship

work? But what was the alternative? Saying good-bye was unthinkable.

When the group took a break, spreading out to pick wild strawberries, Evan found it easier to avoid Jess than to deal with his complicated feelings. He wandered over to Madisun. "Things okay at home?" he asked quietly.

She shrugged. "Yes and no." Side by side, they moved farther away from the group.

"He never came home last night," she told him. "But he will eventually. I'll handle it." She touched his arm. "Thanks for the pep talk yesterday. It helps, knowing you had a rough home life and made it out."

"You will, too." An idea had been percolating in the back of his head. He'd thought about the Gimme a Break Foundation, but there'd be too much red tape, especially considering she was a Canadian. Besides, he wanted this offer to be personal.

"I have a proposition for you," Evan said. Then, quickly, "A business proposition."

Madisun tilted her head.

"I'll loan you the money to go to university."

"What? You can't do that!" Her young forehead screwed up in a frown.

"I can, and I want to. I'll give you funds for tuition, books, living expenses."

She was shaking her head bemusedly.

He went on. "I know you'll need to send money home for the kids, but I don't want you waitressing. You can work for me, when it fits your school schedule. And I'll expect you to e-mail me once a week with a progress report about what you're learning, and what you're thinking in terms of the future."

This time her head shake was vigorous. "That's no deal. There's nothing in it for you."

"I'm an investment counselor. I'm gambling that one day Madisun Joe is going to be a successful businesswoman and she'll be involved in an enterprise that's a good investment."

She gazed at him as if he were out of his mind. "I can't let you do this. I was just venting when I said what I did yesterday, about never getting out. I *will* make it. On my own."

"I have no doubt. But it could take another year. That's wasted time, for you and for me. I want you in university this fall." He paused. "Unless, of course, you don't want that."

Her face lit up. "Of course I want it!" Tears spilled over, and she flung herself into Evan's arms.

He hugged her briefly, then eased away. "Hey, we'll get people gossiping."

She swiped at the tears. "I can't believe it. But, Evan, my dad'll never let me."

"I'll talk to your parents. We'll work it out."

"Madisun?" It was Jess calling.

The girl scrubbed away the last of the moisture on her cheeks. "Time to get back on the trail. Oh, Evan, I'm so excited!"

"Figure out a time for me to meet with your parents. In the meantime, best keep this a secret."

After lunch, Jess and Madisun prepared for another session on communication and horse care. When the girl dropped the box of grooming supplies for the second time, Jess said, "What's up with you today?"

Madisun stared at her, and then a smile lit her face. "Oh, TJ, I'm just so happy, I can't keep it a secret."

This was a turnabout from yesterday. Jess smiled back. "What's happened, Madisun?"

"I'm sure Evan wouldn't mind if I told *you*."

"Evan?"

"He's going to finance me to go to university! This year!"

"Oh, my gosh." Stunned, Jess let it sink in. "That's incredible."

"Isn't he the best?"

Oh, yeah. "He really is." It was the girl's big break, and she deserved it. Jess hugged her. "I'm going to miss you so much, but I'm so happy for you." And then a thought struck her. "Have your parents agreed?"

Madisun's face clouded a little. "Not yet, but they just have to. Evan's going to talk to them. Mom will want me to do this; she doesn't want me getting caught up in the same cycle she did. Dad . . . Well, I have to believe Evan can persuade him."

Jess hoped so, too. But maybe she could do more than hope.

She went through the communication session, getting Madisun to assist, and then they set the guests to work grooming their horses.

When the horses had been turned out, the guests headed up the hill. Evan lingered, as usual, and returned Madisun's wave as she hurried to her truck. No doubt she was eager to get home and set up a meeting with her parents.

"Guess you have to rush back to the ranch and do chores before the hayride tonight," he said to Jess.

"Yeah." She studied him, tanned and strong and handsome in his shirt and jeans. The urge to hug him was a physical ache. She wanted to invite him home for dinner; she wanted to make love with him and make him a part of her life. She took a slight step backward. "Madisun told me about your offer. That's just wonderful, Ev."

He shrugged awkwardly. "She's a good kid. She deserves her chance. Not all of us can get scholarships to Cornell."

"You could have an uphill battle with her father."

"He hits her." His voice was icy.

A cold shiver rippled through her, and she hugged her arms

across her chest. "I didn't know or I'd have done something. She doesn't talk much about her family."

"Battered kids don't."

Their gazes met. *Oh, Evan, I wish I could fix every bad thing that ever happened to you.* She cleared her throat. "It might help if I come with you. The Joes know me, and you're a complete stranger. I could reassure them you're trustworthy, and—"

"Not some kind of sicko like him?"

She studied his clenched jaw. "If you hit Mr. Joe, it won't help Madisun."

He swallowed hard. "You may have to remind me."

Jess had no problem imagining Evan laying into Madisun's father with his fists. The thought should have disgusted her, but instead it made her heart race. Evan would never be a brawler, but he'd fight to protect someone he cared about. "You're a fine man, Evan Kincaid."

He shook his head impatiently. "I'm happy to help her. What was she doing telling you, anyhow? She's supposed to keep quiet about it."

He was embarrassed by praise. This, too, was endearing. Why in holy blue blazes did every dang thing about the man have to be so appealing?

"It's hard to keep secrets when you're close friends," she muttered, thinking guiltily about the huge secret she'd been keeping from Evan.

As Jess played her role at the evening hayride, watching Evan out of the corner of her eye and catching him watching her, she couldn't help but remember their kiss a week ago. So much had happened since then, but they hadn't kissed again.

Of course she didn't want to kiss Evan. Well, her brain didn't, but every other part of her—her heart, her soul, and her sexual being—wanted him very much.

She spent the evening trying to pretend he was just another guest, but even when she was talking to someone else, or in the middle of dancing a sprightly jig with Jimmy B, she was 100 percent conscious of Evan.

It was almost a relief when Hank and Gavin struck up a slow number and Evan tugged her into his arms. She wasn't sure she could have gone another moment without touching him. In fact, it was all she could do to keep from plastering her body up against him.

"I haven't told you about Cynthia," he murmured.

"Cynthia?" He was going to ruin this one dance together by talking about his girlfriend?

"We broke up."

Chapter Thirteen

Jess stumbled and gaped up at him, ashamed and terrified at the way her heart leaped. "What happened?"

"We had a civilized chat. She called me a square peg in a round hole."

"She dumped you?"

He wrinkled his face in an exaggerated grimace. "Could we avoid the word *dumped*?" Then he smiled. "Actually, I started it, then she finished it. We don't belong together and we both figured it out at the same time."

"You're okay then?" He was sounding, and acting, remarkably calm. If she'd just broken up with her fiancé, she'd be a mess.

"Yes. And I think Cynthia is, too."

"Well . . . that's great. Better to find out before you got married." *And where does that leave us?* Jess wondered. Then she answered her own question: *On opposite sides of the country.*

"I think Cynthia and I may end up as friends. I value her a great deal."

Value her? "I thought she was your perfect woman. If she isn't, then what are you looking for?"

He frowned slightly. "I . . . haven't gotten that far."

She tilted her head back. "Try it. Now that you're all grown up, what's your idea of the perfect woman?"

It was his turn to stumble. When he'd regained the rhythm, he said, "Well, obviously, someone with brains and ambition, someone who loves New York as much as I do."

"Sounds like Cynthia." Did he hear the edge in her voice?

"Uh . . . maybe I'd like more, uh, spark. Playfulness, fun. The last week has taught me that life doesn't have to be serious all the time."

"Good." He still hadn't said anything about love. It seemed Evan still wanted to keep his feelings locked up.

"And you, Jess," he said, "what's your idea of the perfect man? You're young, beautiful, vibrant. L-loving." His voice tripped over the last word. "You're not going to stay single forever."

"I don't fall in love easily," she said grimly.

"And if you did, it'd be with a man who was into all that home on the range stuff. Someone who'd be part of your life here."

She nodded. "It's a good life. Rob, my parents, Dave, family and friends."

"Horses," he said softly. The corners of his lips curved up a little, but his eyes were sad.

Oh yes, Evan had feelings for her, too. It wasn't just physical between them. If either one of them were a different person, they might have had a future. She forced herself to return his smile, and confirmed, "Horses." Not just the animals themselves, but the country, the whole lifestyle she'd grown up with; she couldn't imagine surviving anywhere else. And Evan, though he'd learned to enjoy his time here, clearly felt the same essential bond to New York City.

Suddenly, Jess was so tired her feet felt leaden. She'd been through an emotional wringer more than once this week. She stopped moving. "Ev, I'm beat." She glanced at her watch. "Time to wind things up."

Evan noticed how Jess waited for him to find a place in the hay wagon, then hoisted herself up on the opposite side. He told himself it was just as well. He was feeling as confused as he'd been a week ago.

The strangest thing had happened. When Jess had asked him to describe his perfect woman, an image had flashed into his mind. Jess, pulling Knight up after a fast ride. Turning to him as he rode beside her on Rusty, her eyes sparkling, her face alight with the same joy he was feeling. It was absurd. Yes, he was attracted to her, but she had no place in his world except on the fringes.

And deep in the center of his heart.

The Thursday ride wasn't planned to start until late in the morning because it involved another picnic lunch. Though he could have slept in, Evan woke early, restless. His time at the Crazy Horse was nearing an end. He felt good about a lot of things, yet had a sense of unfinished business.

He joined the others for breakfast, but only picked at his food and couldn't concentrate on the conversation. He'd more or less resolved things with Jess, but what about Brooke? If he returned to New York without seeing his mother, would he always wonder what they might have said to each other?

Damn. He'd opened his heart to his mother so many times as a boy, and each time she'd stomped on it. Why should he try again? He told himself it was just curiosity. Jess said his mother had changed, and maybe he'd like to see for himself because he had one hell of a time believing it.

Rising from the breakfast table, he sought out Will in

the office. "Can you call me a cab? I'm going in to Caribou Crossing."

"It'll take half an hour to get a taxi out here, and Marty's heading in for groceries shortly. Why not go with her?"

Marty tried to make conversation during the drive, but Evan wasn't feeling chatty and she gave up. "Where shall I drop you?" she asked as they reached the outskirts of town, which had a few new gas stations and fast food outlets since he'd last been here.

"Anywhere on the main street." He hoped the heart of Caribou Crossing would still be small enough that all the shops would be in walking distance of each other.

He was right, he saw as she stopped at a red light and he glanced around. Small, but more picturesque than he remembered.

Marty let him off in front of the drugstore, and he strolled the couple of blocks to where the beauty salon had been located. Several heritage buildings, including Dave Cousins's Wild Rose Inn and The Gold Nugget Saloon, where his parents used to drink, had been restored since his time. Flowers and fresh paint made the town look charming.

But he was stalling, assessing Caribou Crossing rather than focusing on the reason he'd come.

Standing across the street from Beauty Is You, Evan took several deep breaths and reminded himself he wasn't a man to back down from a challenge. His heart hammering in his chest, he strode across the street and opened the door. A bell jangled and several faces looked up.

His eyes went immediately to one. God, but she looked young. Beautiful. His gaze took in glossy blond hair in shoulder-length waves, a lightly tanned face and arms, a slender body wrapped in a cream-colored, multi-pocketed smock with Beauty Is You written on it.

Had he ever seen her look so good?

Brooke's hand went to her throat. "Evan?" Her voice was shaky, so soft he could barely hear it. She came toward him, moving in the uncertain manner of a blind person in an unfamiliar place.

"It's me," he said.

She gave a choky gasp and burst into tears.

Quickly another woman, also clad in a Beauty Is You smock, with curly brown hair highlighted with gold, dashed over. "What's going on?" She put a protective arm around Brooke.

"I'm her son. We haven't seen each other for a while."

"Oh my heavens! You're Evan!" She released his mother and put out her hand. "I'm Kate Patterson. I've heard all about you."

Distractedly, he shook her hand. Then he said to Brooke, "Are you all right?"

With her fingertips she whisked at the tears on her cheeks. "I can't believe it."

"When you get a break, can I take you for coffee?"

"Go now," Kate urged. "I'll finish Madge's blow-dry."

"Are you sure?" Brooke asked, but she was already pulling off her smock, her hands shaking, tousling her hair in the process. The other woman—Jess's aunt, he realized—reached out to smooth it. Under the smock, Brooke wore a blue sleeveless blouse and khaki skirt.

It felt more like a dream than real life—or like he was observing, not acting—as Evan and his mother walked side by side, untouching and unspeaking, to a coffee shop a couple of doors down the street. He endured the curious gazes of several people along the way, reminders that he was in a small community where all the locals knew each other, not big, anonymous NYC.

He and Brooke took a seat in a back corner and ordered coffee from a middle-aged man who greeted his mother by name and eyed him sharply through wire-rimmed glasses. When the coffee came and they were finally alone, Brooke asked urgently, "Are you all right?"

"All right?" How on earth could he answer that question?

"Are you . . . sick?"

He shouldn't be surprised that she might assume that, after he'd stayed away for so long. "No, I'm fine."

She let out a long breath and the tension in her face eased. She studied him across the table as if she was drinking him in. "Let me look at you, Evan Kincaid. I can't believe how handsome you turned out."

"You're looking good yourself, Brooke." In fact, despite a few tiny crinkles around her eyes and mouth, she seemed younger than she had ten years ago. She had chosen simple styles for her hair, make-up, and clothing, and they suited her. In the past, she'd either been completely run-down or fancied up in a too flashy way. Now she looked wholesome, almost classy.

He had spent so much time being angry at her. Now, when he looked at her, he had trouble recognizing the woman he'd known. "You look really different."

She nodded. "I am." She took a breath. "What are you doing here?"

"I came to the Crazy Horse partly on a job for a client and partly on holiday." He paused, realizing he'd firmed his jaw. "I've been here a week and a half."

"You didn't . . ." She dropped her head.

"No, I didn't call or visit. I didn't . . ." He decided on honesty. "I didn't want to see you, and figured you wouldn't want to see me. Things were over between us a long time ago, Brooke."

Tears overflowed her eyes, but she lifted her head and met his gaze. "You have a right to hate me."

"I don't know that I hate you. I was mad, hurt. It was you who hated me."

Her mouth dropped open. "Hated you? How could you think that?"

She certainly had a selective memory. Grimly, he prodded it. "You said I ruined your life."

"No!"

Anger, hurt, all the emotions he'd buried now burst through to the surface. "You said that if you hadn't gotten pregnant, you'd be back in L.A. having the time of your life. Instead, you were stuck in some hokey little hick town with a whiny kid."

As he spoke, she dropped her head again, burying her face in her hands. For a moment, they sat like that. Then, slowly, she lifted her head. Tears slid down her cheeks. "I'm so sorry, Evan. I got depressed sometimes. I guess I said some awful things. But I didn't mean them. Especially about you."

"You made them sound damned believable."

She winced. Then she straightened. "I apologize, from the bottom of my heart. I was a mess. That's no excuse, I'm just saying how it was. My brain . . . wasn't in the right place half the time."

The apology seemed genuine, and his anger began to dissolve. "Jess Bly—Cousins—told me about the bipolar and alcoholism. She said you were on medication and going to A.A."

"I should have done it years ago."

"Yes, you should have."

She met his gaze, her eyes, the blue-green ones he'd inherited, swollen and red-rimmed. "I'm so sorry. I was a horrible mother."

He didn't deny it, and he didn't sense she was looking for a polite disavowal. He sighed. "I'm glad you got things sorted around, Brooke."

"Is it too late?" she asked quietly. "Too late for us?"

He studied her face. There was a dignity there that he'd never seen before.

A week ago, he would have said it was too late. When he came here this morning, he hadn't known what he intended. He still didn't.

"One of the things you're supposed to do in A.A.," she went on, "is get in touch with the people you've harmed. Apologize and, if possible, make amends. I did it with everyone but you. Well, you and your father, but I have no idea how to reach Mo, and even if I did, I don't think it would be a good idea."

"That's sure the hell right."

She nodded. "You . . . yes, I certainly knew how to reach you, but I didn't have the guts to do it. And you were the one I hurt the most."

"So if I say I forgive you, that will square it with God and A.A.?" Yeah, he sounded bitter. No wonder she flinched.

Then she leaned forward again, shoving her untouched coffee mug aside and resting her forearms on the table. "Of course it won't. And I'm not doing it so much for me as for you. I want you to know it was never about you, Evan. The bad things I did, the horrible things I said, they were never because you deserved them. You were a fine boy. You were the only thing in my life that I loved."

He snorted. "Loved? You didn't love me."

"Oh, yes! But it still wasn't enough to . . . make me get my head on straight. I'm so sorry, Evan."

Yes, she did have dignity. It was present in each gesture, each word. She'd earned it, too. All by herself.

"For what it's worth," he found himself saying, "I do forgive you. I never understood what you were going through. As a kid, I probably couldn't. But as an adult, maybe I should have looked back with a little knowledge and perspective."

A smile flickered on her lips.

He went on. "I've been doing some thinking this week. Reexamining parts of my life."

"That sounds healthy."

"I guess you've done a lot of that, too."

This time the smile arrived and actually stayed a second. "You can say that again."

"Jess says you talk about me."

"I boast." Her lips curved again. "I'm so proud of you, Evan. You were the most ambitious kid in town, even though you got no encouragement at home. You worked so hard and you made it all happen. You're such a big success."

"I've done okay. But it could be more rewarding." Now why had he told her that?

"Really?" She cocked her head to one side. "How so? Oh, Evan, I really hoped you'd found everything you were looking for." She looked genuinely concerned.

In that moment, Evan realized he was having a real conversation with his mother. One where she focused on him, and apparently cared about his happiness. The thought stunned him. He dropped his head, fiddled with his coffee cup, blinked a few times to fight back tears.

Then he looked up at her. "My definition of success had to do with money and status. Oh, it also had to do with being the best at what I do, but I've been using my skills to help rich people get richer."

Her brows drew together. "Mmm. I'm sure you can make a lot of money doing that, but I can see why it might not be so satisfying. What would you rather do?"

"Help average people achieve goals that are meaningful to them. Like owning their own home, having enough money to retire comfortably, and so on."

She had a really nice, warm smile. "Most people need that kind of help. We're pretty hopeless about saving, setting priorities. It's not that we don't want to, it's just so intimidating figuring out how."

"Exactly." He grinned at her. "As for the rich people, I kind of like helping them part with some money to fund worthwhile causes."

"Well, sure. And I bet that makes them feel better about themselves, too."

She got it. His smile widened.

She smiled back, eyes looking misty. Then she said, "Evan, I'm so sorry, but I have clients booked and I can't leave Kate on her own."

A sense of responsibility. Time management. Hard to believe this was Brooke Kincaid.

"Of course. It was rude of me to show up without calling, but—"

"But you were afraid you'd . . ."

"You can say it. Chicken out. Yes, I was."

"I'm so glad you didn't."

"Me, too."

He threw a few dollars on the table beside the still-full cups. "I'll walk you back."

Outside the door to Beauty Is You, she stopped and he looked down at her.

"About A.A.," she said softly, "and making amends to people we've harmed . , . I'd like to do that, Evan. I know I can never make up for all the hurt I caused you when you were a boy, but I do love you and I want you to know that if there's anything I can ever do . . ."

"You've done a lot today. Mom." It was the first time he'd called her that since he was a little kid, and the word felt unwieldy on his tongue.

"It sounds good to hear you call me Mom," she said, voice thready with tears.

He didn't remind her that she'd never wanted him to. Perhaps she remembered, perhaps not. Today, it didn't matter. "It's been good, both of us being able to speak the truth to each other. Having you really listen and try to understand."

"It's been wonderful." Voice still trembling, she asked, "Will I ever see you—hear from you—again?"

"I . . . wouldn't be at all surprised."

"I'll understand if you decide not to contact me. And I'll always be grateful for today. Gosh, sweetheart, it's the nicest thing that's ever happened to me." Tears slipped down her cheeks.

His eyes filled again. "It's been nice for me, too."

So far, neither had touched the other. Now, as tear-drenched eyes gazed into tear-drenched eyes, his mother took an awkward step forward. Evan lifted arms that felt clumsy, and they hugged.

She felt strange in his arms, small yet not fragile, and the scent of some tropical flower drifted up from her hair. Her arms tightened around him. His mother was hugging him. Like she really meant it.

They broke apart, both swiping at their eyes. Then, without another word, she hurried inside the beauty salon.

Evan strode down the street, not seeing a thing, blinking to control the tears.

That afternoon, as the group rode back into the barnyard, sun kissed and windblown from hours in the fresh air, Jess glanced worriedly at Evan. He'd been so quiet all day. He didn't look sad or worried, just thoughtful. Was he planning the best strategy for tackling Madisun's parents? They had agreed to make their visit later today.

When the guests streamed up to their cabins, Evan said to Madisun and Jess, "Give me fifteen minutes?"

"Sure," Madisun said, her voice ragged with nerves.

"We'll make your father listen to reason," Jess reassured her.

The two women were cleaning tack when Evan reappeared. Madisun let out a whistle, and Jess stopped dead. Here she was in grubby jeans, and Evan was wearing a charcoal suit, crisp white shirt, and classy tie. He looked almost like a stranger, and very handsome in his business clothes. New York Evan.

She glanced down and had to laugh. He wore his cowboy boots, but he'd polished them until they gleamed under the thin coating of dust. "Hey, cowboy, you gonna wear those things when you get back to the city?"

He grinned back. "You never know. It'll give Angelica, my assistant, a laugh."

Yup, he had an office, staff, clients. A business. A life. She had to keep remembering those things.

Madisun said, with a note of hero worship, "I think you look wonderful, Evan."

"Thanks, but will I make the right impression on your parents?"

"They'll be blown away."

Her parents had damned well better be blown away, Evan thought. He'd do everything in his power to make them agree to his proposal. He knew Madisun was old enough to leave home if she wanted, but he also knew she took her responsibilities to her siblings seriously, so it was important that her parents supported his plan.

Jess took her own truck, and Evan rode in Madisun's decades-old Chevy. She took the highway into town, then branched off on a back road, ending up in a downtrodden area where the houses were shacks or trailers in poor repair, and most of the yards grew junk rather than flowers. "I lived one street over and two blocks down," he said, and she darted him a nervous smile.

They parked and got out, waiting for Jess, behind them, to do the same. Together, with Madisun in the middle, they walked up the front steps of a run-down shack where shabby toys littered the yard and a few flowers struggled to bloom. The door was open, but a ripped screen blocked the doorway.

Madisun knocked on the door frame and called, "Mom, Dad, we're here."

She opened the screen door and ushered them in. "Wait here."

Evan studied the cluttered room with its shabby furniture, dirty dishes, and overflowing ashtrays. A cute black-haired baby wearing a diaper and nothing else sat on a corner of the stained rug, chewing on an unclothed Barbie doll with straggly hair. A pair of brown eyes studied them curiously, but the baby didn't make a sound.

He glanced at Jess, who looked grim. The sound of raised voices came from another room, and then a flushed Madisun returned. "My parents will be right out. The kids—except for Susie here—are at the park." She scooped the baby up in her arms, and the little girl cooed with pleasure.

The three of them sat, not saying anything, for about five minutes. Then a woman came in, followed by a man. Mrs. Joe's pants and sweatshirt were faded but clean, and her hair was neatly combed and held back with a red band. Mr. Joe wore a tattered undershirt and jeans that sagged under a beer belly. His gait was none too steady, and he clutched an open beer bottle.

Evan's gut clenched. This was a man who beat his wife, his daughter.

Madisun sprang to her feet, gripping the baby, but clearly didn't know what to do.

Jess took control of the situation. Rising, she said, "Hello, Mr. and Mrs. Joe. It's nice to see you again. I'd like you to meet Evan Kincaid, an old friend of mine. He grew up here, but lives in New York now."

Evan stood, too, and moved toward them with his hand extended. They seemed surprised, but returned his handshake. No one offered food or drink, and he was relieved. He didn't want this visit to last any longer than it had to.

"Mary-Anne says you have some notion of paying for her schooling?" Mrs. Joe said, barely loud enough to hear.

"Let's sit down and talk about it," Evan said.

When everyone was settled, he outlined his plan.

"Why wouldya do this?" Madisun's father said suspiciously, slurring his words.

His wife darted a glance under her eyelashes at her husband, then another one at Evan. "She's a good girl." Again, her words were spoken quietly, but her voice was firm.

"I know she is," Evan said. "She deserves a chance to get an education and explore her options."

"You can trust Evan," Jess broke in. "I know this arrangement sounds unusual, but believe me, he respects Mad—Mary-Anne—and won't do anything to hurt her."

"He's tryin' to buy the girl," Mr. Joe huffed.

"No!" Evan and Jess said at the same time, as Madisun, who'd been hovering in a doorway, gasped. Perhaps she squeezed Susie, because the baby let out a cry.

"It's not like that," Jess said. "All he wants from Mary-Anne is that she go to school and study hard."

"I want that for her," Mrs. Joe said softly, sadly, "but the thing is, she helps us feed the kids. I don't see how we can do without her."

"She'll have part-time work," Evan said. "She'll send money home. As long as you"—he broke off and fixed Mr. Joe with a level gaze—"leave your wife and children alone."

He heard Jess and Madisun both give soft gasps, but he didn't take his eyes off Mr. Joe.

The man glared at him, face going bright red, and Evan tensed. *Just give me an excuse*. He'd never in his life punched a man, but he was ready to. The fact that he'd enjoy it shocked him.

After a moment, the other man dropped his gaze and muttered, "Dunno what in hell you're talkin' 'bout."

Evan realized his hands had fisted. He forced himself

to unclench his fingers. He swallowed hard, then said it. "My father hit me and my mother. I do know what I'm talking about."

Another soft gasp from Jess.

Mr. Joe's eyes lifted, fixing on his face with sullenness and a touch of fear.

Evan went on. "A real man doesn't hit women or children. If a coward does that, someone will stop him. Like the cops. That's what happened to my father. Do you understand me?"

Mr. Joe gave a grunt.

Evan knew it wouldn't be that simple, but it was a start.

The Joes didn't ask for further details. Evan imagined Jess's parents if a strange man had offered a similar deal. The questions would have gone on for days, and they'd have demanded references and checked them in detail.

It had been the Blys who had turned the police on his father. Who had protected him. He thought he might call Wade Bly and have a chat about Madisun's family. Jess and her mom tried to shelter him from stress, but from what Evan had seen, Wade was still a strong man. A man who'd prefer to protect than be protected.

Madisun walked Evan and Jess out to Jess's truck. She still clutched Susie in her arms, but suddenly she handed the baby to Jess. She wrapped her arms around Evan and hugged him tight, her whole body trembling. "I didn't think they'd actually agree. And, Evan, thanks for what you said about him leaving Mom and the kids alone."

He hugged her back. "I'll make sure someone keeps an eye on him." Then he pushed her away a foot, holding on to her shoulders and gazing down at her. "It's going to be hard. Leaving your mom and your brothers and sisters. Leaving Jess, the horses, Kathy and Will."

"I know." She met his gaze unflinchingly. "But I want to do it. I need to. I won't let you down."

He smiled at that, and released her. "You won't. Just realize,

I don't have any specific expectations. I want you to be true to yourself, work hard, keep in touch with me. I'm not going to second-guess your decisions, but if you ever want input, I'll be glad to provide it."

"I'll count on that." She darted a glance at Jess. "I hope we can keep in touch, too."

Jess grinned and handed the baby back. "That's for sure."

Fat raindrops began to patter on their shoulders and Jess said, "Best get Susie inside, Madisun."

The girl sprinted for the door as Evan and Jess climbed hurriedly into the truck. She started the engine and turned the wipers to high because the rain was now pouring down. The radio came on, some twangy country song, but Jess clicked it off.

They drove in silence for a few minutes, and then she rested a gentle hand on his arm. "We'll keep an eye on the Joes. Dave and I, and Mom and Pa."

"Thanks." Dave again. The man she was always able to count on.

She left her hand on his arm until she had to shift gears at a corner. "Only a couple more days until you're back home."

"I've had an amazing time."

As she pulled onto the highway, she asked tentatively, "You're not going to see Brooke?"

He remained silent until she turned to him, and saw his grin.

"What?" she said.

"Saw her this morning."

"Evan!"

"Jess, watch the road!" The truck had swerved onto the shoulder.

She slammed on the brakes, causing the truck to fishtail in the gravel, and then it jolted to a stop. "You saw her and you didn't tell me? I'm going to kill you!" She examined his face. "It went well?"

He nodded. "We actually talked. I see what you mean about her having changed."

"So, what now? You're going to stay in touch?"

"I . . . think so. We left it up in the air but . . . well, we hugged each other. It . . . felt good."

Jess flung herself across the seat and gave him an awkward but enthusiastic hug of her own. "That's so great!"

He held her close—the third woman who'd been in his arms today, each of them special to him in her own way. But Jess was the one who made his blood zing. He let out a groan. "Damn, woman, it's hard to be just friends."

She raised her head. "I know. Since you arrived I feel as . . . hormonal as a teenager."

"Me, too." He wanted to stroke raindrops from her soft cheek, kiss those full lips, the same pink as the wild roses. Pull her over on his lap and make out like teenagers. "And since Cynthia and I have broken up . . ."

"I know. But there's no point in starting a relationship when I'm here and you'll be in New York."

"No. It couldn't work."

She shoved herself away from him, and back over to the driver's seat. "I'm not usually so sensible. But as it is, it's going to be hard enough letting you go."

"I know." He forced a smile. "This time we really will e-mail."

She rolled her eyes and started the truck.

He felt like asking her to have dinner with him so they could spend just a little more time together, but he didn't think he could handle the temptation.

By the time she dropped Evan at the Crazy Horse, the rain was thundering down. Jess was grateful she'd driven the truck today, rather than ridden Conti. As it was, she could barely see the road as she drove to the feed store for supplies, then to the drugstore, and finally home to Bly Ranch. A wind had come up, too, and she had to struggle against it as she made her way from the truck to the kitchen door.

Soaked and breathless, she slammed the door behind her and shook herself like a dog, spraying the Blue Heeler for a change, before she bent to greet him. The empty, dark room reminded her she had the place to herself. Her parents were out for supper and bridge, and Robin was spending the night with Dave so they could work on her science project.

"It's just you and me, boy," she murmured to Pepper as she let him out to do his business. And she'd keep busy with chores, because otherwise she might brave the storm, hop back in the truck, drive over to the Crazy Horse, and give Evan the passionate kiss that had been building inside her for days.

The message light on the answering machine was blinking. She'd turned off her cell earlier, when visiting Madisun's parents. She should turn her cell back on, and check the answering machine as well, but really she just wanted to change and get on with a whirlwind of chores.

The home phone rang, and she stared at it indecisively. It was probably for her parents. She let it go through to message, and heard Dave's frantic voice. "Jess? Jessie, where are you?"

She grabbed up the receiver. "Dave? I'm here."

"Oh, Jessie-girl . . ." Dave's voice broke, and in that moment her world turned upside down.

Not Robin, please don't let it be Robin. I'll do anything if it's not Robin. But she knew it was. Tears slid down her cheeks. "How bad?" she whispered.

"Bad. But not . . . hopeless." She heard him suck in a raspy breath, obviously fighting for control.

Not hopeless? My God, how bad is it?

"She was hit by a car," he said. "It's my fault, Jessie. It was raining and I should have picked her up from Kimiko's. She walked, wearing dark clothing. A car came around the corner too fast. The driver braked, the car skidded, and . . . Jesus!" He drew another wavery breath.

"Dave! How badly is she hurt?"

"They think her spleen's lacerated, maybe ruptured. Blood may be leaking into her abdominal cavity. They need to operate, may have to remove it."

"Spleen." What the hell was a spleen? "You can live without a spleen, can't you?"

"Yes, but if they operate she may need a transfusion."

"Oh, my God! And they don't have enough blood?" It was something they'd feared ever since baby Robin's blood had been typed.

"No, the blood of hers we had frozen isn't enough. They've contacted the rare-blood banks and they're flying some in, but it'll take hours. Might not even be able to land a plane or helicopter here if this weather keeps up. They thought of taking her out by helicopter and getting her down to Vancouver, but that'd take time, too, and be a real bumpy ride."

She sucked in a breath and let it out. "Evan." She said the word with dread.

"Yes. There's no one in Caribou Crossing with the same blood type. Evan and his dad were the only ones."

"I know!" she snapped. Her panicked mind couldn't think straight. "We don't have a choice, do we?"

"I'd give anything if we did. But it's Robin's life."

"Oh Lord, Dave, I never wanted him to know."

His laugh was the essence of bitterness. "Nor did I."

She swallowed. "We're wasting time. I'll drive over and get him."

"You'll tell him?"

"I can hardly haul him off to the hospital with no explanation," she said grimly. "Yeah, I'll tell him."

She slammed the phone into the cradle.

Robin. Oh, God, let Robin be okay.

Still in her damp clothing, she threw open the kitchen door, barely noticing when Pepper darted inside, and ran for the truck. She had no idea how she made it to the Crazy Horse, and it seemed only seconds had passed before she was pounding at the door of Evan's cabin. *Please let him be here, not up at the lodge.*

The door opened and she darted in. He took one look at her face, then grabbed her shoulders. "What's wrong?"

She shook off his hands. "Robin's been in an accident."

"Oh, no. I'm so sorry. Is there anything I can do?"

"She needs blood."

He nodded slowly, obviously not comprehending. "A transfusion? Is the hospital low on blood? You need donors?"

"Yes!" If only it were that simple. Could she let him go on thinking it was?

"Of course I'll help." He was reaching past her for the jacket that hung on a peg by the door. Then he stopped and pulled his hand back. "I might not be able to donate. I have an incredibly rare blood type."

She stared up at him. Her panic stilled as she realized the moment had finally come. Now that it had, she felt almost calm. "I know. So does Robin," she said.

He frowned. "Really? But it's so rare. Dave's the same type?"

A reprieve? She could let him believe it.

No. It was time for the truth. She shook her head. "No one in town is the same type. Just Robin. And you."

"But . . . Oh, my God!" His face went dead white and he groped for the back of a chair.

Unable to meet his eyes, she stared instead at his clenched fingers. She spoke the words she had never wanted to say to him. "She's your daughter."

"But . . ."

Jess's sense of urgency returned. "I know you want an explanation, but, Evan, she's hurt. She needs blood. Now!"

"Yes," he said slowly, unwinding his fingers from the chair back. Then, more quickly, "Yes, of course." And he was in motion, thrusting his feet into his boots.

At the truck, he yanked open the passenger door. "Get in. I'll drive. You're crying."

She was?

He ran around to the driver's side as she leaped in.

Concentrating on the immediate, the physical, Evan adjusted the seat, slammed the shifter into first gear, and hammered his foot down on the gas pedal. The truck fishtailed in the muddy gravel, then he shifted into second, the tires gripped, and they were off. Rain thundered down and there was a wicked wind, too, strong enough to shake the sturdy truck.

"She was in an accident?" he asked. "How badly is she injured?"

"Spleen. Maybe ruptured. They have to operate."

Spleen. Upper abdomen, left side. Once he'd had a mild case of mononucleosis and his spleen had been swollen and painful. What the hell did the spleen do?

In a raspy voice, she said, "They say she can live without her spleen. It's the surgery, the blood, that's the problem."

The blood. That damned, weird blood he'd inherited. Why the hell did he have to pass it on to his daughter?

Daughter. *She's your daughter*, Jess had said. Daughter. Daughter. The word rang in his head.

Jess's daughter was his daughter.

The ripped condom. But Jess had said she was okay.

She hadn't *told* him. She hadn't even told him, because she wanted Dave Cousins—the guy all the girls thought was perfect—to be her child's father.

"Does Dave know?" he asked harshly.

"About the accident? Yes, he's the one who called me."

"Not that! Does he know I'm Rob . . . Robin's father?"

Robin. He had a daughter named Robin. That cute kid with the ponytail, that accomplished rider, the girl with poise beyond her years—that kid was his.

"Of course Dave knows," she snapped.

Great, the only one she'd left in the dark was the sperm donor. He could throttle her.

But when he glared over at Jess, the lights of a passing car reflected off the tears on her cheeks. Crap. The only thing that mattered right now was the girl. He had to get to the hospital and let them stick a needle in his arm. Everything else . . . he'd think about later.

When he pulled the truck up under the EMERGENCY sign, he and Jess leaped out and raced for the door. He flung it open and Jess flew past him, straight into a man's arms. Dave Cousins. An older version of the boy Evan had secretly admired.

His daughter's father. Another man he'd like to punch out.

Jess and Dave clung together as Evan walked slowly toward them. They were in a private cocoon, oblivious to him. Jess sobbed and Dave's eyes leaked tears as he said brokenly, "It's my fault. I'm so sorry."

His fault? It was Dave's fault that Robin's life was in danger? Evan's hands formed fists.

Jess raised her head, glared at Dave, and said fiercely, "Don't blame yourself, Dave. Just don't do that!" Then she burrowed her face back into his shoulder.

As Jess sobbed, Dave murmured, "Oh, Jessie, I can't stand to think of her hurting, not our little girl."

Evan had never felt more superfluous. They were family—this woman, this man, and the girl who lay in a bed somewhere nearby. And yet he was here because his blood ran in the child's veins. He was necessary, yet unwanted.

As if he'd spoken aloud, Dave raised his head and stared at him over Jess's bent head.

Dave drew in a breath, audibly. "Evan," he said evenly. His eyes were red and swollen, his cheeks wet, yet there was immense dignity in his face. As easily as Evan read the other man's agony over the accident, he recognized how much Dave hated having to ask for his help. How much he feared having Evan enter his daughter's life.

His anger died. "Dave." He nodded an acknowledgment. "Where's the doctor?"

Jess peeled herself from Dave's arms and wiped a forearm haphazardly across her sodden face. "Where's Robin? I want to see her. And the doctor. Let's get on with this."

Chapter Fourteen

A gray-haired nurse took Evan to a cubicle, and soon the blood was draining from his arm as she grilled him about HIV and hepatitis.

"My blood's okay," he said. "I'm often called to donate, and they're always testing it."

"That's a relief." She patted his shoulder.

Did she know he was Robin's biological father? If so, how had Dave explained that to her? And why was he even thinking about this stuff? All that mattered was for Robin to be okay.

After he'd donated, rested, eaten, and drank juice, Evan was finally set free. When he walked into the waiting room, Jess and Dave were huddled together on a couch and didn't acknowledge him.

He sat on a chair across the room, out of their line of vision, and waited, deliberately trying to keep his mind a blank. After an hour or so, a surgeon went over to Jess and Dave. Evan eavesdropped, to hear that Robin had had a splenectomy and was in recovery doing very well.

Their arms wrapped around each other, Jess and Dave followed the doctor to the recovery room.

So. Evan had served his purpose, and without even seeing

Robin. No one here needed—or wanted—him anymore. And he was damned tired. Relieved, pissed off, exhausted.

He called a taxi and waited just inside the hospital door, watching the still-pouring rain until it arrived. The driver wanted to talk but Evan slumped back and closed his eyes, feeling utterly drained. He'd had a bucket of blood pumped out of his body, which could certainly account for some of it. Then there was Jess and Dave's intimacy, which depressed him for no good reason. And his fear for the safety of a girl he didn't even know.

But mostly, what had knocked him for a loop was finding out—a decade late—that he was a father.

Jess had lied to him, back then and for the last week and a half.

When the cab pulled up at his door, Evan reached into his pocket. Empty. He'd left his wallet and key inside the unlocked cabin. He went in, found the wallet, and paid the driver.

Then he stood aimlessly in the middle of the living room. On the coffee table, he saw a note and a covered tray. The note read: *Evan, are you OK? Did you go out for dinner like you did last week? Here's a snack, in case you're hungry. Don't forget—we're showing* Return to Snowy River *in the lounge tonight!* It was signed "Kathy," with a happy face.

He stared at the curving smile, then lifted the lid off the tray and studied the artful arrangement of cold meats, cheeses, home-baked buns, fruit, and cookies. He had no appetite. Not for food, nor for company.

He opened the fridge, saw that she'd left some fruit drinks, then closed the door again and poured a glass of cold water, which he drained in one long swallow.

He glanced at the time. They'd still be up, probably just finishing the movie. Maybe he should walk over and tell them he was okay, but instead he put the cover back on the tray, sank into a chair, and switched off the light.

Why hadn't Jess told him?

His aching heart supplied an answer. She might've had a crush on him, wanted to share a special night with him, but it was Dave she'd loved.

Why should that bother him? He hadn't wanted Jess to love him, hadn't wanted to have a child. But how could she have been so callous about his rights, his feelings?

And what about now? Where did he stand now? Where did he want to stand?

They obviously didn't want him in their lives. Well, Jess wanted him as a friend. A casual friend. Not only had she resisted a physical relationship, she'd gone to pains to make sure he never met Robin, and she'd refused his assistance with her dream project. What kind of friends did that make them?

Could he possibly be friends with a woman who had deceived him so cruelly?

He groaned, rose, and began to pace. Why had he listened to Gianni? Why had he come here?

If he hadn't come . . .

Jesus, if he hadn't come, Robin might not have received the blood she needed. He drew in a shaky breath. Thank God for Gianni.

He couldn't remember ever feeling so tired. He ached, too, somewhere deep inside. Jess was right; as a child he'd learned to block his feelings. He had a good brain, so he'd focused on reason and intellect. This week he'd begun to think maybe emotions could be good, too. Now he remembered how painfully they could hurt.

He stumbled into the bathroom on heavy legs and bent down to turn on the bathtub faucet. On the marble ledge around the deep-set tub was a wicker tray holding an assortment of aromatic oils and bath salts. He chose a packet at random and tossed it into the water. Peeling off his clothes, he felt so slow and clumsy it was like he'd been drugged.

The air filled with an appealing aroma. He couldn't define

it exactly, but it smelled like the outdoors here. Mostly green scents, like pine and hay, but also something flowery, like those heady wild roses. He sank into the water. Once in, he wondered how he'd ever find the energy to rise again. He was too tired to even think, and that was a good thing. He wadded up a towel and leaned back, resting his head on it.

Tomorrow, there would be things to think about, and to discuss with Jess. Tomorrow, maybe he'd let himself feel anger and hurt and God knows what else, but for now he welcomed oblivion.

Some time later, he woke to the sound of a soft knock on the door of his cabin. Kathy, he figured. He should answer, but he didn't feel like talking to anyone. The water was cold, though. He should get up.

He heard the cabin door open. "Evan?"

It was Jess. Jesus, had something gone wrong with Robin? He should have stayed, should never have surrendered to his childish hurt feelings. He lurched to his feet, splashing water all over, and dashed out of the bathroom. "What's wrong?"

Jess stared at about 170 pounds of lean, muscled, dripping, naked male.

This wasn't what she had in mind when she decided to drop by, see if he happened to be awake, and, if not, leave a note.

Her gaze dipped from his face to his chest, down to his abs and past. Oh man, had he grown up and filled out. A blush heated her cheeks and she forced herself to look at his face.

"Is Robin all right?" he demanded.

"Oh! Oh, yes. Did you think . . . ? Jeez, Ev, I'm sorry. I didn't mean to scare you. Or, uh, disturb your bath."

She tried to control her eyes but they seemed to have a mind of their own and kept shifting their gaze downward.

He turned on his heel and stalked off to the bathroom,

giving her a perfect opportunity to confirm that his butt truly was world class.

He returned, tying a navy terry bathrobe. "You're sure she's fine?"

Embarrassed by the attention she'd been paying his body, Jess snapped, "Of course I'm sure. Do you think I'd be here otherwise? Dave's with her. I'm on my way home to change my clothes and get some things for her." She smiled at a memory. "She even gave me a list. And she said I should stay there and get some sleep, because I've been looking so tired lately."

"She's awake?"

"She was, for long enough to order me around."

"And she's really okay?"

"Physically, she'll be fine. Out of the hospital in less than a week, but not back to her normal activities for six to eight weeks. If we can tie her down that long."

"I gather she's an active kid?"

"You can say that again. Rob's had her share of broken bones and bumps and bruises because she's fearless. But she's always back up, back at it. It drives Dave crazy, he worries so much." She smiled. "I was exactly the same as a kid."

"And you're different now?"

"Uh, maybe not."

They were both quiet a moment, and then he said, "Jess, you should have told me." His expression had gone cold. Bitter.

Why had she come? She was too tired to talk about this. "When I found out I was pregnant?" she asked defensively. "Evan, I knew you didn't want kids."

He looked almost as exhausted as she felt. "That's true. But I had the right to know."

How could she argue with that? She shrugged helplessly, feeling overwhelmed. "I can't do this. Not now. Please?"

After a moment he gave a grudging nod. "Okay. You've been through a lot tonight. And the other night, with Petula."

Petula. Jess closed her eyes suddenly. *Jesus, Robin could have died, too.* She gulped against a surge of nausea.

A speeding car, a dark afternoon, rain, and she could have lost her precious daughter. She drew a breath and it came out as a choky sob. Unable to control the tears, she buried her face in her hands.

Strong hands touched hers gently and drew them away. Then Evan pulled her into his arms. "Hey, I'm sorry," he murmured as she rested her face just over his heart and let soft terry cloth absorb her tears. His heartbeat was strong and regular, a soothing presence, just like the hands that stroked her back. And his voice, saying, "It's okay now, Jess. Everything's fine. Robin's going to be all right."

She lifted her head an inch. "I know, I really know. It's just . . . relief, I guess."

"You said she was awake and talking? What did she say?"

She gave a shaky smile. "She was mad at herself for being careless. Already thinking ahead to being back on her feet, back riding. It was such a relief to hear her sounding so normal."

"Your parents know what's going on? I didn't see them at the hospital."

"They were at friends' playing bridge. I called them there. The doctor said they couldn't visit Rob tonight, and Mom and I worry about Pa getting upset, so I told them not to come to the hospital. They'll be there tomorrow."

She frowned. "I want to be there, too, but it's the guests' last day at the Crazy Horse, and it's not fair to make Madisun handle it all on her own."

"Robin will probably sleep most of the day. Your parents will be there."

"And Dave."

"Yeah."

"He's with her now. He said Rob was right and I should go home and get some sleep, but I don't see how I can."

"Is he the only one who knows I'm, uh, Robin's biological father?"

She pulled back in the circle of his arms and gazed up at him. "Yes. When I found out I was pregnant, he was the first person I told. When we decided to get married, we wanted Robin to know how much we both loved her. We didn't want her—or anyone—having doubts. We wanted her to be secure in a happy, loving family."

A corner of his mouth tilted down. "Yeah, I'd have wanted that for her, too. She's a lucky girl."

Jess could almost feel his pain. She knew him so well. He was thinking of his own parents. He was happy for Robin, but sad for himself and all he'd missed.

Something occurred to her and she stiffened. "Your parents denied you a happy childhood," she said slowly.

He shrugged. "That's old news. I'm long past it."

She doubted it very much, but that wasn't what was on her mind right now. "And then I denied you Robin. Yes, it *was* your right to know. I shouldn't have decided for you." Dang, she wasn't saying this right. "Does that make any sense?"

"You're beating yourself up because I've now struck out twice. I didn't have a happy childhood, and I didn't get to see my own daughter have a happy childhood."

Her eyes flooded again. "And it's my fault."

He sighed. "I admit I was pissed when I found out, but I've also got to admit you were probably right. I didn't want kids. God knows what I'd have done."

Jess remained quiet, and he went on. "Okay, maybe your intentions were good. Mostly you wanted the best for Robin, and you gave it to her. I'm sure Dave made a better father than I ever would have."

She winced. "I think you'd be a fantastic father."

"Yeah, well . . . You're my most loyal supporter. You always have been."

That's because I love you. The words leaped into her mind so forcefully she was scared she'd said them aloud.

She glanced at his face again, seeing how tired and sad he looked. He was suffering, and it was because of her. She'd do anything if she could take the pain away.

Yes, she loved him. Always had. Likely always would. How could she ever have fooled herself into thinking otherwise? She hid her face against his chest, afraid he might read the truth in her eyes.

He rested his chin on the top of her head. "Oh, Jess."

"I should go."

"You shouldn't be driving. I'll take you home. Or . . . you could stay here."

"Stay?" Her voice quavered. What was he suggesting?

"We're both exhausted. It'd be nice to hold each other. Maybe you'd get a little sleep."

And suddenly Jess was so tired she couldn't stay on her feet a moment longer. "Yes, please," she murmured as her knees began to sag.

He scooped her up, carried her into the bedroom, and eased her onto the bed. "Is there anyone you need to call?"

"No. My folks think I'm at the hospital and Dave thinks I'm home sleeping." She yawned widely. "I have his cell. He'll call if anything happens."

"Good." He tugged her boots off, went to turn off the light, then came to lie beside her in the dark.

"Oh, yes," she sighed as his body curved protectively around hers, fitting his front to her back. And just that quickly, she drifted off.

* * *

Jess woke as suddenly as she'd fallen asleep. Her clothing was too confining, she was thirsty, there was a warm presence at her back. . . .

Her body froze as she catalogued the sensations. A delicious outdoorsy scent, the roughness of terry cloth, the whisper of breath against her neck. Evan. She was in Evan's arms.

Robin! It all came back in a flash, and adrenaline surged. Dave's cell phone was in her bag. Had it rung, and was that what had woken her?

Hurriedly, she scrambled off the bed. She heard Evan call her name as she darted into the living room and, by the light of moon and stars through the uncurtained windows, found her bag. She pulled out the phone and checked the display. No messages, thank God, and less than an hour had passed since she'd arrived at the cabin. Still, with the phone in her hand, she couldn't resist calling the hospital.

A nurse reassured her Robin was fine, sleeping soundly. Dave was asleep, too, on a cot beside Robin.

"Everything all right?" Evan had come to join her.

"She's fine."

He stood in front of her, hair tousled, bathrobe askew. The man she loved. The man she'd made a baby—a wonderful daughter—with.

She knew what she wanted that night at Zephyr Lake. One perfect memory, before the boy she loved left town. But that memory had been ruined by his denial, his abandonment.

Now she knew with absolute clarity that she wanted the same thing again. Just one night.

She stepped forward and leaned against him, her mouth touching his chest. She didn't kiss him, just rested her lips there, feeling the warmth of his skin, the sexy tickle of curls of hair. She blew a soft puff of air against him.

He gave a start. "Jess?"

She put her arms around him and, after a moment, his came up to circle her, holding her loosely, tentatively.

She thought about the fact that he was naked under the bathrobe. Thought about how amazing he'd looked, wet from the bath. Every cell in her body was aware of him.

And awareness was moving toward yearning. For him, too. Under the robe, she felt his arousal growing. She pressed her lower body closer.

He sucked in a breath. "Jess?"

Her body flirted with his as she tilted her hips from side to side. She raised up slightly on her toes and pressed a kiss into the hollow between his collarbones. His pulse jumped erratically, and his hands found her backside and pulled her tight against him.

She loved him and she wanted him.

She eased away so she could look into his eyes. Before she could say anything, he leaned down and kissed her. It was like coming home. His lips were the perfect combination—soft yet firm, gentle yet demanding. They caressed, teased, and nibbled. Then his tongue stroked the crease between her own lips, and she opened for him—opening not just her mouth but her heart.

His body shuddered and, in response, hers did, too.

His tongue seduced hers in a mating dance that set her hips to moving in an echoing rhythm. Her jeans were too confining. She wanted to be rid of the restrictive denim. She wanted to free him from the bathrobe and feel every inch of his skin against hers.

But first she needed reassurance. "Ev? If we do this, promise me we won't lose our friendship. It can't be like last time."

He shook his head. "It won't be. I won't lose you twice."

She pulled back and fumbled with the belt of the robe. He'd secured it with a loop that pulled free easily. The strip of cloth fell to the floor. She yanked the robe apart and gazed her fill at his strong, beautifully masculine body.

After a few seconds he said, in a rough voice, "You just

window shopping or did you want to try something on for size?"

"All of it. I want all of it."

"Greedy," he murmured, pulling her back into his arms.

The robe hung loose from his shoulders and she slipped her hands down to curve around that firm butt.

He reached for the front of her shirt.

"They snap," she murmured.

"Hmm?"

"They're not real buttons, they're snaps." She hooked one hand in the top of each half of her Western shirt, tugged gently, and the top snap popped open.

"Got it." He moved her hands away and replaced them with his. His first tug was too gentle. He tried again and the next snap popped. He grinned.

Then he leaned down and kissed the bare skin he'd just revealed. He pulled open the snaps one by one—"Love this shirt"—and kissed, then licked, then kissed again. His lips and tongue blazed a path of fire straight down the center of her body, and she squirmed with need.

He pulled the shirt out of her jeans and finished unbuttoning it. Then he undid her belt and the button at her waist, eased the zipper down an inch, and tongued her navel.

Needing to feel his hardness against her again, she tugged on his hair, urging him to his feet. As he stood, she slid the robe from his shoulders.

She rose on tiptoe to rain kisses on his cheeks, his nose, finally his lips.

His mouth opened under hers and he kissed her hungrily. Then he broke the kiss and eased her down so she stood flat on the ground. He rested his lips against her forehead, and she felt warm air against her skin as he breathed in rough pants. His chest rose and fell against hers, both of them heaving as hard as if they'd just run a race.

He put his hands on her shoulders and separated their

bodies. "Jess, are you sure? If we're going to stop, we have to do it now."

She felt glorious. He wanted her, unreservedly. Yes, this was the night she'd wanted when she was seventeen. *Oh, Lord!* "Tell me you have condoms."

"Oh yeah, I have condoms." He picked her up and swung her around. "How many do you want, Jess?"

She threw back her head and laughed. "That depends more on you than on me, doesn't it, big boy?"

He put her down, but only to change his grip. He hoisted her into his arms as he'd done when he'd carried her to bed before, but this time she wasn't the slightest bit sleepy. She savored every moment. It made her feel feminine, almost delicate. He was so much bigger than she was, so much stronger. She loved it.

"Caveman," she purred as he strode toward the bedroom.

He growled in suitably primitive fashion and tossed her onto the four-poster bed. She bounced once, then settled into the softness of the duvet. When she tried to sit up, the puffy spread enveloped her like a cloud.

"Stay still," he ordered as he pulled off one of her socks.

She grimaced. There was absolutely nothing erotic about old socks and sweaty feet.

But Evan apparently thought differently. His hands lingered on her right foot, the last one he'd desocked. He pressed gently, kneaded, massaged, and she groaned with pleasure. At the end of the day her feet always hurt, and this was sheer bliss. Almost, it distracted her from the ache between her thighs.

"Feel good?" he murmured.

"Mmm-hmm." The bedroom was dim and she could barely see his face, but she thought he was smiling. "Do the other?"

"Your wish is my command."

When he finished with her feet, she said, "Turn the lamp on. I want to see you."

"Good idea." He clicked the switch, then slid her jeans zipper the rest of the way down. She thrust her heels into the bed and raised her hips to help him pull the jeans off. Dang, how embarrassing. They were decorated with horse drool and other substances she'd rather not think about.

Evan didn't show any signs of squeamishness as he slowly drew the denim down her thighs, over her knees, and finally pulled the jeans free of her body.

She watched him as he studied her. The dim golden light must have been flattering. His face told her he found her beautiful, even before he murmured, "God, but you're lovely, Jess."

She glanced down at her body and for a moment thought of Cynthia. Model thin, chic, and no doubt she had expensive, sexy lingerie.

Jess was lean enough, but muscular for a woman. Boring blue cotton sports bra and bikini panties. And, horror of horrors, stubble on her legs. Illuminated clearly by the lamplight. Why on earth had she asked him to turn on the light?

She glanced at his erection. It didn't seem daunted by her stubble.

Oh yeah, this was why she'd wanted the light. So she could study his body, in all its perfection. She gave a little growl of desire. "You really have filled out, Evan Kincaid."

"Like a puppy. I had big feet. You ought to have known I'd grow into them."

"It's not your big feet I'm interested in, buster. Come here."

Obediently, he lay down beside her.

She turned on her side and her body met his with a soft impact that made her shudder with desire. Freed from denim, her lower body pressed firmly against his, with only a thin strip of cotton between them. She moved, jockeying for the perfect position where he could rub . . . Yes! Right there.

And then she remembered. "Condoms," she murmured against his lips.

"Damn, I forgot."

His struggle to rise as the duvet imprisoned him had her chuckling. When he went into the bathroom she climbed under the comforter, hiding her unshaven legs. She pulled the cover to her neck and smiled demurely up at him when he returned. He tossed a couple of packets onto the night table and lifted a corner of the duvet.

"Ready?"

"Yup."

She expected him to slide in beside her, but instead he gave a mighty tug and hurled the whole duvet onto the floor. She gasped.

"Cold?" he asked.

"Freezing." She fought the urge to hide those stubbly legs again. "I need a warm body. Can you find me one?"

He came to join her, both of them lying on their sides, and again their bodies came together, head to toe, in a lingering embrace. The fire, banked temporarily, restoked itself in a flash, and Jess moaned as she pressed against him. He pressed back, moving slowly against her, and tension built inside her.

He touched her breasts through cotton. Her nipples, hard and aching, strained for his caress. "Let's take this off," he murmured.

She sat up and raised her arms above her head as Evan kneeled beside her and slowly peeled her bra upward. He held the stretched cotton at shoulder level, imprisoning her. "Look at you. So beautiful."

She glanced down. Saw breasts, stretched high and firm, with shameless nipples thrusting forward. Maybe she really was beautiful. "Just window shopping?" She repeated his words in a husky whisper, aiming for sultry and coming pretty darn close.

"I like window shopping when I know that, whenever I want, I can touch."

"Touch?" She imagined his touch, and the ache between her thighs intensified.

"Ca . . . ress." He drew the word out, itself a caress that made her skin tingle.

"Lick," he murmured, and Jess realized her tongue was running across her lips as she watched his face.

His throat moved as he swallowed. "Suck." It was the softest of whispers.

She squeezed her thighs tight. Could a woman come just from the sound of a man's voice?

"I want you." It was her own voice. She hadn't even been aware of speaking.

"I want you, too."

In a quick motion, he stripped her bra the rest of the way off. Then he lay her back on the bed, leaned over, and began to fondle her breasts, using his lips, his tongue, his breath, and driving her crazy.

Impatiently she reached down, needing to touch him and to inflict the same delirious pleasure and pain.

He pulled away. "Don't. I'll explode."

She glared at him. "Well, I'm close, too, and you're not showing me any mercy."

He gave a rough chuckle. "I'm a man."

"That was my theory. I was testing it out."

"Oh, Jess, allow me some dignity."

"Stop torturing me then."

"Soon."

He slid his hand down her belly and she tensed, expecting him to slip inside her panties. Instead he ran his hand over the outside and cupped her in his warm palm, his fingers firmly pressing the damp cotton between her legs.

"Evan!" she cried. "I want you inside me."

At last he moved quickly, yanking off her panties and

sheathing himself. In mere seconds he was sliding slowly and gently into her. Her slick, eager body took him in, reveling in the sensations. This was Evan. She could hardly believe it. But who else could make her feel this way?

He was torturing her, yet he was fulfilling a deep need. He was her dream lover, yet he was her oldest friend. He was her love.

Now he began to move faster, harder. Her brain shut down. Her body took over and rose to meet his. She was tripping close to the edge, almost ready to tumble, when she heard him groan and felt him shudder. His movements, so intense, so uncontrollable, pushed her over the edge and she climaxed gloriously.

When she opened her eyes, it was to see him gazing into them. "Oh, Ev, that was—"

"Too quick. I'm sorry, Jess. I've been wanting you all week. I lost control."

"Good."

"What?"

"Seems to me control's the last thing you want when you're making love." She gave a shivery sigh. "It was wonderful."

"God, it felt good. You're fantastic."

She felt a twinge of melancholy. If he really was her dream lover, he'd be whispering words of love.

He rolled off and got up. She sighed. Back to reality. From the bathroom she heard the tub gurgle as he let the water out. She hauled the duvet back on the bed and climbed under it. He returned and handed her a glass of water. It was cold and tasted wonderful.

"I'm starving," she said, surprised to realize it.

He laughed. "How romantic."

Just about as romantic as saying, "God, it felt good" and draining the tub, she figured, but sometimes a gal needed to keep her mouth shut.

"No dinner?" he asked.

She shook her head.

"Me neither. Hang on a minute."

When he returned, she crowed with delight.

"Scoot over," he said.

When she did, he placed a platter in the center of the duvet. Her stomach growled at the array of cold meats, cheeses, and buns, as well as fruit and cookies. He went out again and this time came back with a couple of bottles. "Mango–passion fruit or strawberry-ginseng?"

"Yum. Mango–passion fruit. Where did all this come from?"

"Kathy. It was here when I got back from the hospital."

He retrieved a couple of pillows that had fallen on the floor and they propped themselves up, covers to their waists, torsos bare.

"I love picnics," she said.

"I've never had a picnic in bed."

Aha, that was one thing she had over sophisticated Cynthia.

Picnicking with a naked Jess was a sensual, fun experience. They licked crumbs from each other's chests and fed each other strawberries. When they'd polished off everything Kathy had brought, Evan took the platter out to the living room and deposited it on the coffee table.

He realized he'd never drawn the curtains and was standing there naked. He moved closer to the window. Outside, there was nothing but tall trees, twinkly stars, and a fat crescent moon. The view was serene and lovely. He wanted to share it with Jess, then felt foolish. She saw this sky every night of her life.

A sense of unreality hit him. He had just made love with Jess Bly Cousins. And it had felt perfectly natural. Perfectly . . . perfect. Much better than it had ever been with any other woman. More arousing and intense, but also more comfortable, more fun. He could be himself with Jess. He could even laugh.

When he went back to the bedroom, she greeted him with a jaw-stretching yawn. Obviously, she figured she could be herself with him, too.

For a moment he thought of all the problems that remained unresolved. Robin, and what role he might play in her life. His mission for Gianni. Jess's career plans. He was sure there were more issues between them, but for the moment his brain didn't want to explore them.

The duvet covered her to the waist. Above it, her breasts were pale and delectable, contrasting attractively with the tanned skin of her neck, face, and arms. Her long, shiny hair lay tangled on her shoulders and her cheeks were flushed. He could have stood in the doorway and watched her forever, except that she was beckoning him back to bed. Between yawns.

He climbed under the covers and she cuddled into his arms.

"So tired," she murmured as he reached to click the light off.

When Jess woke again, the bedside clock told her she'd been asleep less than an hour. She slipped from the bed and checked in with the hospital. When she came back, Evan's voice came out of the darkness. "She okay?"

"Yes." She slid in beside him and clicked on a bedside lamp. "Evan, what do you intend to do about Robin?"

He whistled softly. "That's a good question." He propped himself up on pillows and stacked his hands behind his head. "I haven't thought it through, but . . . There's no point arguing about whether you should have told me or what I might have done. The fact is, Robin grew up believing Dave to be her father."

Where had her passionate lover gone? This man was

speaking evenly, dispassionately. The old Evan, who made rational decisions, not emotional ones.

"You say Dave's been a great father, right?"

"Yes," she murmured, feeling sorry for Evan.

"The important thing is Robin. Not my ego, not Dave's."

"Yes."

He nodded, and maybe it was just a trick of the lighting, but she thought he looked sad. "I can't see how it would help her to learn that the man she's called dad really isn't, and her true father's a stranger who ran out on her mom and her."

"You didn't run out on her. You never knew."

He shrugged. "Robin's best off believing what she's always believed. There's no reason for anything to change."

No reason. "Don't you . . . care?" she ventured.

He shook his head impatiently. "How can I care? I don't know Robin. You made sure of that. I've barely laid eyes on her."

His words stung, and she sensed they hurt him as much as they pained her. Yes, he was trying to be objective, but his emotions were engaged. Testing, she said, "You don't want anything to do with her?"

He drew in a shaky breath and, before he blinked, she thought she saw moisture sheen his eyes. "I'd like to know how she's doing. I'll donate blood so you can keep more on hand. I want you to promise that if there's ever anything she needs, anything you and Dave can't provide, you'll let me know."

Jess's heart ached for the boy, the man, who'd never had a proper family. But her first priority was Robin. She touched Evan's shoulder. "You okay?"

"Of course." But he didn't sound it.

With a sigh, she rested her head on his chest. He didn't drop his arm to curve it around her. Instead he clicked off the light. "Get some sleep, Jess."

The idea was tempting, but this would likely be the only night she spent with him. She didn't want to waste it. If only she could find a way of reaching Evan across the invisible barrier he'd erected. She combed her fingers through his sprinkling of chest hair—so much more masculine than a bare chest—deliberating. Then inspiration struck. She pulled away and slid out of the bed.

"Jess? Don't go. Not yet."

Well, that was a hopeful sign. "Oh, I'm not going far." She put on a drawl. "Just hold your hosses, pawdner."

She retrieved Evan's bathrobe from the floor and slipped it on. Then she found the cowboy boots he had pulled off her feet. She headed for the cabin door, shivered in the night air, and scampered for her truck.

Chapter Fifteen

Two minutes later Jess was back in the bedroom. Evan was sitting up in bed under the duvet, his arms folded across his chest. "What's going on?"

She grinned at his puzzled expression but didn't respond except to slide the robe off her shoulders.

"Okay, I'm awake," he said, his gleaming eyes telling her she'd succeeded in breaching that invisible barrier. "Get in here."

She reached outside the door for the old Resistol hat she'd brought in from the truck, and planted it on her head. "Boots and a hat—a cowgal's necessaries," she said. "Who needs clothes?"

He was grinning now, too. "Let me guess, you're planning on doing a little riding?"

Relieved that she'd pulled him out of his funk, she ran the tip of her tongue around her lips. "If I can find a worthy mount."

"A noble steed?"

"Smooth gaits," she murmured. She wished she could leave her boots on, but they were too dang dirty. She yanked them off and climbed onto the bed beside him. "Stamina. Vigor. A sweet personality, but lots of spirit. Perfect breeding."

She tilted her head to study him. "Strong teeth . . ."

He laughed.

She leaned forward to drop a kiss on his laughing mouth.

"Good breadth between the eyes." She kissed his forehead. "Suggests there's a brain in there."

"Ears . . ." She stroked back his hair and examined one. She kissed it, ran her tongue around the edge, and he twitched and gave a little groan. "Sensitive, receptive. All very good." She teased his other ear, then finger combed his hair. "Glossy coat."

Sitting back on her heels, she peeled the duvet down a few inches. "Powerful shoulders." She gave each a kiss, then stripped him down to his waist and nodded approvingly. "Good depth of chest. Yes, stamina should be just fine."

His body shook with laughter.

It stopped when she leaned forward to take a nipple in her mouth. Holding the Resistol with one hand so it didn't tip off, she sucked and felt him writhe. Felt a matching surge of arousal in her own body. She released him and murmured, "Nice markings." She sucked his other nipple, then sat back and said, "Roll over."

"What?"

She yanked the duvet off, noting the proud thrust of his erection, feeling the tingly ache in her sex. She whacked him gently on the hip. "Over now, there's a good boy."

He chuckled and obliged. She ran her hands over his buttocks. "Well muscled," she murmured in appreciation. "Oh yeah, you're a strong one."

She nipped one of his butt cheeks and he yelped. Then she ran her hands down the back of his legs, stroking and massaging the muscles. Desire was building in her, and it was all she could do to stop herself from moaning the way he was.

"Let's see the other side again," she said.

Obligingly he rolled for her. She glanced from his eye-catching erection to his face, and smiled at the gleam in his eyes.

"So far, so good?" he asked.

She pursed her lips and pretended to consider. "Yes, I'd have to say this is looking to be a fine specimen." She let her glance flick below his waist. "Measuring up quite well."

He was indeed, and she was dying to have him inside her, but it was fun prolonging the torture.

She worked down the fronts of his legs with her hands, enjoying the firmness of his muscles, the tickle of little hairs against her fingers. "Well-shaped legs, well-muscled. Good balance, I'd guess, as well as strength."

He chuckled. "Are you almost done with this inspection? Or is there something you've overlooked?"

She straddled his thighs and reached down between them, finally allowing herself to caress the soft skin that covered his strong shaft. He sighed with pleasure and she gave a contented "Mmm."

"So, lady, are you buying this horse?"

"Not without taking a test ride."

He gave a sexy chuckle. "Going to put me through my paces?"

She grinned back. "Am I in for a wild ride?"

"Only if that's what you want." His voice was husky. "The rider's in control, right?"

"But the mount has ultimate power, because he's bigger and stronger."

"All this mount wants to do is please you."

"Oh, Evan, you definitely do that."

"Then tell me what you'd like me to do. Or better still, show me."

She reached for a condom package. "I'd love to ride you bareback, but . . ." As she said the words, an image of herself pregnant with Evan's child flashed into her head. She sucked in a shuddery breath. She could do it again—get pregnant—this time deliberately. It was the right time of month. It had happened before from making love with him just once.

No! What was she thinking?

She put the packet to her mouth and ripped it open with her teeth, then flung the wrapper to the floor. With painstaking slowness, she sheathed him.

"Am I allowed to touch the rider?" he asked.

She considered, then shook her head. If he caressed her breasts, ran those seductive fingers up her thighs, she'd lose control. This time, she wanted to set the pace.

"Trust me," she murmured. "Let me take you for a ride and I promise you'll enjoy it."

She grasped him confidently and he groaned. "I don't doubt it for a moment. Just try not to torture your mount, okay?"

"I'm a very considerate rider. For example"—she lifted up and leaned forward, hovering over him—"we'll start out nice and slow. You always start a ride with a nice slow walk, to get warmed up."

She lowered her body slightly, guiding the tip of him inside her. She eased down a touch more, then again, absorbing him with a slowness that was both ecstasy and agony.

Evan put his hands behind his head and watched as she finally seated herself fully. "You're beautiful, Jess."

She straightened, feeling the warmth of his gaze caress her body.

"Beautiful posture," he murmured. "Now, how does it go? Ear, shoulder, hip, heel? Seems to me, your heels are a little far back."

She pressed them into his legs. "The better to spur you on."

She rotated her hips and flexed muscles deep inside her body, and he groaned and thrust upward. She patted his hip gently. "Slow down now."

"You spurred me on," he pointed out. "With those bony heels of yours."

"They aren't." She twisted back to look at one. "Okay, maybe they are." And then she got down to business, setting a slow, tantalizing pace that soon had both their bodies slick with sweat. Evan obeyed her, lying still—or as still as he could—as she raised and lowered, pressed and released, curved sideways then straightened. She used her own arousal as her guide, building the pitch, then easing off again, somehow trusting that Evan's needs, his self-control, would match hers.

"Ready for a little trot?" she murmured.

"Ready for a full-out gallop." His voice was husky with desire.

"All things in good time."

Jess speeded her motion, feeling both their bodies tense as they neared the finish line. She rested a hand on his chest over his heart, palming the throbbing pulse, and breathed deeply, filling her nostrils with the musky tang of their passion. She was close, so close.

"Are we ready for that gallop?" He ground out the words between clenched teeth.

She forced herself to slow, then stop moving. She sat across his body, feeling the strong jut of him inside her, pulling herself back from the edge. "Remember my lessons? You don't go straight from a trot to a gallop. You collect the horse first."

His face was flushed; his eyes were bright.

"Are you collected, Evan?"

He gave a growl of frustration, but she saw the twinkle in his eyes. He was enjoying this game as much as she was.

She lifted slightly and reached below her, capturing his firm balls and squeezing gently.

His head went back and his body bucked under her.

"Trying to throw me off?" she teased.

"This horse wants to gallop. Now."

"Well, if you're that full of energy . . ."

She moved again, quickening the pace until he could no longer hold back and his body lifted from the bed, thrusting uncontrollably into her, reaching the deepest parts of her body and soul, bringing her sensations and emotions all rushing together as she and Evan raced toward the same goal.

She tossed off her hat and let out a whoop, and he laughed with joy. Then his breath caught and he gasped, "Oh, Jess!" just as she began to climax around him. She threw back her head, letting the waves of pleasure surge through her as he thrust hard, again and again, into her very core.

After, when they'd both ridden out the tremors, she collapsed in a mindless heap on top of him.

His chest heaved, slippery with sweat, curls of hair tickling her breasts. Her own body still throbbed with sensation. Occasional spasms, aftershocks, rocked her. Evan's arms were around her, holding her as if he'd never let her go. How she wished it were true. Finally, both their bodies settled and they lay still.

Somehow she found the strength to slide off him and lie beside him.

He dealt with the condom, then put his arm around her. "Jess?"

"Hmm?" It came out as a contented, sleepy purr and she smiled against his chest.

"About this boot camp thing . . ."

She tensed. Didn't he have any damned sense of the moment? He was supposed to be feeling all mellow and loving. "Uh-huh?" she muttered warily.

"Are you really serious about it?"

She moved away from him, sitting up, reaching up to drag her fingers through her tangled hair and pull it back. "Well, sure. What do you mean?"

He lay on his side, watching her. "You used to have all those dreams. Racehorses, rodeo, riding schools. I just wondered if . . . you like having a dream to . . . well, dream, or if you really do want to make it work."

She released her hair, letting it tumble to her shoulders. "I've thought about that, this past week. I really want it and I'm prepared to do whatever needs to be done. This isn't just another dream." No wonder no one else had taken her dreams seriously, when she never had herself. Firmly, she added, "This is the one I'm going to make a reality."

"All I'm saying is, be sure. You have a good job here, and you're terrific at it. There's nothing wrong with chucking an old dream in favor of a new one."

Oh, Evan, would you please listen to your own words?

"I agree. But I *do* want this one. I believe in it. I've just been too gutless to go after it." She narrowed her eyes. "It was another self-fulfilling prophecy, you know? We created these stereotypes about you being a klutz and me not being so smart."

"I'd never thought of it that way. I'm sorry."

"Hey, we did it to each other. But I bought into it, Ev. Thought I didn't have any business sense. Well, I'm not that bad. I ran the ranch for Pa for more than a year."

He pushed himself up to a sitting position, too, wadding pillows behind his back. "And there's nothing wrong with asking for help."

"No." Why hadn't she before? Had she been scared to try too hard in case she failed? Or afraid reality wouldn't live up to the dream? It was a heck of a lot easier to dream than to put the effort into making something work. It was a lot safer than taking the risk. If not for Evan, she might never have figured this out.

She'd once suggested that he had to come back to Caribou Crossing to find himself. Maybe she'd needed him to come back so she could find herself, too. "You're right. I talked to Dave on the weekend and he's going to help me."

"Oh. Well, that's good." He looked taken aback.

Dang, she didn't want to hurt his feelings. "I know you offered, too, and that was really sweet. But it'd be so impractical, with you in New York and me here."

"It's all right, Jess," he said evenly, crossing his arms over his bare chest. "You don't have to make up excuses. You already said you didn't want my help. I'm just glad you weren't too proud to ask for help from *someone*."

Oh yes, he was definitely hurt.

"I'll provide a few guidelines," he said coolly. "I'm sure Dave is exceptionally capable, but I doubt he's ever put together a proposal for this kind of funding."

"That would be great, Ev," she said meekly, hoping that Dave would at least deign to look at the material Evan was going to send.

"There's an idea you—the two of you—might consider," he said slowly. "If you want to provide scholarships to people who can't afford to attend but could seriously benefit, you might look into setting up a charitable foundation. Instead of, or as well as, running it as a business."

She frowned in puzzlement as he spoke, his voice gathering animation and speed as he went on. "With a charity, what you'd be offering people like Gianni and Elena isn't an investment that will give them a return, but a tax deduction that will save them money. Plus, if they want it, involvement in doing something worthwhile."

Her eyes widened as she tried to take this in. "Like that Gimme a Break Foundation you talked about." Excitement sparked inside her. "That sounds amazing. Would a businessman like Gianni really go for something like that?"

"Many do." He glanced away, and his tone was formal again when he said, "You and *Dave* can discuss it with him."

His arms were still crossed over his chest, but that didn't stop her from reaching for his hand. "Evan, thank you. This is brilliant. I knew there was a problem with my business model, and that's one reason I could never figure out a solid plan. I didn't want it to be all about making money, yet I needed to attract investors. Getting people to donate to a charity is a way different thing. And I'd love to involve people like Gianni and Elena in the planning, and in deciding who gets the scholarships. Maybe they could be on the board?" New ideas crowded her mind, energizing her.

As she gushed on, his hand lay warm and unmoving in hers.

Then, slowly, he threaded his fingers through hers. "I've set up a number of these kinds of foundations. The offer of help is open anytime—to you, and to Dave. It would mean a lot to me to help you achieve your dream."

So much that he'd even work with Dave. She stared into his eyes, trying to understand. And then suddenly she did. Evan did love her and this was as close as he could come to acknowledging it. They might never again be together as a couple, but he wanted to offer her a loving gift.

She leaned over and touched her lips to his. "Thank you. So much."

She thought about the joy and pain of working with Evan. Would he visit again? Would they make love again? She wanted so much from this man. Then she thought about what a coward she'd been in pursuing her dreams. And not just her career ones.

When she was a teenager, pregnant by the love of her life, what had she done? Copped out, rather than tell Evan. She'd never given him—them—a chance.

Here she was again, in love with that one special man, and ready to let him walk away without telling him how she felt. She had never said the words to him.

Jess bowed her head, feeling ill prepared. She was sweaty and tousled, she had mauve bags under her eyes, and her dang legs were stubbly. Cynthia would have been perfectly groomed, wearing some fetching concoction of silk and lace. But Evan had broken up with Cynthia. He'd made love with plain-old Jess Bly Cousins. He'd even stripped off her day-old socks and grubby jeans to do it.

She straightened her spine and looked him in the eye. She took a deep breath, then said it: "I love you, Evan."

His mouth opened, and then his face went expressionless. She knew this look. It meant he was processing information, analyzing, and deciding how to react. Damn! She wished he would just, for once, react with his heart rather than his brain.

"I love you, too, Jess," he said carefully, and she knew it wasn't going to be all right. "I always have. You're a . . . special friend and I'm so glad we've found each other again. And sharing tonight has been really . . . special. Another wonderful gift."

He was sending a clear message. Maybe she should accept it gracefully. That's what the old, cowardly Jess would have done.

She took another deep breath. "I love you that way, too, Ev. But I love you another way. That once-in-a-lifetime way. I know it would be difficult, but we could make it work."

His expression didn't change: flat and controlled.

She was going to have her say, whatever the cost. For once, Evan Kincaid was going to know exactly how she felt. "I want you to stay. I know you love Manhattan, but you fit in really well here. You've had a good time—I've seen you. You're planning to move your business in a new direction, so do it here. It wouldn't be so high powered, but you'd find plenty of challenges. We could have a wonderful life. Stay."

He didn't say anything for a few seconds. Then he gave a sigh that moved through his whole body. "I'm flattered, Jess. Honored. But my home is in New York, just as yours is here."

Was her home really here? Or was it with Evan? How could she ask him to move from the place he loved if she wasn't prepared to do the same thing?

She weighed her love for Caribou Crossing against her love for Evan, testing the competing aches in her heart. "I honestly don't know if I could live in New York, but I'd try. If you wanted me. We could work out something with Robin and Dave—"

"No!" He shook his head violently. "No, Jess, don't even think about it. You and Robin belong here. You're . . . wild roses."

His gaze met hers, his eyes as sad as the ache in her heart. "As for love—well, I've never cared for anyone as much as you, but I'm not sure I even know what love is."

He reached out to touch her cheek. "You'll always be so special to me. I'd do anything for you. I want you to be happy, Jess."

She was going to fight this one to the end, bitter or sweet. "Being with you makes me happy."

Evan closed his eyes.

He was wrong, just plain wrong. Why couldn't he see it? "And being with me makes you happy. Doesn't it?"

"Yes, but—"

"Give yourself—give us—a chance. Let yourself love, Evan. I know it's inside you." She felt like she was pleading for her life.

"Jess, you belong here and my life is in New York."

A life where he worked too hard at a job that didn't bring him fulfillment. A life where he had acquaintances rather than friends. She bit her lip and held back the comments. She didn't want to sound spiteful. Besides, it was clear she'd lost. He wasn't ready—maybe wasn't able—to open his heart. She felt sorry for Evan, maybe even more than for herself.

She would have cried, but she'd run out of tears tonight.

Jess removed his hand from her cheek, kissed the palm, wrapped his fingers around the kiss, and gave his hand back to him. "I understand. At least this time I tried, rather than run away."

She glanced at the bedside clock. Almost dawn. And she was glad. Her night with Evan was definitely over. Right now she was calm, but she sensed it was the lull before the storm. No way would she fall apart in front of him. She slid out of bed. "I have to go."

He bit his lip.

Methodically, she gathered the clothes he had removed earlier.

"Jess, I . . ."

She pressed the snap buttons of her shirt together, remembering how he'd pulled them open. "I'll see you in a couple of hours."

The storm was approaching, her eyes growing damp. She yanked on her boots and headed for the door.

Behind her, she heard him say, "I'm sorry."

Sorry. What a pathetic word. Keeping a tight grip on her frayed emotions, Jess drove to the hospital, compelled to see her daughter. Robin, sleeping, looked unusually pale in the artificial light. Dave slept beside her bed, and Evan's blood coursed through her veins, her two fathers protecting her. Jess bent to kiss her forehead.

Rob's eyelids twitched. Slowly, her eyes opened and focused. "Mom? Can I go home?"

"Not yet, hon. How do you feel?"

Robin shrugged, winced, said stoically, "No biggie." She yawned. "Where's Dad?"

"Sleeping right over there. You go back to sleep now."

"Okay," Robin mumbled. "Don't forget to feed Concha and Pepper." She was asleep before Jess could answer.

Feeling reassured and more grounded, Jess drove home. She gave herself a mental pat on the back for courage. She refused to let the tears come, or to feel stupid. She had *not* made a fool of herself, and she knew Evan loved her as much as he would let himself.

Too bad it wasn't enough. . . .

When she neared the ranch, she turned the engine off and let the truck coast to a halt. She eased into the silent house. She was so tired, and her body ached in places that hadn't hurt in years. In the shower she stood motionless, letting the hot water cascade over her. When the tears came, she closed her eyes and lifted her face to the spray.

She had lost him. Again.

Though she told herself friendship was much better than nothing at all, right now it felt like hollow comfort. She wanted Evan Kincaid—heart, soul, and mind—forever more.

She had cried so much in the last few days that the wellspring soon ran dry. When she twisted the taps off and reached for a towel, she felt shaky, shivery. Well, to hell with feeling like crap. She refused to give in to it.

Jess scrubbed the towel across her body, rubbing hard, bringing pink heat to her skin. She reminded herself that she was brave and strong. Her life was so full, so rich, even if she would never have a man to love. She had her family, her friends, and she would damned well have her "Riders Boot Camp," with that cowboy boot logo Robin had designed.

She strode into her bedroom and selected one of her nicest embroidered cowboy shirts and, because they were spunky just like her, the red dress cowboy boots she wore when she went dancing.

She collected some things for Robin, then went downstairs. The kitchen smelled of bacon and coffee as Jess walked in.

Her mom turned from the stove. "How's Robin?"

"Doing well. She'll be pretty much out of commission for a while, but the doc says she'll be fine."

Her mother enveloped her in a hug. Those damned tears threatened again, and Jess pulled away to pour a mug of coffee.

Her dad, who'd been sitting at the kitchen table with his own mug of coffee, said, "That's what the hospital said when we called. Glad to know it's true. A splenectomy sounded pretty serious."

He shook his head. "Rob's topped even you, Jess. I haven't been so scared since the time Ranger balked at that fence and you went flying over."

"I didn't break a bone," Jess boasted.

"You concussed yourself," her mother reminded her.

"Oh yeah, I forgot."

Her parents exchanged amused glances.

"Didn't hear you come in," her father said.

She tried not to blush. "I snuck in so I wouldn't wake you."

"You look tired," her mother said. "Better make it an early one tonight."

"You bet I will."

Her mother whipped plates of scrambled eggs and bacon onto the table. "Wade, get moving with the toast."

"Yes, ma'am," he said, sticking four slices of multigrain bread into the toaster and flipping down the switch.

Jess picked up a strip of crisp bacon and nibbled it. "I hate it that I have to work today. I want to be at the hospital with Rob."

"I'm going in when we finish breakfast," her mom said.

"I'll come over, too," her pa said, "as soon as I give the ranch hands instructions for the day's work."

"We'll watch over her," her mother assured her. "And I'm betting her dad'll be there, too."

Her dad. Dave.

The doctor had suggested he go home and get some sleep last night, but he'd flat out refused. Yes, Dave would definitely be there to reassure himself Robin was all right. He blamed himself for her accident and would turn even more overprotective, which would make Robin chafe. Jess heaved a sigh.

Her mother touched her hand. "You go to work, honey, and don't worry about a thing."

Go to work and see Evan. Her heart lurched. Could she handle it?

Then she took a deep breath. Of course. And he'd do his best to make it easy on her. They'd be awkward with each other, but it would wear off. By now they'd been through enough that she knew both of them wanted to be friends, forever.

The fact that she longed for them to be so much more was something she'd deal with. She was an expert at facing reality, focusing on the positive, putting on a brave face. She lifted her chin. "By the way, I haven't told you about Madisun Joe. Ev's going to put her through university. I went with him to talk to her parents so they'd understand he's not some kind of pervert."

Her father whistled. "That's generous of him."

"He's a good boy," her mom said.

"Man," she corrected. Evan really was a man now. He was open-minded and flexible; he cared about other people and wanted to help them. He was a man who was worthy of her love, even if he didn't know what to do with it.

"Madisun deserves a break," her mother went on. "But I'm surprised her father agreed. Her income's important to that family."

"Ev's going to make sure she has money to send home."

Her mom smiled. "Yes, I suppose he would."

Jess drained her mug. Still needing caffeine, she got up to refill it. "It's important she get out of that house as soon as possible. Her father hits her. She never told me, but she opened up to Evan."

"Damn!" Her father whacked the table with his fist.

"Makes you want to go and punch him out, doesn't it, Pa?"

"It does. Or at least call the police."

"Madisun's getting out."

"There are other kids," he said grimly, and her mother came to stand behind him, resting her hands on his shoulders.

"I know. Evan told him there'd be no money if he harmed Mrs. Joe or the kids, but we should keep an eye on them."

"Damn right."

She studied her father's determined face and, above it, her mother's firm jaw.

At the moment she might feel like hell, but life really did have its wonderful moments. "I love you two, you know."

Chapter Sixteen

In the morning, Evan felt groggy from lack of sleep, and totally confused. Too much had happened in the last few hours.

He had a daughter. Jess had asked him to stay. She'd offered to come to New York. They'd become lovers.

She'd said she loved him.

His daughter was in the hospital after major surgery, and he'd yet to meet her. Probably never would.

Shaking his head, he stumbled to the bathroom for a shower, starting with hot water, then edging it over to cold in hopes it would help him make sense of the mess in his mind. It didn't.

The easiest thing would be to catch a cab to the airport and wait for the next flight out of here. That's what the old Evan would have done.

Instead he dressed in clean jeans and a fresh shirt and went over to gaze out the glass balcony doors. Sunlight filtered through the trees. He opened the sliding door to catch the fresh scent of morning. A rat-a-tat sounded some distance away, but he didn't see his woodpecker. Everything was so peaceful in contrast to the turmoil inside him. Barefoot, he walked out on the deck and took a deep breath.

"Morning, Evan," a voice called softly.

He glanced next door to see Ann, sitting on her own balcony with her feet propped up on the railing. "Morning."

"We missed you last night."

"Sorry. Something came up unexpectedly and . . ." He shrugged, hoping she wouldn't pursue the matter.

"It was another great evening. It's going to be hard to leave."

It would be. So much harder than ten years ago. "Yeah."

"Right now I've half a mind to chuck it all and move here. Set up a family practice. But I suspect, once I get back home, I'll change my mind. It's tempting, though."

"Yes, it is." He wasn't lying. "Remember the first couple of days, when George kept saying this place got into your blood?"

"Now we're as annoying as he was."

This was nice, hanging out on the deck and chatting casually to Ann. Putting off the moment when he had to face Jess.

Ann glanced at her watch. "Breakfast time."

He went inside to pull on socks and boots, then headed for the lodge. If he phoned the hospital, would they tell him how Robin was doing? Likely not, because he wasn't *family*. Jess would let him know if there was a problem, though. Wouldn't she?

When he made his apologies for the previous night, the others were polite enough not to pry. No one mentioned Robin and he figured Jess must not want them to know as it might cast a pall on their last day. Certainly everyone was in high spirits.

Evan mostly kept quiet. There was so much on his mind. He had a daughter—and he'd promised to stay out of her life. Jess had said she loved him—and he'd hurt her.

Yesterday his mother had said she loved him. Two women in two days. And he'd never thought of himself as lovable.

After breakfast, Kathy said, "We've got treats for you to take to the horses." She brandished a big bowl heaped with dark-colored balls.

"I remember these," Thérèse said. "What are they made of again?"

"Oatmeal, molasses, carrot, and apple, with a little flour and oil to hold them together. They're good for the horses, and they love them."

Each guest stuffed a few in a baggie, then headed back to their cabins to prepare for the morning ride.

When Evan walked into the barnyard along with the group, and saw Jess all rigged out in fancy Western gear and sexy red boots, his heart rolled painfully in his chest.

She greeted them with a bright smile. "It's your last day, and I want to congratulate you. You've come a long way."

The others began the now-familiar process of matching tack to horses, but Evan went over to Jess. Up close, he saw that her eyes were a little red and puffy. "How's Robin?"

"Doing great."

"And how are you, Jess?"

"Fine," she said with a quick, forced smile. Then her face softened, and the smile became real. "Honestly? I'm tired and a little depressed. But I'm okay."

He wanted to hug her, but the yard was filled with guests. "It was a special night. Thank you. I'll never forget it."

She nodded.

He couldn't let it go at that. "Regrets?" he asked.

She closed her eyes for a moment, then opened them and shook her head. "No, I don't regret anything I did."

Odd phrasing. Did she mean she regretted something he'd done, or not done?

"Oh, Evan," she said on a sigh. She reached up to touch his

cheek, then turned and headed for the barn. A couple of feet away from him, she stopped and turned back. "Evan?"

"Yes?"

"Don't tell the other guests about Rob, okay? Madisun knows, but this is private."

He nodded, then got on with the routine that by now felt like second nature.

It was the oddest morning. Despite his tiredness, his senses were heightened—maybe because it was the last day, the last time he'd be doing these things.

He was aware of how lightly he sprang into the saddle, of the warm roughness of Rusty's neck under his hand. Of the dappled patterns of light and shade as he rode through the woods, and the chitter of squirrels and squawk of birds.

And when he and the others in Jess's group galloped across rolling hills, he knew he would hold this memory, like last night's, in his heart forever. Poignant, yet joyful.

He gave a whoop and caught up with Jess. She turned to laugh at him, tossing back her head, letting her hat bang against her back, reaching up her free hand to untie the cord that bound her ponytail. She was wild, she was beautiful, and last night she'd been his.

Every time he looked at her, he thought, *This woman loves me. She offered to spend her life with me*. He couldn't take it in, any more than he could cope with the idea of having a daughter.

The ride took the group past lakes they'd visited before and rolling range land where cattle grazed. They stopped to pick wild strawberries and bury their faces in rosy pink blossoms. Then Jess led them up a twisting wooded path to another rocky viewpoint, where they gazed in awe at the landscape spread beneath them.

The awe soon gave way to hunger, as enticing smells drifted their way. Kathy, Will, and Marty had gone all out, with a brunch that offered a bit of everything, from pancakes to barbecued ribs.

There were pitchers of mimosas, made with nonalcoholic champagne and fresh-squeezed orange juice, and real crystal flutes to drink from. They drank rounds of toasts—to their hosts; to TJ, Madisun, and Marty; to the guests themselves; and to the horses.

From time to time, people wandered off to check on their horses. Kathy said, "Don't tell TJ, but horses like pancakes." So of course they all started feeding their horses pancakes. Sandy picked yellow and orange wildflowers and threaded them into her gray horse's dark mane, and the other women followed her example.

Evan stood beside Rusty, tearing a pancake into pieces and feeding them to the horse. "Girl stuff, huh, big fella?"

All the same, he plucked a wild rose and held it to his face, memorizing the scent, then offered it to Rusty. The horse studied it for a moment, then opened his mouth and took it between his teeth. He crunched, looking absurd as a pink petal hung outside his huge dark lips.

Evan laughed and slapped the horse's neck. He stood contentedly, stroking Rusty and watching others as they stroked their horses, too.

He'd barely spoken to Jess today. There was something different about her. She must have been physically and emotionally exhausted after a week that had included Petula's death, Robin's critical accident, and his own . . . he didn't want to call it rejection, but what other word applied?

And yet Jess seemed serene. More confident? Proud, almost. Like she'd gone through hell and come out the other side, even stronger. It made his heart ache to think he'd been part of her hell.

When everyone was ready to go, the picnic packed away, cinches tightened again, Jess said, "Madisun, will you lead us home?"

The girl beamed. "Sure will!" She urged her horse to the head of the line.

Evan hung back, pulling into line just before Jess. There was no opportunity to talk for the first half hour, as they rode down a switchback mountain trail. Then the group came out on a country road where they could ride two abreast. He held Rusty back until Jess brought Knight up beside him.

"Madisun likes being trail boss," he said. "It's nice of you to let her."

"She deserves it. She really pulls her weight around here. I'll miss her when she goes off to school."

"We made a good team, talking to her parents."

"Yes, Evan. We make a good team."

He glanced over but she was looking straight ahead, not at him. After that, it seemed neither of them had anything to say.

When the group returned to the barnyard, Jess hurried to find a private corner and, for the fourth time that day, called the hospital. Just as she got a reassuring answer, the batteries to Dave's cell died. She'd borrowed his phone last night at the hospital and this morning had forgotten to retrieve her own, which was still plugged into the charger at Bly Ranch.

When she walked back into the barnyard, she noted how the guests went about their tasks in slow motion. "Last-day syndrome," as she and Madisun called it. Everyone was reluctant to leave, to end the holiday. To say good-bye to their horses, new friends, and, perhaps most of all, the people they'd become at the Crazy Horse.

She collected good-bye hugs and handshakes.

Evan said, "Feel like having dinner tonight?"

She shook her head. In her heart, she'd already said good-bye to him. "I want to be with Rob for as long as they'll let me stay. And you can't miss Kathy and Will's farewell dinner. I'm so beat, when visiting hours end I'll just go home to bed."

"I understand."

She couldn't tell whether he was relieved or sad. She just knew she couldn't contemplate another night with him. Last night had been special; she'd leave it to stand on its own. Finally, ten years late, she had the memory she'd longed for.

And yes, it was a poignant one. Not because Evan didn't love her, but because she honestly believed he did. He was just too stuck in the past to let himself realize it.

A person had to change, to grow. That was the lesson Kathy and Will tried to teach here at the Crazy Horse, and she'd only just applied it to herself.

And so, while the guests milled around in the barnyard, reluctant to leave, she headed up to the lodge to use the office phone.

After closing the office door behind her, she pulled her hair back into a neat ponytail and set a pad of paper and pencil in front of her on the desk. Then she took a deep breath and dialed a number she had memorized but never used.

After a few rings, a male voice said, "Vitale."

She gulped. "Gianni? This is TJ Cousins, from the Crazy Horse."

"TJ! It's good to hear your voice. Brings back good memories. How are you?"

"I'm fine. And you?"

"Trying to remember there's more to life than work. Elena keeps reminding me."

"Please say hello to her." She swallowed. "I know Evan Kincaid will be talking to you, but I wanted to speak to you directly. He says you're still interested in the no-frills boot camp?"

"Yes, but I understand you're not so far ahead with the planning as I'd hoped."

She winced, then straightened her shoulders. "That's correct. I admit I've never done anything like this before.

Though I have run a ranch, as well as the very successful riding program at the Crazy Horse."

"Evan said he would provide you with guidelines for what we need."

"He told me that. I appreciate it. I've already enlisted the help of one of our most successful local businessmen, and I hope to have something to you shortly. Let me ask, though, what do you think of the idea of a charitable foundation that would provide scholarships to deserving people who can't afford to go but would really benefit?"

"Evan ran that by me, and I think it has a lot of potential. I talked to Elena, and she loves the idea."

"That's great. I didn't realize Evan had talked to you about it."

"He wanted to, because of the potential for a conflict of interest. You being an old friend and all. But I said I trusted his judgment."

A conflict of interest. She'd never thought of that, and clearly had a lot to learn. "I trust his judgment, too," she said.

"Then what do you think of this idea, TJ? How about we start treating this as a team project, and figuring out how we can make it work? Elena wanted to do that from the beginning, and she was right, but old habits die hard. That's partly why I need you, and the horses. To keep reminding me."

Her heart leaped. "Really?" She wanted to sing and dance with joy, but struggled to keep her focus. "Gianni, I promise I'll be totally businesslike and professional. I have resources here to draw on, and I welcome your and Elena's input. And Evan's, of course." She could work with Evan. Things would get easier with time. "He's the expert."

"About some things." He chuckled. "Tell me, TJ, how did Evan make out on horseback? He's one of the most uptight guys I've ever met, though he's top notch at his job."

"He loosened up surprisingly well. I think he'll bring a

new perspective back to his work. He'll have you to thank for that."

"You, too, I imagine."

She laughed. "And a horse named Rusty."

He laughed, too. "Horses are the best teachers, aren't they?"

It seemed to take forever for the other guests and Madisun to say their good-byes and head on their way, but Evan waited patiently.

Jess had gone up to the lodge for a few minutes, and since she'd returned he had sensed a barely contained excitement. She must be looking forward to spending the rest of the day with her daughter.

When finally it was just the two of them, he said, "I'll walk you to your truck."

She grabbed his hands, gripping tight. Voice bubbly, she said, "Ev, I phoned Gianni."

"You did? When?"

"Just now. Oh my God, I can't believe it! He wants to make a go of it, all of us working together as a team. With him and Elena in from the ground floor, so that they're part of putting the charitable foundation or business or whatever together."

His mouth fell open. "Seriously?"

"He sounds serious. And excited." She wriggled like a puppy, excitement rippling through her own body. "He says it'll be a team project. All of us, and especially you. He trusts you and so do I."

His heart warmed. "You're saying you want me to help?" Jess trusted him to help her achieve her dream.

She gave a little grin. "If you and Dave can figure out how to get along."

He'd made that offer and he'd follow through on it, no matter how awkward it might be.

"He's a good guy," she said.

Evan sighed. "Yeah, I know he is. He always was. I was the jerk." Okay, so Dave was a better man than he was. He could at least try to stop being a jerk about it.

"Yup, you were. But you've grown up some."

His heart lifted, for he knew it was true. He gave her a playful sock on the shoulder. "Thanks for that. You, too."

She nodded. "I know. It's about time."

Then her expression sobered and she gazed down at the ground. "Well, I should get going."

"I know you're anxious to see Robin." He was almost tempted to ask if he could come along, but what point would it serve? Before, he'd been curious to meet Jess's daughter. Now that he knew Robin was his, things had changed. Because, of course, she wasn't his; she was Dave's. They all agreed it was in Robin's best interests.

If he met her, talked to her, there'd be more to miss.

There was one thing, though, that he needed. "Will you send me a photograph?"

Her head jerked up and she studied his face for a long moment, then walked over to the truck, unlocked it, and reached inside. She came back to him holding a slim, battered wallet. From it she extracted something and handed it over.

It was a snapshot of Robin, bareback on her horse, a big smile on her face. "Thanks."

"Let me know if you want more. Or . . . anything."

"Will I see you again before I go?"

She dropped her head. "I don't think so. We've said everything, haven't we?"

"I suppose so."

He knew she wanted to get to the hospital. Even more than that, he figured she needed to get away from him. Her eyes were swimming and he wasn't far from tears himself.

She leaned forward and touched her lips to his. Briefly, so very briefly. "Bye for now, Ev."

"I love you, Jess." The words came out of his mouth before he realized he was going to say them.

Her face went still, and he wondered what he'd done. Then she just nodded calmly. "I love you, too." She cleared her throat. "Now get out of here before I cry."

He gazed at her, memorizing every inch of her lovely face. Then he backed slowly away. The tears were beginning to slip down her cheeks. He wanted to hold her tight, comfort her, but nothing he could say would ease her pain. Or his own.

He wrenched himself away and strode up to his cabin without a single glance over his shoulder. He slammed the door and turned to lean against it, resting his forearms on the rough wood and his forehead against his hands. Hands that were tanned and calloused. A country legacy he would carry back to New York.

Along with cowboy boots, a Resistol hat, a tenuous relationship with his mother, and a horde of memories.

Jess gunned the truck down the road, trusting the tires to find the gravel tracks. She blinked against tears, but they refused to quit, so, before pulling onto the highway, she stopped the truck and let herself have a good cry. When she was done she drove to the hospital, where she hurried to a ladies' room and bathed her face with cold water.

"Pull yourself together, girl," she muttered to her reflection. She'd definitely had better days. She was thrilled about Gianni and her boot camp, yet even that couldn't override her sorrow that Evan was going home. As she'd always known he would.

He'd said he loved her. Spontaneously. That was a bit of a shocker, even though she knew he didn't mean the word *love* the way she wanted him to.

They were going to be friends forever. She smiled at her face in the mirror and saw the lines of strain ease.

He was going to work with her and Dave, and Gianni and Elena, and "Riders Boot Camp" was going to be a reality. At long last, her dream was coming true. One dream out of two wasn't bad at all.

Best of all, she was a new woman. A stronger, braver one. She freed her hair from its tail, gave it a toss, and strode in her sassy red boots to Robin's room.

The scene inside was balm to her battered soul. Her parents and Dave sat around Rob's bed, talking in soft voices. Her daughter saw her first. "Mom, you're here!"

Jess went over to hug her carefully. "It's good to see you, sweetie."

"I want to go home now."

"How did I know you were going to say that?"

Dave was watching them, a troubled expression on his face. She smiled reassuringly. "Well, that's good-bye to another batch of Crazy Horse guests."

"What about our old classmate?" His voice had an edge.

"He had a good time, but he'll be glad to get home. There's nothing here for him." *He won't come between you and Robin*, she tried to tell him with her words and her eyes.

Dave's face cleared and he smiled. It was almost the old sunny smile of the Dave she'd known before Anita's illness.

She was tempted to tell them all about her phone call with Gianni but guessed the excitement would be too much for Robin right now. The news could wait.

Shortly after Jess arrived, her parents headed home for dinner, and it was just she, Dave, and a worn-out Rob. Despite her protests over having to stay in the hospital, it was clear the girl was in pain and exhausted.

When visiting hours ended, Jess walked out with Dave.

"It's really all right?" he asked. "With Evan?"

"I think so. He doesn't want to mess things up."

"He doesn't want a mess himself, you mean."

"Maybe. But I honestly think he's concerned about Robin's best interests."

They had left the hospital and were walking toward her truck. "Jessie-girl, are you still in love with him?" His tone was sympathetic.

Her shoulders sagged. "I guess. Seems to be my fate."

He put an arm around her. "Poor kid."

"It's not that bad. At least now we're friends." Her words sounded hollow to her ears, and she guessed, from the way Dave squeezed her tight, he heard them the same way.

"If you want to talk about it . . ."

He was such a sweet man. "Thanks, Dave. I'd rather talk about my good news, though. I didn't want Rob getting overexcited, but I'm busting to tell someone." She filled him in on what she and Gianni were planning.

Though he scowled at the idea of working with Evan, he gave her a big hug and kiss. "I'm so happy for you. And happy that I can help."

She drove home slowly, barely able to keep her eyes open. Once there, she forced down a few bites of dinner, not even knowing what she was eating. Then she ran a hot bath and climbed in, only to wake an hour later in cold water. Chilled despite the summer warmth coming through her bedroom window, she pulled on a pair of winter flannel pajamas.

Last night it had been a cowboy hat and a naked body; tonight it was flannel jammies.

Last night it had been Evan. She closed her eyes on that memory, hoping it would follow her into her dreams.

Chapter Seventeen

Evan woke on Saturday with a hangover for the first time in his life. The final dinner had indeed been a banquet, and the guests went through bottles and bottles of champagne and wine. He hadn't bothered to say no when people offered to refill his glass.

He'd been in a weird mood. Sometimes he felt a quiet pleasure at the week's accomplishments and the new direction he planned to take in his life. Other times, he was depressed. He tried to drown his gloom with wine and not think about Robin, and an e-mail relationship with Jess.

When he made it into the lodge on Saturday morning, his stomach churned at the smell of bacon and sausages. Kathy handed him a glass of a brown concoction. "Drain it," she ordered, "before you talk to me."

A hangover cure? It tasted foul, but at least his stomach didn't rebel.

"I never drink too much," he grumbled, annoyed at himself.

"You're not the only one who overdid it. You'll feel better in a few minutes."

Her words were prophetic. In ten minutes, he was chowing down with the rest of the guests, blithely shoving slices of crisp-skinned sausage into his mouth.

Last night, the talk had all been about the Crazy Horse holiday. Today, there was a distinct change in tone. Even in appearance. Hair that had gone uncombed was now carefully styled. Jeans had been replaced with traveling clothes. Conversation focused on flights and what was waiting back home. Work that would have piled up. Business issues that might or might not have been resolved.

Evan thought of the pages of material Angelica had sent that he needed to go through on the plane. She'd sent only the most urgent stuff. There would be heaps of mail and hundreds of e-mails to deal with.

Oh well, he had lunch with Gianni and Elena to look forward to tomorrow. They could swap Crazy Horse stories, talk about Jess, brainstorm ideas for the boot camp.

And on Monday he'd make Angelica giggle when he described his first day on a horse. He had the photograph she'd requested, of him up on Rusty's back.

He was taking home several photos, including some with Jess in them. And two of Jess and Robin riding together. He now had three pictures of the daughter he'd never met.

After breakfast, people lingered near the front door of the lodge. The Crazy Horse van was making two trips to Williams Lake, one for the morning flights and one for flights later in the day. Evan had left it so late to book, the only flight he'd managed to get was at four o'clock. He said his good-byes to those who were departing before him, and for the first time, business cards came out.

"Don't forget to send us news," Kathy reminded them, "so we can put it in our quarterly newsletter."

When people still seemed predisposed to linger, Will said, "We're leaving in half an hour, folks. If you haven't finished packing, get a move on."

Guests hurried away, but Evan followed Kathy when she returned to the kitchen. "Got any of those horse treats left?"

"Heading down to say good-bye to Rusty?"

"And the others. Treats all around, if you please."

"Coming up."

He took an apple from the always stocked bowl while she assembled a plastic bag full of the round balls.

She handed him the treats. "Here you go, horse lover."

He pondered the label as he walked down the hill to the fenced pasture. Never in a million years would he have considered himself a horse lover.

Mickey and Raindance, the appaloosa Madisun rode, grazed near the fence, but he didn't see Rusty. Mickey whickered as Evan went through the gate, a couple more horses emerged from the trees, and then Rusty trotted toward him.

Soon he was surrounded by horses and he fed every one, handing out treats until the bag was empty. He stuffed it in his pocket and stroked noses, patted necks. Gradually the horses drifted away until it was just him and Rusty, who showed no inclination to leave.

The horse put his head down, puffed air on Evan's boots, then lifted his head again and gently butted Evan's chest. Evan stroked his neck and fingercombed his coarse mane. The horse's skin was warm in the sunshine, and so were Evan's shoulders and the top of his head—bare today rather than topped with the cowboy hat he'd grown used to. The air smelled of clover and, more mildly, horseflesh. Just when, in the past two weeks, had the odor of horse become appealing? He breathed deeply, wishing he could hold this scent in his lungs to take back home with him.

NYC. Exhaust fumes and imported cigars. The hustle-bustle of life in the fast lane. He loved New York. And yet . . . it was so peaceful standing here doing nothing but pat a horse.

He remembered how restless he'd felt his first few days here. "You've taught me a lot," he murmured to Rusty. "You and Jess."

The horse's ear twitched.

"I've learned how to relax, but I've also got a new sense of direction."

Rusty snorted gently.

"You're a good boy. Even if you did stomp on my foot the first day." He smiled at the memory, and the recollection of Rusty blowing apple froth on him and Jess howling with laughter. He took the apple from his other pocket and held it out on his palm. "No tricks today," he warned.

It was only the second time he'd offered the horse an apple. Rusty took it neatly and politely.

Every time he ate an apple, Evan would remember Rusty showering him with applesauce. He'd also remember apple pie cooked by Miriam Bly and shared around a kitchen table where people treated him like family.

Warmth, affection. Fun.

Jess, in her forthright way, had said it didn't sound like he had much fun in New York. She was right. Yes, he dined with lovely women, went to parties, had drinks at clubs, and went to the theatre, but he'd had more out-and-out fun in these two weeks than in all the years in New York. He'd definitely have to make some changes when he got back.

Back. Home. Manhattan. Traffic fumes, honking horns, designer food.

Damn, he should be concentrating on the good things. The things he loved. A doppio and the *New York Times* all by himself in the morning. Wheeling and dealing across continents and time zones.

Yes, he loved those things, but now he found himself thinking of Kathy's hot chocolate and Miriam's plain Colombian coffee. Of helping Madisun and Jess achieve their dreams, and helping Wade and Miriam create a bit more financial security. Maybe even helping Brooke deal with the financial matters she found intimidating. Perhaps actually getting to know and like his mother.

But mostly, he thought of Jess. Of her infectious laugh, her soulful brown eyes. Of her naked on top of him, with a sexy sparkle in her eye and a cowboy hat on her head.

Rusty head-butted him and he resumed stroking the horse's neck.

He'd felt more love and passion with Jess than with any woman he had ever met. Or could ever imagine meeting.

"I love her." He spoke the words aloud, realizing as he said them that he really meant them. Meant them not just in a friendly fashion, but in the way Jess had talked about. That once-in-a-lifetime way.

"My God, I've been a fool."

Rusty regarded him curiously. The horse's head went up and down once.

Evan laughed. "Yeah, you agree. Jesus . . ."

Then he laughed louder. "I love Jess Bly. I've loved her since the day I met her, back when we were both seven. But I never realized . . . Oh hell, twenty years."

Suddenly, his knees were weak, and he leaned against Rusty for support. He'd thought he didn't know what love was, but in fact it had been in his heart all along; he'd just been too scared to recognize it.

He loved Jess the way she loved him.

He'd loved her for twenty years, and he'd wasted the last ten of them. And he'd been prepared to waste even more. Been willing to toss her love away. All because he'd been stuck in childish patterns formed back when love had been a scary proposition.

Yes, he was crazy about New York, but he could be crazy about Caribou Crossing, too; he was already more than halfway there. What he knew, finally, was that the true dream in his heart was Jess. Her and her horses and cowboy hats, her grubby fingers and manure-coated boots. Her generosity, her marshmallow heart. Her saucy breasts, her curvy butt, the whole damned package.

Daughter and all.

"Robin," he murmured, for the first time tasting the name slowly and allowing himself to fully envision the girl. He could get to know Robin. Not only could he let himself love Jess, but he could love his own daughter.

He wouldn't have to dither around anymore about whether he should have kids, whether he'd be a good father. Robin existed, and he would, with Jess's help, make her a fine stepfather. Maybe down the road, he and Jess would even have kids of their own. But first, there was Robin.

The crunch of gravel broke into his thoughts. He turned to see the Crazy Horse van, heading for the airport. On impulse, he raised his arm, flagging Will down.

"Talk to you later," he said to Rusty, then vaulted over the fence. "Can I hitch a ride into town?"

The back door opened and they let him inside. "Last-minute souvenir shopping?" Sandy asked.

"Something like that."

Will drove to the airport first, with all the guests chattering excitedly while Evan nursed his own thoughts. He waited impatiently through another round of farewells at the airport. Perhaps picking up on his mood, Will was quiet as he drove into town and parked at the grocery store.

"Thanks," Evan said. "I'll find my own way back."

Then, on legs that trembled, he walked the few blocks to the hospital. He didn't know what he'd say, just that he needed to finally meet Robin Cousins.

He got directions from the nurse at the front desk and found Robin's room. Hoping Dave wasn't there, he peeked around the door. The girl was alone, propped up on a heap of pillows, watching the TV that was suspended above her bed.

He forced himself through the doorway before he had time to change his mind.

She looked up. Big chocolate eyes like Jess's. "Hi," she said. "Looking for someone?"

His daughter. She was his daughter. He had to clear his throat before he could get the words out. "You, actually."

"Me? But . . . Oh wait, I saw you at the Crazy Horse last Saturday. Right?" Her voice was strong, her manner confident. She did look a lot like her mother, but her personality made the familiar features into something unique.

"Yes, I've been staying there."

She used the remote to click off the TV. "Isn't it the greatest?"

"It sure is. And I really enjoyed the show you and your mom put on. You're a wonderful rider."

"I've been riding since before I could walk," she said cockily.

He chuckled. "Your mom used to say the exact same thing."

"She did? You know Mom? Oh wait, you're the man who came over for dinner last week when I was at Dad's."

"That's me. I grew up here. With your mom. And your dad." He forced the last word out.

"Cool." Was he imagining it, or did he see himself in the tilt of her jaw? "Where do you live now?"

"New York City."

"Wow! That's, like, so awesome! I absolutely have to go there one day."

He smiled, thinking of showing her and Jess his city. They'd ride horses in Central Park, go to the theatre, explore Greenwich Village, and stop at the Magnolia Bakery for cupcakes. There were things about New York both Jess and Robin would love, just as long as Jess knew they'd be coming home to Caribou Crossing afterward.

He closed his eyes briefly. Was he being too confident? Jess had said she loved him. She'd asked him to stay. She would be happy, wouldn't she?

Or was this a dream she didn't really want to come true? She might turn him down. He broke out in a cold sweat.

"Hey, mister, are you okay?"

He ran a shaky hand over his face and tried to smile. "I'm fine. How about you? I heard about your accident."

"I'm okay. Right now it hurts when I move. Well, it hurts even when I don't move. But I'll be back up on Concha soon."

If Jess did accept him, he'd have years of worrying about this girl. First she'd be the reckless tomboy, then the teenage heartbreaker. "I'm glad you're going to be okay."

"So did you come here to see Mom?"

"I came because I wanted to meet you."

"Cool. Hey, you haven't told me your name."

"It's Evan Kincaid."

"I'm Robin Cousins." She held out her hand and he reached out, his own hand trembling, and for the first time touched his child. She had a firm grip, and he hated to let go of her small, warm hand. When he did, his palm was tingling and his eyes were damp.

He had actually fathered this girl.

From the hospital, he walked back to the center of town. He thought about stopping in to tell Brooke what he was planning, then decided it could wait. They'd have lots of opportunities to talk. He figured the new Brooke would be thrilled to welcome Jess and Robin into the family.

Besides, he'd already begun resolving things with Brooke.

It had occurred to him earlier, in Will's van, that there were some things he needed to do to prove himself worthy of Jess. A few of them, he could already tick off. Like learning to ride, and to appreciate the country she loved. And reconciling with Brooke.

That left two more things. One was meeting Robin. And the other issue involved one more person who was intrinsic to Jess's life. And Robin's.

He squared his shoulders and walked into the Wild Rose Inn.

The lobby was a classy version of rustic "cowboy" crossed with gold-miner days, and it worked nicely. Behind the desk, a middle-aged woman stopped clicking away on a computer keyboard and looked up with a welcoming smile.

"I'm looking for Dave Cousins."

"In his office, down that hall, on your left."

He followed her instructions and stopped in the open doorway. "Dave?"

The man looked up from his desk. "Evan," he said warily.

Evan squared his shoulders. "When we were kids, you offered me friendship and I was fool enough to turn you down. Is the offer still open?"

Dave had one of those faces that reveal emotion. Evan read his mistrust—and fear. The other man rose, walked quickly to the door, and closed it. "This is about Robin."

"Yes. And Jess." He hadn't been invited to sit, and he didn't want to. Nor, it seemed, did Dave. The other man stood by the door, arms folded across his chest.

"I love Jess," Evan said. "I guess I always have. I think she loves me, too."

Dave closed his eyes, and when he opened them again his face had aged a decade. "She always has," he said softly.

In that moment, Evan respected him immensely. He knew Dave saw what was coming, yet he didn't protest or deny.

"I'm going to move to Caribou Crossing. I want to marry her, if she'll have me."

Dave sucked in a breath and Evan hurried on. "We won't

tell Robin about . . . anything. I'll be her stepfather. You'll still be her father."

Dave ran a shaky hand over his jaw. "I appreciate that."

"You *are* her father. You raised her, loved her. I just want to be part of her life, too. We can work this out, Dave. It'll be okay."

"Okay," he echoed in a flat voice.

Evan winced at his own choice of word. All this man had, since his fiancée died, was Robin and Jess. How could it be "okay" for Evan to interfere with that?

"I love Jess," he said again, as justification.

"Yeah, I see that. And Jessie deserves . . . everything. She's the best."

"I know. I can't believe I was so stupid I didn't realize it before." He gave a nervous laugh. "I'm not even sure she'll accept. I've been such a jerk, she may think I'm not worth the hassle."

A corner of Dave's mouth lifted. "She's not one to hold a grudge," he said thoughtfully. "She might make you do some real fancy talking, but I'm guessing she'll come round to seeing things your way. When are you going to ask her?"

"I was thinking about tonight. I have this idea. . . ."

"You always did plan things out in detail." There was a hint of humor in the other man's voice.

"Dave, will you keep this a secret? I want to surprise her, and there are some things I need to do first."

"Like buy a ring?"

"Yeah, like that."

Dave studied him, his face solemn. "Be sure about what you're doing. Don't hurt her, Evan."

The "again" hovered in the air between them, unsaid. "I won't. I promise you." An impulse made him stick out his hand.

Dave paused a mere second before shaking it firmly. Then he said, “Sit down. Tell me what you’re planning.”

Evan paused. Could he really talk to Dave about this? But the guy had made the offer, basically an offer of friendship, and Evan wasn’t about to turn that down.

Chapter Eighteen

Jess smiled tiredly as she walked out of the hospital late in the afternoon. It was always tough dealing with Robin when she was sick or injured. The poor kid never wanted to acknowledge how bad she felt and always wanted to be back on her feet.

She glanced around, hunting for Dave. It was sweet of him to suggest a quiet dinner at the little Italian bistro. She had lots to tell him. Besides, it was another way of distracting her mind from the knowledge that Evan was on a plane, winging his way back to New York. The love of her life would be her e-mail penpal and business associate. Oh well, it could be much, much worse.

Ev had dropped by to meet Robin. When Rob had told her, Jess hadn't known what to think, but she did know Evan was a man of his word. He wouldn't go back on his promise to keep the secret of Robin's parentage.

Jess looked around again. Where *was* Dave? His truck sat at the front of the parking lot, the cab empty. She was tired and knew the doors would be unlocked, so she walked over and climbed into the passenger seat. She stretched, resting her head on the headrest, and closed her eyes.

She barely stirred when noise and motion told her he'd

climbed in beside her. "Hey, good-looking," she murmured, but he didn't reply.

He was making a clumsy job of starting the truck and backing it out of the parking spot, and normally she'd have teased him, but right now she didn't have the energy to bother. She would just let herself drift until he parked at the restaurant. "You're going to buy us a very fine bottle of red wine," she said.

"Actually, I had something else in mind."

The voice was Evan's. She jerked upright and gaped. "You're not gone!"

He glanced down at himself. "Apparently not."

He was wearing jeans and his boots, which were polished to a gleam. His crisp white shirt had the sleeves rolled up and several buttons undone. He was tanned, healthy-looking, and there was a twinkle in his eye when he grinned at her.

She frowned, not comprehending. "You're here, and you're stealing Dave's truck."

He laughed. "And I'm kidnapping his ex."

She glanced out the window. He was on the highway, heading north. She couldn't get her head around this. "What's going on?"

"Relax. All will be revealed."

He turned onto a dirt road. The old twisty, turny road that led to Zephyr Lake. Evan Kincaid was here in Caribou Crossing and he was taking her to Zephyr Lake. Did she dare hope . . . ?

The lake came in sight, flashing blue through a screen of aspens. Theirs was the only vehicle.

He parked and she climbed out, her knees weak. When he handed her a wicker picnic basket, she took it automatically and followed him. He carried a plaid rug that looked brand new, and a blue and white cooler with a Wild Rose Inn sticker on it.

She wanted to ask again what this was all about. On the other hand, if she didn't ask, she could let herself hope.

He led her to a level spot by the lake and spread the blanket. She set down the picnic basket, tugged off her boots, and sank down. He pulled off his boots, too, and sat beside her. He lifted the lid off the cooler and extracted two crystal flutes, which he handed to her.

"It's not red wine," he said, pulling out a bottle of champagne. Dom Pérignon. She recognized the label from her parents' twenty-fifth anniversary party. He ripped off the foil that covered the cork.

Zephyr Lake and champagne. Had she fallen asleep in Dave's truck, and this was all a crazy dream?

The cold glasses sweated in her hands. The chilly dampness convinced her she was awake.

But her hands trembled and her heart thumped so fast she could hardly breathe. Now, fear was warring with hope. This was still Ev, the New York guy, the one who wouldn't let himself love. She had to know before she exploded from tension. "Evan?"

He eased the cork out. "I thought we might do it right, this time around."

"It?" Her voice squeaked. She cleared her throat. "Last time we had take-out chicken and beer, and I seduced you."

He concentrated on filling the glasses so the bubbles frothed but didn't overflow.

"Let me guess," she said, her voice wavering. "This time *you're* seducing *me*?"

He stowed the bottle back in the cooler, took one glass from her hand, then set it on top of the cooler lid. "That comes later. First, I'm going to propose."

The breath rushed out of her. "Propose?" Marriage? Was there any other kind of proposal? Well, a business proposal, but—

"Hey, don't spill the champagne." He reached out quickly

to rescue her tilting glass, and set it beside his own. "I had a little talk with Rusty this morning. You know what they say about horse sense? Well, that old boy has more than his fair share."

Yes, she'd been right to hope. Jess began to laugh as tears rolled down her cheeks, trickled over her lips. When she smiled, she tasted salt on her tongue. "Do you mean . . . ?"

He smiled gently. Lovingly. "I love you, Jessica Bly Cousins. You're my once-in-a-lifetime love. You're my dream. I want to move back to Caribou Crossing and marry you."

"Oh, Evan . . ." Could she believe in this? Tentatively, she said, "But you love New York."

"I do. And you will, too, when I take you and Robin to visit. But I can love Caribou Crossing. The last two weeks have shown me that."

She'd seen him changing in front of her eyes. "I know you can," she breathed.

He took her hand, gripping it between his, and she felt him shaking. He was actually scared she wouldn't accept.

"You said you loved me, Jess. Is it true? Will you marry me and be my best friend and only love, forever and ever?"

"I . . ." Her heart wanted to say yes, but she had one question. "What about Robin?"

He smiled. "She's wonderful. I'd be honored to be her stepfather."

"Oh, Evan. Yes. Yes, I'll marry you." She hurled herself into his arms, knocking him over backward.

His arms came around her, pressing her so tight she could barely breathe. "Jesus, Jess, I love you so much. I've been such a fool."

"Yes, you have. But I love you anyhow, Ev. Forever and ever."

AUTHOR'S NOTE

I grew up in a city (Victoria, British Columbia) and have lived in both Victoria and Vancouver, so maybe it's natural that I've mostly written about urban settings. However, I've also spent a lot of time in the country and I love it, and I was one of the many girls who fell in love with horses as a child and never lost that feeling. So now I figure it's high time to indulge my adult self with a little country-style romance.

Rather than set the story in a real town, I made up Caribou Crossing. It's a composite of a number of small towns in the interior of British Columbia. Set along the old Cariboo Wagon Road, it has a gold-mining history and now its economy is based on ranching and tourism. (And if you're wondering if there's a typo in the last sentence, no, it's just one of our weird BC things. The animal is a caribou and the region was named after it, but it's spelled Cariboo.)

Home on the Range is a departure for me in a second way. Usually, my muse has led me to write about strangers who meet and fall in love, but this time she pointed me in the direction of a reunion story. I found that there's a different dynamic when the heroine and hero have a shared past (and one big unshared secret). I had a lovely time writing Jess and Evan's story and I hope you enjoy reading it.

I hope you'll also look for Jessica's parents' love story, in the novella *Caribou Crossing*, and for Evan's mother Brooke's brand-new romance, in *Gentle on My Mind*.

I'd like to thank all the people who helped bring this book

to life: Audrey LaFehr and Martin Biro at Kensington; Emily Sylvan Kim at Prospect Agency; and my critique group, Michelle Hancock, Betty Allan, and Nazima Ali.

I love sharing my stories with my readers and I love hearing from you. I write under the pen names Susan Fox, Savanna Fox, and Susan Lyons. You can e-mail me at susan@susanlyons.ca or contact me through my website at www.susanfox.ca, where you'll also find excerpts, behind-the-scenes notes, recipes, a monthly contest, my newsletter, and other goodies. You can also find me on Facebook at facebook.com/SusanLyonsFox.

Learn how Jessica Bly and her family
first came to Caribou Crossing
and how Jessica and Evan
first met in this special prequel novella,
printed here in its entirety.

Also available as a Zebra eBook.

Turn the page to begin!

Chapter One

Late February 1995

Miriam Bly lay in darkness, her eyelids heavy, shuttering her from the world. Dimly, she was aware of an ache in her belly, another in her heart, but the sensations were dull, muffled. A cocoon wrapped her, protecting her from . . . From what?

This wasn't normal not-quite-awake-yet sleep. She felt almost like she'd been drugged. What could have . . . But the thought faded before she could follow it through.

She wanted to open her eyes.

No, maybe she didn't. Instinct told her there was something she didn't want to face.

A male voice prodded the border of her safe cocoon. "Honey, I'm here."

Wade. It was Wade.

A sense of peace filled her. She was with Wade, safe and loved.

"I'm with you, Miriam," he said softly. "Now and forever."

She smiled. No need to open her eyes, because his beloved face was crystal clear in her mind's eye.

Heaven, *Miriam thought as she swayed in the arms of her brand-new husband to "The Yellow Rose of Texas." This was sheer heaven.*

The male singer's voice sang the last line, vowing that the yellow rose of Texas was the only girl for him, and a fiddle echoed the plaintive melody.

"That's how I feel," Wade said, his chocolate eyes warm and sparkly as he smiled down at her. She'd shed her high-heeled sandals when he'd taken off the jacket of his rented tux, so he was a good six inches taller, making her feel feminine and protected. "You're the only girl for me. Now and forever, Miriam."

"Oh, Wade." Her heart skipped. He could always make her heart skip. "That's exactly the way I feel."

Two hours ago, she and her high school sweetheart, Wade Bly, had been joined in marriage just across the street in the historic church that dated back to Caribou Crossing's gold rush days. Now, after a buffet dinner set up in white tents in the town square, the reception was in full swing to tunes played by The Lonesome Cowboys, a local country and western band.

The clear, velvety September sky showcased a dazzling array of stars, but Miriam was sure they couldn't rival the ones in her eyes as she gazed up at her nineteen-year-old husband. He had rolled up the sleeves of the slim-fitting white pleated shirt, and unbuttoned it at the neck, so she had ample opportunity to admire his strong muscles and the tan he'd acquired working on his parents' ranch. His rich chestnut hair was freshly cut in a style that complimented his rugged features.

She nestled as close as the puffy white skirt of her wedding dress allowed, and followed his lead as the band started to play "Stand by Your Man."

As they circled slowly, she gazed around the square. Surrounded by friends and family—had they invited half the town to their wedding?—she felt loved, blessed, blissful.

One of her best friends, Connie, who was dancing nearby with her steady guy, caught Miriam's eye and gave her a thumbs-up.

Miriam smiled at her, grateful to Connie and the rest of the gang who'd decorated the town square, making it magical and romantic. They'd threaded the trees with strings of sparkly lights, set out big urns of roses in all shades of pink, and weaved flowers through the lattice of the band shell. Even the statue of gold-panning Richard Morgan, one of the town's founders, had a wreath of roses decorating his miner's hat, and the wire-framed caribou set out by the chamber of commerce to promote tourism wore rosy headdresses on their antlers.

The square was the heart of the small town of Caribou Crossing, which itself was near the center of British Columbia's Cariboo, a ruggedly scenic patchwork of rolling hills and grasslands adorned with indigo lakes, sparkling rivers, and patches of forest.

A gold rush town in the 1860s, Caribou Crossing could easily have turned into a ghost town as many had, but an enterprising minister and a handful of miners saw the potential for ranching, and the town entered a new era. Now, more than a century later, there was a growing tourist industry as well, with the locals playing up the gold rush history and the country and western theme.

Miriam had moved here at age ten when her dad's

bank transferred him from Edmonton, and she'd fallen in love with everything: the magnificent scenery, horses and riding, the small-town sense of community, even the Western attire.

She glanced over to see Wade's parents heading onto the dance floor. His rancher dad was stocky and handsome in a Western-cut suit and shirt. His mom, whose health was a little fragile, looked vibrant today in a full-skirted blue dress. "It took our wedding to get your dad out of his Stetson."

"And me out of my boots," Wade said. "In these dress shoes, I'm as tottery as a new foal finding its feet."

"Seems to me you're doing just fine."

A number of their guests, including some of the females, were wearing cowboy boots and hats. Others, like her mom and Wade's had taken the opportunity to wear fancier clothes. Miriam loved how folks here were so easygoing and, though they were nosy as all get-out, they weren't judgmental.

"Warm enough?" Wade asked.

"As long as you keep holding me." She'd have preferred to get married in the summer, but in Caribou Crossing life was controlled by the seasons. An early September wedding meant that haying was finished at Bly Ranch, and it would be another month before the calves had to be weaned. Oh yes, she was a country girl, for sure. No, make that a country wife!

The song ended and the singer said, "This next tune's a special request."

Miriam's eyes widened and she gazed up at her husband. "Oh, Wade, did you—"

"Not me." He tipped his head toward the band

shell and rotated their bodies so she could see. "It's your dad."

Her suit-clad father, Henry Torrance, who was more at home in his office at the bank than on a public stage, looked uncomfortable but determined as he mounted the band shell steps and took the microphone. "This song is for the two ladies in my life. Rosie, my beloved wife of twenty-five years, and with any luck another twenty-five and more to come. This is her favorite song, and I think it's the right one for my other special girl tonight." He swallowed and the lights on the band shell revealed a gleam of moisture in his eyes as he gazed across at Miriam.

"You're my oldest child but you're also my little girl," he said, his voice gruff. "I hate to see you grow up and leave my house, but you couldn't be doing it with a better man. So here's a song for you and Wade, to start off your new life together."

Touched, Miriam blinked back tears of her own as she blew him a kiss and mouthed, "Thank you, Daddy."

The members of the band took up their instruments again. Before the first note sounded, she knew what they'd play: "We've Only Just Begun," a song made famous in the 1970s by The Carpenters. Hokey and sentimental, sweet and romantic, it was a perfect wedding song.

Wade gathered her close as she watched her mom, beautiful and elegant in a rose-colored sheath, step into her dad's arms as if there was no other possible place to be. "That's going to be us one day," she told Wade.

He glanced at the older couple. "Twenty-five years married, with lots more to come? Same as my parents."

He nodded to where his mom and dad swayed in each other's arms. "Yeah, for sure."

"Still as in love as we are today."

"More in love."

"If that's possible." He filled her heart so completely, he'd given her his love and pledged his future, how could her feelings be any stronger and truer? Imagining the future, she said, "One day, you'll be requesting that very same song when our daughter gets married."

"You think I'm going to let our daughter get married? What guy could possibly deserve her?" he teased.

She sighed contentedly. "Four kids, right? Two boys, two girls."

"Yeah, but not for a while. I want time alone with you first."

"Time." She gave a happy shiver. "We have so much time. Time to do it all. Our honeymoon, our first apartment. Living together, Wade. It's going to be so much fun."

"Being able to make love whenever, wherever, we want." He kissed her, sweet and warm with a touch of tongue to fire her blood. "Starting with the honeymoon." In an hour or two, they'd drive to a neighboring town to spend their wedding night in the bridal suite of a historic inn. Then they'd head down to Vancouver to explore the big city for a few days.

"It'll be different," Miriam said. "Making love when we're married. Knowing that we're really, truly, totally joined together. Forever. It'll be better than ever before."

"Tough to imagine." He tugged her closer. "But I know what you mean."

Glancing around the open-air dance floor, crowded with kids they'd gone to school with, the parental generation, even a few grandparents, Miriam's gaze lit again on Wade's parents.

"That was so sweet of your folks," she said, "giving us their old ranch truck when they bought a new one." That truck had carried her and Wade on many, many dates and been the site of loads of make-out sessions—a fact that she hoped his parents had never guessed.

"Pa needs me to show up on time for work, now that I won't be living at the ranch anymore."

His folks had a big cattle ranch and Wade had been helping out since he was a toddler. Now he was a full-time paid employee. Bly Ranch was a family business, started by Wade's granddad, and one day he'd inherit it.

Though Miriam's parents—her banker dad and high school teacher mom—were town folk, she'd fallen in love with Bly Ranch the first time Wade invited her out to ride. There was nothing she enjoyed more than galloping side by side across the open grassland, then spreading a blanket by the creek under the shade of the cottonwoods for a picnic and a little fooling around.

"You do know," Miriam teased, nestling against his strong, sexy body, "I just married you for the ranch?"

"Oh, was that the reason?" He gave his hips a subtle pump against her belly.

"Well, there might have been one or two other things."

They laughed softly together and she thought how amazingly compatible they were. They had the same values, the same interests, the same joy in life. They had all the same dreams.

She could see the future ahead of them, clear as day. Those four children. Living together in town, close to her parents, her and Wade's friends, and the kids' schools. Going out to the ranch on weekends to ride and have Sunday dinner. Then eventually, many years from now, she and Wade would be the Blys of Bly Ranch, owning that incredible piece of property and taking care of it so they could pass it down to their own children.

All those beautiful dreams—and they were coming true, starting today.

"It's all going to be so perfect," she sighed, going up on her toes to kiss her husband as he held her in the circle of his arms, safe and loved.

Chapter Two

Wade Bly walked down the hospital corridor, running a hand over his stubbly jaw, and swallowed a yawn. The wall clock said five past ten. Outside the window, blustery snow whirled down from a slate-gray sky. February at its nastiest.

He'd had only a couple hours' sleep during the last thirty. Though he was used to staying up all night when there was a problem with the livestock, this was a whole different thing. He had never, in his entire twenty-seven years, felt so exhausted, drained, and downright shitty. His eyes ached from holding back tears, and his throat burned with unuttered curses and screams.

He fed change into the coffee machine and bought two cups, then returned to Miriam's room.

His mother-in-law glanced up from where she sat by the bed, holding Miriam's left hand.

"Any sign of her waking up?" he asked, handing her one of the cardboard coffee containers.

Rose shook her head. Bleak light from the window fell across her face. A high school teacher, she was usually cheerful and energetic, but on this dismal morning she looked as bad as he felt. "Just as you left, her eyelids rippled, but she didn't open her eyes. She's smiled a couple of times." Rose stared at him somberly through swollen, bloodshot eyes.

He bit his lip. Once Miriam woke, she wouldn't be smiling. He sank down in the chair on the other side of the bed, took a sip of coffee, grimaced, and put the cup down. Threading his fingers through Miriam's, he thought how small and lifeless her hand felt.

Her hands were usually in action, tending their daughter, holding a horse's reins, baking cake, squeezing his butt, stroking him with lazy sensuality.

Rose's voice broke into his thoughts. "You found someone to feed the cattle and horses?"

"Yeah. Ted Williamson's going to go over."

"Did you call your parents?"

"No. I'll wait until Miriam wakes up." He wished his mom was here now, though. He could use one of her hugs. The phone just wasn't the same.

Thinking of his mom's health, his parents' move, all the changes over the past months, he asked quietly, "Do you think it was too much for Miriam? Us moving to the ranch and all?" He'd vowed to protect his wife, and he'd failed.

"She's not like your mother, Wade." Her voice was even. "She's strong, she's always been healthy."

His mother was strong-minded and loving, but physically frail. Back in the fall she'd had a really bad spell and the doctor said the climate was too harsh for her. That's when his folks decided to retire early and move to Phoenix.

"You and Miriam always knew Bly Ranch would be yours," his mother-in-law went on. "It just happened a lot sooner than you expected." She stifled a yawn and rested her head against the back of her chair.

"A hell of a lot sooner." His pa wasn't even sixty yet, and Wade had figured that it'd be another twenty, thirty years before he and Miriam would take over Bly Ranch—and that they'd inherit it, clear title.

"It was the only thing that worked for everyone."

"Yeah." His parents had had to finance their move and buy a home down south, not to mention anticipate their living expenses for the rest of their lives, so they couldn't afford to just give the ranch to Wade and Miriam. They'd given them half, though. Using the down payment he and Miriam had been saving for a house in town, the two of them had obtained a mortgage. A hellacious mortgage that'd have them pinching pennies for years to come.

Rose's voice broke into his musings. "Last time I spoke to your mom, she said she was feeling so much better."

"I know. It's great."

"She said they're both learning golf." She closed her eyes and this time a yawn did escape.

Wade yawned, too, trying to fight against his exhaustion so he'd be awake when Miriam opened her eyes. "So I heard." He couldn't picture his hardworking rancher pa on a golf course. But his father would do anything to look after his mom. That was what husbands did for the women they loved. Wade reached for the foul coffee, took another sip. It did nothing to combat his weariness or his sense of guilt.

In a drowsy voice, Rose said, "Miriam loves the ranch."

"I know." He'd close his eyes and rest them for just a second.

"She was so excited about moving out there last December."

"She was." He smiled as a memory came into his mind.

Wade unlocked and opened the front door of the log ranch house. On this crisp December afternoon two weeks before Christmas, the sun glinted off the snow, making sparkles that matched up with Wade's mood. Anticipation—not just of the next moments but of the years ahead—coursed through him. He hoisted his wife, heavy winter coat, boots, and all, into his arms.

Miriam laughed. "Really? You're going to carry me over the threshold?"

He gazed at her, even more beloved than on the day he'd married her eight years earlier. Miriam was everything to him: vital, cheerful, loving. "You got an objection, Mrs. Bly?"

She beamed at him. "Not a single one, Mr. Bly."

An impatient girlish voice from behind them said, "Hurry up. I want to get changed and go riding."

"Hold your horses, Jessie," he said. This was momentous and he wanted to savor it. Bly Ranch—his childhood home, his heritage—was all theirs. Well, theirs and the bank's, with a mortgage so huge he didn't even want to think about it. And he wouldn't, because everything would work out. It always did, for him and Miriam.

Look at Jessica, their seven-year-old. No, they hadn't planned on having kids until much later, but she'd come along anyway. And they'd hit the jackpot with this beautiful girl who had his chestnut hair and brown eyes, and her mom's plucky spirit and generous heart.

He wasn't much of a guy for speeches, but he said, "Okay, family, this is our new home." Pride and love made his voice a little rough. "We're going to look after it and each other, and it's going to be good to us."

He took a booted step across the wooden frame. The front door was used only for special occasions. Normally, everyone went in the back through the mudroom, shedding boots and coats on the way, but if ever there was a special occasion, this was it.

Carrying Miriam, he walked into the front room, wood-paneled and cozy. Quiet now, after the past couple days' bustle of moving. The fire he'd laid an hour ago, before they left to pick up Jessie at his in-laws' place, just needed a match.

He tilted his head and kissed his wife, then slowly let her down.

"Can I go riding now?" Jessica demanded.

Their daughter loved to ride. Sun, rain, or snow, and there was lots of snow in the middle of winter in the Cariboo. She was a skilled rider and a natural with horses, and she'd been going out on her own for the past year.

Miriam glanced at Wade. "They're forecasting more snow tonight."

"Mommyy." Jessie drew the word out in a protest. "It's not tonight yet."

"Take Whisper," he told his daughter. "She's good in snow. And watch the sky," he cautioned. "If you see clouds the color of your horse's coat, you head straight back. And promise to be careful."

"I'm always careful."

Yeah, right. Jessie was a tomboy. But she'd never done herself any serious damage. Scrapes and bruises were part of life in the country, and they toughened you up.

"Even if the sky's still clear, be back by four, no later," Miriam added. "You know how quickly it gets dark at this time of year."

With their daughter gone for an hour or two, he'd have time alone with Miriam. What better way to celebrate their new home than by making love?

Perhaps his wife was thinking the same thing, because she squeezed his hand and shot him a mischievous smile as Jessie took off up the stairs, her ponytail bouncing, to change into riding clothes.

"I'll light the fire," Wade said.

Miriam shook her head. "Later. I have other plans for right now."

"Oh, yeah? Will I like those plans?"

"Guaranteed." She peeled off her coat and tossed it over the back of the big couch his parents had left behind when they moved. Next, she unbuttoned his coat and he obligingly shrugged out of it and let her heave it on top of hers.

"This is going in a nice direction," he said, as they both took off their boots and lined them up on the hearth.

"And it'll continue." She stepped close, so their jean-clad hips touched. "Crossing the threshold is one big step. The next one's making love in the master bedroom."

He slipped his arms around her. "Thanks for not calling it my parents' room."

She grinned and looped her arms around his neck. "It does feel weird, doesn't it? But it's ours now. Thank God they took their bed."

"You can say that again."

She glanced around the living room. "The house doesn't feel like ours yet, but it will."

They, together with his pa and a bunch of friends, had loaded some of his parents' stuff into a U-Haul and moved Wade and Miriam's belongings from their tiny rental house. His old family home was now a mishmash and he thought it looked nice. "It will."

"I hope things work out for your folks."

"Me, too." This morning, his parents, along with the ranch Border Collie, Shep, had headed off in their new Honda CR-V, towing the U-Haul, on their way to Phoenix. He'd really miss them, but he sure hoped that his mom's health improved, and that his pa found something to keep him busy.

Wade rested his hands on his wife's shoulders. "And now we own Bly Ranch." He still couldn't quite get his head around that fact. "Us and the bank," he amended ruefully.

"We can handle the mortgage," Miriam said, stretching up to kiss him.

He took his time enjoying her soft lips. "You bet we can." There was no question. Together, they could handle anything.

They broke apart when Jessica hurried down the stairs. "I'll be back by four. Bye!"

They called good-bye as she headed for the kitchen. A couple of minutes later, the mudroom door slammed.

"Alone in our new home." Wade smiled down at his wife, thinking how pretty she looked in figure-hugging jeans and a tan sweater that matched her hair. "Someone mentioned the bedroom?"

"That would be me." She took his hand and they headed up the stairs.

His grandparents had built the house and, though his parents had modernized the kitchen and bathrooms, the place still had a rustic, comfy feel. It had always felt like home, and now that's exactly what it was. Home for another family. His family. Yeah, it was starting to sink in and feel right. Really, this was good timing. Better to take over the ranch when he and Miriam were young, strong, and full of energy rather than when they had gray hair.

Holding hands, they walked down the hall to the end, the big corner room. The largest window faced out on what in summer was a peaceful meadow where the ranch horses grazed and played, but now was a field of pristine snow.

He glanced around the room. "Hey, you've been busy in here," he said. Yesterday, she and her friends

Connie and Frances had spread tarps over everything and painted the room sunny yellow. This morning, he and the guys had moved his parents' furniture out and his and Miriam's in. At that point, his wife had kicked him out.

Now he saw that she and her girlfriends had set the room up in a completely different layout than when his parents had occupied it. There were lots of personal touches, too. On the dresser, alongside a Christmas cactus with vivid red blossoms, sat their wedding photo and the photo of them in the hospital with Jessica the day she was born. The cushion his mother-in-law had cross-stitched rested on the rocking chair where Miriam had nursed Jessie and would one day nurse their other babies. The painting they'd bought on their honeymoon—of an aspen grove in early morning light—hung on the wall facing the bed. His wife's Dick Francis mystery novel and alarm clock were on one bedside table, his clock radio and change jar on the other.

Yes, it was their room now, not his parents'. There was only one more thing they needed to do, to make sure of it.

He turned to Miriam, who smiled and said, "I love you, Wade."

"I love you, too, honey." Gazing into her beautiful face, he reflected, "You know, when we got married at nineteen, it kind of felt like we were playing at being grown up. Now it's real. A ranch and a kid. It doesn't get more grown up than that."

Her eyes sparkled and the corners of her mouth curved. "Then let's have grown-up sex."

"Twist my arm." Before she could do that, he reached for the hem of her sweater and hoisted it upward.

The fabric cleared her face and she grinned. "Hey,

just because you're married to me, that doesn't mean you get to skip the foreplay."

"Never," he vowed. "But foreplay's more fun when we're both naked."

"Can't argue with that." She unhooked her bra before he could reach behind her to do it, and then she was naked from the waist up.

He gazed in appreciation. She had a firm, compact, curvy body. So beautiful. In summer she always had a tan, but the past months had faded her skin back to its natural creamy shade. A flush colored her cheeks, and her dusky nipples had tightened into buds. Her curly, shoulder-length hair was the sandy brown of cottonwood, her eyes the blue-gray of an October fog settling like a quiet blanket over the hills. "You're the prettiest thing I've ever seen," he said honestly, knowing he'd say the same thing ten, twenty, fifty years from now.

Her lips, naturally pink and full, curved. "That's not a bad start on foreplay. But I thought you were going to get naked. 'Cause I know you're *the handsomest thing I've ever seen, Wade Bly."*

"Hey, whatever my wife wants . . ." Quickly, he peeled off his clothes as she stripped off the rest of hers.

*"The handsomest," she said, "*and *the sexiest."*

The chill of the room made them shiver and quickly slide under the covers. As they met in the middle of the bed, body heat against body heat made a sharp contrast to the cool sheets. He wrapped his arms around her, felt the soft press of her breasts against his chest, and sighed with pleasure.

They'd started dating when they were thirteen and first made love when they were sixteen. As teens, sex had been a new, amazing thing. Now, after years of marriage, it was a regular part of life, yet it was still pretty damned amazing. They knew each other's bodies so well and there was a whole other level of intimacy. When they were together, naked, nothing else in the world existed. Miriam was *his world. She was the only woman he'd ever made love with and he couldn't imagine wanting anyone else.*

He tugged a wayward curl off her face, touched his lips to hers, stroked down her side and the womanly curve of her hip.

She hooked her leg over his, pressing against his growing erection, and squeezed his ass. "Sex in the afternoon. I like it."

"Me, too." It was a rare treat, what with their jobs, Jessica, and all the chores it took to keep a family going each week. Usually, sex was snatched in a heady, breathless rush first thing in the morning before the alarm went off, or savored with lazy intensity at the end of a busy day after their daughter had gone to bed.

"This feels luxurious." She stretched, her whole body rippling like a cat's. "Decadent."

"I'll show you decadent." Wade pressed a kiss to the pulse point along the side of her throat, then the secret spot behind her ear that made her moan. Her familiar scent of crisp apples and sunshine made him smile against her skin. Sliding down under the covers, he made his way, with kisses and caresses, to her breasts, so full and firm, the skin soft and delicate under his lips. He licked around and around her areola, sucked her nipple, teased it with the tip of his tongue. She tasted just the way she smelled, all sweet and fresh.

Her breathy little moans and the way her fingers thrust through his hair to cup his head were all so familiar and such a turn-on.

He was hard now, his body urging him to enter her and drive toward release, but he ignored the demand and took his time kissing her smooth belly and tracing from memory the silvery stretch marks and faint scars from her C-section. Miriam bemoaned them, but to him they were a reminder of how miraculous her body was. It had carried their child—and would again.

Oh, man, it was a good life, being with Miriam.

He ran his fingers through the soft brown curls at the apex of her thighs, feeling the firm flesh beneath and smelling the distinctive, womanly scent of her arousal. His tongue traced the familiar, ever fascinating path between her legs to lick until she whimpered and her body tensed. Then he sucked her taut little bud and she surged against him in climax.

Bringing Miriam this kind of pleasure was a total high.

Before the spasms faded, he rose above her and slid into her, making her gasp and clutch at his shoulders. Her body sheathed him and pulsed around him in a hot, slippery, sensual embrace that made him swell even more.

Their bodies found an easy, erotic rhythm. Then, as the tension built too high inside him, he slowed to the tiniest of movements and touched his lips to hers. Her tongue flicked into his mouth, tangled with his, and she gave a breathy, sexy little laugh.

Then she raised her butt, changed the angle, challenged him to meet her pace as she pumped her hips. "So good, Wade," she murmured.

"Oh yeah," he answered fervently. It was such a basic, primal act, two bodies mating, yet each time was unique and incredible.

His wife's arms held him tight, her internal muscles hugged him, and the pressure built within him, the drive to stop teasing and to come. He fought it off, but it intensified.

When he reached between their bodies, she shifted

to give him easier access to her clit. He strummed that sensitive bud with his finger.

She caught her breath and gazed into his eyes. "I love you."

"I love you, too, Miriam."

Then he plunged deep and hard, taking them both over the top as they clung and shuddered together.

Drained, physically satisfied, full of love and joy, he slowly collapsed on top of her. Before his weight could get too heavy, he eased his body off hers and lay beside her.

Sprawled on her back, Miriam stretched and gave a contented sigh. "You haven't lost your touch, Mr. Bly."

"Good to know." He rolled onto his side and studied her profile. Her lips were curved in a contented smile. "You look happy."

She turned her head to look at him, her blue-gray eyes soft, almost luminous, in the pale afternoon light. "Very happy. I have something to tell you."

Something good, he gathered, so he smiled expectantly. "Yes?"

"You know when you carried me across the threshold?"

"Yeah?"

"It wasn't just me." Now her smile turned radiant. "Wade, I'm pregnant!"

"What? Oh my God, Miriam, that's terrific." A year ago, they'd decided it was time to go off birth control and have a second child. And now it was happening. "Wow."

He leaned over to kiss her and she met his lips eagerly. Then he ran his hand down her body, across her flat belly. "You just found out?"

"Two days ago. I suspected, did a home test, then went to the doctor. I'm barely six weeks along."

A little hurt, he asked, "Why didn't you tell me right away?"

"I wanted to wait until everything was settled. Your parents on their way south, us in our home here. It seemed like the right time."

The right time. To tell him—yes, he heard what she was saying and it made sense.

But . . . was it the right time to have a child? When they'd decided to have a second kid, he had a salary from his pa, Miriam was working part-time at the vet's, and they were saving for a small house. Now they had a huge mortgage. He'd have to be careful how much money he took out of the ranching business, and they really needed Miriam's income. But when she had Jessie, they'd both agreed she'd stay home for three or four years. With this baby—

"Wade?" Concern tugged at her brow. "You are happy about it, aren't you?"

What expression had she read on his face? Quickly, he said, "Of course I am." No, he wasn't going to share his worries. In fact, he wasn't going to worry. He and Miriam wanted more children, another girl and two boys if they got their way. There was no point waiting. They were together, they loved each other, they were healthy and happy.

He patted her tummy gently, thinking about the little boy or girl he was going to love like crazy. "It's terrific news, honey. The best."

Her face cleared. "In two weeks, it'll be Christmas. Christmas in our new home. You, me, Jessica, and this little one growing inside me. It's going to be wonderful. Oh, Wade, when I think of everything that's ahead of us, it's so exciting."

"It is. It really is." He glanced at his bedside clock.

"Jessie won't be back for another hour. What do you want to do?"

A dimple flashed. "I really should start on dinner."

"I didn't ask 'should,' I asked 'want.' "

"Well, in that case . . ." She rose lithely and straddled him.

Oh yes, with this wonderful woman as his partner, everything was going to work out just great.

Chapter Three

Sounds penetrated the woolly borders of Miriam's safe cocoon. Jarring noises. Loud voices, the clatter of something metal, feet thudding down the hall. Noises that made her anxious. Something was wrong, very wrong.

No, she didn't want to face it. Couldn't deal with it.

Running feet.

That sound could be a good thing. She believed in focusing on the positive.

Running feet. Waking to the sound of running feet . . .

She remembered waking once before to hear that sound in the hallway, as she lay cozy and warm beside Wade on a very special day.

Miriam woke to the sound of running footsteps thudding down the upstairs hall toward the staircase. That would be Jessica, hurrying downstairs to see if Santa had filled the stockings.

She rolled over and spooned her sleeping husband, wrapping her arm around him. "Wake up, sleepyhead."

"Hmm?" He stirred, clasped her hand.

"Merry Christmas, sweetheart."

"Oh, right." He turned over to face her. "It's Christmas. Cool."

"Our first Christmas in our new house." She loved Christmas, and this one was going to be extra special. Oh yes, she could relate to her daughter's eagerness to get the day under way.

She and Wade kissed, but when he teased his tongue between her lips, she pulled back regretfully. "Don't get carried away. Our daughter's on the move."

They pulled themselves up in bed, propping pillows behind their backs and straightening their flannel pajamas. He clicked on the light just as Jessica flung the door open. Normally, there was a "knock first" rule, but rules went out the window on Christmas morning.

"Santa found us!" Jessica cried, clutching three overstuffed red stockings with fluffy white trim. "He ate all the cookies, too."

Wade, who'd eaten most of those Christmas cookies himself, said, "Told you I sent him a change-of-address notice."

Jessica flung herself on the bed between them and handed out the stockings. "I can't wait to see what he brought us." She upended her stocking so the goodies poured out haphazardly.

Miriam's gaze met Wade's and they smiled as their daughter pawed through the little toys and candy, exclaiming happily. She and her husband had been raised to be frugal, and Jessica didn't have as many fancy toys as some of her friends, but she wasn't a greedy child. Besides, she was so in love with horses that being in the barn or going riding was her idea of heaven. Miriam couldn't wait to see their daughter's face when she found out about her big Christmas present.

"Mommy, Pa, what did you get?" Jessica demanded,

drawing her mom's attention. "Why aren't you opening your stockings?"

"We were enjoying watching you," Miriam said. "But it's my turn next." She emptied out her stocking, delighting in the combination of treasures her husband had put together for her: a Sue Grafton mystery, a cassette tape of Christmas songs by Willie Nelson, a framed photo of Wade and Jessica on horseback, a small box of chocolate-covered cherries, and the obligatory mandarin orange in the toe of the stocking.

Wade took his turn, beaming over the tooled leather key fob that read "Bly Ranch," the Faith Hill cassette, and hand warmers to go inside his gloves when he took hay to the livestock and mended fences.

They all trailed downstairs in pajamas, robes, and slippers to eat a Christmas breakfast of pancakes and bacon. Then it was present time, in the front room. While her husband got the fire going, Miriam put her new Willie Nelson tape in the cassette deck and Jessica plugged in the lights on the Christmas tree.

Bly family tradition was to put up the tree on Christmas Eve. Yesterday, Wade had cut the tree on their own—my God, she still couldn't believe Bly Ranch was theirs!—property, a perfectly shaped Douglas fir that reached the ceiling and filled the room with a green, outdoorsy scent. They'd decorated it after dinner, stringing chains of popcorn and cranberries and hanging the ornaments they'd accumulated over the years, with the best display space going to ones Jessica had made at school. This year's were pictures of horses cut out of magazines that she'd mounted on cardboard and decorated with glitter. Miriam had snapped photos all evening, and this morning had her camera ready for the present unwrapping.

Under the tree were their own gifts to each other, together with presents from Wade's parents and other relatives and friends. Miriam and Wade sat side by side on the couch, with Jessica delivering wrapped packages, then crouching on the hearth to open her own.

Most of the gifts were practical: pretty new sweaters and scarves, new cowboy boots for the ever-growing Jessica, a cookbook for Miriam. But she'd also scrimped to buy Wade the binoculars he'd been wanting, and she discovered that the gorgeous silver-wrapped box contained a skimpy lacy negligee.

"Mommy," Jessica said critically, "that nightie's not going to keep you warm."

"You're right," she said, "but it's the thought that counts." She tossed her husband a wink, very much appreciating that thought. Even though they'd been married eight years, Wade still made the occasional romantic gesture, letting her know he found her attractive and sexy.

Jessica unwrapped a children's book about raising a foal, a present from Grandma and Grandpa Bly, who knew what Wade and Miriam had planned. But it wasn't until she opened the final gift, a miniature halter—just the right size for a foal—that her mouth opened and she stared at her parents. "Who's this for?"

Miriam squeezed Wade's hand. "You tell her."

"Your first horse, Jessie," he said. "We're giving you Whisper's foal." The mare, one of the Bly Ranch horses, was a dark dapple gray, in foal to a midnight black stallion named Rapscallion. Miriam and Wade figured that raising a foal would be a great exercise in responsibility for their horse-crazy daughter.

Jessica gave an earsplitting screech as she sprang from the hearth and rushed over to throw her arms around her parents. "Can I go see Whisper now? I want to tell her."

"Sure," Wade said. "And you can feed and water the horses while you're out there."

Their daughter ran off, abandoning the pile of gifts and wrapping paper.

"We made our girl happy," Wade said contentedly.

"We did. I only hope she's half as excited when she learns she's going to have a baby brother or sister."

He chuckled. "I'm excited. Does that count?" He pulled her into the curve of his arm. "When do you want to tell people, hon?"

"After the new year? Right now, I kind of like it being just between the two of us."

"Sounds good to me."

She snuggled close. God, how she loved this man and their life together. But it would be a busy day—everything a pleasure, but still involving effort—so she separated herself again and rose. "Better get going. Loads to do before we head into town." They were going to her parents' for a snack-style lunch and another round of gift giving.

"I'd rather you tried on your Christmas present," he groused good-naturedly as he started to collect wrapping paper.

"Tonight," she promised. "If you're a good boy."

She went into the kitchen to make stuffing for the turkey, and he headed out to feed the cattle. With snow on the ground, he couldn't go a day without harnessing the draft horses and toting hay to the hungry beasts.

Kitchen chores finished, Miriam showered and dressed in figure-hugging black pants and a long red sweater. As she was putting playful Christmas tree earrings in her ears, Wade rushed in and headed for the shower. She laid out clothes for him: charcoal cords, a sage green shirt, and the new green sweater his parents had given him. Then she went to make sure Jessica was dressed. They called Wade's parents in Phoenix and shared Christmas greetings and thank-yous, and then it was time to go.

They loaded the car with gifts and tins of mincemeat tarts she'd baked, and then the three of them drove west into Caribou Crossing. They were ten miles out of town, and the drive was scenic: split-rail fences lining the road, an occasional house with outbuildings, vast expanses of rolling ranch land now blanketed with snow, and a backdrop of low hills.

Reaching town, Wade drove down the main street. Caribou Crossing was a bit of an odd mix. Several heritage buildings had been restored, other storefronts had a tired fifties look, and some, like The Gold Nugget Saloon, were tawdry. Still, today everything looked festive with garlands of holly and strings of white lights. Firefighters, using their ladder truck, had decorated the huge fir in the town square where she and Wade had held their wedding reception. On the snowy lawn of the town hall, a jolly Santa waved from a sleigh towed by wire-framed creatures that anyone outside Caribou Crossing would call reindeer, but here were called caribou.

Too bad these wire beasts were the only caribou ever seen in town. Though the chamber of commerce had set out road-crossing signs—like the ones in school zones but with "Caribou Crossing" and a black silhouette of the mammal on them—those were purely for tourism. The caribou that had once roamed free had fled to more remote territory long ago.

Caribou might be scarce, but a number of people strolled the sidewalks, decked out in colorful hats and scarves, many carrying gaily wrapped packages. As Wade cruised slowly down the main street, Miriam opened the window on the passenger side to let in crisp, snowy air and warm holiday greetings.

Her friend Jane, who'd gone to school with Miriam and Wade and was now a lawyer in town, said, "Lunch next week?" and she happily agreed. Elderly Mrs. Vey asked when the vet's office, where Miriam worked part-time, would be open, and Miriam told her, "The twenty-seventh. But if it's an emergency, call Dr. Christian." Main Street was always like this; you couldn't go twenty feet without stopping for a chat.

Wade made a couple of turns, entering one of the nicer areas of town, then pulled up outside her parents' two-story wood-framed house, where multicolored lights sparkled at the windows and eaves. It was the family home where they'd raised four kids. Only their fifteen-year-old daughter, Andie, still lived at home.

Most days, her mom complained that the three of them rattled around in all that space, but today the downstairs was full. Andie's longtime BFF was there. Logan, who lived down in Vancouver where he went to college, had brought his girlfriend—a student from India—home for the holidays. Joan, the middle sister, was there with her husband, baby, and in-laws. Add in a few close friends of their parents' and it was a noisy, cheerful crowd, rosy cheeked from excitement, the warmth of the fire, and Miriam's mom's brandy-spiked eggnog.

Jessica lost no time telling everyone she was now a horse owner. "Or at least I will be as soon as it's born this spring," she added. "I think my horse is going to be a rodeo star. Or maybe a racehorse."

"Can't say she isn't ambitious," Miriam commented to Wade.

"I'd say she's a dreamer," he said dryly.

"There's nothing wrong with that," she defended her daughter. "Look at us. Remember all those dreams we had, the day we got married? Now they're all coming true." Gently, subtly, she touched her belly, thinking of baby number two and not for one moment regretting that she'd have to turn down her mom's delicious eggnog.

Her dad clapped his hands and announced it was time to open presents, and they all settled in for another round of tearing off wrapping paper. The highlight, for Miriam and Wade, was their gift from her parents: a personal computer. They'd wanted one—a few of their friends had them and raved about e-mail and games—but they hadn't been able to justify the expense. "Thanks, Mom and Dad. This is terrific!" Miriam exclaimed.

"Here." Her father handed her another parcel. "This goes with it."

She opened it eagerly, expecting a game, and found a box with the label QuickBooks. Inside was a CD and a hefty manual. A bookkeeping program? "Um, thanks," she said dubiously. Though her dad was a banker, she'd never been fond of math and had always been grateful he didn't talk shop at home.

"You're operating a business now," he said. "You need the proper tools."

"My pa did all the books by hand, in ledgers," Wade said. "But this, uh, I guess it'll be great."

Her father shook his head. "You're the younger generation. You're supposed to be into technology. Get with the program, kids."

Everyone laughed. Miriam exchanged a glance with Wade, who hated math worse than she did. Her husband was a proud man and liked being in charge, yet after only two weeks of living at Bly Ranch, she'd seen how much he had on his plate. Being a ranch owner wasn't the same as being an employee. She was his wife, his partner in this venture, which was a lot different from visiting the ranch on weekends to ride. She needed to pull her weight, too.

She said, with resolve, "You're right, Daddy. I'll take this on."

Wade's grateful smile was her reward.

"I'll sign up for a bookkeeping course and learn how to use this program." Bookkeeping was just about adding and subtracting, wasn't it? Her dad was right. She and Wade owned not only a massive number of acres, more than a hundred head of cattle, and half a dozen horses—they were running a business.

All of which, if she thought about it that way, sounded pretty intimidating. Almost overwhelming. She took a deep breath. They could handle it. Wade had worked for his father forever, and she'd learn whatever she needed to know.

"Talk to the ranch's accountant," her father advised. "He'll tell you what records you need to keep and what reports he needs from you at fiscal year-end."

"Uh, okay." The ranch had an accountant? And what was fiscal year-end? Okay, she was officially intimidated.

She looked around the room at the brightly lit tree, cheerily dressed family and friends, platters of Christmas snacks on the table, then down at the box on her lap. "QuickBooks," she muttered under her breath.

Chapter Four

The sound of a closing door made Wade jerk to alertness. It was Rose, returning from a trip to the ladies' room. "Any change?" she asked quietly.

"I dozed off," he admitted.

They both peered at Miriam. There was movement under her eyelids. "Shouldn't she be awake by now?" he asked. "I know Dr. Mathews says it varies, but . . ." As he spoke, Miriam's head shifted on the pillow like she was shaking it in a "no" gesture.

"Let her rest, Wade." Rose sank heavily into her chair and reclaimed Miriam's left hand.

He nodded. If he was Miriam, he wouldn't want to wake up. And, much as he needed the reassurance of seeing her open her eyes and speak, he had no idea what he'd say to her.

"All that commotion a little while ago?" Rose said. "The patient's fine now. His heart stopped, but they got it going again."

"Good to know." When they'd heard the calls and running feet as doctors and nurses raced down the hall with the crash cart, he'd feared the worst.

Miriam's fingers twitched in his and she muttered something.

"What was that?" he asked Rose. "It sounded like . . . QuickBooks?"

"It did. That's the bookkeeping program she's been learning, isn't it?"

"It's giving her some trouble, but she's really working at it. She's got half the old records onto the system."

"I wonder why she's thinking about it now?" Rose mused.

He shook his head. A memory flickered. "I remember when you and Henry gave us that program. On Christmas day."

"It was a good Christmas." Rose's voice was soft.

"A great one." And memories of that day were a comforting place for his mind to dwell. He closed his eyes and let them flow.

Christmas morning, stockings in bed, breakfast, present opening. The drive through gaily decorated Caribou Crossing . . . Lunch with Miriam's family and more gifts . . . Then they realized they were running late.

Wade helped his wife and daughter gather the gifts they'd received. Bundled in their coats and scarves, the three of them headed out to the car. It was snowing, in big, lacy flakes that Jessie caught on her tongue.

He stowed their stuff in the trunk. As he started the car, he thought about setting up that computer. When it came to ranch machinery, he was a whiz. He was pretty good with plumbing and electricity, too. How hard could a computer be?

Bookkeeping, though . . . He was as happy as a tick on a hound dog that Miriam had volunteered to take that on. His father had always handled the books, and, though he'd given Wade a crash course before heading to Phoenix, it was a little mind-boggling. Orders to place, bills to pay, regulations to comply with, all sorts of taxes, year-end reports—the list went on and on.

There was a lot more to running a ranch than the things he'd always been involved in: breeding and tending cattle, growing hay to feed them, shipping them off to sale, looking after the horses, and maintaining the barn, fences, and equipment.

His pa had said he could call for advice anytime, but hell, when had Wade ever heard his father beg help from anyone? Wade was a grown-up; he could handle the ranch, with Miriam's help. The two of them made a great team. And Jessie was always happy to help with any chores involving horses.

Momentary concerns brushed aside, Wade hummed along happily to John Denver's "Christmas for Cowboys" on the local country and western station. Personally, his idea of Christmas wasn't to be out in the snow driving cattle, like the song said, but he wasn't a city guy either. Here in Caribou Crossing, he had the best of both worlds. Open range and an independent way of life, plus the comforts of a small town: a nice restaurant to take his wife on her birthday, folks to chat with at the feed store, good schools for his kid. Kids, soon.

"Pa, you need to turn up there."

"Oh, right." He was on autopilot, heading for Bly Ranch. Instead, Wade made the turn Jessie indicated. They'd arranged to bring a friend of hers home with them for Christmas dinner. They were running late, too.

Evan, an only child, was also in second grade. His family was new to town and the kid didn't exactly fit in. As Miriam put it, their softhearted daughter—who was also one of the most popular, outgoing children in her class—had picked up another stray. The two had formed a bond, which Wade didn't really understand as they were so different. Evan didn't like the country or horses, and refused to ride, but he was supersmart and actually loved homework. Jessica was a country girl at heart, totally horse crazy, and preferred anything active over doing homework—yet she'd sit down at the kitchen table and work with Evan.

"I can't wait to tell Ev what I got," Jessica said eagerly from the backseat of the car.

"Honey, go easy with that, okay?" Miriam said. "His family probably doesn't give gifts."

"Santa doesn't even visit?"

"Well, Evan said his family doesn't celebrate Christmas," Miriam answered. "Santa probably knows that." His wife, as softhearted as his daughter, had asked Evan if his family would like to join the Blys for dinner. Evan reported back that his folks said thanks but no thanks. They were fine with him coming, though.

The area of town Wade was driving through was far different from the one where Miriam's parents lived. Here, the houses were trailers or shacks, mostly rentals and in poor repair. A few yards had flowers, but more were full of rusting junk. Though Evan said his dad was a mechanic and his mom worked part-time as a waitress, it was pretty clear that they struggled to make ends meet. Heading down the block where the boy lived, Wade saw him standing outside the run-down rental cottage. He wore a jacket far too thin for the weather and had his ragged backpack slung over one shoulder.

When Wade pulled up, Evan quickly opened the door and hopped in, shivering.

"Merry Christmas, Ev!" Jessica said.

Miriam and Wade echoed the greeting, and then his wife said, "I'm sorry we're late. You should have stayed inside, where it's warm. Besides, I'd like to go wish your parents a happy holiday."

She opened the passenger door to get out, but Evan said, "No, don't. They went out for a walk."

Wade hadn't met the parents and Miriam had met

only Brooke Kincaid. Just once, briefly. When Evan first started coming to their place, Miriam had walked home with him one day. He didn't invite her in but brought his mother to the door. She was wearing a ratty bathrobe, and her blond hair was unwashed and tangled. The woman apologized, said that she'd been in bed with a bad headache, and that she was glad to meet Miriam and happy their kids were friends. Miriam told Wade that, even unkempt and sick, Brooke was beautiful, and looked too young to have a seven-year-old child. Perhaps that was why Evan called her Brooke, rather than Mom.

Now, as Wade drove away from the rental house, Miriam said, "Evan, don't you have a warmer coat? Or at least a heavy sweater to wear under it?"

"Brooke says I grow so fast she can't keep up with me."

"Kids have a habit of doing that," Wade said. Still, the boy was no bigger than Jessica, and skinny. But maybe he'd been even smaller and had a growth spurt this year. Wade cranked the rattly heater up as far as it would go, which still wasn't great. They'd bought the car used, back when Jessie was born, because Wade needed the truck pretty much full-time. He sure hoped the vehicle would last until they could afford something nicer—which, given the size of their mortgage, wouldn't be any day soon.

The kids—mostly Jessie—chattered away in the backseat, the radio played country versions of Christmas music, and the heater clattered like it was working its butt off. Miriam rested her gloved hand on Wade's corduroy-clad thigh and leaned close. Whispering, she said, "Jessica got three new sweaters, and that navy pullover isn't the least bit feminine. I bet she wouldn't mind passing it on to Evan."

"His parents might see it as charity," he murmured back.

"It'd be a Christmas gift," she said. "I'll check with Jessica, then wrap it up and sneak it under the tree."

He patted her gloved hand, thinking how much he loved her. "You're a good woman, honey."

When they reached the ranch, she said, "Wade, why don't you get Evan to help you with the fire?"

Right. Like the little egghead had any talent for stuff like that. But Wade knew it was a ploy to keep the boy occupied while his wife could talk to Jessica, then deal with the sweater, so he went along with it.

A few minutes later, Jessie ran into the front room. "Ev, come out to the barn and see Whisper, the mare who's carrying my foal."

"Bet she looks like any other horse," he teased as he let Jessie drag him away.

"No, she's much prettier. And smarter."

Miriam hurried down the stairs shortly after they left, carrying a new parcel. "Kids out in the barn?"

When Wade confirmed, she stuck the gift under the tree, and then they both went to the kitchen. She put on her apron, basted the turkey, and started trimming Brussels sprouts. Wade plunked down at the table to peel potatoes. Couldn't say he cared for the task, but he did love Miriam's mashed potatoes and gravy, not to mention hanging out with her in the kitchen.

The children tramped into the mudroom, shed their outdoor clothing, and went to play by the fire. Wade and Miriam finished up, then poured mulled apple juice into four mugs and joined them.

"Evan," Miriam said, "Santa must have been a little mixed up. It seems he didn't know you don't celebrate Christmas, because he left a couple of gifts for you under our tree."

The boy's face lit with excitement, but he quickly banked it down and frowned. "Dad says there's no such thing as—" He broke off, glancing at Jessica, then said, "Santa brought me something?"

"Here," Jessica said eagerly, reaching under the tree to pull out the remaining packages.

"I brought you something, too," he said hesitantly. "They're not much, but . . ." He reached into his pack and pulled out a bundle wrapped neatly in tissue paper and handed it to Miriam.

Wade recognized the paper. It was the same stuff Jessie had wrapped some of their gifts in. The kids had made it as an art project at school, taking leaves and drawing or spray painting around them.

"Evan, that's so sweet of you," his wife said. She separated the tissue.

When she saw the contents, her mouth fell open. "These are beautiful." She held up a few. They were Christmas tree ornaments, the same type Jessie had made in school, but even a proud father had to realize that the boy's were made with more care and attention to detail. Also, where Jessie's had all been horses, Evan had cut out a variety of pictures, from cottages with smoke rising to glittering big-city high-rises, from trees to animals to models in fancy clothes. He'd applied glitter with precision.

"They're miniature works of art," Miriam said. "And oh, my! Look at these snowflakes. They're exquisite."

The ornaments she held up now did look like snowflakes. They'd been cut painstakingly from white paper, each in a distinctive and elaborate pattern. Wade glanced down at his big, calloused hands and couldn't imagine them wielding scissors to create anything like that.

"Where did you learn to make these?" Miriam asked. "This wasn't a school project?"

"No. I checked out a library book on making Christmas ornaments."

"They're amazing. You're a talented boy."

He shrugged. "I know."

Wade choked back a snort. The comment was typical, and it was one reason he had trouble warming to the boy. Evan could be arrogant, a know-it-all, and he made no bones about calling Caribou Crossing Hicksville.

"Open your presents," Jessica ordered.

The boy fingered the shiny red bow on one, then meticulously untied it and put the ribbon on the coffee table. Where Jessica ripped into parcels, he was the opposite, peeling off the tape so it didn't tear the paper. Finally the box was revealed. It was a jigsaw puzzle with a thousand pieces. Miriam did them occasionally, and one day when Evan had stayed at their place for dinner she'd started a puzzle. They bored Jessica, but Evan was fascinated, and clever about finding pieces.

For herself, Miriam always chose country scenes, but for Evan she'd picked one of Manhattan, all high-rises, giant advertisements, and sparkling lights.

"Santa's smart," she said. "He knows you like big cities."

"Wow," Evan breathed. His blue-green eyes, pretty much his only good feature, widened. "Where is this?"

"New York City."

"I'm going there one day," he announced as if there was no doubt about it. "Maybe I'll even live there. It sure beats Hicksville."

"Not me," Jessica announced. "I'm going to stay right here and breed horses. Here, Ev, open this one." She handed him another parcel.

When he saw the navy sweater, Miriam quickly said, "Santa brings sweaters to everyone in Caribou Crossing.

He knows how cold it gets here."

"I got sweaters, too," Jessica said.

"It's really nice. And warm."

"There's one more," Jessica said, "and it's heavy!" She passed him the rectangular package.

When he peeled back the paper to reveal a hardcover dictionary, Jessica said, "Oh gee, it's a dictionary. That's no fun."

Wade agreed, but Miriam had insisted it was the right gift. The boy had a great vocabulary and liked to use it, and he'd complained that the library wouldn't let him check out a dictionary. From the expression on the boy's face, his wife's judgment was spot on.

Evan touched the front cover lightly, almost reverently. "My very own dictionary? To keep?"

"Santa said so," Miriam told him.

"This is the best present ever." His tone left no doubt he believed that.

"You're weird, Ev," Jessica said affectionately.

"Says the girl who's obsessed with horses," he teased back. But his smile, when he looked at her, lit his face with the same emotion.

He was a strange-looking boy with a scrawny face and big ears, and his personality was downright odd, but his affection for Jessie was obvious. That was why Miriam liked him, and Wade had agreed to having him around—along with his positive influence on Jessie's schoolwork.

Evan turned to Wade and Miriam, his expression serious again. "Thank you, Mr. and Mrs. Bly." A quick grin twitched his lips. "I mean, if you run into Santa Claus, would you tell him thanks?"

"We certainly will," Miriam said.

Wade rose to poke the fire and toss another log on.

The turkey smelled so good, he was hungry again. "Is it almost time for dinner?"

Evan didn't say a word, but turned to Miriam eagerly.

She rose, tugging her red sweater over her curvy hips. She looked so sexy in those black pants and the bright sweater. "I'll get the vegetables going. Then I want all three of you in the kitchen in ten minutes to help."

Soon they were all working together. One thing Wade would say for Evan: He was always eager to help and he followed instructions precisely. Unlike Jessica, who was willing but more haphazard. Wade knew his own role after all these years of marriage, so he carried and carved.

Once they were all seated and had dished out the first serving, there was little conversation. When they went back for seconds, Evan said, "You're an excellent cook, Mrs. Bly. I've missed your cooking."

"Thanks. I'm sorry we haven't had you out to the ranch before, but we've been so busy getting settled."

In town, Evan had walked home with Jessie after school a couple of times a week. They played together and did homework, and Evan often stayed for dinner. He could put away food like no one's business. God knows where it went; the boy was as skinny as barbed wire.

"It's okay." Evan's busy fork paused and he hung his head. "It's not like I can walk here, like I did when you were in town. But at least Jess and I will still see each other at school after New Year's."

"But that's not enough," Jessie protested. "You have to come out here sometimes."

"We'll work it out," Miriam promised. "I can bring you out to the ranch when I pick Jessica up after school,

you can stay for dinner if it's okay with your parents, and then Wade can drive you back after." Clearly, she'd thought it out, though she hadn't discussed it with Wade. He had better things to do with his evenings, like chop firewood and repair equipment, not to mention bring himself up to speed on the latest government regulations and figure out his pa's antiquated filing system.

"It'd be okay with my folks," Evan said quickly. "Are you sure?"

The kid looked so eager, so hopeful. Jessie had said he didn't make friends easily, which didn't surprise Wade one bit. Oh hell, maybe he was getting as soft-hearted as his womenfolk. "Hey," he said, "we need you, Evan. Without you, how's Jessie going to pass second grade?"

"Pa-a." Jessica rolled her eyes.

"I suppose that's true, sir," Evan said thoughtfully.

Wade and Miriam exchanged a glance of mutually suppressed laughter.

Jessica snorted. "Horses are more fun than homework."

"Schoolwork's important," the boy said. "You have to learn and get good marks if you're going to get ahead in the world."

Was he parroting his parents? Parents had dreams for their kids. Wade's had been that Jessica would love ranching as much as he did, but his girl had a mind of her own and it was set on horses, not cattle.

"Well said, Evan," Miriam commented. "You're right."

"Yeah, well," Jessie grumbled, "Ev's a klutz when it comes to the stuff I'm good at."

The boy shrugged awkwardly. "Yeah. I suppose we all excel at different things."

Wade stifled a grin at the adult phrasing. Now that the kid had his own dictionary, God knows what might come out of his mouth.

"And it's nice of you to help Jessica," Miriam said. "Now, who wants more stuffing?"

They ate until they were as stuffed as the turkey had been. Then the kids went up to Jessica's room to play with some of her new toys. While Miriam tidied up the kitchen, Wade went out to tend the horses. When he came back in, he called upstairs, "Evan, I should take you home now. It's getting close to bedtime."

The pair came downstairs a few minutes later, Evan wearing the navy sweater under his thin jacket, his backpack showing the outline of his dictionary, and the jigsaw puzzle clasped tightly in his arms.

As usual, Miriam handed him a plastic bag of leftovers, which he accepted with a muttered "Thank you, Mrs. Bly."

Jessie was yawning and Miriam said, "Bedtime for you, my girl. I'll tuck you in and we can start reading one of your new books." His wife and daughter liked snuggling up together with a book at bedtime—and he liked sneaking a peek from the doorway while they did it.

Tonight, though, by the time he made it back from town, singing along to songs on CXNG, the local country and western radio station, he found his wife waiting for him in the front room.

"Jessie asleep?" he asked.

"Couldn't keep her eyes open." She rose and came into his arms. "Mmm, you smell of snow, all crisp and fresh." She rubbed her warm nose against the cool skin of his throat.

He dipped his head and kissed the top of her silky hair. "And you smell of turkey."

"Turkey? That's not so romantic."

"Sure it is. It's delicious." He dropped a kiss by her ear and murmured, "Edible."

She chuckled, then said suggestively, "Well then, if you're not too full from dinner . . ."

"There's always room for more dessert. When it's you." Talk about the perfect way to end a wonderful day. His lips moved across her cheek to meet hers for a long, sizzling kiss.

She smiled up at him. "You still make my heart skip."

"Good to hear." She made his heart do cartwheels. Her effect below his belt was pretty spectacular, too. "Let's go upstairs and you can try on your new nightie."

"Mmm, but what if it doesn't keep me warm?" she teased, her dimple flashing.

He grinned, remembering their daughter's innocent comment. "Wife, you're going to be plenty warm."

They broke apart and she cast one long look at the Christmas tree before he unplugged the lights. "Our first Christmas at Bly Ranch," she said. "I'd say it was perfect."

He twined his fingers with hers. "It'll be perfect once we're in bed together."

Hand in hand, they went up the stairs. At the top, he kissed her again and said with satisfaction, "This is going to be the best year yet."

Chapter Five

Again, Wade woke with a jerk, his neck stiff from falling asleep in the chair by Miriam's bed. He checked her face. Still and white, almost as white as the hospital sheets. Her eyes were closed, but the fingers twined through his felt reassuringly warm.

His gaze went to Rose. She was awake, her face almost as pale as Miriam's and far more strained.

"She moved a little and her eyes almost opened once," she said. "I think she's coming back to us."

He glanced at his watch. Almost noon. Yes, Miriam was sure to be awake soon. "What are we going to tell her?" The words grated out.

"The truth." Her bloodshot eyes filled with tears and she pressed trembling fingers to her brow and temples. Then she stood abruptly, said "Ladies' room," and went out the door.

The truth. Yeah, they had to tell Miriam the truth. And it would break her heart.

It was his fault. He was supposed to take care of her, and he hadn't.

Like him, she'd been working flat out. She was energetic and didn't exactly complain, but she'd joked more than once that owning the ranch was sure different from going out there for weekend rides. He saw her yawn over dinner, pick at her food, rub her back, move slowly and painfully. Though he hated to see her like that, what choice did they have? They needed the money from her job, he worked as many hours as he could stay awake, and they sure couldn't afford to hire anyone to do the housework or bookkeeping.

Still, he'd been raised to believe that a man took care of his woman. Maybe it was an old-fashioned notion, but Caribou Crossing was ranch country and he was a rancher. Ranchers weren't exactly known for being newfangled. Yeah, it had hurt his pride to know that his pregnant wife had to work her pretty little butt off so they could make ends meet. But he hadn't found a solution. And now, here she was.

"I'm sorry, honey." He squeezed her hand gently.

Why hadn't he recognized the signs that she was more than just tired? Like they said, hindsight was twenty-twenty.

But damn it, if he could only go back in time. Maybe even one day would have been enough.

He thought back to last night's dinner. It was only sixteen, seventeen hours ago, yet it seemed like a lifetime.

"Love this dessert," Wade told his wife, digging into the rich devil's food layer cake that followed a spaghetti and meatballs dinner.

"I know you do." She smiled at him.

"The cake is stupendous," Evan enthused. "Everything you make tastes like ambrosia, Mrs. Bly."

Miriam met Wade's gaze for a second. A sparkle of humor brightened her eyes as they shared the thought: Evan's been using his dictionary again.

"Thanks," she said. "You three are an easy audience to please."

She'd given herself only a tiny piece of cake, Wade noticed. Though she was eating for two, lately she hadn't had much of an appetite. He hoped it was just one of those weird phases of pregnancy.

He stretched tired muscles. Winter wasn't as strenuous as summer on the ranch, but his days were still packed. With snow on the ground, he had to take feed to the cattle every day, break up ice on the creek so they could drink, and put out salt. He kept an eye on the animals' health, checked and mended fences, tended to the outdoor horses and the ones they kept in the barn, and kept the outbuildings and equipment in order. Chopping firewood was another never-ending task. The only break from the daily routine was the couple of times a week that he drove the truck into town for supplies and met up with friends for coffee at the Round-Up.

Reluctantly, he swallowed the last bite of cake and shoved his chair back from the table. "Got to get back to work. Miriam, I'm going out to the office to tackle Pa's files again." They'd both been working in the ranch office out in the barn. She was putting financial information into the computer program, and she needed Wade to locate the papers that corresponded to the notes in his pa's ledger. The handwriting was hard to read and his father used abbreviations that made no sense to Miriam, and sometimes not even to Wade.

"I'll look after the horses," Jessie volunteered. She was happy to do any task involving horses, and Wade was mighty grateful for her assistance.

"Have you finished your homework?" Miriam asked, looking not at her but at Evan for confirmation.

"We have," the boy said.

She turned back to her daughter. "Okay, then. But, Jessica, I want you in bed by the time I get home from class." Miriam drove into town two nights a week to take a bookkeeping course. She sighed. "Wish I didn't have to go out. A warm bath and early to bed with a book sounds way better."

Her days were as busy as Wade's. They were both up before dawn on these short winter days. She made breakfast and packed lunches, then drove Jessica to school and went to her job at the vet's office. She finished midafternoon when the vet's mom came in for two or three hours, which meant Miriam could pick Jessie up at school—with Evan on the days of her evening classes. She did whatever shopping was needed, then came home to cook dinner and do housework. After dinner, she was either back into town for her classes, or at home doing homework or entering financial data into the computer.

Even with both of them working flat out, they were barely making ends meet. And there'd be more expenses when the baby came.

But Wade couldn't worry about that. Miriam was pregnant, and they both loved kids. They'd manage somehow. Once the long, cold winter was over, things would look brighter.

"Pa?" Jessica said impatiently. "Are you coming?"

Wade realized Evan was clearing the table and Miriam was at the sink, rinsing the dishes he handed her. When she bent to put them in the dishwasher, her movements were slow, and she paused to rub her lower back.

"Yup, I'm coming." He rose and went over to kiss his wife. "Drive safe and stay warm, hon. Bye, Evan, see you soon." Miriam would drop him at home or the library before going to her class. "Okay, Jessie-girl, let's head out to the barn."

In the mudroom, as they pulled on boots and heavy coats, his daughter said, "I've been thinking, maybe I won't be a horse breeder."

"No?"

"I think I should go on the rodeo circuit."

"Uh-huh." He didn't bother trying to talk her out of it. Her dreams changed every week or so. He'd bet, though, that whatever she ended up doing, it would relate to horses, not cattle. "Sure hope your baby brother or sister turns out to be rancher material." He wanted one of his kids to carry on the tradition. He'd hate to see Bly Ranch leave the family.

"I can't wait for the baby to come. And to get big enough so I can teach it how to ride!"

"Me, too." He smiled contentedly at the thought of another bright, healthy, enthusiastic child like Jessie. Yeah, things were a little tough now in terms of work and finances, but life was great and there was so much to look forward to.

Chapter Six

This time it was pain that prodded Miriam's cocoon. It tugged at her belly and she shifted position, trying to ease it.

The baby . . . She remembered now, it was the baby moving. . . .

It really was a kicker, this little one.

Wincing as the baby kicked out again, Miriam pulled on her heavy down coat, scarf, woolly hat, and gloves. She said good night to several fellow bookkeeping students as they passed her on their way to the door of the high school, and wondered if they were as overwhelmed by the classes as she was. It turned out that while bookkeeping did involve adding and subtracting there were a bunch of other concepts that confused her. Too bad she hadn't inherited her dad's aptitude. Though she hated to beg him for help, she just might have to. The instructor, Mr. Benson, a retired accountant, really wasn't very good at explaining things.

A humorous thought made her lips quirk. Too bad Evan Kincaid wasn't ten years older. She'd bet he could figure out all these accounting concepts and tutor her.

She hurried across the plowed parking lot to the car. At

least its engine roared to life, though the heater had packed it in last month and they couldn't afford to fix it. Even bundled up as she was, tonight the chill seeped into her bones, aggravating the nagging ache in her lower back that had bothered her for the last couple of days, along with the crampy twinges in her belly.

When the baby had first stirred, with a gentle fluttering, she'd been so happy. Now the little one had graduated to doing aerobics in her body, which was far less pleasant. Jessica had been an active baby, but not like this. Oh well, just as long as the baby was moving, all was well.

Still, bed was going to feel awfully good tonight. Especially if it contained her husband's warm, firm body to curl up against. She hoped he wouldn't work too late.

It used to be Wade put in long days at the ranch working for his dad, but he usually made it home for dinner and didn't go back. They'd play with Jessica, maybe watch a child-friendly TV show. After tucking their daughter in, they'd cuddle up on the couch together, watching something more adult and chatting about their day. Every week or so, her parents or sister Andie would come baby-sit so Miriam and Wade could go to a movie or to the Lucky Strike, their favorite country and western bar. But most of the time they were content to stay home. Often, they'd go to bed early themselves—but not because they were sleepy.

Miriam smiled at that thought as she drove through the town center. Caribou Crossing was quiet at this hour, though lights glowed through the windows of the Roadhouse restaurant and the Round-Up coffee shop. Gaudy neon marked the windows of The Gold Nugget Saloon, a sleazy bar she always avoided. The door of the bar opened and a couple came out, voices raised in what sounded like a drunken argument. Light gleamed briefly on the woman's blond hair as Miriam drove past them, grateful that Wade was her husband. The two of them rarely disagreed, much less out and out fought.

A few blocks down, the Lucky Strike was humming. Nostalgically, Miriam remembered Valentine's Day the previous year. She and Wade had sent Jessica to a sleepover at Bly Ranch—a treat she always loved—and had a wonderful dinner at the Roadhouse, along with other romantic couples of all ages. Then they'd walked over to the Lucky Strike and danced until the place closed. Tipsy, laughing, arms tight around each other, they'd tramped home in the snow and made love until dawn.

This year, he'd given her a dozen red roses. The grocery store kind, not from a florist. But that huge mortgage hung over their heads, and at least her hubby, who had so much on his mind these days, had remembered it was Valentine's Day and told her he loved her. They hadn't made love until dawn, but they'd had some pretty fine sex all the same.

Wade might not be as romantic as he used to be, but he was a loving husband and the sex, when they were both awake enough to indulge, was still terrific.

Her spirits rose as she left town and headed east on the dark secondary highway that led to the ranch. Traffic was light and, despite the chill, the winter night was lovely: A clear, starry sky illuminated the crisp white snow that coated each rail of the roadside fences and blanketed the rolling ranch land.

She was so lucky to live in this beautiful country, with her wonderful husband. Tonight, despite tiredness and aches and pains, she was going to seduce Wade. First, though, she'd get him to massage her sore lower back. That thought warmed her enough to survive the fifteen-minute drive.

She pulled the car next to the Bly Ranch truck in the garage, then hurried into the house. Wade was in the kitchen, putting the dried dishes away.

"Thank you, sweetheart." She came up behind him and wrapped her arms around his waist. "Jessica in bed?"

"Reading a horse book and waiting for a good-night kiss.

Speaking of which . . ." He turned and gathered her close for a long, slow kiss.

When their lips parted, he said, "You feeling okay? I saw you rubbing your back earlier."

"The baby's finding its feet. Nothing major." She winced as another of those weird cramps tugged at her insides.

"Say good night to Jessie, then have a bath and I'll give you a massage."

He'd volunteered; she didn't even have to ask. "You're the best," she said gratefully. Then she squeezed his backside. "You know what else relieves pain and relaxes me?"

"Orgasm," he said promptly. "I can help you out with that."

Feeling better by the moment, she said, "I knew I could count on you."

"Always glad to be of service."

Laughing softly, she headed upstairs, stopping to press a hand to her side as the little one acted up again. "Go to sleep, you," she murmured, before going to say a quick good night to her daughter. Jessica, at least, was drowsy. The girl was so active all day, she dropped off to sleep quickly and slept soundly.

In the bathroom, Miriam turned on the water in the tub. She'd love it hot, but stuck to warm because it was better for the baby. In went a handful of Epsom salts, a trick her doctor had taught her during her first pregnancy. And thinking of the doctor, it was good she had an appointment this week. She was past the first trimester danger zone, so the achy back and crampy twinges were no doubt just symptoms of pregnancy, but best to make sure.

After brushing her teeth, she stripped, tossed her clothes in the laundry hamper, and with a sigh of expectation stepped into the tub and sank down. Bliss. What utter luxury to be doing absolutely nothing.

She must have dozed off because the next thing she knew, Wade's hand was on her shoulder. "Hey, wife, you can't spend the night in there."

Blinking to focus her tired eyes, she saw that he'd changed into pajamas. Even in striped blue and gray flannel, the man looked sexy.

"I can think of a better place." She yawned, and reached gratefully for his hand as he helped her up and steadied her when she stepped out of the tub.

He rubbed a towel gently over her body.

"You're a good husband."

"Have to treat you well or you'll find some other guy."

She chuckled. "Not gonna happen." As he well knew. They were made for each other, the two of them. Maybe they were working harder than she'd like, and didn't have as much time for romance as they once had, but there were still wonderful moments like this. And once they got the ranch under control, there'd be more of them. "Especially not if you give me that massage you promised."

"Climb into bed." With a warm hand on her lower back, which didn't ache quite as much now, he steered her into the bedroom.

"Door locked?" she asked.

"You bet." They never took the risk Jessica would forget the "knock first" rule and catch them making love.

She slid between the covers, then rolled onto her side. At four months, her baby bump was still small, but she'd rather not lie on her stomach.

Her husband flicked off the light and climbed in behind her. When his leg brushed hers, she realized he'd taken off his pajamas. With slow, warm hands, he kneaded the muscles in her back, from her neck to the curves of her butt, loosening knots and relaxing tension she hadn't even realized she was carrying.

"You're very good at that," she murmured. She'd always loved Wade's hands, so capable when it came to work, so deft at massage, so knowing and seductive when it came to touching her in the most intimate ways.

They switched position so that she lay on her other side, and he continued to massage.

Then his hand, which had been working the muscles of her butt cheek, slipped between her legs. "How tired are you?"

"Not too tired." In fact, she was exhausted, still a little achy, and the baby kept kicking. But this time together was special and she didn't want to lose it. Besides, orgasm did often help when she had menstrual cramps or a headache, so maybe it would tonight.

She wriggled her backside toward him, and he came forward to meet her. He was hard already, a number of steps ahead of her in the arousal department. But she'd catch up, because now he'd looped an arm over her hip and his fingers teased her pussy.

Any thought of aches and pains fled as sensation centered under his seductive touch. Sweet heat filled her. Wanting to kiss him, she rolled over again, warning, "Don't stop."

He kept up the arousing strokes and caresses as she leaned into him, circling his lips with the tip of her tongue, then dipping inside. His tongue flirted with hers, drawing it in.

She touched his cheek, ran her fingers through his thick hair, cupped the solid strength of his shoulder. Knowing his body by touch in the dark, she worked her way down, revisiting all her favorite places and the ones that made him moan.

As their kiss deepened and heated, he stroked her body in a whole different way than when he'd massaged her. He was gentle with her breasts, knowing that pregnancy made them sensitive. His hand caressed her tummy so lovingly, she knew he was thinking of their baby growing inside her. Now, when his fingers again slipped between her legs, she was soaking wet for him.

Usually, they made love with one of them on top, but tonight that would put a strain on her back. Wade must have realized that, because he slid down under the covers, kissing all the places his fingers had caressed.

She raised her leg, an invitation for him to bury his face between her legs where she was slick and swollen.

He settled his mouth at the entrance to her body and her thighs gripped him, encouraging him as he licked and sucked, teasing her toward climax.

She lifted the covers. "Two can play that game, mister."

Quickly he shifted under the bedding until he'd reversed direction so his feet were at the head of the bed. His mouth, though, was in the very same place, the exact place she wanted it.

In the warm, dark cave created by the sheet and duvet, their bodies adjusted to match each other, having done this so many times before. She smelled the enticing musk of mutual arousal, then closed her mouth on him, sucking him in.

He moaned with pleasure.

He'd long ago taught her exactly the way he liked to be touched. Exactly where and when to lick, how to pump her hand on his shaft, when to suck and slide.

Once, after he'd been out drinking with some guy friends, he told her that the single ones said it must be boring always having sex with the same woman. He told her the guys were such losers; they didn't get it. Perfect sex could never be boring. And that was what the two of them had together.

Oh yes, perfect.

Her thighs clenched, her breath caught. Wade knew exactly what she wanted, and gave it to her: that final firm suck of the taut bundle of nerves that controlled her pleasure.

When she spasmed and shuddered against his mouth, he held her, gentled her through it.

Her own mouth and hands had stopped their erotic play while she gave herself over to her climax, but when her body relaxed and her thighs released him, she got back to business.

Chapter Seven

Rose hadn't returned yet, and Wade guessed she was calling her husband to give him an update. Henry'd been at the hospital earlier, after dropping Jessie at school, but then had gone to work. This afternoon, he'd pick Jessie up from school and take her to his and Rose's house, where Andie would baby-sit.

Alone with Miriam, Wade leaned forward to kiss her forehead and murmur, "I love you, honey."

Her lashes fluttered and she smiled, but she didn't open her eyes.

She was in a world of her own, one where he couldn't join her.

He rested his head on the pillow beside hers. Just for a moment. Just to breathe her in, to feel the tickle of her hair against his cheek. He wished he could take off his clothes and slip into bed with her, to cradle her in his arms and keep her safe.

She made a little *mmm* kind of sound.

It reminded him of last night, when they'd been naked together in bed. He closed his eyes, remembering. So good . . . Making love with Miriam was always so good. . . .

And last night, man had it been special.

In the dark world under the covers, Wade gave himself over totally to sensation. The world held only him, his wife, and their love. There wasn't a single thing to worry about.

With the taste of her climax sweet on his lips, her slender hand pumping his swollen shaft, and her warm, wicked tongue and lips licking and sucking him, pressure built quickly. He had no reason to hold back, so he didn't, letting his own orgasm pour through him and into Miriam's mouth.

After, he could barely move. Exhausted and boneless, he somehow managed to drag himself back up the bed so his head was on his pillow. "Love you, honey," he said. "Sleep well."

"Love you, too, sweetheart." She yawned, then turned and wriggled herself into the curve of his body as he spooned her. "Morning's going to come far too soon."

He kissed her shoulder, yawned widely, closed his eyes . . . and he was gone.

How much later was it when he woke in the darkness, feeling the bed shift as Miriam climbed out? He didn't bother checking the clock, just rolled over, ready to go back to sleep. When she was pregnant, she often had to pee in the middle of the night.

A few minutes later, his wife's voice called from the bathroom, bringing him to alertness. "Wade? Are you awake?"

"Yeah. Are you okay?"

"I . . ."

That hesitation had him whipping back the covers and climbing out of bed. "Miriam?" He strode to the closed bathroom door. "Can I come in?"

"Yes."

When he did, she was standing by the toilet, clad in flannel pajamas, one hand across her middle. Her face was white and she gestured wordlessly to the toilet.

He looked inside and saw that the water had swirls of red. "Jesus, you're bleeding!"

"Spotting. It's just spotting. I think." But her eyes were huge and scared, and her voice was uncertain. With a gasp, she curved forward suddenly, hunching over the way she'd done when she was in labor with Jessica.

He put his arm around her shoulders, steadying her. "Miriam, what's going on? The baby's acting up?"

"I guess. It's like cramps. Or c-contractions. Like when I went into labor. It's probably normal, right?"

"It didn't happen when you were pregnant before."

"The doctor says each pregnancy's different." She straightened. "It's eased off now. I have an appointment with Dr. Mathews in a couple of days. I'll ask her."

Wade felt inexperienced and helpless. His wife was in pain. She was bleeding. He hated asking for help, always figuring he should handle things himself. But what did he know about pregnancy? "We should call her now."

"We can't do that. It's the middle of the night. It's not an emergency."

How did they know whether it was? "I'm calling your mom."

Miriam put a restraining hand on his arm. "We shouldn't wake her up." But he could tell from her tone that she'd love her mother's reassurance.

"She won't mind. It's not negotiable, Miriam."

"Okay," she said softly, sounding relieved.

He helped her back to bed and got her settled, then yanked on his pajamas and dialed the phone. When her dad answered, sounding sleepy and worried, Wade said, "Miriam's feeling a little under the weather. Could we talk to her mom? We have some pregnancy questions." His mother-in-law had given birth to four kids, which to his mind made her an expert.

When Rose came on the line, he passed the phone to his wife, who described the pains she'd been having. Miriam listened, then said, "If you're sure, Mom. Yes, we'll call you back." She hung up and turned to him. "She says to call the doctor."

The number was programmed into their phone. When she made the call, Wade listened to her side of the conversation, gnawing on his bottom lip as he saw the worry on Miriam's face. Wordlessly, she handed him the phone.

"Wade," Dr. Sonia Mathews said calmly, "as I told Miriam, it may be nothing at all, but I don't think we should wait until morning to find out. Bring her to the hospital and I'll meet you there."

"Sure. Of course. But you think it's nothing?" He begged for reassurance.

"We'll hope. She's healthy, and her last pregnancy had no complications, at least not until she was in labor."

That had been a little scary. They'd planned for natural childbirth, but Jessie's umbilical cord had slipped into the birth canal. Dr. Mathews said it would be compressed during birth and cut off the oxygen supply, so she'd had to perform a C-section. But mom and baby had both come through beautifully.

While he'd been talking to the doctor, Miriam had climbed out of bed again and was pulling warm clothes from the cupboard. After making sure she looked steady on her feet, he dialed her parents back. "The doctor says it could easily be nothing," he told Rose, "but we're going to the hospital. We'll have to take Jessie with us, but—"

With relief, he listened to his mother-in-law say that they'd come to the hospital and her husband would take Jessica home to their place while Rose stayed with Miriam and Wade.

He thanked her, then hurriedly threw off his pajamas and dragged on clothes. "I'll get Jessie," he told his wife. "Don't go downstairs by yourself. Wait for me." The baby might kick and Miriam might slip.

He'd do everything in his power to look after his family. . . .

Wade snapped out of his daydream as Rose returned to the room. He lifted his head from Miriam's pillow and settled back in his chair as Rose reclaimed her own.

He remembered his promise to himself that he'd do anything to look after his family. Well, he'd done a shitty job of it, hadn't he?

Anger—at circumstances, partly, but mostly at himself—burned through him, bringing him to his feet. Though he was exhausted, he had to move. To walk, to get out of this room, to . . . "Back in a few minutes," he said gruffly, and strode out the door. He headed down the long corridor, toward the entrance to the hospital. Hell, he wanted to run, to open the door and head out into the snowy day. To escape.

To return to the ranch and ride out into the snow, where the world was cold and pure and simple. Where nothing existed but the crunch of a horse's hooves breaking the snow, the jingle of the bit, the creak of the saddle, his breath and the horse's puffing out in clouds. It was damned hard to feel crappy when he was riding.

But he deserved to feel crappy. And he couldn't abandon Miriam. He loved her more than life itself. He had to be there when the going got tough, and right now it was about as tough as he could imagine.

Just a few minutes to himself, though.

When he reached the hospital door, he opened it and stepped outside. Clad in only a flannel shirt and jeans, he was immediately chilled by air that was many degrees below freezing. But that icy bite was fresh and invigorating.

He glanced past the plowed, slushy parking lot in the direction of the ranch. The hills east of town were clad in snowy blankets. Gaze fixed on the hills, ignoring everything else around him, he stood and breathed in and out, slowly. His nostrils and throat tingled with a sensation like burning, his lungs expanded, and a sense of calm filled him.

Miriam was alive, and so was Jessie. Their family would return to Bly Ranch and they'd heal.

He took one last bracing breath, squared his shoulders, then opened the door and returned to the heat, the noise, the smell of the hospital.

Chapter Eight

The cocoon was thinning and Miriam struggled to hang on to it, to still her fluttering eyelashes and keep her eyes closed. Instinct told her that she was safe inside, that something bad waited for her if the cocoon dissolved. Yet her body had its own ideas, and her eyelids lifted of their own volition. Vision blurry, eyes sore, she blinked. Where was she?

Her mom's face sharpened into focus. "Hello, baby," she said, and squeezed Miriam's hand.

"Mom?" Miriam gazed around, taking in her surroundings, and realization sank in bit by bit, in fierce jabs of agony. The contractions, the rush to the hospital, her doctor examining her. The sadness and pity in Dr. Mathews's eyes when she said there was a serious problem with the baby.

Miriam's eyes filled and her voice quivered. "I lost the baby?" She didn't really have to ask; the sense of an aching void inside her told her it was true.

Her mom's eyes squeezed shut for a moment, and when she opened them again they were glazed with moisture. "I'm afraid so."

"Why?" she asked plaintively, not bothering to wipe at the tears that streaked down her cheeks. "What did I do wrong?" She wanted her husband. Where was Wade? He should be here, holding her. How could she get through this without him?

"Nothing. But there was a problem with the baby. You couldn't have prevented it."

A nurse came in and checked the monitors. "Your doctor's in the hospital, Mrs. Bly. I'll let her know you're awake and she'll come see you as soon as she can."

When she left, Miriam turned back to her mom. "Where's Wade?"

"He just stepped out for a minute. He's been here by your side."

Reassured, she returned to the one thing that most mattered. Trying to understand, she said, "But I was past the first trimester. You're supposed to be safe then."

Her mother bit her lip. "Sometimes miscarriages happen later."

"My baby," she sobbed. Her abdomen hurt, but the real pain was in her heart. "Was it a boy or a girl?"

"A boy."

Two girls, two boys. That was what she and Wade wanted. All their dreams had been coming true and now they'd lost their son. A quick stab of anxiety made her ask, "Jessica? Is she all right?"

"She's fine. Your dad took her to school and he'll pick her up this afternoon and take her to our house. Andie will baby-sit."

Reassured, Miriam said, "Thanks." For the first time, she realized how tired and worn her mom looked, though the love and concern in her eyes touched Miriam's broken heart. "I want to go home, Mom. I just want to go home." Actually, she wanted to go to her parents' house and have her mother look after her. But she wanted Wade there, too. "When can I leave the hospital?"

"Not quite yet." She seemed about to say something else when Wade stepped into the room.

His eyes widened and he rushed to the bed. “You’re awake.”

Miriam had seen him after he’d been up all night with ranch emergencies, but never had he looked so drained. When he took her hand, she gripped his fiercely. “We l-lost our son,” she wailed, fresh tears sheeting down her cheeks.

He leaned over and kissed her on the forehead. Rather than lift his head again, he rested it on the pillow next to hers. “I know, honey.” His voice was choked. Slowly, as if it took superhuman effort, he raised his head and glanced at her mother. “Have you . . . ?”

She shook her head. “The nurse says her doctor’s coming.”

“Okay.” He sank down in the chair on the other side of the bed, still holding Miriam’s hand. “You’re going to be all right. That’s the most important thing.”

He didn’t think losing their son was important? But no, that was unfair. Of course he did. He was just trying to make her feel better. As if anything could.

“I love you, Miriam,” he said. “Our love’s strong enough to get us through anything. Right?” His deep brown eyes looked wounded and pleading.

Could they—could she—get through this? Women did. Miscarriage wasn’t all that uncommon. But she’d made it past the first trimester. She’d felt the baby move. “Right.” She hoped that saying it would make her believe it, but grief, pain, drugs had muddled her brain. Except for the one thing she was sure of. “I do love you, Wade.” She squeezed his hand, gently this time. “And our Jessica.” Then she turned to her mom. “And you and Dad, and my sisters and brother.” Right now, that love was the only thing holding her together.

Darn it, she was an optimistic person who tried to see the bright side of life. She really would get through this and, somehow, life would get back to normal. There’d be another child. Not one to replace the little boy they’d lost, but a new, unique individual.

Her mind could recite those facts, and one day, surely, her heart would believe them and start healing.

Dr. Mathews, dressed in blue scrubs, walked into the room. She was so beautiful, with gorgeous red hair and emerald green eyes, she could have been a model. When Miriam had told her that, she'd laughed and said that as a toddler she'd plastered Band-Aids over her dolls' imaginary wounds, and her fate was determined. She was a warm, caring doctor who always took the time to explain things and to listen to patients' concerns.

Now her green eyes were shadowed, and her face was strained as she touched Miriam's shoulder. "How are you feeling, Miriam?"

"Sad. And sore. I want to go home."

"I'm sure you do, and we'll get you there as soon as we can." Her gaze shifted to Miriam's mom, the doctor's raised brows conveying a question.

Miriam's mom shook her head, her throat moved as she swallowed hard, and tears seeped from her swollen eyes.

The doctor nodded. She pulled up another chair, beside Wade's.

"What went wrong?" Miriam asked. "Was it something I did?"

"No, not at all. These things happen. You couldn't have prevented the miscarriage."

The words confirmed what Miriam's mom had said, but how could she not feel guilty? She'd carried this child, and she'd lost it. "If I'd called you earlier?"

"The baby had problems. He wouldn't have made it, no matter what you did. I'm so sorry."

More tears slipped down. So sorry. They were all so sorry. And none of that "sorry" could save her little boy.

Dr. Mathews began to describe what had happened, but Miriam couldn't take it in, or maybe she just didn't want to.

Perhaps one day she'd want to understand, but for now, only one thing mattered: Her baby was dead.

The doctor was talking about the surgery they'd done, and Miriam's brain slowly grasped that something had gone wrong. "You had a rare condition called placenta percreta," the doctor said. "The placenta had penetrated the uterine wall and attached to your bladder."

Miriam's brain couldn't make much sense of this. It didn't sound good, though. Her insides were messed up. Not just her insides, but her reproductive organs.

She was vaguely aware of both Wade and her mom gripping her hands tightly, but she focused on Dr. Mathews's face.

The doctor leaned forward, her expression sympathetic, and again rested a hand on Miriam's shoulder. "It's a serious condition, Miriam. And during surgery, the placenta ruptured. There was a hemorrhage and"—she stopped, took a breath, then went on—"we had to do a hysterectomy. I'm so very sorry."

Miriam's breath caught in her throat. Hysterectomy? Women with uterine or cervical cancer had hysterectomies. A hysterectomy meant that they took out . . . No. No, it wasn't possible.

Wade made a choked sound and there was a rushing in Miriam's ears like busy traffic on a wet highway, almost drowning out the doctor's next words.

"You won't be able to get pregnant again."

And then, mercifully, Miriam's world went black.

Chapter Nine

Late April 1995

It hit Wade out of the blue every now and then. He'd be focused on work, and suddenly there it would be. The pain.

Today, he'd been on the move since dawn. The cows were starting to calve, so he rode around regularly, checking for problems. The older cows usually gave birth easily, but complications could always arise, and he kept an eye on the heifers—the first-timers. When they were close to their time, he moved them to the small maternity pasture close to the ranch house, where he could check them every few hours, day and night.

When he'd ridden Romany, a sturdy bay gelding, along a section by the creek, he saw that the previous night's windstorm had brought down a dead cottonwood, the top of it damaging the fence. He'd had to ride back to fetch the small chainsaw so he could get the tree off the fence. One day, when he found time, he'd buck up the cottonwood and cart it back to chop for firewood, but now the urgent priority was mending the fence.

He tackled the task with practiced motions. Just part of a normal day's work. And the thought came: *My son will never do this with me*. It was like a punch in the gut. He gripped the fence post with one gloved hand as he doubled over in pain.

A few minutes later, glad no one was there to see, he slowly straightened and stared around him. Snow clung persistently in shady patches, but the rangeland was mostly clear now, the yellowed grass welcoming the pale spring sun. The cattle had come through the winter well, and he took an owner's pride in surveying the sturdy animals dotting the landscape, especially the dozen new calves. But the panoramic view, so familiar and always so pleasing to his eye, brought another reality home to him.

While he grieved the loss of his and Miriam's tiny boy, there was a bigger picture on top of that. There'd be no more kids to share his soul-deep love for this breathtaking, demanding land. No more kids to tuck in at night, to teach to ride, to nag to do their homework, to have snowball fights with.

No Bly to take over the ranch, not unless Jessie suddenly switched loyalty from horses to cattle, and he didn't see that happening.

He and Miriam could adopt, he reminded himself. Maybe, at some point. Right now, that was beyond imagining. For him, and, he was dead certain, for her.

If only he'd paid attention to the signs and taken her to the doctor when she first started feeling achy, maybe she wouldn't have needed a hysterectomy. If only he'd protected his wife.

Sucking in a breath, he realized the air had chilled off. The sun was dropping toward the horizon. Quickly, he finished repairing the fence, then put the chainsaw and tools into saddle panniers, tightened Romany's cinch, and mounted up. As he made a final inventory of the cattle in the fading light, he wished he had a dog to help, and for company. What was a ranch without a dog? But his parents had taken good old Shep, the ten-year-old Border Collie, to Phoenix. Wade had figured on getting another dog this year, and knew Jessie'd love it, but he wasn't sure Miriam was up to it.

Normally a healthy woman, she'd been slow to recover from the surgery. She just didn't seem to care. Not about her health; not about getting back to normal life. Wade might've liked to share his grief with her, but she couldn't even talk about the baby without crying. Hell, she couldn't get through the day without crying. Anything would set her off.

Thank God for Rose. For the first couple of weeks, she'd taken leave from her job as a high school teacher to care for her daughter, and since then she'd come out every day after school.

Wade tried to help, but he felt like a bull in a china shop, tiptoeing around his wife and always seeming to do or say the wrong thing. So he focused on work, and there was plenty of that to do.

Dr. Mathews said emotional healing took time. He and Miriam were both strong people, and they'd get through this.

He didn't identify any heifers that needed to be brought to the maternity pasture, so it looked like he stood a chance of getting a decent night's sleep. Yawning, he rode into the barnyard at dusk, but the sight of his mother-in-law's car woke him up in a hurry. Usually, she picked Jessie up after school, bought groceries, did a little housework, got dinner going, then headed home in the late afternoon. Anxiety filled him. Had something happened to Miriam?

Quickly looping Romany's reins over a hitching post, he rushed to the back door and into the mudroom, then flung open the door to the kitchen. Rose was slicing carrots at the kitchen counter. Jessie sat at the kitchen table, a schoolbook in front of her. The scent of tuna casserole—a childhood favorite of Miriam's—filled the air. Things seemed normal. He took a breath, let it out, then said, "Hi, Rose. I thought you'd have left."

She turned to him. "I wanted to talk to you before I go."

A slight frown. "You still have your coat and boots on. Do you have to go back out?"

"Only to get my horse settled. I'll be back in a few minutes."

As he went to deal with Romany, he wondered what Rose wanted to talk about. Sure hoped she wasn't going to say she couldn't help out anymore.

Ten minutes later, he was back at the house, shedding his heavy outerwear in the mudroom. This time, when he opened the kitchen door, Rose was seated at the table with Jessie.

Wade walked in sockfooted, rested a hand on his mother-in-law's shoulder for a moment, then bent to kiss the top of his daughter's head. "Hey, Jessie-girl."

"Hey, Pa. Any new calves today?" She might not be as keen on cattle as on horses, but she loved baby animals of any kind.

Rose said, "You and your pa can talk ranching later. Right now, I need him for a few minutes. Would you go up and tell your mom that dinner will be ready in half an hour? Then you can read a book until it's time to eat."

When she'd gone, Wade sat down across from Rose. "Is Miriam okay?"

Rose frowned. "She picks at the lunches I leave, and half the time she's not even dressed when I get here. I hate to see her like this."

"Me, too."

She tilted her head, and blue-gray eyes very like his wife's studied him. "How are you doing, Wade?"

What could he say? If he'd been a little boy and she'd been his mom, he'd have broken down in tears. She'd have hugged him and fixed whatever problem was bothering him. But he was an adult. His mom was in Phoenix, and when he talked to his folks on the phone he tried to be upbeat rather than worry them.

He shrugged. "It's hard." Knowing this was tough on Rose, too, he asked, "How about you?"

She nodded. “Like you said, it’s hard. Hard losing the baby, and hard seeing my own child this way.”

“But we have to carry on.” Gruffly, he added, “Can’t tell you how grateful I am for the way you’ve been here for us.” It pained him that they needed that help. He should be able to look after his wife and child.

“I’d do anything for Miriam and her family.”

He saw the sincerity in her eyes. “I know you’re hurting, too,” he said softly. “I wish there was something I could do.”

Rose shook her head, looking tired and sad. “It’ll just take time. For all of us. And that’s sort of what I wanted to talk to you about.” Her shoulders lifted and fell as she took a deep breath, then let it out. “You know that Henry’s the manager at the bank.”

“Yeah, of course. Has been since he was promoted . . . when was that anyhow? Four or five years ago?”

“Seven. He’s been offered a promotion, to a job in commercial lending that he’d really love to do.” She gazed steadily across the table at him. “It’s in Winnipeg.”

“Winnipeg?” Manitoba was one hell of a long way away. What would he do without them? Rose, Henry, even teenaged Andie who was always happy to baby-sit Jessie.

“He says he’ll turn it down. But if he does, he won’t likely be offered another opportunity. Not at his age. We just don’t know what to do, Wade.”

He scrubbed his face with his fingers, trying to think. It was his job to look after his family, not Rose and Henry’s. They had their own lives, their own needs. Trying to work this through, he asked, “Is it just Miriam that’d keep you here?”

“You three. Yes. Caribou Crossing is a nice town and we stayed here because it’s a good place to raise kids. But we don’t love it the way Miriam does. Henry and I like city life, and we’re getting older. Our son’s in college in Vancouver, our second daughter’s married and settled, and as for Andie, I’m pretty sure she'd love to move someplace with shopping malls and more activities for teens."

"You've been here how long?"

"Seventeen years."

"That's a long time to be in a place you don't really love." He tried to imagine living without the wide-open land and ever-changing skies that nourished his soul, the community where everyone knew everyone.

"It is," she said firmly. "But Caribou Crossing is your home. It's where Miriam and Jessica belong." She raised a hand and scraped silvered brown hair back from her face. "If Miriam was healthy, I think we would move. We'd plan to visit often. Very often. But she's not well and the thought of leaving her . . ."

She was saying that he couldn't look after his wife. That he couldn't honor the vows he'd made on his wedding day. And she was so damned close to the truth that it shredded his pride as painfully as if he'd run into barbed wire. "When would you go, if Henry took the promotion?"

"The job starts at the beginning of June. That's not much more than a month off. He'd go out first, and I'd pack up the house, finish out the teaching year. Andie would finish grade nine."

His in-laws had thought this through. Well, of course they had. It was the promotion his father-in-law had long wanted, and the kind of life that would make both of them happy.

"Have you mentioned this to Miriam?" he asked.

"No. We haven't told any of our kids. I wanted to discuss it with you; then Henry and I will talk again. If we stay, there's no need to tell our children about the job offer."

Wade blew out air on a long exhale. What would Miriam say? If they asked her today, she'd burst into tears and cling to her mom. But later, when she was back on her feet . . . "If Miriam was healthy," he said slowly, "she wouldn't let you make such a big sacrifice for her."

"She's our daughter. You'd do the same for Jessica."

He nodded. He'd do anything for Jessie. And for Miriam. But his wife was strong and capable. She would heal, and once she did, she'd find out what her parents had done. She'd feel guilty; she'd be mad. Mad at her mom and dad, and mad at Wade for letting them do it.

"I think you should go." The words came out heavily. How would he manage? How could he take on anything more? But he had to do the right thing.

"Really?" Something lit in Rose's eyes, like a spark of hope she hadn't before allowed herself.

"Really." This could work out. It had to. "You'll still be here for two months. We'll be able to manage then." They'd have no other choice.

"Miriam will be feeling better. Her body's healed now, and she'll get over her depression. And if you still need help, I could always stay another few weeks."

He'd hate to ask it of her, but it was nice to know there was a fallback.

"I'd feel like I'm abandoning her," Rose said softly.

Wade knew that feeling. It hung on his shoulders every morning when he drove Jessie to school, leaving Miriam curled up in bed. It crept under the covers with him at night when he slid in beside his wife and realized that, for yet another day, he hadn't seen her smile. But then, he felt abandoned, too. When Miriam looked at him, her gaze was distant, like she didn't see him; when he hugged her, he held her body but her spirit was missing. Things had to change, though. As everyone said, time healed wounds, even if scars remained.

He sighed and reached over to touch Rose's hand. "Think how she'd feel once she gets better if she found out what you'd given up. Think how upset she'd be."

Her lips opened in surprise. "Oh! I hadn't thought of that.

Thank you, Wade, you're right. That'll make Henry feel so much better."

She rose, came over, and leaned down to hug him from behind. That maternal embrace was affectionate and comforting. He pressed his arms over hers, where they circled his neck. He wasn't a boy and she wasn't his mom, but for the moment his mother-in-law's hug felt pretty darn good.

"You'll look after Miriam," she said. "Ever since you first started dating, I've known you would look after my daughter."

Yeah, like he'd done such a great job of it so far. "I will, Rose," he assured her. "I always will." Even if it meant working twenty-four/seven to keep the ranch afloat, put food on the table, get Jessie to and from school.

Quick footsteps sounded on the stairs, and Rose straightened. "That's Jessica."

"How do you want to tell Miriam about the transfer?"

"Let's wait awhile. Until she's stronger. She won't find out from anyone in town because she's not returning her friends' calls."

Used to be, Miriam loved getting together with her girlfriends for lunch or an occasional girls' night out, and she'd come home bubbling with stories. Now, she wouldn't even talk to them on the phone.

Jessie trotted into the kitchen. "Is it dinnertime? Mommy says she's not hungry."

Rose stood. "When I cook dinner, people eat. I'll go get her. Then I need to get home to Henry and Andie." She hurried out of the kitchen.

Jessie pulled the milk container out of the fridge and poured three glasses. "Daddy, when can Ev come out again? I miss playing with him."

To his surprise, Wade missed the boy, too. The kid might be odd, but he grew on you. "I know, but right now your mommy's not up to company."

"We'd be quiet." Jessie put on her best wheedling tone. "We'd even do homework."

He smiled for the first time that day. She was so normal. She really didn't understand the loss they'd suffered and she was so wrapped up in her own life. He tugged affectionately on her ponytail. "Sure you would." Who knew, maybe Evan would be good for Miriam, too. He certainly wouldn't create more work. He always more than pulled his weight when he was around. Maybe the kid would set up a jigsaw puzzle. Miriam used to enjoy doing those with him.

Besides, Jessie was entitled to be happy even if her parents were going through a rough patch.

"We'll get him out here again just as soon as your mommy's up to it," he promised.

Life would get back to normal.

Soon.

Chapter Ten

July 1995

Miriam rested her forearms on the handle of the grocery cart and studied the shopping list again. Last year, she'd have had a mental list of what they needed and remembered everything. Now, even a written list was confusing.

She'd bought milk, now she was way over in the produce aisle, and the next thing on the list was butter, which was back near the milk. Oh well, she'd get it later. The next item read "desserts." Like a dim memory, Miriam recalled bustling about the kitchen, kneading pastry dough, blending cream and sugar, spreading chocolate frosting. Sneaking a taste, imagining the pleasure on her husband's and daughter's faces as they ate the treats she baked.

The idea of making a pie or cake seemed as impossible as . . .

Well, sometimes just the thought of making it through the day seemed impossible.

She refocused on the list. Dessert. She'd buy ice cream and cookies.

"Miriam!" A female voice made her turn to see Connie Bradshaw, bright and pretty in denim shorts and a pink tank top, holding a bag of peaches. A kindergarten teacher, this was summer holiday for her.

"Hi, Connie." Belatedly, she remembered to smile at her old friend.

"I haven't seen you in ages." The petite brunette cast a quick up-and-down gaze over Miriam, making her realize that she hadn't changed out of the sweats she often wore at home.

"No, it's been awhile."

"I called, but . . ."

Connie'd left messages. Other friends had, too. "Sorry, I've been busy," Miriam said.

"It's okay." There was concern, a question, in Connie's eyes.

Now that Miriam was coming into town again to shop, she of course ran into people she knew. Some mentioned the miscarriage, but others didn't, probably figuring it best they didn't remind her of it.

As if it wasn't the single biggest thing in her life, the heavy dark blanket that weighed her down so that she could barely manage to get through each day.

"I'm meeting Jane and Frances for lunch," Connie said. "Why don't you come?"

Lunch. She used to do that when she was working at the vet's office. Meet up with girlfriends for lunch. She was supposed to be doing the things she used to, supposed to be getting back to normal life. That was what the doctor said, and her mom, who called every day from Winnipeg, and Wade. They were always nagging her to do things, to try harder, to heal faster. Even Jessica, always at her to come see her foal, to read a story together at bedtime. So much pressure.

But she loved Wade, Jessica, her mom. She tried to do what they wanted, even though it felt like she was plodding through quicksand every day, trying to make it all the way to bedtime without sinking. Then she could take the pills the doctor had prescribed and sink into blissful oblivion.

"Miriam? Come on, join us for lunch."

If she did, she could tell Wade and her mom. It would make them happy. "Okay." She began to push her cart toward the checkout.

"Wait a sec." Connie stopped her and took the milk out of the cart. "I'll put this back. It's so hot out, it'll go sour in your car. You can come back to the store after lunch."

"Right. Thanks."

They both paid for their groceries and Connie helped Miriam load bags into her car. Then, swinging her bag of peaches, the other woman led her down the street. "Tourism picks up each year," Connie commented.

Though Miriam had been coming into town for a couple of weeks now, she realized she'd never really looked around. Now she noted that there were indeed more strangers than usual on the street, many carrying cameras and wearing souvenir T-shirts with the "Caribou Crossing" road sign logo. She hunted for an appropriate comment. Making conversation had turned into an effort. It was hard to remember what she was supposed to say, and why it mattered. "That's good for business."

"Sure is. The town's booming right now."

Good. That should mean the ranch was doing well, too.

Miriam hadn't gotten back to the bookkeeping. She'd been halfway through her course, partway through inputting figures into the computer system. No way could her brain cope with that kind of work right now. One day she'd get back to it, and in the meantime she had total confidence in Wade.

"This place opened a couple of months ago," Connie said, stopping in front of a coffee shop called The Gold Pan. "Have you been here yet?"

"No." It occupied the space where a rather old-fashioned gift shop had been.

"It has classy versions of miners' food."

As they went in, Miriam glanced at the huge sepia prints

of old mining pictures that decorated the walls, and the rustic wooden tables and chairs.

Jane and Frances hadn't arrived yet, and Miriam went into the ladies' room to use the facilities. When she washed her hands, the reflection that stared back at her was a shock. When was the last time she'd actually looked in a mirror? And how long had it been since she'd had her sandy brown hair cut? Or washed it?

Frowning, she combed her hair vigorously and, finding an old scrunchie of Jessica's in her purse, fashioned a ponytail. Pulled back, her hair didn't look so lank. At least her face was tanned from working outside in the vegetable garden. She added lip gloss and thought she didn't look too horrible.

But when she saw her three former classmates chatting around a table, she knew she didn't measure up. They looked young and fresh in pretty summer clothes, their hair gleaming, their faces bright and animated. In comparison, Miriam, at twenty-seven, felt like a middle-aged hag.

Well, she'd lost a child. She'd lost her uterus, damn it. Let them go through that and still look young and vibrant.

Their conversation stopped when they saw her coming. They'd been talking about her. Of course they had.

She took a deep breath and tried to get a grip. It wasn't healthy to resent other people's happiness, or to get angry when they pitied her. Her focus was supposed to be on getting healthy. So she forced a smile. "Hey, girls, it's great to see you."

"You, too, Miriam," Frances said. A striking blonde, she wore a lovely blue sundress, no doubt from the clothing shop where she worked.

Jane, tailored and professional with her short, stylish auburn hair, sleeveless white blouse, and tan linen pants, nodded in agreement and asked tentatively, "How are you?"

"Okay. Fine. Keeping busy."

Looking relieved, Jane said, "That's great. Just great."

They were all silent for an awkward moment; then Frances grabbed a menu. “Have you been here before? They have some fun things.”

“I haven’t. What do you recommend?”

“The skillet sourdough bread’s terrific. So are the soups and the native greens salad. If you want hearty, the chili is amazing.”

“I’m starving,” Jane said. “Chili for me.”

Miriam used to know what hunger felt like. Now, she ate because she knew she had to. After listening to the others’ selections, she chose the same thing as Connie: the salad with a side of skillet sourdough.

Orders placed, there was another moment of silence. It was because she was there. No one knew what to say around her. Before anyone could ask her a question, she said brightly, “Tell me what you’ve all been up to.”

Then, rather than let herself drift off into a fog, as so often happened, she forced herself to concentrate and offer the occasional comment, as she also forced herself to eat every tasteless bite of food.

Jane, a lawyer with a firm in town, had just gotten engaged to another lawyer, and when they married in the spring, they would set up their own practice together. Connie and her husband of two years were planning a holiday in Hawaii at Christmas break, and trying to decide between Maui and Kauai. For the past few months, Frances had been dating a man who lived in Vancouver, traveling down for long weekends and holidays, and she was thinking about getting a job there.

Their lives seemed so fun, so exciting. They had dreams; they were so enthusiastic about everything; they had so much to look forward to. Miriam was the same age as them. Why didn’t she have any of that? Even before she lost the baby, all she’d done was work, ever since they’d moved out to Bly Ranch.

"You're not back at the vet clinic, are you?" Jane asked. "I took Libris in last week and Mrs. Christian was at the desk."

Dr. Christian was holding Miriam's job for her. His mom was filling in, though she really didn't want to work full-time.

"Not yet," Miriam said. "Soon, though." It was the same thing she told Wade when he asked. She'd enjoyed the job, used to come home full of stories about the pets and their humans. It felt like years ago. Like she'd been a different woman. Now it took all her energy to make it through the day, what with meals to prepare, housework, the garden.

Her energy was coming back, though. Slowly. Her enthusiasm for life would surely come back, too.

Her love for Wade would—No, what was she thinking? Her heart raced and she put a hand to her chest, pressing against that wild flutter. Of course she hadn't lost her love for her husband. She would never stop loving him. Just like she'd never stop loving Jessica, or her parents or siblings.

It was just that love, right now, was more of a knowledge than a feeling. She knew she loved her family. She knew she loved sunny mornings and wild strawberries and riding across open meadows. She just didn't feel it. Not physically, not emotionally. Her mind recalled what it was like. How sometimes it was a warm glow that settled deep in her bones, and other times an overpowering rush that filled her heart and brought tears of joy to her eyes. Surely one day she'd experience that again.

And yes, sometimes she did resent Wade and Jessica. Not just for the demands they made on her, but for the way they carried on with life as if there'd never been a baby. As if she hadn't lost her ability to have children. As if she weren't a hollow shell.

That was why she couldn't feel, couldn't taste, couldn't even focus on a task. She was a shell, a dry husk. Empty. Empty but for grief, resentment, anger, guilt.

Everyone said there was nothing she could have done to

save her baby. But she knew differently. She should have known something was wrong. Should have gone to the doctor earlier. And even if her poor tiny boy was doomed, she wouldn't have needed a hysterectomy. One day, there could have been other children. But she'd been stupid, irresponsible. She hadn't paid attention to the signs her body was sending her. It was her fault.

All her fault.

Did Wade blame her? He was so careful with her, like he was tiptoeing on eggshells in his Roper boots. She was never sure what he was thinking. Of course, even when he did talk to her, she had trouble focusing on what he was saying.

Speaking of which . . . Damn. She'd completely tuned out her girlfriends. This was what always happened. She tried to concentrate, but then her mind turned inward and she lost the drift of the conversation.

"I need to run," Jane said. "I have an appointment at one."

They settled the bill and the four women left together and said their good-byes on the street. Miriam couldn't wait to get back to the ranch and take a nap. Lunch had worn her out.

"Don't forget that milk," Connie said.

"Oh, right." Yes, she'd forgotten that she hadn't finished grocery shopping.

Walking back to the store, Miriam pulled out her list. Milk, butter, desserts. And there, in Jess's printing with a big star drawn around it, was something else she'd forgotten: "Pick up Ev at library at 12."

She was an hour late. Okay, she'd get him first, then go back for groceries. One thing about Evan: He wouldn't complain. He was the most polite child.

It was a nuisance driving him to and from the ranch, but he really was a nice boy and a good influence on Jessica. Besides, her daughter deserved some fun. She sure wasn't getting it with her mom these days.

And that made Miriam feel guilty. Everything made her

feel guilty. She should be healing faster. If only she could pull her feet out of the quicksand and shed the heavy gray blanket that weighed her down.

Maybe she couldn't yet stop feeling like an empty shell, but at least she could pretty up the exterior. She had to make more of an effort. When she got back to the ranch, she would shower, wash her hair, and put on clean clothes. When Wade came in from haying, she'd be more animated. She'd tell him about lunch with her friends, share all the news. Make him happy. Wade, too, deserved some happiness.

Chapter Eleven

Body aching from a long day of haying—thank God the early crop had done well—Wade headed into the house for a quick dinner.

Miriam was in the kitchen, and his heart lifted at the sight of her. She'd changed from her usual sweats into shorts and a green T-shirt, and her long, curly hair was clean and shiny. Combined with the tan she'd acquired in the garden, she looked almost like his real wife, the pretty, vibrant, happy one. "Hey, honey, you're a sight for sore eyes."

She smiled. "And you're so covered in hay you look like a scarecrow."

He chuckled. "Let me grab a quick shower and I'll be right back." Though his muscles were exhausted, he still took the stairs at a run, fearful that by the time he returned, she'd have lost her rare sparkle.

But no, when he came down, clean and changed, and gave her a hug, she returned it warmly. Standing in the bright kitchen, his arms around her and hers around him, he wanted to never let her go, to hang on to this one perfect moment.

But Jessie and Evan came in from outside, and Miriam broke away to greet them. "Dinner's almost ready," she said. "You two wash up, then please set the table."

Normal. It felt so blessedly normal—the old, wonderful normal—as Miriam sliced beans, Evan put dishes and cutlery on the table, and Jessie poured milk for all of them. Wade leaned against the counter near his wife. "How was your day?" he dared to ask.

"I went in for groceries, and to pick up Evan, and I ran into Connie. I had lunch with her and Jane and Frances. At that new coffee shop, The Gold Pan. Have you been there?"

He shook his head. The days were so full, he barely had time to whip into town for supplies once a week. Besides, there was no spare cash for restaurant meals. Not that he begrudged her one bit; seeing her girlfriends had invigorated her.

She started talking about Jane, who was now engaged to another lawyer, then Evan said, "Excuse me, Mrs. Bly, but the potatoes are boiling dry. Do you want me to serve them?"

"Oh!" She spun, gazed at the stove. "No, thanks, Evan. I'll get them."

Quickly she drained the boiled new potatoes, which were soft, almost mushy now, rather than firm. But they'd taste fine with butter and salt, which Evan had already put on the table.

Miriam put the green beans in the microwave and took a baking dish of pork chops from the oven, and within minutes they were all seating themselves at the table.

Wade smiled across the table at his wife. "Dinner looks great." He missed the days when she served meatloaf, lasagna, casseroles, and stir-fries, but at least she was shopping for groceries and putting dinner on the table each night. "Finish what you were saying about your friends, hon. You told me about Jane. What are Frances and Connie up to?"

"Frances is dating a guy who lives in Vancouver, so she's down there every weekend. They eat at great places, go to shows. She's having so much fun. And Connie and her husband are going to Hawaii during Christmas break. Doesn't that sound great? We should do something like that."

He stared at her. She couldn't be serious. "Uh, you know

the cattle and horses need feeding every day. We can't just up and leave them."

She frowned. "Your parents went to Mexico one winter, and you came out to feed the animals. You could hire someone to do it."

Hire someone? Yeah, like he could hire someone to help with the haying? Or he could've hired someone to help when the cows were calving, so he wouldn't have had to work twenty-four/seven? Hiring people required money, which they sure as hell didn't have. "Don't think that'll be in the budget this year," he said gruffly, hating to burst her bubble. Hating that he wasn't a better husband who could give her the things she wanted.

Jessie said, "Oh, who wants to go to Hawaii anyhow? It's way more fun here, with the horses." She began to gush about the latest exploits of Rascal, her foal.

Wade smiled affectionately at her. Though she was impulsive and not the most organized kid in the world, she was turning into a mighty fine ranch hand. At the age of eight, she did a lot of the work with the horses, helped care for sick animals, and rode out to check on the cattle. The best thing was, she didn't resent spending her summer holiday that way; she thought it was fun. Who knew, maybe he'd make a rancher of her after all.

She was a good kid and he was more than happy to agree when she wanted to have Evan come out to the ranch to play, or to go riding with other friends from school. Or when she persuaded their neighbor, a retired rodeo rider, to teach her roping and barrel racing.

Listening to Jessie boast about how Rascal was the smartest foal in the entire world, he glanced across the table at Miriam. In the old days, they'd have shared an amused smile. Now, Miriam stared at Jessie as if she was listening, but her lack of expression told him she wasn't taking in a single word. She'd withdrawn again.

His pleasure in the evening faded and Wade quickly finished the tough pork chops. He rose to see what they might have for dessert and found the usual. When he put a carton of Neapolitan ice cream on the table, Evan scooted to his feet to clear the dinner plates and bring bowls and spoons, and Jessie found a package of chocolate chip cookies in the cupboard.

Miriam didn't comment when their daughter scooped out only chocolate ice cream for herself and added three cookies. When Jessie passed the carton to her, Miriam waved it away. Evan served himself equal amounts of chocolate, strawberry, and vanilla and gave the carton to Wade.

It was cold and wet in Wade's hand. Yes, ice cream was a perfectly normal summer dessert, but he was sick of it. He put the lid back on the carton and got up to return it to the freezer. Once, there'd been homemade cakes, pies, and cookies in this kitchen. He sat down again and took a couple of cookies, so dry and flavorless compared to the ones Miriam used to make.

She'd taken some big steps forward today, he reminded himself. He shouldn't be impatient.

But he felt so helpless. He loved Miriam, but these days he barely recognized her. He wanted to fix her, to heal her. But then he hadn't managed to heal his own sorrow either. All he could do was carry on, and hope things improved for both of them.

Jessie was now telling Evan about her rodeo lessons, and how she planned on riding the rodeo circuit when she got older. She and the boy were both big dream spinners. For her, it was horse training, racing, rodeoing, being on the Olympic team, or working with rescue horses. Evan's dreams spun off in the opposite direction. The top student in grade two, the kid who treated the library as his second home, he was already planning on a scholarship to some big-name university like Harvard, Yale, or Cornell. Evan had his heart set on New York

City, too. Ever since Miriam gave him that jigsaw puzzle at Christmas, he'd been researching the city.

"I'll get at least a master's degree," he said now, "and maybe a Ph.D. I might be an investment banker, or maybe a securities lawyer. I'll have an office in the Big Apple, and live there, too. Perhaps on Park Avenue."

The kid probably would, too. He had smarts, discipline, and a maturity way beyond his years.

"You'll do it, Ev," Jessie said confidently. "You're so smart, you can do anything."

Wade grinned at his daughter's echo of his own thoughts.

Evan gave her a big smile, those striking blue-green eyes of his glowing. "And you're so accomplished with horses, you can do whatever you choose."

They were each other's biggest fans, these two youthful dreamers. Wade glanced at Miriam, who was staring into space, her face as blank as a mask. Once, the two of them had shared dreams. He remembered their wedding night, when they'd mapped their future as if dreams really did come true.

Now, he had no time for dreams. His mind was full of worries. And he sure couldn't share those with Miriam, when she was in such rocky shape. No way he could tell her he'd had to sell Rapscallion, the ranch's most valuable horse, in order to make the mortgage payment. Or tell her that, out of the blue, some small thing would hit him like a punch in the gut and he'd have to fight back tears. Besides, he felt so guilty, so dang inadequate. How could a man confess that kind of shit to his wife?

He heaved a sigh and rose, stretching his aching shoulders. Time to get back to work. There were bills to pay, if he could figure out where to find the money to pay the minimum amounts due. The ranch's finances were in a mess, worse off than before Miriam had started entering things into that computer program. If there were more hours in the day, he'd try to learn QuickBooks himself, but he kept hoping she'd get back to it. Couldn't she find a measly half hour a day to get that stuff organized?

Then, gazing at his wife's drawn face, he felt guilty for even thinking it. Thank God she had recovered physically from the surgery. Hell, thank God she'd survived, period. He'd lost his son and the possibility of future kids, but he could have lost his wife, too. He should be grateful, every moment of every day. And he was.

"Miriam?"

She didn't look up.

He rested his hand on top of her head, enjoying the silky smoothness of her sandy hair. "Miriam, honey?"

Slowly, she turned her face toward him. "Hmm?"

"Can you take Evan back to town?" He hoped it was one of the nights she'd have the energy for it.

Huge blue-gray eyes gazed at him soulfully. "Take him to town?" She made it sound like an impossibly exhausting task. "I suppose I—"

Evan broke in. "I can walk, sir. I don't want to be any trouble."

Wade knew the latter part was true. He'd come to like, even respect, this odd little boy.

Jess snorted. "It's ten miles into town, Ev. If you'd only climb on a horse, you could ride behind me and I'd take you."

The boy still adamantly refused to ride. That was probably a good thing, because, as Jessie often said, he really was a klutz. It was strange that he could be so precise about handling plates and glasses, yet he managed to trip down steps and fall over coffee tables. He had almost as many scrapes and bruises as Jessie.

"You're not riding into town in the evening, Jessie-girl," Wade said firmly. "Evan, I'll give you a lift." He had to wonder why the kid's parents never once offered to drive him out or pick him up.

To his daughter, he said, "You get the dishes done and help

your mom with anything else she needs before you go hang out with Rascal."

He pressed a kiss to Miriam's silky hair. "Back soon. Love you, hon."

Her eyes focused on him, but when she said, "Love you, too," the words sounded hollow.

How long would it be before she wanted to make love again? At night in bed, she slipped into a drug-induced slumber and he spooned her, holding her warm body, remembering the intimate connection they'd once shared. Praying it would return.

He and Evan headed outside. Though Wade preferred driving the truck, he used the car whenever possible, as it used less fuel and gas was expensive.

When they were out on the two-lane highway to town, both windows down so a breeze would cut the summer heat, Evan said, "I'm sorry to be a bother."

"Stop saying that. You're good for Jessie."

"But it's summer vacation. We don't have homework to do."

Wade turned to him. "Son, it's not just about helping her with homework. You're Jessie's best friend and you're a good kid. We all like having you around."

Color rose in the boy's thin cheeks and he blinked quickly. His "thanks" was so quiet Wade barely heard it.

They drove in silence. The car radio had packed it in along with the heater.

After a few minutes, Evan said, "Mrs. Bly seemed happier tonight, for a while."

"Yes, she did. It's a good sign."

"It was nice to hear her recount stories about her friends."

Recount? Seriously? "It was."

"She used to talk about the animals that came to the vet clinic, too. Is she returning to her employment there again?"

No, Evan couldn't just say "going back to work," like a normal person. "I hope so," Wade responded. It would be another sign that she was healing, and they sure could use the money. Her salary was one of the factors the bank had considered in approving their mortgage.

It made him feel guilty for thinking that way. His mother'd never had to go to work. Though there had always been times the family needed to scrimp, his pa had always supported them. Of course, his father hadn't had a hellacious mortgage.

No, but he'd paid Wade and another ranch hand or two, and he'd dealt with the same issues Wade faced: unexpected vet bills, machinery that needed to be replaced, family stuff like Wade's impacted wisdom tooth and Jessie needing a new coat. A car that was packing it in, bit by bit.

Every now and then, when Wade spoke to his parents on the phone, he thought about asking his father for advice. But damn it, he was a man, not a needy child. Whenever his folks asked how things were going at the ranch, he lied and said, "Just fine."

He'd figure things out. And Miriam would get better. Soon.

"Would you please drop me at the library, Mr. Bly?" Evan asked.

"Sure." Other kids spent summer evenings riding or playing ball but not this little egghead.

Wade felt a surge of affection for this strange but good-hearted boy. When he pulled up in front of the library, he said, "Night, Evan," and reached out to ruffle the boy's hair.

At first Evan flinched away, but then, when Wade's hand settled on his head, he froze and color again rose in his cheeks. "Good night, sir. And thank you for everything." He slipped out of the car and trudged, backpack hanging from his narrow shoulders, up the walk to the library.

The boy looked very alone in that moment. Almost like he carried the weight of the world on his frail back. Wade's back was a lot stronger, but he knew the feeling well.

Chapter Twelve

October 1995

Miriam and her little helpers dumped bags of groceries on the kitchen table. "You kids put things away," she told Jessica and Evan, "and I'll get dinner going."

"What are we having, Mommy?"

"Meatloaf."

"Oh, goodie! We haven't had that in a long time," Jessica said.

No, they hadn't. Miriam had been making basic meals: throwing pork chops, chicken, or steak into the oven; boiling or baking potatoes to accompany the meat; and getting Jessica to pick some kind of vegetable from the garden. But today, she wanted to do something more interesting.

"I remember your meatloaf, Mrs. Bly," Evan said. "It's superlative."

She smiled, a spontaneous one rather than a forced one. Yes, she was slowly getting better, just as the doctor had promised. "If you two peel the potatoes, I'll make mashed potatoes."

"Yummy!" Jessica said. Then, "Where did Pa go? The truck's gone."

"I noticed. Guess he had to go into town for something. Too bad I didn't know, or we could have picked it up." She'd expected Wade to be out with the cattle. He was finishing off the weaning, so all the calves would now feed from troughs. It wasn't long until they'd be shipped off to auction.

Though she preferred summer weather to winter, she was glad Wade would be able to slow down a little. He'd worked himself to the bone over the past months.

Before sitting down to peel potatoes, Jessica clicked on the radio, which was set to CXNG. Miriam realized how long it had been since she'd listened to music. Since the hysterectomy, she'd avoided it because the songs depressed her. All the songs: the cheery ones, the love songs, the achy-breaky-heart ones. Now, though, she found herself moving to the beat of a tune she didn't know as she mixed the ingredients for meatloaf.

The radio host said, "Y'all been listening to Tim McGraw's 'I Like It, I Love It,' and next up's Miss Shania Twain singing 'Any Man of Mine.' " Another new song she didn't know, but as she caught the rhythm and hummed along, she thought of Wade. Of the patient way he'd eaten the pathetic meals she'd prepared, thanked her for whatever tasks she'd managed to do, even told her she was pretty when she knew she looked like a hag.

Whenever he turned to her in bed, she pretended to be asleep. Her body felt so empty and unwomanly, and she always thought of the last time they'd made love. It was the night they lost the baby.

But no, that was all in the past. She'd walked around under a cloud for too long, and now the sun was peeping through. Miriam felt like a frozen stream thawing after a long, cold winter.

Maybe it was time to go back to her job at the vet's office, to set up regular lunches with her girlfriends, to buy some new clothes. Perhaps she could even work on Wade to take her and Jessica to Hawaii over the Christmas holiday.

Shania was singing that any man of hers would be a breathtakin', earthquakin' kind of guy. Yes, that was exactly how Miriam had always felt about Wade.

Tonight, she wasn't going to take a sleeping pill, and she was going to hug her husband in bed and see where things went from there.

She put the meatloaf in the oven, then chopped up the potatoes the kids had peeled, and put them in a pot of cold water. When Jessica begged permission to go see Rascal, Miriam laughed. "Nice try. You know the rule. Homework first. Right, Evan?" She cocked an eyebrow in his direction.

"We'll do it, Mrs. Bly. Come on, Jess, the sooner we commence, the sooner we consummate."

Miriam choked back a laugh. Should she tell Evan to read *all* the meanings of that word in his dictionary? No, she wasn't about to raise the subject of sex with an eight-year-old, no matter how advanced he was.

"I swear, Ev," Jessica said, "I don't know what you're saying half the time."

Thank heavens!

Miriam went upstairs to take a leisurely shower, shave her legs, and apply the apple-scented body lotion Wade had always loved. She donned a denim skirt and a figure-hugging coral tee, brushed her hair until it fell in shiny waves, and applied glistening coral lip gloss. Oh yes, there'd be some *consummating* going on in this house, after Jessica went to sleep.

When she returned to the kitchen, the enticing aroma of meatloaf filled the air and the kids were working diligently at their books. She went out to the garden to pick tomatoes and a cauliflower, and by the time she'd washed them, Jessica and Evan had finished their homework. "Okay," she told them, "you can go out and play."

A few minutes later, Miriam was grating cheddar to melt

on top of the cauliflower when she heard the outside door. She put down the cheese grater as the mudroom door opened and Wade stepped through. It was like she saw him clearly for the first time in ages. He was a hunk, her tall, strong cowboy in well-faded denim jeans, an even paler denim shirt worn open at the neck, and a dark brown Resistol cowboy hat set atop shaggy chestnut hair. He'd lost weight, though, and looked tired.

Love, a warm, poignant feeling that contained tenderness, lust, and appreciation, filled her. "Hey, sweetheart," she said softly, going to give him a big hug and a firm kiss.

"Hey." He gave her a perfunctory squeeze, then stepped past her. "Gonna grab a shower."

Miriam sighed. That wasn't the reception she'd hoped for, but he'd no doubt had a long, hard day. He'd feel better after a shower, and even better when he saw dinner on the table. He'd always loved her meatloaf.

She put the potatoes on to boil, cut up the cauliflower to steam, and sliced the tomatoes. When the potatoes were ready to mash, she called the kids in.

Wade—who'd taken a really long time with that shower—came back and they all sat down together. Evan and Jessica raved about the food, and Miriam enjoyed every bite herself. Wade, though, shoveled it in mechanically as if he didn't notice or care what he was eating. When she tried to make conversation, he seemed to be off in his own world and sometimes didn't respond.

It dawned on her that this must have been what it had been like for him, all these months he'd lived with her depression. Was he just tired and distracted, or was something wrong?

When dinner was finished and the kitchen tidied, Wade said, "Why don't you kids go play upstairs until it's time to take Evan home?"

When the two children left, he turned to Miriam and said heavily, "We need to talk."

Anxiety fluttered uncomfortably in her full tummy as they settled back at the kitchen table in their usual chairs across from each other. "What's wrong, Wade?" She reached over to rest her hand on his bare forearm. How warm and strong he felt, and how long it had been since she'd appreciated that. "Whatever it is, we'll work it out, sweetheart."

"It's my fault." He pulled his arm away, rested his elbows on the table, and buried his face in his hands. "I messed up," he said from behind his hands.

"Messed up how?" she asked cautiously. Wade never messed up. He was such a capable guy.

He lowered his hands and gazed at her, his face bleak. "We're caught up now but I missed two mortgage payments."

"What? You missed mortgage payments?" She shook her head disbelievingly. "How on earth did that happen? Did you forget to mail the checks?"

A hard swallow rippled his Adam's apple. "There was no money in the business account to write checks on."

Stunned, she gaped at him, then asked, "Where did it go?"

He gave a ragged laugh. "It went on life. Ranch expenses, food, electricity, gas for the car and truck, my impacted wisdom tooth. I've been selling livestock, trying to cover expenses, but I'm way behind on the bills. Taking the cattle to auction will carry us through for a few more months, but the bottom line is, there just isn't enough coming in."

What? She hadn't had a clue about any of this. "But . . . why? I mean, the ranch is supposed to make money." She'd never gotten far enough into the bookkeeping to understand the ranch's finances. "It always made money for your parents, right?"

"It did okay. Ranching's a tough business and there were some lean years, but they always managed."

"Then what's changed?" None of this made sense to her. Were they going to lose the ranch? No, that was impossible. She just wasn't understanding.

"What's changed?" he repeated, his voice grating. "We've got that damned mortgage. And, well, it's not Pa in charge anymore. It's me."

The mortgage. Yes, she knew it meant they had to be careful with money. But what did he mean about him being in charge? Frowning in puzzlement, she said, "But you know the ranch. You've always worked here. Aren't you doing the same things your father did?"

"I think so."

She tried to work this through. "Didn't you phone him and ask?"

Wade flattened his hands on the table and used them to thrust himself to his feet. He paced across the kitchen. With his back to her, he said, "I thought I could handle it. I didn't want to ask for help like some little kid."

She stared at his oh-so-familiar back. Wade was independent. Proud. She'd always known that. But now she realized he was insecure, and too mule-headed to get past it and ask for help. A bubble of anger churned in her tummy. Because of his stupid pride, he'd put them at risk of losing their home. "Why didn't you tell me what was going on?" she demanded, voice shrill.

He spun around. "Because you were so damned out of it, Miriam. You were so depressed, so unfocused. You could barely keep up with the house and Jessie, you didn't go back to your job, you'd given up on the bookkeeping, you just—"

"You're saying it's my fault?" She sprang to her feet, disbelieving and furious. "I lost my *baby*, Wade! I lost my *uterus*!" And maybe that was her fault, too, a guilt she'd live with for the rest of her life.

"I lost my baby, too. And all the other babies we might have had."

"But you handled it. You went back to work like it didn't even matter!" She hadn't realized until now how much she'd resented that. How alone she'd felt in her grief.

"It mattered. Jesus, Miriam, it shattered something inside me."

"It did? But you never said anything." And that hurt; he'd shut her out.

"You were sad enough without me dumping my sorrows on you. Besides, there was work to do. I guess my way of handling things was to keep busy."

Her anger faded as the truth sank home. Wade had grieved, too, and hadn't been able to come to her. Quietly, she admitted, "And my way was to fall apart. I'm sorry I wasn't there for you."

"Aw, honey." He crossed the kitchen and caught her hands in his. His rich chocolate eyes were anguished.

His grief, their financial troubles, he'd had to deal with everything by himself. If she hadn't abandoned the bookkeeping, she'd have known their situation all along. If she'd gone back to her part-time job, they'd have had more income. Guilt put a sour taste in her mouth. "I should have helped more."

"We both did the best we could."

That was generous of him, but had she? Yes, she'd told herself she was too depressed and tired to deal with those things, but if she'd known the truth, maybe she'd have somehow found the energy to help. "I feel so bad that you couldn't tell me because you thought I couldn't handle it."

"Well"—he swallowed—"it was also that I felt, you know, inadequate. Like I was letting you down."

Those words sank in slowly, penetrating her guilt. She frowned. "So, because of your pride, you went ahead and missed two mortgage payments without telling me? We're supposed to be partners, aren't we?" She tugged her hands free and rubbed her head, which had begun to ache. Maybe she'd have been a better partner if he'd treated her like one.

Another bubble—no, more of a knot—of anger was

growing, but she fought it down. “Why tonight? Why are you telling me now, if you got the mortgage caught up?”

“Because the bank manager told me I had to.”

“You saw the bank manager?”

“This afternoon. She said no one wants us to lose the ranch, but defaulting on the mortgage was a red flag and she wanted to discuss it.”

Miriam shook her head. She, a banker’s daughter, had defaulted on her mortgage. If her dad found out, he’d be shocked and disappointed. Laying blame on Wade or herself was pointless now; there was only one thing that mattered. “We have to make sure it never happens again.”

“Exactly. The manager said”—he scowled—“she said I’m in over my head, trying to run the ranch. She said, if you find yourself in a hole, the first thing to do is stop digging.”

“Makes sense. So what do we do?”

“She said I had to discuss it with you, and—”

“She’s right about that,” she interrupted. How could he have let things go this far without telling her? “What else?”

“We have to ask for help,” he added grudgingly.

Help? “A loan? My parents might give us a loan.”

“Uh-uh. More debt isn’t the answer.”

“I guess you’re right. What kind of help, then?”

“Advice on ranching from Pa and other ranchers. Your dad could help us work out a budget. The bank manager said we need a solid business plan. She’s right. We have to figure out a way to keep paying the mortgage, or else they’ll foreclose.”

“Foreclose,” she echoed. Such a nasty, technical word for losing your home.

“We can’t lose Bly Ranch,” he said. “We have to find a way of keeping it.”

“We can’t lose our home,” she agreed, though the work involved in keeping it sounded overwhelming and unbelievably stressful. A year ago, life had been so easy.

Wait a minute . . . what did *home* mean? It was the place

where husband, wife, and daughter lived, laughed together, and loved each other. They'd had that last year, before the move. Bly Ranch was . . . vast acreage, more than a hundred cattle, a bunch of horses.

Responsibilities. Huge ones. And debt.

She and Wade weren't even thirty yet. Their friends were building careers, falling in love, having fun. They weren't faltering under a crushing load of debt and the intimidating challenge of finding some way of turning things around. Even her parents, who both had careers, worked regular workweeks; they didn't slave away every evening and weekend.

She gazed up at her husband, noting the lines of tiredness and strain carved into his handsome face. Where was the lighthearted, romantic guy she used to dance with at the Lucky Strike? She thought back to their wedding night and all the dreams they'd shared, the bright future they'd envisioned. Things had gone so badly off course this past year, and some dreams—their four children—were lost forever. Maybe this was the time to abandon another dream—Bly Ranch—and envision a different future.

"What if we don't?" she asked tentatively.

"Don't what?"

"Don't try to keep it. What if we let it go?" She speeded up as she went along, and it felt like another weight was lifting from her shoulders. "We could sell, see if we can get out with at least some of the money we put in. Start fresh."

Fresh. That word opened up so many possibilities, new dreams that could heal their wounds, weave their family tighter together, bring back the joy in their lives.

Chapter Thirteen

Wade gaped down at his wife as she gazed up at him from her seat at the kitchen table. Had she lost her mind? "You can't mean that."

"Maybe it's too much for us. We can't handle it. All this responsibility and worry . . . We're not even thirty, Wade."

"But you love the ranch. Don't you, Miriam?"

"I don't know." Expression troubled, she said, "I did, but Wade, it's too much for us."

"It's our home." The home they were building together. Yes, losing the baby had been a big setback, and so was the financial trouble, but they'd get back on track. She couldn't lose faith in that. Faith in him.

Miriam shook her head. "Home is wherever we make it. We could get a small house in town, just like we planned a year ago."

"But we talked about this when Mom and Dad decided to move. You agreed." He scowled at her. "I'm not a quitter, and I didn't think you were either."

"A quitter?" She came to her feet, took a couple of steps away, then turned back to face him. "It's not quitting to realize you've made a mistake. When we decided to buy the ranch, we didn't know how hard it would be."

"This isn't a mistake." The words ground out as pressure throbbed at his temples. "We just have to work harder. If you did the bookkeeping and went back to work at the vet's, that'd be a big help, and—"

"I know, I know. I should have done those things, but you didn't tell me we were in trouble."

"I figured you'd get back to them as soon as you could."

"Look, I know you were trying to be considerate, but you can't just keep secrets from me."

"Keep secrets? You were in no shape to hear the truth." His voice had risen along with his temper.

"So now it's all my fault?" Her eyes flashed.

"I'm not saying that! Damn it, Miriam. We both have to work harder."

"Wade, you already work from before dawn until late at night. Every day. Seven days a week. You have no life except for work!"

He dragged his hands through his hair. "Work smarter, then. Whatever it takes." His parents had given them half of this ranch. He couldn't lose it. Didn't she understand how important Bly Ranch was to him and his family? Wasn't *she* part of this family?

"Whatever it takes? No!" Hands fisted on her hips, she glared at him. "Don't be so stubborn! Sometimes it's better to just admit you were wrong and move on."

"Wrong? I'm not wrong."

"Ooh! I don't even know you. You're not the man I married!"

"Well, this marriage sure isn't what I thought it would be." When he married Miriam, he never could have imagined they'd be fighting like this.

"What's that supposed to mean?"

"I thought that we were partners. That you'd stand by me."

"I would if what you were doing was reasonable, but it's not!"

They glared at each other across several feet of kitchen floor. For months Wade had wished that his wife was *present*, that they could have a real conversation. Well, she was dang well present now, and pissing him right off.

"Mommy? Pa?" Jessie's quavering voice made him spin on his heel to see her in the kitchen doorway, tears streaming down her face.

"Jessica," Miriam started, and then their daughter was running toward her, yelling, "We can't lose the ranch! You can't get divorced!"

Divorced? The word was a slap in the face, a shock icier than the first plunge into Zephyr Lake each spring.

"Divorced?" Miriam echoed the word disbelievingly as she gathered their sobbing daughter in her arms and they both sank to the kitchen floor. Over the top of Jessie's head, Wade's wife's agonized gaze settled on his face. Silent tears slipped down her cheeks.

He strode over and dropped down on his knees to wrap his arms around the two of them. Oh God, he loved them so much. He'd only wanted to look after them, yet he'd hurt them so deeply.

Forcing words past a lump in his throat, he said hoarsely, "We're not getting divorced, Jessie-girl. I love you and your mom more than"—he struggled to find words to convey the truth—"more than life itself."

More than Bly Ranch, he realized.

And that was what Miriam had been trying to make him realize.

Their daughter raised a wet, blotchy face to focus on him, like she was wondering whether to believe him.

Miriam drew a quavery breath, but smiled through her tears. "And that's exactly the way I love both of you. I'm sorry we were yelling, honey."

"We h-heard you from upstairs," their daughter said, her words punctuated by a hiccupy sob. "Evan s-said parents fight all the time, and we should stay in my room. But you guys d-don't fight. So I came down and then I h-heard you saying those things."

"Stupid things," Miriam said firmly. "Sometimes when people are upset, they say stupid things they don't really mean."

"We're really sorry," Wade said, giving them another hug, then slowly easing his death grip on his family and standing up.

Then he noticed Evan hovering in the doorway, shifting from foot to foot.

Embarrassed as hell, Wade nodded awkwardly at the boy. "Sorry, Evan."

Miriam looked over, too, brushing dampness off her cheeks. "Oh, Evan." She rose and went to him. When she reached out to touch him, he flinched away. "We're so sorry," she said gently. "We didn't mean to upset you."

"It's okay," he said cautiously. His solemn gaze fixed on her face, then traveled to Wade's, and then landed on Jessie's. "Are you okay?" he asked.

She sniffled, nodded, then went over to take his hand.

Though he'd sure rather Evan hadn't witnessed their family drama, Wade was still glad that Jessie had this friend who looked out for her.

"I'm sorry, Miriam." Wade went over to rest his hand on his wife's shoulder.

"Me, too." She gave him a shaky smile. "We'll figure things out, Wade. The important thing is, we love each other. We *are* partners, and we have to start acting like it."

"Agreed," he said wholeheartedly. He put his arms around her and she hugged him back. For a long minute he held her tight, wishing he never had to let go. They kissed gently, an apology and a promise.

When he turned again to the kids, he saw they were taking

it all in, Jessie with a smile and Evan with a serious expression that was more an adult's than a child's.

"I should drive Evan home," Wade said. "Is that okay, Miriam?"

"Of course, sweetheart. I'll put Jessica to bed."

"And I'll come kiss you good night when I get back," he said to his daughter. Then, to Miriam, "And then we'll talk. Like grown-ups."

Evan got his things, and then the two of them went out to the car. Wade drove down the ranch road and turned onto the two-lane highway into town. He said, again, "I'm sorry about that. We've had some troubles lately, but that's not an excuse for fighting."

"You need an excuse?" The question sounded genuine.

Wade shook his head. "There's never a good excuse. Not when you love someone."

The boy didn't respond, and Wade glanced over to see him staring out the windshield, his brow furrowed.

"It won't happen again," Wade promised.

Would the kid tell his parents about the fight? Wade had met them both, but only briefly. Blond Brooke had a vivacious personality. Mo, a half-Asian man, was more taciturn. Both were very good-looking, which made him think that one day skinny, big-eared Evan might turn into a handsome guy. They didn't seem overly concerned about their son's activities, maybe because he was so mature for his years. All the same, tonight had to have been troubling for the boy. "Want me to come in and talk to your folks?"

Evan's thin body jerked; then he turned and fixed those big, solemn blue-green eyes on Wade. "Why?"

"To reassure them everything's okay. I don't want them worrying about you coming out to the ranch."

"Oh," he said slowly. Then, "It's okay. They won't worry. Besides, they won't be home right now."

Evan never said much about his parents. Wade knew that

Brooke waitressed part-time, and Mo worked at an auto repair shop, but that was pretty much it.

When Wade pulled up at the shabby rental house, he reached over to touch Evan's shoulder. The boy tensed and turned his face toward Wade, expression giving nothing away.

"You're a good friend to Jessie," Wade said. "And to her mom and me. We'll see you again soon."

The boy gave a stiff little nod. "Yes, sir. Thank you." He slid out from under Wade's hand and opened the car door. "Good night."

Wade drove home quickly, then went upstairs. Jessie was tucked in bed, her mom beside her with an arm around her, reading from one of their daughter's favorite horse books. This, Wade thought, was what mattered. Yes, he loved Bly Ranch and would hate to lose it, but he could survive anything if he had these two females.

He hugged them, kissed Jessie, then took his wife's hand as they walked from the bedroom.

She turned to him and said quietly, "I'm exhausted. Let's never fight like that again."

He shook his head. "Guess we both have some issues. But fighting's sure not the way to solve them. Are you too tired to talk tonight?" He hoped not. If he had to give up Bly Ranch, he'd rather know now than worry about it overnight.

To his relief, she said, "No, I'll never sleep unless we do. Let's go down and light a fire."

"Great." That would set the right mood. He and Miriam had enjoyed a lot of good times in front of a fire.

She went to make tea while he got a blaze going. Then they settled side by side on the couch.

"So," he said, "where do we start?"

She took a sip of tea, then touched his shoulder. "I think I've figured out why we fought."

"You mean, because we were both upset and we're dealing with huge issues?"

"True. But also, we don't know how to solve problems."

"We don't?"

"Think about it, sweetheart." Her eyes were as gentle as her warm hand. "Until this year, we were starry-eyed kids and all our dreams were just handed to us on a silver platter. We agreed on everything. Even buying the ranch. Looking back, I remember that my dad tried to make us look at some cold, hard facts, but we were so excited, we just leaped into it. We both love the ranch, we'd always figured we'd end up here, and we assumed everything would work out."

As she spoke, he felt the truth of her words, deep inside him. "Guess that's true."

"We can't be starry-eyed kids anymore. Yes, we still have dreams, but the silver platter's gone."

"Sure as hell is," he said ruefully. "And in its place, there's a hellacious mortgage."

"Now we have to work for what we want. We have to learn new things. If we keep the ranch, I have to master the bookkeeping. You maybe have some things to learn about ranching, and have to learn to ask your dad and others for advice. We have to figure out how to do a business plan. And most important of all, we have to share our worries and problems with each other and decide together what to do about them."

He rested his hand on her thigh, which was covered by her denim skirt. "You're pretty smart, wife."

"You might have shared your worries if I wasn't so out of things."

He shook his head. "Don't blame yourself. We each heal in different ways, and you needed time. It was a horrible thing, what happened with our baby."

"It was. And it would've gone easier for each of us if we'd talked about it. But we didn't." She studied his face. "Would you be willing to do that now?"

He swallowed. He'd wanted to before, yet it meant showing Miriam a side of him she'd never seen. But she was his wife. The person he loved and trusted most in the world. "Yes." Wryly he added, "You're determined to see all my weaknesses, aren't you?"

Her eyes crinkled as she gave a small smile. "You've seen mine, all these months. And you're still here. I'm so glad of that."

"Me, too."

Her smile faded and her blue-gray eyes darkened. "What was the worst part for you? About my miscarriage?"

Oh, hell. The grief was something he wouldn't mind sharing. But it wasn't the answer to her question. He swallowed again, and when the two words came, they grated out as if he were dragging them over barbed wire. "The guilt."

Her brows drew together. "You mean, my guilt?"

Confused, he shook his head. "What do you mean? No, mine. I didn't protect you. I saw the signs there was something wrong. Should've gotten you to the doctor earlier."

Miriam's face paled. "Dr. Mathews said nothing could have saved our son."

"I know, but maybe you wouldn't have needed a hysterectomy." He reached for her hands, hoping she wouldn't pull away.

And she didn't. Instead, she gripped his fiercely. "It was my fault. My body. I'd even been pregnant before. I should have known."

Seeing the pain in her eyes, he realized something. "You've been blaming yourself. And so have I."

Her eyes glittered with unshed tears. "You're right, I might not have needed a hysterectomy. We could have had more children." A tear slipped free and ran down her cheek, then another.

His own eyes were damp. "Yes. That haunts me. Even more than losing our son."

She nodded, the tears running free now. "Me, too."

He pulled her into his arms, her face resting against his shoulder. Dampness soaked through his shirt. He clutched her tighter, rested his chin on top of her head, and now tears slid freely down his cheeks. "It's our fault, both of ours," he choked out. "And we can't go back and fix it."

"We can't. It breaks my heart."

"Mine, too." And yet, talking about it, sharing the guilt, holding Miriam . . . He actually felt a little better. He hoped she did, too.

Taking her shoulders, he eased her gently away from him until she gazed up into his face. "We can't go back, but we can move forward."

She sniffed back tears. "We have to." Then she slipped free, found a tissue in her skirt pocket, and blew her nose. "As partners," she said firmly.

With rough fingers, he brushed the tears off his cheeks. "As partners."

"We said those vows, for better or worse. We weren't thinking about the worse, but no marriage is all silver platters. We're in this together. If one of us has a problem, then it's the other person's problem, too, and we need to work together to solve it."

When she put it that way, it seemed so obvious. "Yeah, I guess that's what marriage is all about."

Then he took a deep breath, gripped both her hands again, and took the plunge. "You were right. Home isn't a place. Home is us. You, me, and Jessie. If we have to give up Bly Ranch, if it's going to hurt our family to keep it, then we have to let it go." Though the words sent stabs of pain through his heart, he meant them.

She studied his face for a long time, and he hoped she saw the truth. Then she gazed over at the fireplace. "Remember our Christmas tree?"

"Yes." And what did that have to do with anything?

She turned back to him. "Wade, I love it here. I've loved the ranch since the first day I saw it. I never grasped what was involved in owning it, and I still don't know all of it. But I think it could be worth all the challenges and all the work. Let's not give up. We'll do what the bank manager said. We'll talk to everyone who might possibly help us, we'll put together a plan, and we'll do our very best to hang on to this place."

It would mean humbling himself in front of his parents, Miriam's, the neighboring ranchers. Caribou Crossing was a small town. Everyone would know. But then folks probably already knew he was out of his depth and were just waiting for him to admit it and ask for help.

Maybe they could hang on to the ranch. Build their home here, in the place all three of them loved so much. And in the struggle to do that, he'd have Miriam beside him every step of the way.

He squeezed her hands. "That sounds mighty good to me."

Relief and hope filled him, followed by a surge of love so powerful that had he been standing it would have brought him to his knees. He leaned over, cupped her beloved face between his big, calloused hands, and touched his lips to hers.

She returned his kiss eagerly.

Miriam was back, fully present. His warm, giving, sensual, sexy wife. Her lips and tongue told him that.

When they broke the kiss, he said, "Tomorrow, we'll get to work. A new day, a fresh start. Tonight, I want to make love with my wife."

He prayed she'd say yes.

Chapter Fourteen

Miriam felt a little like Dorothy in *The Wizard of Oz*. She'd survived a tornado of experiences and emotions and emerged safely back home, where she'd started. And yet "home" was a different place and she was seeing it through new and very grateful eyes.

She touched Wade's cheek. "Then take me to bed, husband." There was nothing on earth she wanted more than to be naked in his arms.

He rose to adjust the fireplace damper and close the glass door, then came back and held out his hand to her.

She grasped it and he pulled her to her feet. Arms around each other, they headed up the stairs. As they walked, he tugged her T-shirt free from her skirt on one side. His warm, calloused fingers teased the skin at her waist. For so long, her body had just been an object, a thing she had to tend. Now, it awakened and she felt feminine, sensual. Something tingled through her, the stirrings of arousal.

Wade locked the bedroom door and turned on the lamp.

Suddenly, nervousness overcame arousal. She'd lost weight, and she was scarred. Before, Wade had said he loved her stretch marks and the scar from her C-section, but the new scars were ugly symbols of her barrenness. "Turn off the light," she said, her voice high and strained.

He studied her, then said quietly, "My wife's back and I'm not letting her out of my sight."

"I look different." She *was* different. Barren. Empty. What would it feel like for her, for him, to make love now?

He smiled, his deep brown eyes warm with love, and smoothed his hand over her hair. "You're beautiful, Miriam. You were beautiful on our wedding day, and you're beautiful in that T-shirt and the skirt that shows off your pretty legs. When you're old and gray, you'll still be the most beautiful woman in the world."

Then he touched his lips to hers, and made her believe him.

In that moment, her nervousness fled. This was Wade. When the kiss ended, she said, "And you'll still be my handsome love, the only man I could ever imagine being with."

They'd shared a bedroom and bathroom all these months, but she saw him with new eyes as she reached up to undo his shirt buttons and peel the edges back to reveal his firmly muscled chest. She shoved the shirt off his shoulders and with wondering hands explored his powerful shoulders, firm pecs, sensitive nipples. He was thinner, yes, but still so handsome.

She touched her tongue to his nipple, licked.

His body jolted in reaction.

It had been months since she'd even thought of sex, but now warm tingles raced through her blood.

Wade eased her away from his body so he could pull her tee over her head. Then he took off her bra and gathered her close until her breasts pressed against his chest. He groaned. "God, I've missed you, Miriam."

He was erect already beneath the fly of his jeans. Feeling his rigid length press against her sent more quivers of heat racing through her.

Emotionally and physically, she was suddenly hungry, desperately hungry, for this man. She unfastened his belt buckle, then went for the button at the waist of his jeans. Eagerly, she yanked down the zipper, pulled down his boxers, and clasped his length like a prize, a treasure. The treasure that would restore her sense of womanhood.

"I want you inside me," she whispered.

He jerked and thrust in her hand. "Jesus, Miriam. I want to go slow, to make this good for you."

"It'll be good." She was already aching and damp between her legs, her body crying out its need. "I need you, Wade. I need *us*."

"Oh, honey. I need that, too. But you have to stop touching me or I'll explode."

Reluctantly, she let go as he fumbled for the fastenings of her skirt. Then denim slid down her hips, hit the floor. Wade's hands thrust into the sides of her panties and yanked them down, and now she was naked in front of him.

Quickly, he peeled his jeans and underwear off, then tossed back the duvet.

Before the duvet settled, she was scrambling onto the bed, holding up her arms in welcome.

The last time they'd made love—No! She wouldn't think back; she'd live in this moment. "Now, Wade," she urged as he eased down on top of her. "Take me now. Hard and fast. So nothing else exists but you and me, together."

He groaned, then kissed her, fusing their mouths together as his tongue thrust demandingly inside hers.

She spread her legs, he slipped a hand between them, tested her dampness, opened her folds, and then—"Oh God, yes!" she cried against his mouth as he plunged into her, heated steel driving into her body. And she took him greedily, her hips lifting and tilting to urge him even deeper.

Her hand thrust into his hair, gripped the back of his head, held him tight. Her other hand stroked frantically down his back, grasped his backside, dug her nails in. "Faster," she gasped. “Harder.” She wanted this, only this, just the two of them. Man and woman, raw and primitive.

They weren’t kissing now, just breathing hard against each other’s mouths, him in raw pants, her in needy whimpers.

Her hips twisted, ground against him. It had been so long since she’d last been aroused that now the building tension was so fierce it almost hurt.

Wade reached between them, not gently the way he usually did, but she didn’t care. The rough press of his thumb against her clit almost made her scream with pleasure. “Yes, yes, more.”

Under her hand, his butt muscles clenched and his body drew back for a moment; then with a wrenching groan he plunged into her again and again as he climaxed. Pressure on her clit, pressure on her channel, pulsing jets of come exploding inside her—and everything came together and shattered and she buried her cry against his neck as she came in shuddering waves of ecstasy.

It took awhile for the world to come back into focus. She gazed up to see Wade’s chocolate eyes.

“Are you okay?” he asked softly. “That was, uh . . .”

“Exactly what I needed. I love you, Wade.”

“I love you, too.” He kissed her tenderly, then sat back on his heels beside her on the bed. “That wasn’t exactly how I’d planned for that to go.”

She studied her gorgeous husband. “No? Well, I believe in second chances. So if you’d like to try again . . .” She grinned at him.

He grinned back. “There’s that dimple of yours. I haven’t seen it in a long time.”

“There are other parts of me you haven’t seen in a long time.” She stretched seductively, feeling the return of her feminine power and confidence.

“You’re not too sore?”

“Not if you take it easy.”

"Slow and easy this time. That's a promise, honey."

He eased down and, starting with her lips, began to fulfill that promise. It was like he was determined to kiss every inch of her body. She felt cherished and sexy, melty and aroused, absolutely blissful.

When he reached her tummy, Wade paused. Then, deliberately, he kissed her scars. The ones from when she'd had Jessica, and the ones from the lost baby. She was no longer embarrassed about them, and she liked that he didn't pretend they weren't there. They were part of her. Part of her and Wade, too. Of their grief, their guilt, emotions they now shared.

He dropped his face against her skin and she felt new moisture—from tears, not from his exploring tongue.

She clasped his head to her soft flesh and tears seeped from her eyes, too.

They stayed like that for a long moment, and then he began to kiss her again. Each touch of his lips was a healing one, a step toward their new life together.

Chapter Fifteen

Christmas Eve 1995

"Jessica," Miriam chastised teasingly, "stop nibbling that popcorn. It's for the popcorn chains."

"We already have enough chains," the girl said, undaunted.

"I don't know how you can have any room left in your tummy, Jessie-girl." Wade paused in stringing lights. "Not after that delicious meal your mom cooked."

Miriam smiled from her perch on a two-step ladder, where she was hanging chains of popcorn and bright red cranberries on the full branches of the fir Wade had cut down. Her husband was such a sucker for her lasagna, not to mention the pumpkin pie she'd made for dessert. It felt so wonderful to be full of energy again.

And joy. This afternoon, she and Wade had knocked off work early and gone riding with Jessica. Crisp air, dazzling sunshine on clean white snow, the jingle of harness and puff of the horses' breath—simple pleasures, but oh how lovely it was to enjoy them again.

Now she said, "That was a beautiful ride this afternoon."

Her daughter gazed up from hanging her handmade

ornaments on the tree. “It’s nice to have you come riding again, Mommy.”

“Yes, it is,” Wade said.

“I’m so glad we’re keeping the ranch,” Jessica said.

“We’re all glad,” Miriam said. It was going to be tough, but they had a viable plan in place, thanks to their parents, neighbors, and friends. She and Wade were determined to make it work—and to keep talking, rather than nurse secrets and worry about things in private. As part of that plan, they had let Jessica, and by extension her friend Evan, know that the budget was tight and everyone had to pull his or her weight. That was true of their new addition, too: the Border Collie pup sleeping in a basket by the fire. The dog, named Dandy-girl by Jessica, would more than earn her keep as a working cattle dog.

Riding their own acreage this afternoon, seeing the gentle sweep of the land under its snowy blanket and listening to the chitter of birds in the evergreens, Miriam had felt a new sense of wonder. She’d always loved the ranch, but now she was coming to understand it in all its complexity. The demands it made and the rewards it offered to those who loved and tended it.

Wade touched her jean-clad leg in a soft caress. “Let me finish that up. You hang those ornaments Evan gave us last year. I don’t dare touch them.”

She climbed down and he caught her by the waist for a hug and a surreptitious pat on her backside. With careful fingers, she picked up one of Evan’s paper lace snowflakes.

“I’m glad Ev’s coming for Christmas dinner again,” Jessica said.

“So am I,” Wade said. “He’s a good kid. Just wish the boy liked cattle.” He shot Miriam a sly look, and she winked at him. They’d already speculated whether as the children grew up friendship might turn into something more. There was nothing Wade would like better than for Jessica to marry a man who wanted to be part of Bly Ranch. Right now, Evan Kincaid seemed determined to leave Caribou Crossing and head for New York City, but the boy was young. Things changed, as he and Miriam well knew.

Chatting lazily about this and that, the three of them finished putting the decorations on the tree. "Now," Wade said, "we get our reward." He flipped a switch and the sparkly tree lights came on.

"Ooh, it's so pretty!" Jessica said.

"It's lovely," Miriam agreed as she took a few pictures. "We did good, family."

Wade came to stand behind her, wrapping his arms around her. "We did very good."

She crossed her arms over his and leaned against his warm, muscular body. She'd always found him so strong, so capable, and so sexy. In the past couple of months, she'd learned a lot more about him: sensitivities, vulnerabilities, compassion, creativity, humor. A thought struck her, one she would share with her husband when they were alone.

Jessica came over to lean against her side, and she and Wade tucked her into their small circle as they all gazed at the tree.

Then their daughter broke free again. "Stockings! We have to hang the stockings. And put out the milk and cookies." She ran toward the kitchen, then paused to look back. "Santa knows we're here to stay, right?"

Wade hugged Miriam closer. "I made very sure he knows that."

They all made quick work of getting the stockings hung, and then Miriam and Wade tucked Jessica in. Their daughter figured that the sooner she went to sleep, the sooner she'd wake up to Christmas, and they were happy to encourage that belief.

Once they were back downstairs, they let the puppy out to do her business, then got her settled in the kitchen, filled the stockings, and tucked wrapped gifts under the tree. Miriam put on the Willie Nelson Christmas tape and turned off the lamp, so that only the fireplace and tree lights illuminated the room. Wade poured them both glasses of eggnog and added a hefty splash of brandy. Shunning the couch, they settled on the rug in front of the fire.

Miriam tasted the eggnog, and it took her back to the previous Christmas, at her parents' house. She touched her tummy and said, "Last year, I didn't drink Mom's eggnog because of the baby." She glanced at the red stockings hanging on the mantel. "There were supposed to be four stockings."

He rested his hand, that strong, calloused, yet gentle hand, on top of hers. "I know, honey. I miss him so much."

"Me, too."

They were silent a moment, and then he said, "The year sure didn't turn out the way we thought it would."

"No. But we've come out stronger, sweetheart."

He linked fingers with her. "Very true. You and me, Miriam. Now and forever."

She smiled, remembering how he'd said those words to her when they danced at their wedding. They meant even more now. Their bond had been tested by fire.

Though they were both working hard, somehow it didn't seem like a burden now that they had a plan and clear goals. Dealing with the animals and owners at the vet clinic actually invigorated her, as did having regular lunches with her girlfriends. She'd finally mastered QuickBooks, and whipping the ranch's books into shape gave her a huge sense of accomplishment.

Her grief and depression hadn't entirely gone, but she'd found a support group and Wade attended now and then, too. But what helped her most of all was a sense of true partnership and intimacy with her husband. They could talk finances, help Jessica with her foal, and chuckle over Evan's latest word of the day. They could play with the puppy, share worries, shed a tear for their lost baby, and turn to each other in bed.

Earlier, when they'd been admiring the tree, she'd thought of something she wanted to tell him once they were alone. "Remember our wedding night?"

He winked. "Very well."

She chuckled. "Not that part. Though I'm glad you do remember that part. But when we were dancing in the town square, we were talking about how we'd love each other over the years. Then, I didn't think I could possibly love you any more than I did at that moment."

He tilted his head, his beautiful eyes glowing in the firelight. "And now?"

"I know you on a deeper level. There's so much more to you than I ever realized."

"Some not so great stuff," he said wryly.

"You're human, just like I am. And you're an amazing person. You're my lover, my partner, my love. My past, present, and future. I love you so very much. And you still make my heart skip. You always will."

"Aw hell, Miriam," he said roughly. "Keep that up and you're going to make this tough old rancher cry."

That wasn't what she wanted, only to let him know how deeply she cared. So she teased, "Can't have that. Let's move on to later on our wedding night, when we were in the bridal suite at the inn."

"I remember. . . ." His eyes danced. "Let's see. I was with the most beautiful, sexiest woman in the world." He leaned over to reach under the tree, and pulled out a small package. "Speaking of which, here's your first Christmas present."

She studied those dancing eyes and grinned. "I take it this isn't for Jessica's eyes?"

"Uh-uh."

Eagerly, Miriam tore off the paper. Like last year, it was a box from the classy lingerie store in town. But when she opened it, it wasn't another negligee. She held up an abbreviated black lace bra and matching thong. "Wow." Amazing that after all she'd put him through this past year, he still thought she was a sexy babe.

"There's a note," he pointed out.

She unfolded the gift card to read his messy scrawl: *Once a month, wear these under your regular clothes—and tell me you've done it. All my love, Wade.*

She grinned. "Why Wade Bly, you kinky man, you. What do I get if I do?" Then she had an idea. "No, wait, don't tell me."

She grabbed the box and hurried to the downstairs half bath.

Less than five minutes later, she emerged, knowing she looked just the same as when she'd gone in, except for the flush on her cheeks. "I'm wearing them." She pirouetted in her jeans and flannel shirt.

He sat up, all attention. "Do they fit?"

"See for yourself." She raised the hem of the shirt and gave him a flash of lace-clad breasts.

"Oh, man, Santa's come early this year. Come here, wife."

As she went to her husband, she remembered something else from their wedding night. The song her father had chosen for them: "We've Only Just Begun."

It had never been more true.

If you enjoyed *Home on the Range*,
you won't want to miss Susan Fox's
next deliciously sexy Caribou Crossing romance:

GENTLE ON MY MIND.

Read on for a little taste of this exciting romance.

A Zebra mass-market paperback
on sale in September 2013.

Brooke Kincaid hung up the phone and hugged herself. Beaming, she danced a few steps across the kitchen floor in time to Glen Campbell's "Wichita Lineman," the song playing on Caribou Crossing's country and western radio station. Her marmalade cat, Sunny, watched from a windowsill, tail twitching, golden eyes asking a question.

"A grandmother!" Brooke told him. "I'm going to be a grandmother."

Well, in fact she'd become a grandmother last fall when her son, Evan—newly returned to Caribou Crossing—married Jessica and became stepdad to her daughter, Robin, a wonderful ten-year-old. But now Jess was pregnant!

Oh Lord, Jess was pregnant. Brooke stopped dancing as all the fears rushed into her mind. Would Evan let her near the baby, given what a terrible mother she'd been to him? And would the baby be okay? What if Evan did have a predisposition for bipolar disorder even though the disease had never manifested itself in him, and he passed it on to the baby?

Sunny yowled, breaking Brooke's train of thought. He hopped down from the sill and came to wrap himself around her ankles.

The gesture calmed her, and so did bending to stroke his sun-warmed fur. She'd acquired Sunny four years ago as a rescue cat, but the rescuing really worked the other way around.

"You're right," she told him. "I need to focus on the positive." Evan and Jess had made the decision to have a child, they knew about her own bipolar and alcoholism, and the decision was theirs to make. And yes, of course they would let her be involved. Her son had called her right away, the morning after Jess had shared the news with him and Robin. Brooke beamed again, remembering the joy in his voice.

As for her, at the age of forty-three she'd been granted a second chance, and she'd do things right this time.

She was fourteen when she got pregnant. Naively, she'd expected a pink-and-white girl doll, but what she'd received was a bellowing, demanding boy-child. She had messed up royally with Evan, and she blessed him for being generous enough to forgive her.

After ten years of estrangement, she had her son back, plus a wonderful daughter-in-law, a delightful granddaughter, and now a brand-new baby on the way. No clouds of worry were going to spoil this amazing day.

Johnny Cash's "I Walk the Line" came on the radio and she smiled. "So do I, my friend, so do I." She had stayed sober, gone to A.A. meetings, and taken her bipolar meds for almost five years. Now, she had even more motivation.

She ran her hand down her cat's golden coat and tugged gently on his tail. "It's all good, isn't it, Sunny?"

He pulled his tail from her grip and narrowed his eyes in mock annoyance, then began to purr.

Brooke laughed at his game. Until Evan had come back, she hadn't laughed—not this way, with genuine pleasure—in at least a dozen years. Now laughter came easily. "Life just couldn't be more perfect," she told the cat, reaching out to stroke him again.

But Sunny's ears twitched and he shook her hand off. His hair rose, his eyes slitted, and he stared intently into space, at nothing visible to her.

Jake Brannon clung desperately to the handgrips of his Harley, fighting to stay conscious. He'd been losing blood for going on an hour now. Thank God for the fierce pain in his side; it helped him focus.

When he'd made his getaway he'd left his helmet behind, and now the wind made his eyes water and whipped strands of hair across his face. He squinted to see the road. It twisted away in front of him like a snake. A rough-skinned snake. Every time he hit a pothole the bike jerked and a fresh wave of pain radiated from the wound.

He hoped to hell the bullet wasn't still in there. If only he could stop to examine the injury and staunch the bleeding. But the man in the black truck was chasing him, and by now there were probably others.

His own fault. He'd been sloppy. Should have been in and out without anyone seeing him. Should be back in his motel room right now, sound asleep. Instead of riding the never-ending snake in the frail light of dawn toward, toward . . .

Damn, he was losing focus again. Where the hell was he? He'd avoided the main highway in hopes of evading his pursuers, but the roads out here in the middle of British Columbia's Cariboo country were a maze. Would he ever find his way to the Gold Rush Trail Motel, to the sanctuary of that kitschy little room where sepia photos from gold rush days decorated the walls?

Jake narrowed his eyes against a pale rising sun. The sun

was off to his right, which meant he was riding . . . north? He groaned. His brain was so damned fuzzy.

The bike's tires skittered over a spill of gravel and jounced into another hole. Pain slammed through him and he let loose with a string of curses. The wind whipped them away, and he imagined them streaming behind him in a series of little balloons like the speech in cartoons.

Focus, damn it. Best as he could figure, he needed to head northeast. The sun rose in the east, and the sun was hitting the corner of his aching right eye, so northeast had to be straight ahead. As the crow flies. If only the Harley were a crow . . .

Straight ahead. He tried to grasp that thought and hang on to it. But damn, his vision was as blurry as his mind. He blinked but the view got foggier, not sharper. There was something white . . . vertical white shapes marching in a row straight ahead of him. A fence? Oh, Jesus, the road curved and he was heading straight for a fence!

He tried to yank the bike around the curve, but his sweaty hands had no strength. His world was turning gray and he was barely aware of the bike going down, spilling him free. Screaming pain roused him momentarily as his leg and hip scraped along the road. His head hit next and the gray turned charcoal. He heard his bike crash into something, then the engine abruptly cut out.

His eyes closed and the blackness took him.

"Sunny, what's wrong?" Brooke asked, just as the peaceful country morning was shattered by a horrible screech of metal, then a crash. Not metal on metal but metal on . . . wood?

Wood? "My white picket fence!" She dashed to the front door, flung it open, and darted down the steps in her bathrobe and flip-flops.

A huge black motorbike was jammed partway through her

fence amid a confetti of shattered white wood. Where was the rider?

Brooke rushed through the gate and found him sprawled on the gravel verge of the road, facedown, like a broken, abandoned toy. He was dressed in black—sneakers, jeans, and leather jacket. No helmet over that tumble of shoulder-length black hair.

Mo. He looked just like Mo. She flashed back to the age of fourteen, when she'd been utterly fascinated by the sexy nineteen-year-old bad boy. Back then, she'd had no idea how bad he'd turn out to be.

"Get a grip," she told herself. This man was *not* Mo, and he might be dying. She had to call 911. But what if he died while she was phoning?

Staring at the biker, she forced herself to take a deep breath. Although she'd taken a first-aid class, she couldn't remember a blessed thing. Another breath. She had to control the crippling panic.

Pulse. Yes, make sure he was breathing. If not, she'd have to start mouth-to-mouth and CPR.

Kneeling, she stroked his hair out of the way and slipped two trembling fingers around his neck to press against his throat. His pulse leaped strongly, so strongly that she jerked back in shock. Then she let out her breath in a low whistle of relief.

The man groaned and his body moved convulsively, turning so he lay on his back.

No, despite having bronzed skin, he didn't look like Mo, who'd been half Indo-American. He didn't look like a thuggish biker either. In fact, he was strikingly handsome, with strong, carved features. His mouth, framed by a dark beard, added contrast with full, sensual lips. If she'd had to administer the kiss of life . . .

Her cheeks burned. The thought of touching a man's lips with her own was shocking. It had been more than fifteen years since she'd shared any degree of physical intimacy with a man. Her ex-husband had soured her on men so thoroughly that she was positive she'd never be attracted to another one.

And yet there was something enticing about this particular face, this mouth.

She shook her head briskly, trying to recall the checklist the first-aid trainer had taught them. Immediate danger. Make sure he wasn't in immediate danger.

There was blood—he'd scraped himself up pretty badly—but no arterial spurts. He wasn't bleeding to death. He wasn't likely to be run over either, as he was well onto the gravel shoulder of the road. This end of Wellburn Road was quiet, down past the entrance to Bly Ranch. Her little patch of rented land was on Jessica's parents' ranch, and past her there was only Ray Barnes's place and a couple of other small spreads. Horses and riders often used this road, and people knew to drive cautiously.

So the motorcycle man was in no immediate danger. Now she needed to assess his injuries so she could tell the ambulance crew what to expect.

She studied his sprawled body. No broken limbs, as far as she could see. Head injuries? She rested her fingers gently on his skull and his eyes flickered open.

They were unfocused, dazed. An intriguing shade of gray with hints of blue and mauve. Wood smoke, she thought, on an October day. Gentle, dreamy eyes, belying the beard and black leather.

"Hello," she said. "Can you hear me?"

The muscles around his eyes twitched as his gaze sharpened. She read confusion, pain—then something that looked like fear. And then anger. Wood smoke turned to storm clouds.

When Jake's eyes first opened he figured he'd died and gone to heaven. Lord knows why a sinner like him would end up there, but a fair-haired angel was peering down at him. His vision was still blurry but he could see that her eyes sparkled blue-green like a tropical ocean. Rose-petal pink lips opened and she said something, but he was so entranced by her face that he didn't catch the words.

He wanted to reach out and touch a strand of that curly golden hair and see if it felt as silky as it looked. Or maybe she was a vision with no substance and his hand would slide right through her. The thought that he might never touch his angel almost made him cry.

No, damn it, that was pain that brought a rush of moisture to his eyes. Pain, shrieking through his body. He couldn't isolate it, couldn't assess his injuries; he was on fire in so many places. He wasn't dead—or if he was, this was hell, not heaven. What the fuck had happened? He must have been hit by a semi. No, he'd been riding his bike . . . And it crashed. But he was a good rider. . . .

Ah, now he remembered. He crashed because he'd been shot. He'd messed up when he snuck into the grow op in the dark hours before dawn. Someone had heard him, come after him, shot him. He'd barely made it to his bike and escaped.

Hellfire and damnation! Drug traffickers were after him and if they found him they'd kill him. If he was right, one of them was the man who'd murdered Anika, the teen prostitute whose body had been tossed in a Dumpster down in Vancouver.

His body was in agony, a killer was after him, and his angel was either a hallucination or a real live woman he was somehow going to have to deal with. He had three choices: cry, scream, or cuss. For a man, that narrowed down to one. He let loose with a string of curses.

She froze like a terrified animal poised for flight.

Hell, all he'd done was cuss a little. What was her problem? He studied her more closely, realizing his vision had sharpened. Now he saw the fine lines around her eyes and mouth. The angelic face was older than he'd thought, and fear etched the lines even deeper. Damn it, she really was scared of him. The black leather, the bike, some foul language . . . Did she think he was a member of a biker gang like Hell's Angels or Death Row?

Her eyes closed briefly, and when they opened their expression was calm. The tension in her muscles eased as she breathed deeply. But Jake sensed she hadn't truly relaxed; she was disciplining her body to hide her anxiety.

"I can see you're conscious and more or less lucid," she said evenly. "I'll go call for an ambulance."

An ambulance. Hospital, doctors, the Royal Canadian Mounted Police. He suspected the killer he sought was a prominent, supposedly respectable member of this community. Maybe even a member of the local RCMP detachment. Caribou Crossing was a small town; chances were, this woman knew the man. His angel might even be the devil's woman. Maybe that was why he made her so nervous.

Shifting her weight, she started to rise.

His hand shot out and grabbed her arm. "No!"

She tried to pull away. Under his firm grip, she was trembling.

He was sorry to hurt her, sorry to scare her, but he had no choice. He had to keep his presence in Caribou Crossing a secret or it would blow the undercover operation. No police; no hospital; no drug-dealing murderers. No one could know he—Corporal Jake Brannon, working U/C for the RCMP—was here.

Except that angel-face already did.

Suddenly she yanked hard, almost pulling her arm from his grasp.

The movement jarred his entire body, and pain made him gasp and bite his lip. She was strong for such a slender, gentle-looking woman.

She jerked again and agony weakened his grip. Exploiting

his weakness, she wrenched herself free and scrambled backward.

He had to stop her from reaching the phone. There was only one way.

Struggling to stay conscious, Jake fumbled for the Beretta in the shoulder holster under his jacket. He pointed it at her. "Stop, or I'll shoot you."

She froze, swaying on her feet.

Grimly he wondered which of them was going to pass out first. "Get back here."

After a long moment, too long for his sanity, she stumbled toward him.

He felt powerless lying there, his only weapons a firearm he would never use against her, and the force of his own personality. But he knew she was afraid of him and he had to play on her fear. "Kneel down." He needed her close, where he could read her face.

She obeyed, her movements jerky. "I was just going to call an ambulance." Her gaze flicked between his face and the Beretta.

"Don't call anyone."

"But you're hurt. You need help."

"I don't need doctors or cops."

She glanced at the firearm again, her eyes wide, and he could almost hear her brain working.

"Got it?" he said.

"You're an escaped criminal!" She spat out the words.

He'd miscalculated; somehow he'd tipped her past fear to anger. When he'd cussed and grabbed her arm she'd been scared, but now she was glaring at him like she'd love to get her hands on his firearm and shoot him between the eyes.

She might get her chance, because his vision was blurring again, his world once more fading to gray. He had to control her. Now. And fear was the key.

He shifted position and got a firmer grip on the Beretta.

The movement hurt his side, but the bright edge of pain helped him focus. "If you call anyone, talk to anyone, you'll regret it." Trusting her was not an option. Even if it had been, he didn't have the time, the strength, to explain. He might pass out any moment, and then she'd have the Beretta. He needed a threat that would bind her even if she got his firearm.

What did every person value the most? Their life.

"They can lock me up, but not forever," he hissed. "I'll get out and come after you."

"Then get it over with and shoot me now," she dared him, and he saw it had turned into a battle of wills. She was stronger than he'd expected. His beautiful, feminine angel was strong. It made her even more appealing.

God, his mind was drifting again. *Focus, man!* Her strength could endanger his mission. He had to find a threat that had meaning to her. "Your family. Everyone you love. If you betray me now, I'll kill your family. I won't be in jail forever. I'll come back."

She flinched as if he'd struck her, and her face went dead white.

Thank God. He'd found the right threat. She had family and she loved them. The threat was a complete lie, but she had no way of knowing that. To her, he was a violent criminal on the lam with a gun he had no qualms about using.

He was so exhausted he could barely think. Was there anyone else in her house? No, or they'd have run outside, too.

"I'm going to tell you what to do." He forced the words through gritted teeth. "And you will obey to the letter, or I promise you, I will kill your loved ones. If you call the police, if I go to jail, I'll come back as soon as I get out. If you leave town, I'll find you. You and all your family."

"I'll d-do it," she stammered, her whole body quivering. "Whatever you want."

"Get me into the house, then hide my bike. You have a garage or shed?"

She nodded.

His world was out of focus but he saw the movement of her head. "Patch up that fence. No one can know I'm here." He knew he was speaking, but the hollow rushing sound in his ears drowned out the words. "Cover up all traces of the accident. They can't find me. They'll kill me."

"The police won't—"

"No! Can't trust the police."

What was he saying? He didn't know anymore. Damn, he was losing it. Couldn't see. Couldn't think. Had to stop talking before he said too much. What else did she need to know? "Then see if you can . . ." He paused, fighting for breath, for the end of the thought. "Keep me alive. Got it?"

GREAT BOOKS, GREAT SAVINGS!

When You Visit Our Website:

www.kensingtonbooks.com

You Can Save Money Off The Retail Price Of Any Book You Purchase!

- **All Your Favorite Kensington Authors**
- **New Releases & Timeless Classics**
- **Overnight Shipping Available**
- **eBooks Available For Many Titles**
- **All Major Credit Cards Accepted**

Visit Us Today To Start Saving!

www.kensingtonbooks.com

All Orders Are Subject To Availability.
Shipping and Handling Charges Apply.
Offers and Prices Subject To Change Without Notice.

Books by Bestselling Author

Fern Michaels

__The Jury	0-8217-7878-1	$6.99US/$9.99CAN
__Sweet Revenge	0-8217-7879-X	$6.99US/$9.99CAN
__Lethal Justice	0-8217-7880-3	$6.99US/$9.99CAN
__Free Fall	0-8217-7881-1	$6.99US/$9.99CAN
__Fool Me Once	0-8217-8071-9	$7.99US/$10.99CAN
__Vegas Rich	0-8217-8112-X	$7.99US/$10.99CAN
__Hide and Seek	1-4201-0184-6	$6.99US/$9.99CAN
__Hokus Pokus	1-4201-0185-4	$6.99US/$9.99CAN
__Fast Track	1-4201-0186-2	$6.99US/$9.99CAN
__Collateral Damage	1-4201-0187-0	$6.99US/$9.99CAN
__Final Justice	1-4201-0188-9	$6.99US/$9.99CAN
__Up Close and Personal	0-8217-7956-7	$7.99US/$9.99CAN
__Under the Radar	1-4201-0683-X	$6.99US/$9.99CAN
__Razor Sharp	1-4201-0684-8	$7.99US/$10.99CAN
__Yesterday	1-4201-1494-8	$5.99US/$6.99CAN
__Vanishing Act	1-4201-0685-6	$7.99US/$10.99CAN
__Sara's Song	1-4201-1493-X	$5.99US/$6.99CAN
__Deadly Deals	1-4201-0686-4	$7.99US/$10.99CAN
__Game Over	1-4201-0687-2	$7.99US/$10.99CAN
__Sins of Omission	1-4201-1153-1	$7.99US/$10.99CAN
__Sins of the Flesh	1-4201-1154-X	$7.99US/$10.99CAN
__Cross Roads	1-4201-1192-2	$7.99US/$10.99CAN

Available Wherever Books Are Sold!

Check out our website at **www.kensingtonbooks.com**

5229

Romantic Suspense from
Lisa Jackson

See How She Dies	0-8217-7605-3	$6.99US/$9.99CAN
Final Scream	0-8217-7712-2	$7.99US/$10.99CAN
Wishes	0-8217-6309-1	$5.99US/$7.99CAN
Whispers	0-8217-7603-7	$6.99US/$9.99CAN
Twice Kissed	0-8217-6038-6	$5.99US/$7.99CAN
Unspoken	0-8217-6402-0	$6.50US/$8.50CAN
If She Only Knew	0-8217-6708-9	$6.50US/$8.50CAN
Hot Blooded	0-8217-6841-7	$6.99US/$9.99CAN
Cold Blooded	0-8217-6934-0	$6.99US/$9.99CAN
The Night Before	0-8217-6936-7	$6.99US/$9.99CAN
The Morning After	0-8217-7295-3	$6.99US/$9.99CAN
Deep Freeze	0-8217-7296-1	$7.99US/$10.99CAN
Fatal Burn	0-8217-7577-4	$7.99US/$10.99CAN
Shiver	0-8217-7578-2	$7.99US/$10.99CAN
Most Likely to Die	0-8217-7576-6	$7.99US/$10.99CAN
Absolute Fear	0-8217-7936-2	$7.99US/$9.49CAN
Almost Dead	0-8217-7579-0	$7.99US/$10.99CAN
Lost Souls	0-8217-7938-9	$7.99US/$10.99CAN
Left to Die	1-4201-0276-1	$7.99US/$10.99CAN
Wicked Game	1-4201-0338-5	$7.99US/$9.99CAN
Malice	0-8217-7940-0	$7.99US/$9.49CAN

Available Wherever Books Are Sold!

Visit our website at **www.kensingtonbooks.com**